Lars Kepler

THE FIRE WITNESS

Lars Kepler is the pseudonym of the critically acclaimed husband-and-wife team Alexandra Coelho Ahndoril and Alexander Ahndoril. Their number one internationally bestselling Joona Linna series has sold more than twelve million copies in forty languages. The Ahndorils were both established writers before they adopted the pen name Lars Kepler and have each published several acclaimed novels. They live in Stockholm, Sweden.

THE FIRE WITNESS

THE FIRE WITNESS

A Joona Linna Novel

LARS KEPLER

Translated from the Swedish by

NEIL SMITH

McClelland & Stewart

M&S paperback edition published 2018

Copyright © 2011 by Lars Kepler
Translation copyright © 2018 by Neil Smith

McClelland and Stewart and colophon are registered trademarks of
McClelland & Stewart, a division of Random House of Canada Limited,
a Penguin Random House Company

Simultaneously published in the United States by Vintage Books,
a division of Penguin Random House LLC, New York. Originally published
in Sweden as *Eldvittnet* by Albert Bonniers Förlag, Stockholm, in 2011.
Published by agreement with the Salomonsson Agency.

Library and Archives Canada Cataloguing in Publication data is available
upon request.
ISBN: 978-0-7710-4879-1
Ebook ISBN: 978-0-7710-4880-7

Printed and bound in the United States of America

Cover design: Henry Steadman
Cover image © somethingway/Getty Images

McClelland & Stewart,
a division of Penguin Random House Canada Limited,
a Penguin Random House Company

www.penguinrandomhouse.ca

1 2 3 4 5   22 21 20 19 18

Penguin
Random House
McCLELLAND & STEWART

THE FIRE WITNESS

... and all liars, shall have their part in the lake which burneth
with fire and brimstone ...

Revelation 21:8

A medium is a person who claims to have a paranormal gift, an ability to see connections beyond accepted scientific limits.

Some mediums offer contact with the dead through séances, whereas others offer guidance with the help of tarot cards.

Trying to contact the dead through a medium is a practice that reaches back through human history. A thousand years before the birth of Christ, King Saul of Israel attempted to ask the spirit of the dead prophet Samuel for advice.

All over the world, the police seek the help of mediums and spiritualists with complex investigations, even though there isn't a single documented example of a medium's helping to solve a case.

1

ELISABET GRIM IS FIFTY-ONE YEARS old and her hair is peppered with gray. She has cheerful eyes, and when she smiles you can see that one of her front teeth sticks out a little farther than the other.

Elisabet works as a nurse at the Birgitta Home, a children's home north of Sundsvall. It's privately run and takes girls between twelve and seventeen years of age.

Many of the girls have problems with drugs when they arrive, almost all have a history of self-harm and eating disorders, and several of them are very violent. For them, there aren't really any alternatives to group homes with alarmed doors, barred windows, and air locks. The next step is usually adult prison and compulsory psychiatric care, but the Birgitta Home is one of the few exceptions, offering girls a path back to society.

Elisabet likes to say that the Birgitta Home is where the good girls end up.

She picks up the last piece of dark chocolate, puts it in her mouth, and feels its blend of sweetness and bitterness tingle under her tongue.

Slowly, her shoulders start to relax. It's been a difficult evening, even though the day started so well: lessons in the morning and swimming in the lake after lunch.

After dinner, the housekeeper went home, leaving Elisabet on her own.

The number of night staff was cut four months after the Blancheford Holding Company bought the place.

The residents had been allowed to watch television until ten. She had spent the evening in the nurses' office, and was trying to catch up with her logs when she heard angry shouting. She hurried to the TV room, where she found Miranda attacking little Tuula, yelling that Tuula was a cunt and a whore, dragging her off the sofa, then kicking her in the back.

Elisabet is starting to get used to Miranda's violent outbursts. She rushed in and pulled her away from Tuula, earning herself a blow to the face, and she had to shout at Miranda that this was clearly unacceptable behavior. Without any discussion, she led Miranda away along the corridor, to the isolation room.

Elisabet said good night, but Miranda didn't answer. She just sat on the bed staring at the floor, and smiled to herself when Elisabet closed and locked the door.

The newest girl, Vicky Bennet, was booked for an evening conversation, but there was no time because of the trouble with Miranda and Tuula. Vicky tentatively pointed out that it was her turn and got upset when she was told it would have to be postponed. She smashed a cup, then slashed her stomach and wrists with one of the fragments.

When Elisabet came in, Vicky was sitting with her hands in front of her face, blood running down her arms. Elisabet cleaned the cuts, which turned out to be superficial, put gauze on her stomach, and bandaged her wrists, then sat and comforted her until she saw a little smile. For the third night in a row, she gave the girl ten milligrams of Sonata so that she'd get some sleep.

2

ALL THE RESIDENTS ARE ASLEEP now, and the place is quiet. There's a light on in the office window; the world outside seems impenetrable and black.

Elisabet is sitting in front of the computer, a deep frown on her face, writing up the evening's events in the log.

It's almost midnight, and she realizes that she hasn't even found time to take her evening pill. Her little habit, she likes to joke. The combination of nights on call and exhausting day-shifts have ruined her sleep. She usually takes ten milligrams of Stilnoct at ten o'clock so that she can be asleep by eleven and get a few solid hours of rest.

The September darkness has settled on the forest, but the smooth surface of Himmel Lake is still visible, shining like mother-of-pearl.

At last, she can switch the computer off and take her pill. She pulls her cardigan tighter around herself and thinks about how nice a glass of red wine would be. She'd love to sit in bed with a book and a glass of wine, reading and talking to Daniel.

But she's on call tonight and will be sleeping in the little over-night room.

She jumps when Buster starts barking out in the yard. He sounds so agitated that she gets goose bumps on her arms.

It's late; she should be in bed.

The room gets darker when the computer shuts down. Everything seems incredibly quiet. Elisabet becomes aware of the sounds she's making: the sigh of the office chair when she stands up, the tiles creaking as she walks over to the window. She tries to see outside, but the glass just reflects her own face and the inside of the office.

Suddenly, in the reflection, she sees the door slip open behind her.

Her heart starts to beat faster. The door was just ajar, but now it's half open. There must be a draft, she tries to tell herself. The stove in the dining room always seems to pull in a lot of air.

Yet Elisabet feels peculiarly anxious, and fear starts to creep through her veins. She doesn't dare turn around, just stares into the dark window at the reflection of the door behind her back.

She listens to the ticking of the computer.

In an attempt to shake off her unease, she reaches out her hand and switches off the lamp, then turns around.

Now the door is wide open.

A shiver runs down her spine.

The lights are on in the hallway leading to the dining room and the girls' rooms. She's just left the office, to make sure that the vents on the stove are closed, when she hears a whisper from the bedrooms.

3

ELISABET STANDS STILL, LISTENING, as she looks out into the hallway. At first she can't hear anything, but then there it is again. A slight whisper, so faint that it's barely audible.

"It's your turn to close your eyes," the voice says.

Elisabet stands perfectly still, staring off into the darkness. She blinks several times but can't see anyone there.

She is thinking that it must be one of the girls talking in her sleep when she hears a strange noise. It's like someone dropping an overripe peach on the floor. And then another one. Heavy and wet. A table leg scrapes as it moves; then another two peaches fall to the floor.

Elisabet catches a glimpse of movement from the corner of her eye. A shadow slipping past. She turns around and sees that the door to the dining room is slowly swinging closed.

"Wait," she says, even though she tells herself it was just the wind again.

She hurries over and grabs the handle but meets a peculiar resistance. There's a brief tug-of-war, and then the door simply glides open.

Elisabet walks into the dining room very warily, trying to scan the area. The scratched table stands out in the darkness. She moves slowly toward the stove, sees her own movement reflected in its closed brass doors.

The flue is still radiating heat.

Suddenly there's a crackling, knocking sound behind the oven doors. She takes a step back and bumps into a chair.

It's only a piece of firewood falling against the inside of the doors. The room is completely empty.

She takes a deep breath and leaves the dining room, closing the door behind her. She starts to head back toward the hallway to the isolation room but stops again and listens.

She can't hear anything from the girls' rooms. There's an acrid smell in the air—metallic, almost. Though she looks for movement in the dark hallway, everything is still. Even so, she is drawn in that direction, toward the row of unlocked doors. Some of them seem to be ajar.

On the righthand side of the hall are the bathrooms, and then an alcove leading to the locked isolation room where Miranda is sleeping.

The peephole in the door glints gently.

Elisabet stops and holds her breath. A high voice is whispering something in one of the rooms but falls abruptly silent when Elisabet starts to move again.

"Quiet, now," she says to the girls.

Her heart starts to beat harder when she hears a series of rapid thuds. It's hard to localize them, but it sounds as if Miranda is lying in bed and kicking the wall with her bare feet. Elisabet is about to check on her through the peephole when she sees that there's someone standing in the alcove.

She lets out a gasp and starts to back away. She feels as if she's in a dream, as if she's wading through water.

She immediately realizes how dangerous the situation is, but fear makes her slow.

She only thinks to run for her life when the floor creaks.

The figure in the darkness moves very quickly.

She turns and starts to run, hearing footsteps behind her. She slips on the rug and knocks her shoulder against the wall but keeps moving.

A soft voice is telling her to stop, but she doesn't—she runs, almost throwing herself down the hallway.

Doors fly open, then bounce back.

In panic, she rushes past the registration room, using the walls for support. A poster falls to the floor. She reaches the front door, fumbles, but manages to open it and run out into the cool night air; but she slips on the porch steps. One of her legs folds beneath her as she lands awkwardly on her hip. The stabbing pain from her ankle makes her yell out loud. She slumps to the ground, then hears heavy steps on the porch and starts to crawl away. She loses her shoes as she struggles to her feet with a whimper.

4

THE DOG IS BARKING AT her, running around, panting and moaning. Elisabet limps away from the house, across the dark driveway. The dog barks again, rough and anxious. Elisabet knows she won't be able to get through the forest—the nearest farm is half an hour's drive away. There's nowhere to go. She looks around in the darkness, then creeps behind the drying house toward the old brewery. She reaches the brew house and opens the door with shaking hands, goes inside, and carefully closes the door.

Gasping, she sinks to the floor and tries to find her telephone. "Oh God, oh God . . ."

Elisabet's hands are shaking so badly that she drops it on the floor. The battery falls out. She has started to pick up the pieces when she hears footsteps crunching across the gravel.

She holds her breath.

Her pulse is racing. Her ears are roaring. She tries to look out through the low window.

The dog is barking outside. Buster has followed her. He's scratching at the door and whimpering.

She crawls farther into the corner, next to the brick fireplace, and tries to breathe quietly as she pushes the battery back into her cell phone.

Elisabet lets out a scream when the door to the brew house opens. Panicking, she tries to shuffle along the wall, but there's nowhere to go.

She sees a pair of boots, then a shadowy figure with a terrible face holding a dark, heavy hammer.

She listens to the voice, nods, and covers her face.

The shadow hesitates, then rushes over, holds her down on the floor with one foot, and strikes hard. There's a flash of pain at the front of her head, just above her hairline. Her vision shrinks to a point, and then disappears. The pain is appalling, but she can still feel the warm blood running over her ears and down her neck like a soft caress.

The next blow hits the same place; her head lurches, and all she can feel now is the air being drawn down into her lungs.

Bewildered, she can't help thinking that the air is wonderfully sweet. Then she loses consciousness.

Elisabet doesn't feel the rest of the blows or how they make her body flinch. She doesn't notice that the keys to the office and the isolation room are taken from her pocket, and she isn't aware of being left on the floor, or how the dog slips into the brew house and starts to lick the blood from her crushed head as life slowly leaves her.

5

SOMEONE'S LEFT A BIG RED apple on the table. It looks delicious, all shiny. She decides to eat it and then pretend not to know anything about it. She'll ignore the questions and nagging, just sit there looking grumpy.

She reaches for it, but when she touches it, she realizes that it's completely rotten.

Her fingers sink into the cold, wet flesh.

Nina Molander wakes up the moment she snatches her hand back. It's the middle of the night. She's lying in bed. The only sound is the dog barking out in the yard. Her new medication often wakes her at night, and she has to get up to pee. Even though her calves and feet have swollen, she needs the pills; otherwise, her thoughts turn very dark, and she stops caring about anything.

She needs something bright, something to look forward to. She's tired of thinking about death.

Nina folds the covers back, sets her feet down on the warm wooden floor, and gets out of bed.

The house is quiet, and the hallway is lit up by the green sign for the emergency exit.

Hearing strange whispering behind one door, Nina wonders if the other girls are having a party without her.

I wouldn't want to go anyway, she thinks.

It smells like someone just burned something. The dog starts barking again. She doesn't bother trying to be quiet. She feels like slamming the bathroom door several times. She couldn't care less if Almira gets angry and throws things at her.

The old tiles creak gently. Nina walks toward the bathroom but stops when she feels something wet under her right foot. A dark puddle is seeping out from under the door to the isolation room where Miranda is sleeping. At first Nina just stands still, unsure of what to do, but then she notices that the key is in the lock.

Very strange.

She opens the door, goes inside, and switches the light on.

There's blood dripping everywhere.

Miranda is lying on the bed.

Nina takes a few steps back, without even noticing that she's wetting herself. Then she sees the bloody shoeprints on the floor and reaches out to the wall for support. She thinks she's going to faint.

She turns around and rushes to the next room. She shakes Caroline's shoulder.

"Miranda's hurt," she whispers. "I think she's been hurt."

"What are you doing in my room?" Caroline asks, sitting up in bed. "What the hell time is it?"

"There's blood on the floor!" Nina shouts.

"Just calm down."

6

NINA IS BREATHING FAR TOO fast as she looks into Caroline's eyes. She has to make her understand.

"There's blood everywhere!" she screams.

"Be quiet," Caroline hisses, getting out of bed.

Nina's cries have woken the others. She can already hear voices from the other rooms.

"Come and look!" Nina says, rubbing her arms anxiously. "Miranda looks funny, you have to come and look at her, you—"

"Can you just calm down? I'll come and look, but I'm sure—"

They hear a scream from the hallway. It's little Tuula. Caroline hurries out. Tuula is staring into the isolation room, her eyes open wide. Indie emerges, scratching her armpit.

Caroline pulls Tuula away but still has time to see the blood on the walls and Miranda's white body. Her heart is beating fast. She stands in Indie's way, thinking that none of them needs to see any more suicides.

"There's been an accident," she explains quickly. "Can you take everyone to the dining room, Indie?"

"Did something happen to Miranda?" Indie asks.

"Yes. We need to wake Elisabet."

Lu Chu and Almira come out from the same room. Lu Chu is wearing only a pair of pajama pants, and Almira is wrapped in the comforter.

"Go to the dining room," Indie says.

"Can I wash my face first?" Lu Chu asks.

"Take Tuula with you."

"What the hell is going on?" Almira asks.

"We don't know," Caroline replies curtly.

While Indie tries to get everyone into the dining room, Caroline hurries to the staff's overnight room. She knows Elisabet takes sleeping pills and never hears any of the girls running around at night.

Caroline bangs on the door as hard as she can.

"Elisabet, you have to wake up," she cries.

No response. Not a sound.

Caroline goes past the registration room to the nurses' office. The door is open, so she goes in, picks up the phone, and calls Daniel, the first person she can think of.

The line crackles.

Indie and Nina come into the office. Nina's lips are white; she's moving weirdly, and her body's shaking.

"Wait in the dining room," Caroline snaps.

"What about the blood? Did you see the blood?" Nina screams, and scratches her right arm.

"Daniel Grim," a tired voice says over the phone.

"It's me, Caroline—there's been an accident, and Elisabet won't wake up. I can't get her up, so I called you; I don't know what to do."

"I've got blood on my feet!" Nina yells. "I've got blood on my feet!"

"Calm down!" Indie shouts, trying to pull Nina out of the room.

"What's going on?" Daniel asks, in a voice that's suddenly very awake and very focused.

"Miranda's in the isolation room; it's full of blood," Caroline replies, swallowing hard. "I don't know what we—"

"Is she badly hurt?" he asks.

"Yes, I think. . . . Well, I—"

"Caroline," Daniel interrupts. "I'm going to call an ambulance, then—"

"But what should I do? What should—"

"See if Miranda needs help, and try to wake Elisabet," Daniel replies.

7

THE EMERGENCY CALL CENTER IN Sundsvall is located in a three-story brick building next to Bäckparken. Jasmin sits in front of the computer with her headset on and blows on her mug of black coffee. It's four o'clock in the morning, and the worst part of the night shift has passed.

Jasmin puts her coffee cup down and takes an incoming call: "SOS 112 . . . What's the nature of your emergency?"

"My name is Daniel Grim, I'm a counselor at the Birgitta Home. One of the residents just called me. It sounds serious; you have to get out there."

"Can you tell me what happened?" Jasmin asks as she searches for the Birgitta Home on the computer.

"I don't know. One of the girls called. I didn't really understand what she was saying. There was a lot of shouting in the background, and she was crying and saying that there was blood all over the room."

Jasmin gestures to her colleague Ingrid Sandén, indicating that they need more operators.

"Are you at the scene?" Ingrid says through the headset.

"No, I'm at home. I was asleep, but one of the girls called—"

"You're talking about the Birgitta Home, north of Sundsvall?" Jasmin asks calmly.

"Please, hurry up," he says in a shaky voice.

"We're sending police and an ambulance to the Birgitta Home, north of Sundsvall," Jasmin repeats, just to be sure.

She transfers the call to Ingrid, who keeps talking to Daniel while Jasmin alerts the police and paramedics.

"Birgitta is a children's facility, isn't it?"

"Yes, a group home," he replies.

"Shouldn't there be staff there?"

"Yes, my wife, Elisabet, is on duty, I'm about to call her. . . . I don't know what happened. I don't know anything."

"The police are on their way," Ingrid says calmly, and from the corner of her eye she sees the flashing blue lights of the first emergency vehicle sweep across the deserted street.

8

THE NARROW EXIT RAMP OFF Highway 86 leads straight into the dark forest, toward Himmel Lake and the Birgitta Home. The grit crunches under the police car's tires.

"You said you'd been out here before?" Rolf Wikner asks, shifting up to fourth gear.

"Yes . . . a couple of years ago, one of the girls tried to set fire to one of the buildings," Sonja Rask replies.

"Why the hell can't they reach anyone on staff?" Rolf mutters.

"Probably have their hands full—regardless of what's happened," Sonja says.

"It would be helpful to know a little more."

"It would," she agrees calmly.

The two drive in silence, listening to the police radio. An ambulance is on its way, and another police car is coming from the station.

The road, like so many logging roads, is perfectly straight. The tires thunder over potholes and dips. Tree trunks flit past as the flashing blue lights make their way far into the forest. Sonja reports back to the station as they pull up in front of the dark-red buildings of the home.

A girl in a nightgown is standing on the steps of the main building. Her eyes are wide open, but her face is pale and distant.

When Rolf and Sonja get out of the car and hurry over to her, the girl doesn't seem to notice them.

A dog starts to bark anxiously.

"Is anyone hurt?" Rolf says in a loud voice. "Does anyone need help?"

The girl waves vaguely toward the edge of the forest. She tries to take a step, but her legs buckle beneath her. She falls backward and hits her head.

"Are you okay?" Sonja asks.

The girl lies on the steps, staring up at the sky, breathing quickly and shallowly. Sonja notes that she's drawn blood from scratching her arms and neck.

"I'm going in," Rolf says firmly.

Sonja stays with the girl in shock and waits for the ambulance while Rolf goes inside. He sees bloody marks left by boots and bare feet on the wooden floor, including long strides heading for the entryway, then back. Rolf feels adrenaline course through his body. He does his best not to stand on the footprints but knows that his primary objective is to save lives.

He looks into a common room where all the lights are on and sees four girls sitting on the two sofas.

"Is anyone hurt?" he calls.

"Maybe a little," a small, red-haired girl in pink sweatpants and a hoodie says with a smile.

"Where is she?" he asks anxiously.

"Miranda's on her bed," says an older girl with straight dark hair.

"In here?" he says, pointing toward the hallway with the bedrooms.

The older girl just nods, and Rolf follows the bloody foot-prints past a dining room with a large wooden table and a tiled stove and into a dark hallway lined with doors leading to the girls' private rooms. Shoes and bare feet have walked through the blood. The old floor creaks beneath him. Rolf stops, pulls his flashlight from his belt, and shines it along the hallway. He quickly looks at the hand-painted maxims and ornate biblical quotations on the wall, then aims the beam at the floor.

Blood has seeped out across the floor from under the door in a dark alcove. The key is in the lock. He heads for it, carefully moves the flashlight to his other hand, and touches the handle as gently as he can.

There's a click, and the door slips open.

"Hello? Miranda? My name is Rolf, I'm a police officer," he says into the darkness as he steps closer. "I'm coming in now. . . ."

The only sound is his breathing.

He carefully pushes the door open and sweeps the light around the room. The sight that greets him is so brutal that he wobbles and has to reach out for the door frame.

Instinctively, he looks away, but his eyes have already seen what he didn't want to see. His ears register the rushing of his pulse as well as the drops hitting the puddle on the floor.

A young woman is lying on the bed, but large parts of her head seem to be missing. Blood is spattered up the walls and still dripping from the dark lampshade.

The door closes behind Rolf, and he's so startled that he drops the flashlight on the floor. The room goes completely black. As he turns and fumbles in the darkness, he hears a girl's small hands hammering on the other side of the door.

"Now she can see you!" a high-pitched voice screams. "Now she's looking!"

Rolf finds the handle and tries to open the door, but it won't budge. The little peephole glints at him in the darkness. With shaking hands, he pushes the handle down and shoves with his shoulder.

The door flies open and Rolf stumbles into the hallway. He breathes in deeply. The little red-haired girl is standing a short distance away, looking at him with big eyes.

9

DETECTIVE JOONA LINNA IS STANDING at the window in his hotel room in Sveg, 450 kilometers north of Stockholm. The dawn light is a cold, pale blue. There are no lights lit along Älv Street. He won't be able to find out if Rosa Bergman lives here for a few hours.

His light-gray shirt is unbuttoned and hanging over his black suit pants. His blond hair is unkempt, as usual, and his pistol is lying on the bed in its holster.

Despite numerous approaches from various elite groups, Joona has remained with the National Crime Unit. His tendency to go his own way annoys a lot of people, but in less than fifteen years he has solved more complex cases in Scandinavia than any other police detective.

During the summer, a complaint was filed against Joona with the Internal Affairs Division, claiming that he had alerted an extremist left-wing organization about a forthcoming raid. Since then, Joona has been relieved of certain duties without actually being formally suspended. The head of IAD has made it very clear that he will contact the senior prosecutor at the National Police Cases Authority if he believes there are grounds for prosecution.

The allegations are serious, but right now Joona doesn't have time to worry about any potential suspension or reprimand. His thoughts are focused on the old woman who was following him outside Adolf Fredrik's Church in Stockholm, who gave him a message from Rosa Bergman. She had passed him two tattered cards from an old Cuckoo card-game deck.

"This is you, isn't it?" the woman said uncertainly. "And here's the crown, the bridal crown."

"What do you want?" Joona asked.

"I don't want anything," the old woman said. "But I have a message from Rosa Bergman."

His heart began to thud. But he forced himself to shrug and explain that there must have been a mistake:

"Because I don't know anyone named—"

"She's wondering why you're pretending that your daughter's dead."

"I'm sorry, but I don't know what you're talking about," Joona replied with a smile.

He was smiling, but his voice sounded like a stranger's, distant and cold, as if it were coming from under a large rock. The woman's words swirled through him, and he felt like grabbing her by her thin arms and demanding to know what had happened, but instead he remained calm.

"I have to go," he explained, and was about to turn away when a migraine shot through his brain like the blade of a knife through his left eye. His field of vision shrank to a jagged, flickering halo.

When he regained his sight, he saw that he was lying on the ground and people were standing in a circle around him. They moved aside to make way for the paramedics.

The old woman had vanished.

Joona had denied knowing Rosa Bergman. But he had been lying.

Because he definitely knows who Rosa Bergman is.

He thinks about her every day, but she shouldn't know anything about him. If Rosa knows who he is, then something must have gone very wrong.

Joona left the hospital a few hours later and immediately began looking for Rosa.

He had no choice but to conduct the search alone, so he requested a leave of absence.

According to official records, there's no one named Rosa Bergman living in Sweden, but there are more than two thousand people with the surname Bergman in Scandinavia.

Joona systematically checked through database after database. His only remaining option was to search the Swedish Population Register's physical archives. For centuries, the register was maintained by the church, but in 1991 it was digitized and transferred to the Tax Agency.

Joona started to work his way through, beginning with southern Sweden. He sat down in the National Archive in Lund with a paper cup of coffee in front of him, searching for a Rosa Bergman born at the right time and place. Then he traveled to Visby, Vadstena, and Gothenburg.

He went to Uppsala and the vast archive in Härnösand. All in all, he searched through thousands of pages of births, locations, and family connections.

10

Joona had spent the previous afternoon in the archive in Östersund. The antiquarian smell of discolored old paper and heavy bindings filled the room, and sunlight moved slowly across the tall walls.

Just before the archive closed, Joona found a girl born eighty-four years earlier who had been christened Rosa Maja in Sveg Parish in Härjedalen, in the province of Jämtland. The girl's parents were Kristina and Evert Bergman. Joona couldn't find any information about their marriage, but the mother, Kristina Stefanson, had been born nineteen years before, in the same parish.

It took Joona three more hours to locate an eighty-four-year-old woman named Maja Stefanson in an assisted-living home in Sveg. It was already seven o'clock in the evening, but Joona got in his car and drove to Sveg. It was late by the time he arrived, and he wasn't allowed into the home.

Joona checked into Lilla Hotellet and tried to get some sleep, but he woke up at four o'clock and has been standing at the window ever since, waiting for morning.

He's almost certain that he has found Rosa Bergman. She's using her middle name and has adopted her mother's maiden name.

Joona looks at his watch and decides that it's time to go. He buttons his jacket, leaves the room, and heads out into the small town.

The Blue Wings assisted-living facility is a cluster of yellow houses around a neat lawn.

Joona opens the door to the main building and goes inside. He forces himself to walk slowly.

She wasn't supposed to be able to find me, he thinks again. She wasn't supposed to know about me.

Joona never talks about how he ended up alone, but he spends every waking moment thinking about it. His life flared up and died away in an instant. It went from gleaming white to smoldering ash.

In the cafeteria, a thin man in his eighties is staring at the television, where a chef is heating oil in a pan and talking about various ways to update traditional crayfish cakes.

The old man turns to Joona.

"Anders?" he says in an unsteady voice. "Is that you, Anders?"

"My name is Joona," he replies in his soft Finnish accent. "I'm looking for Maja Stefanson."

The man stares at him with moist, red-rimmed eyes. "Anders, listen, lad. You've got to get me out of here. It's full of old people."

The man hits the arm of the sofa with a frail fist but stops abruptly when a nurse walks into the room.

"Good morning," Joona says. "I'm here to visit Maja Stefanson."

"How lovely," she says. "But I should warn you, Maja's dementia has gotten worse. She tries to escape whenever she has a chance."

"I understand," Joona says.

"This summer, she managed to get all the way to Stockholm."

The nurse leads Joona down a freshly mopped hallway with subdued lighting and opens one of the doors. "Maja?" she calls out warmly.

11

An old woman is making the bed. When she looks up, Joona recognizes her immediately. It's the woman who was following him, the one who showed him the cards and told him she had a message from Rosa Bergman.

Joona's heart is beating hard.

She's the only person who knows where his wife and daughter are, and she shouldn't be aware of his existence.

"Rosa Bergman?" Joona asks.

"Yes," she replies, raising one of her hands like a schoolgirl.

"My name is Joona Linna."

"Yes." Rosa Bergman smiles, shuffling toward him.

"You had a message for me," he says.

"Oh my, I don't remember that," Rosa replies, sitting down on the sofa.

He swallows hard and takes a step toward her. "You asked me why I was pretending my daughter was dead."

"You shouldn't do that," she says sternly. "That's not nice at all."

"What do you know about my daughter?" Joona asks, taking another step toward the woman. "Have you heard anything?"

She merely smiles into the distance, and Joona lowers his gaze. Though he is trying to think clearly, he notices that his hands are shaking as he goes over to the little kitchen area and pours coffee into two cups.

"Rosa, this is important to me," he says slowly, putting the cups on the table. "Very important."

She blinks a couple of times, then asks in a timid voice: "Who are you? Has something happened to Mother?"

"Rosa, do you remember a little girl named Lumi? Her mother's name was Summa, and you helped them...."

Joona trails off when he sees the lost expression in the woman's eyes, clouded with cataracts.

"Why did you try to find me?" he asks, even though he knows there's no point.

Rosa Bergman drops her coffee cup on the floor and starts to cry. The nurse comes in and soothes her in a familiar way.

"I'll show you out," she says quietly to Joona.

They walk down the hallway.

"How long has she had dementia?" Joona asks.

"It happened quickly with Maja.... We started to notice the first signs about a year ago.... People say it's like a second childhood, which is pretty close to the truth."

"If she...if she suddenly has a lucid period," Joona says gravely, "would you mind contacting me?"

"That does happen occasionally," the woman says, nodding.

"Call me at once," he says, handing her his card.

"Detective?" she says in surprise, pinning the card to the corkboard behind the reception desk.

12

When Joona gets out into the fresh air, he breathes in deeply. Maybe Rosa had something important to tell him, he thinks. It's possible that someone asked her to pass on a message. But she took a turn for the worse before she could tell him.

He'll probably never know what it was.

Twelve years have passed since he lost Summa and Lumi. The last traces of them have been erased, along with Rosa Bergman's lost memories.

It's over now.

Joona sits in his car, wipes the tears from his cheeks, then starts to drive back home to Stockholm.

He's driven thirty kilometers south when the head of the National Crime Unit, Carlos Eliasson, calls him.

"We have a murder at a children's group home up in Sundsvall," Carlos says in a tense voice. "The emergency call center was alerted just after four this morning."

"I'm on leave," Joona says almost inaudibly.

"You still could have come to karaoke night."

"Another time," Joona says, almost to himself.

The road runs straight through the forest. Far off between the trees, a silvery lake is glinting.

"Joona? What's happened?"

"Nothing."

Someone calls for Carlos in the background.

"I'm going into a meeting now, but I want ... I just spoke to Susanne Öst, and she says the Västernorrland Police aren't going to make a formal request for help from National Crime."

"So why are you calling me?"

"I said we'd send an observer."

"We never send observers, do we?"

"We do now," Carlos says, lowering his voice. "I'm afraid this one's pretty sensitive. You remember Janne Svensson, the captain of the national hockey team? The press never shut up about how incompetent the police were."

"Because they never found—"

"Don't start. That was Susanne's first big case as a prosecutor," Carlos goes on. "I don't want to say that the press were right, but the Västernorrland Police could have used you on that occasion. They were too slow; they went by the book, and too much time passed. . . . Nothing that unusual, really, but sometimes the press pick up on it."

"I can't talk anymore," Joona says.

"You know I wouldn't ask you if it was just a straightforward murder," Carlos says, taking a deep breath. "But there's going to be a lot of coverage, Joona. . . . This one's very, very brutal, very bloody . . . and the girl's body has been arranged."

"How? How has it been arranged?" Joona asks.

"Apparently, she's lying on her bed with her hands over her face."

Joona drives on in silence, his left hand on the wheel. The trees flit past on both sides of the car. He can hear Carlos breathing over the phone. There are other voices in the background. Without saying anything, Joona turns off the E45 toward Los, onto a road that will take him to the coast, and then up to Sundsvall.

"Please, Joona, just go up there. . . . Help them solve the case, preferably before the press get hold of it."

13

JOONA LEAVES THE COASTAL ROAD and turns onto Highway 86, which heads up inland along the Indals River Valley.

After two hours of driving, he finally approaches the isolated children's group home.

He slows down and turns onto a narrow gravel road. Sunlight filters through the tall pine trees.

A dead girl, Joona thinks.

A girl was murdered and positioned on her bed while everyone was asleep. The murder was extremely violent, according to the local police. They have no immediate suspects, and it's too late for roadblocks, but everyone in the local police department has been informed. Detective Olle Gunnarsson is leading the investigation.

It's almost ten o'clock by the time Joona parks and leaves the car beyond the police's outer cordon. The forest has opened up into a large clearing. Damp trees are sparkling in the sunlight on the slope down toward the lake. By the side of the road is a metal sign that reads "Birgitta Children's Home."

Joona walks toward the cluster of rust-red buildings gathered around the central yard like a traditional farm. An ambulance, three police cars, a white Mercedes, and three other cars are parked in front of the buildings.

A dog is barking nonstop as it runs along a line tied between two trees.

An older man with a walrus mustache, a potbelly, and a wrinkled linen suit is standing in front of the main building. He spots Joona but shows no sign of saying hello. Instead, he finishes rolling his cigarette and licks the paper. Joona steps over a cordon, and the man tucks the cigarette behind his ear.

"I'm the National Crime observer," Joona says.

"Gunnarsson," the man says. "Detective."

"I'm supposed to follow your work here."

"Fine, as long as you don't get in the way," the man says, looking at him coolly.

Joona looks up at the main building, where the crime-scene investigation is already under way. The rooms are lit up by arc lights, lending all the windows an unnatural glow.

An officer emerges from the door, his face almost white. He claps one hand to his mouth, stumbles down the steps, then leans against the wall and throws up onto a patch of nettles next to the drainpipe.

"You'll do the same once you've been inside," Gunnarsson says to Joona with a smile.

"What do you know so far?"

"Not a damn thing ... We got the call in the middle of the night, from a counselor at Birgitta ... Daniel Grim. That was at four o'clock. He was at his home in Sundsvall and received a call from the girls. He didn't know much. He said that the girls were yelling something about lots of blood."

"So the girls made the call from here?" Joona asks.

"Yes."

"But they called the counselor in Sundsvall rather than the police?" Joona says.

"Exactly."

"There must have been a staff member here?"

"No."

"Shouldn't there have been?"

"Presumably," Gunnarsson says in a tired voice.

"Which one of the girls called the counselor?" Joona asks.

"One of the older residents," Gunnarsson says, looking in his notebook. "A Caroline Forsgren ... But, as I understand it, she wasn't the one who found the body. That was ... It's a hell of a mess—several of the girls have looked into the room. It's horrible. We've taken one of them off to the hospital. She was hysterical, and the paramedics thought that was the safest thing to do."

"Who was first on the scene?" Joona asks.

"Two colleagues, Rolf Wikner and Sonja Rask," Gunnarsson replies. "I got here at around quarter to six and called the prosecutor ... and she clearly pissed herself and contacted Stockholm ... so now we're stuck with you."

He smiles at Joona without any warmth.

"Do you have a suspect?" Joona asks.

Gunnarsson takes a deep breath and says in a didactic tone: "Years of experience have taught me to let an investigation unfold at its own pace. We need to get people out here, start to interview the witnesses, secure the evidence...."

"Is it okay if I go in and take a look?" Joona asks, glancing up at the door.

"I wouldn't recommend it.... We'll have pictures soon."

"I need to look at the girl before she's moved," Joona says.

"We're dealing with an attack with a blunt instrument, very brutal, very aggressive," he says. "The perpetrator's a strong guy. After her death, the victim was laid out on her bed. No one noticed anything until one of the girls was going to the bathroom and stepped in the blood that was seeping under the door."

"Was it still warm?"

"Look ... these girls are pretty tricky to deal with," Gunnarsson explains. "They're frightened, and they're very angry. They object to everything we say, they don't listen, they scream at us, and ... Earlier they were determined to get through the cordon to get things from their rooms—iPods, ChapStick, coats, and so on—and when we went to move them to the other building, two of them escaped into the forest."

"Escaped?"

"We managed to catch up with them. . . . Now we need to get them to return voluntarily. They're lying on the ground, demanding to ride on Rolf's shoulders."

14

Joona puts on a paper suit and goes up the steps to the main building. The fans of the arc lights are working hard, and the air on the porch is already warm. Every detail is visible in their strong glare.

Joona walks slowly along the stepping plates that have been laid out across the floor. A picture has fallen to the floor, and the broken glass glints in the powerful lights. Bloody shoeprints cover the hallway, leading to and from the front door.

The house has retained its original character from when it was a grand farmhouse. The painted panels have faded over the years but are still colorful, and the traditional patterns done by traveling painters curl across the walls and woodwork.

Farther along the hallway, a forensics technician named Jimi Sjöberg is shining a black light on a chair that's already had Luminol sprayed on it.

"Blood?" Joona asks.

"Not on this one," Jimi mutters, moving on with the black light.

"Have you found anything unexpected?"

"Erixon called from Stockholm and told us not to touch anything until Joona Linna gave the go-ahead," he replies with a smile.

"I'm grateful."

"So we haven't really started," Jimi goes on. "We've laid out all these damn plates, and photographed and filmed everything, and ... well, I took the liberty of taking blood samples in the hallway so we could send something off to the lab."

"Good."

"And Siri lifted the prints in the hall before they got contaminated. . . ."

The other forensics expert, Siri Karlsson, has just dismantled the brass handle from the isolation-room door. She puts it carefully into a paper bag, then comes over to Joona and Jimi.

"He's here to take a look at the crime scene," Jimi says, nodding at Joona.

"It's pretty unpleasant," Siri says through her mask. Her eyes look tired and troubled.

"So I understand," Joona says.

"You can look at pictures instead, if you'd rather," she says.

"This is Joona Linna," Jimi tells her.

"Sorry, I didn't realize."

"I'm just an observer," Joona says.

She looks down, and when she raises her eyes again, there's a trace of a blush on her cheeks. "Everyone's talking about you," she says. "I mean ... I ... I don't care about the investigation. I look forward to working with you."

"Same here," Joona says.

He stands still and listens to the whirr of the lamps and tries to focus. He needs to absorb impressions of what he sees without giving in to the instinct to look away.

15

JOONA GOES OVER TO THE alcove. The door to the isolation room no longer has a handle, but the lock and key are still in place.

He closes his eyes for a moment, then enters the small room.

It's brightly lit, and everything is still.

The warm air is heavy with the smell of blood and urine. He inhales to detect any other smells: damp wood, dirty sheets, deodorant.

The hot metal of the lamps ticks. He can hear the muffled sound of barking through the walls.

Joona stands perfectly still and forces himself to look at the body on the bed. His eyes linger on every detail, even though he'd like nothing more than to hurry out into the fresh air and shade of the forest.

Blood has run across the floor and is spattered over the furniture and the pale biblical motifs on the walls. It's sprayed across the ceiling and over to the bathroom. A thin girl in the early stages of puberty is lying on the bed. She has been laid out on her back, with her hands covering her face. She's wearing nothing but a pair of cotton underpants. Her breasts are covered by her elbows, and her feet are crossed at the ankles.

Joona feels his heart beating, feels his blood coursing through his veins as his pulse roars in his temples.

He forces himself to look, register, and think.

The girl's face is hidden.

As if she's frightened, as if she doesn't want to see the perpetrator.

Before the girl was positioned on the bed, she was subjected to extreme violence. Repeated blows with a blunt object to her forehead and scalp.

She's only a young girl. She must have been horribly frightened.

A chain of events has led her to this room, to this group home. Maybe she was just unlucky in her parents and foster parents. Maybe she thought she'd be safe here.

Joona studies every detail until he can't take it anymore. Then he shuts his eyes for a few moments and thinks about his daughter's face and the gravestone that isn't hers, before opening his eyes again and resuming the examination.

The evidence suggests that the victim was sitting on the chair at the little table when the attacker struck.

Joona tries to identify the movements that led to this spatter pattern.

Every drop of blood falling through the air naturally assumes a round shape and has a diameter of five millimeters. If the drop is smaller, it means that the blood has been subjected to external force that's broken it into smaller drops.

And that's where spatter-pattern analysis comes in.

Joona is standing on two stepping plates in front of the small table, probably exactly where the murderer stood a few hours before. The girl was sitting on the chair on the other side of the table. Joona looks at the spatter pattern, turns around, and sees that blood has been sprayed high up the wall. The implement was swung backward several times to gain momentum, and every time it changed direction for another blow, blood sprayed back from it.

Joona has already stayed longer at this crime scene than most detectives would have, but he isn't finished yet. He stands in front of the girl on the bed. He sees the stud in her navel, the lip print on the glass of water, notices that she has had a birthmark removed below her right breast, sees the fine hairs on her shins and a yellowed bruise on her thigh.

He leans cautiously over her. Her bare skin is emitting very faint heat now. He looks at the hands covering her face and sees that she didn't manage to scratch the perpetrator: there's no skin under her fingernails.

He takes a few steps back and then looks at her again. Her white skin. The hands over her face. There's hardly any blood on her body. Only the pillow is bloody.

She's clean.

Joona looks around the room. Behind the door is a small shelf with two clothes hooks beneath it. On the floor are a pair of sneakers with white socks tucked inside them. A pair of washed-out jeans is hanging from one of the hooks, along with a black varsity sweater and a jean jacket. There's a small white bra on the shelf.

Joona doesn't touch the clothes, but they don't appear to be bloody. Presumably, she got undressed and hung her clothes up before she was murdered.

So why isn't her whole body covered with blood? Something must have protected her. But what?

16

Joona is walking in the sunshine, thinking about the extreme level of violence to which the girl was subjected and the fact that her body was as clean and white as a pebble in the sea.

Gunnarsson had said that the violence inflicted on her had been aggressive. Joona is thinking that it clearly required a lot of force, almost desperate force, but it wasn't uncontrolled violence. The blows were focused. The intention was to kill, yet the body had been treated with care.

Gunnarsson is sitting on the hood of his Mercedes, talking on his phone.

Murder investigations don't tend to become chaotic if they're left without direction. They mostly sort themselves out; that's the usual way of things. But Joona has never waited, has never trusted that order would be restored by itself.

Of course, he knows that the murderer is almost always someone close to the victim and usually contacts the police shortly afterward to confess, but he never counts on this.

She's lying on the bed now, he thinks. But she was sitting at the table in just her underwear when she was murdered.

It's hard to believe that could have happened in complete silence.

There must be a witness in a place like this.

One of the girls has seen or heard something, Joona thinks as he heads for the smaller building. Someone probably had an idea of what was coming, identified some sort of threat or conflict.

The dog is whining under the tree, then bites its leash before starting to bark again.

Joona goes over to the two men talking outside the smaller building. One of them is the crime-scene coordinator, a man in his fifties with a side part and a dark-blue police sweater. The other one doesn't seem to be a police officer. He's unshaven and has friendly, if tired, eyes.

"Joona Linna, National Crime," he says, shaking hands with them both.

"Åke," the coordinator says.

"My name is Daniel," the man with the tired eyes says. "I work as a counselor here at the home. . . . I came as soon as I heard what had happened."

"Do you have a minute?" Joona asks. "I'd like to meet the girls, and it would probably be a good idea if you were there."

"Now?" Daniel asks.

"If that's okay," Joona replies.

The man blinks behind his glasses and says worriedly, "It's just that two of them managed to run off into the forest. . . ."

"They've been found," Joona explains.

"Yes, I know, but I probably need to talk to them," Daniel says, then, suddenly, gives an involuntary smile. "They said they won't come back unless they're allowed to ride on one of the police officers' shoulders."

"Gunnarsson would probably volunteer," Joona replies, walking toward the small red cottage.

This first meeting will be his chance to study the girls, see how they interact and what's going on beneath the surface. If anyone has seen something, the other members of the group tend to indicate it unconsciously, acting as compass needles. Joona knows he doesn't have the authority to conduct interviews, but he needs to know if there's a witness.

17

THE FLOOR CREAKS AS JOONA steps over the threshold into the small house. There are three girls in the cramped room. The youngest of them can't be more than twelve years old. Her skin is pink and her hair coppery red. She's sitting on the floor, leaning back against the wall, watching television. She whispers to herself, then hits the back of her head against the wall several times, closes her eyes for a few seconds, and resumes watching the television.

The other two don't even seem to notice her. They're sitting on a corduroy sofa, leafing through fashion magazines.

A woman is sitting on the floor next to the red-haired girl.

"My name is Lisa and I am a psychologist," she says tentatively, in a warm voice. "What's your name?"

The girl doesn't take her eyes off the television. It's a repeat of the series *Blue Water High*. The volume is turned up loud, and the screen casts a chilly glow across the room.

"Have you heard the story of Thumbelina?" Lisa asks. "I often feel like her—the size of someone's thumb. . . . How are you feeling?"

"Like Jack the Ripper," the girl replies without taking her eyes off the screen.

Joona sits in an armchair in front of the television. One of the girls on the sofa stares at him wide-eyed but looks down with a smile when he says hello. She has a stocky build, her fingernails are badly bitten, and she's wearing jeans and a black shirt with the phrase "Razors cause less pain than life" on it. She's wearing blue eye shadow and has a sparkly hair tie around her wrist. The other girl, who looks slightly older, is wearing a ripped T-shirt with a horse on it, and a white pearl rosary necklace. She has old injection scars in the crook of her arm and is using a rolled-up khaki jacket to form a pillow behind her head.

"Indie?" the older girl asks in a subdued voice. "Did you go in and look before the cops came?"

"I don't want nightmares," the heavyset girl says languidly.

"Poor little Indie," the older one teases.

"What?"

"You're scared of nightmares when—"

"Yes, I am."

The other girl laughs: "So fucking selfish."

"Shut up, Caroline," the red-haired girl cries.

"Miranda's been murdered," Caroline goes on. "That's probably a bit worse than—"

"I just think it's nice not to have to deal with her," Indie says.

"You're sick." Caroline smiles.

"*She* was fucking sick. She burned me with a cigarette."

"Stop bitching!" the red-haired girl snaps.

"And she hit me with a jump rope," Indie goes on.

"You really are a bitch." Caroline sighs.

"Sure, I'll say it if it makes you feel better," Indie teases. "It's really sad that an idiot's dead, but I—"

The little red-haired girl hits her head against the wall again, then closes her eyes. The front door opens, and the two girls who escaped come in with Gunnarsson.

18

JOONA LEANS BACK IN THE chair. His face is calm, his muscular body is relaxed, and his eyes are as gray as the frozen sea as he watches the two girls walk in.

The others boo loudly and laugh. Lu Chu is swaying her hips exaggeratedly as she walks, flicking a V-sign with her fingers.

"Lesbian loser," Indie calls.

"We could take a shower together," Lu Chu replies.

The counselor, Daniel Grim, comes into the cottage behind the girls. He's obviously trying to get Gunnarsson to listen.

"I'd like you to take it a little bit more gently with the girls," Daniel says, then lowers his voice before he goes on. "You're frightening them just by being here. . . ."

"Don't worry," Gunnarsson reassures him.

"But I am," Daniel replies frankly.

"What?"

"I *am* worried," he says.

"Well, you can butt out, then." Gunnarsson sighs. "Just get out of the way and let me do my job."

Joona notes that the counselor hasn't shaved and that the T-shirt under his jacket is inside out.

"I just want to point out that, for these girls, the police don't represent security."

"Yes, they do!" Caroline jokes.

"That's good to hear," Daniel says with a smile, then turns back to Gunnarsson. "For most of our residents, the police have only featured in their lives when things were going wrong."

Joona can see that Daniel knows the police officer thinks he's a nuisance, but he still chooses to raise another matter: "I was speaking to the coordinator outside about temporary accommodations for—"

"One thing at a time," Gunnarsson interrupts.

"It's important, because—"

"Cunt," Indie says irritably.

"Fuck you," Lu Chu teases.

"Because it could be damaging," Daniel goes on. "It could be damaging for the girls to have to sleep here tonight."

"Are they going to stay in a hotel, then?" Gunnarsson asks.

"You should be murdered!" Almira yells as she throws a glass at Indie.

It shatters against the wall, scattering water and jagged glass fragments across the floor. Daniel rushes over as Almira turns away, but Indie manages to punch her in the back several times before Daniel separates them.

"For God's sake, control yourselves!" he roars.

"Almira's a fucking cunt who—"

"Just calm down, Indie," he says, blocking her hand. "We've talked about this—haven't we?"

"Yes," she replies in a calmer voice.

"You're a good girl," he says with a smile.

She nods and starts to pick up pieces of glass from the floor with Almira.

"I'll get the vacuum cleaner," Daniel says, and leaves the cottage.

"Did Miranda have any enemies?" Gunnarsson asks the group.

"No," Almira replies, and giggles.

Indie glances at Joona.

"Okay, listen!" Gunnarsson says, raising his voice. "I just want you to answer my questions without shrieking and messing around. It can't be that damn difficult, can it?"

"That depends on the questions," Caroline replies calmly.

"I'll probably stick to shrieking," Lu Chu mutters.

"Truth or dare," Indie says, pointing at Joona with a smile.

"Truth," Joona replies.

"I'm asking the questions," Gunnarsson protests.

"What does this mean?" Joona asks, covering his face with his hands.

"What? I don't know," Indie replies. "Vicky and Miranda were the ones who did all that—"

"I can't handle this," Caroline interrupts. "You didn't see Miranda. That's how she looked. There was so much blood, there was blood everywhere. And ..."

Her voice collapses into sobs, and Lisa goes over and tries to calm her down.

"Who's Vicky?" Joona asks, getting up from the armchair.

"She's our most recent arrival."

"So where the hell is she?" Lu Chu snaps.

"Which one's her room?" Joona asks quickly.

"She probably snuck out to see her fuck-buddy," Tuula says.

"We usually store up Valium, then sleep like—"

"Who are we talking about now?" Gunnarsson asks in a loud voice.

"Vicky Bennet," Caroline replies. "I haven't seen her all—"

"Vicky's just too fucking much," Lu Chu says, laughing.

"Turn the television off," Gunnarsson says, sounding stressed. "I want everyone to calm down, and—"

"Stop shouting!" Tuula screams, turning the volume up.

Joona crouches down in front of Caroline and holds her gaze with calm intensity.

"Which one is Vicky's room?"

"The last one, at the end of the hallway," Caroline replies.

19

JOONA LEAVES THE SMALL HOUSE and hurries across the yard, saying hello to the forensics technicians before going back into the main building. It's gloomy now that the lamps are switched off, but the plates on the floor stand out like stepping-stones.

One girl is missing, Joona thinks. No one has seen her. Maybe she ran away in the chaos; maybe the others are trying to help her by withholding what they know.

The crime-scene investigation has just started, and the rooms haven't been searched yet. The entire home should have been examined with a fine-toothed comb, but there hasn't been time—too much has been happening.

The girls are anxious and scared.

The victim support team should be here.

The team needs reinforcements, more forensics technicians, more resources.

Joona shudders at the thought that the missing girl might be hiding in her room. She could have seen something and may now be so terrified that she won't dare come out.

He hurries into the wing that has the girls' rooms.

The walls and timbers are creaking slightly, but otherwise the building is quiet. The door to the isolation room is ajar. The dead girl is lying on the bed in there with her hands over her eyes.

Joona suddenly remembers that he saw three horizontal marks in the blood on the edge of the door frame. Blood from three fingers, but not fingerprints. When Joona noticed the marks, he was absorbed in structuring his impressions of the crime scene; only now does he realize that they were on the wrong side. There are faint prints from boots, shoes, and bare feet going in all directions, but the three streaks of blood lead deeper into the building.

Whoever left the marks was planning to do something in one of the other girls' rooms.

No more dead bodies, Joona whispers to himself.

He pulls on a pair of latex gloves and heads for the last room. When he opens the door, he hears a rustling sound and stops abruptly, looking around. The sound disappears. Joona carefully reaches for the light switch with his hand.

He hears the noise again—an odd, metallic sound.

"Vicky?"

He feels across the wall and finds the switch. Yellow light immediately fills the sparsely furnished room. There's a creak as the window swings open toward the forest and lake. A sudden noise in the corner draws Joona's attention, and he sees a birdcage lying on the floor. A yellow parakeet is flapping its wings and climbing the roof of the cage.

The smell of blood is unmistakable. A mixture of iron and something else, something cloying and rancid.

Joona lays out some plastic stepping plates and walks slowly into the room.

There's blood around the window latch. Clear handprints show that someone climbed up onto the windowsill, grabbed the frame, and then, presumably, jumped out onto the lawn below.

He goes over to the bed. An icy shiver runs down his neck when he pulls the covers back. The sheet is covered with dried blood. But whoever was lying in the bed hadn't been injured.

The blood has been wiped off onto the sheet, smeared across it.

Someone covered in blood slept in these sheets.

Joona stands still for a while, trying to read the movements.

She really did sleep, he thinks.

When he tries to lift up the pillow, he discovers that it's stuck to the bottom sheet and mattress. Joona pulls it free and finds a bloodstained hammer with congealed brown matter and strands of hair stuck to it.

20

The Birgitta Home is bathed in soft, beautiful light, and the lake is glinting majestically between the tall old trees. There's nothing to indicate that a gruesome murder was committed just hours ago.

Gunnarsson is standing in the yard with Daniel Grim and Sonja Rask. Gunnarsson has opened the trunk of his white Mercedes and laid out the forensics technicians' sketches of the crime scene.

The dog is still barking excitedly, tugging at its leash.

When Joona stops behind the car and runs his hand through his tousled hair, the other three turn to face him.

"The girl escaped through her window," he says.

"Escaped?" Daniel says in astonishment. "Vicky escaped? Why would—"

"There's blood on the window frame, there's blood in her bed, and—"

"Surely that doesn't mean—."

"There's a bloody hammer under her pillow," Joona concludes.

"This doesn't make sense," Gunnarsson says irritably. "That can't be right. The violence was so damn extreme. . . ."

Joona turns back to Daniel. His face looks fragile and naked in the sunlight.

"What do you think?" Joona asks him.

"What? About the idea that Vicky might . . . It's insane," Daniel replies.

"Why?"

"Just now," the counselor says, smiling involuntarily, "the police were convinced this was the work of a grown man. Vicky's small—she weighs less than fifty kilos—and her wrists are as thin as . . ."

"Is she violent?" Joona asks.

"Vicky didn't do this," Daniel replies calmly. "I've spent two months working with her, and I can tell you that she didn't."

"Was she violent before she came here?"

"I have to respect the oath of confidentiality," Daniel replies.

"Surely you can see that your damn oath is costing us time," Gunnarsson says.

"What I can say is that I coach some residents to adopt alternatives to aggressive responses . . . so that they don't react angrily when they feel disappointed or frightened, for instance," Daniel says mildly.

"But not Vicky?" Joona says.

"No."

"So why isn't she here?" Sonja asks.

"I can't discuss individual residents."

"But you don't consider her violent?"

"She's a sweet girl," he replies simply.

"So what do you think happened? Why is there a bloody hammer under her pillow?"

"I don't know; it doesn't make sense. Maybe she was helping someone and hid the weapon?"

"Which of the girls are violent?" Gunnarsson asks angrily.

"I can't identify them individually—you must understand that."

"We do," Joona replies.

Daniel looks at him gratefully and tries to breathe more calmly.

"Try talking to them," Daniel says. "You'll soon see which girls I mean."

"Thanks," Joona says, starting to walk away.

"Bear in mind that they've lost a friend," Daniel says quickly.

Joona stops and comes back to the counselor.

"Do you know which room Miranda was found in?"

"No, but I assumed . . ." Daniel falls silent and shakes his head.

"Because I'm having trouble believing it's her room," Joona says. "It's almost empty. The room on the right, just past the bathroom."

"The isolation room," Daniel replies.

"Why would someone end up there?" Joona asks.

"Because . . ." Daniel trails off and looks thoughtful.

"What are you thinking?"

"The door should have been locked," he says.

"There's a key in the lock."

"What key?" Daniel asks, raising his voice. "Elisabet's the only person who has a key to the isolation room."

"Who's Elisabet?" Gunnarsson asks.

"My wife," Daniel replies. "She was on duty last night. . . ."

"So where is she now?" Sonja asks.

"What?" Daniel says, looking at her in confusion.

"Is she at home?" she asks.

Daniel looks surprised and uncertain. "I assumed Elisabet had gone with Nina in the ambulance," he says slowly.

"No, Nina Molander went on her own," Sonja replies.

"Of course Elisabet went with her, she'd never let one of the—"

"I was the first officer on the scene," Sonja interrupts. Exhaustion is making her voice sound brusque and hoarse. "No one on staff was here," she goes on. "Just a bunch of frightened girls."

"But my wife was—"

"Call her," Sonja says.

"I've tried; her phone's off," Daniel says quietly. "I thought . . . I assumed . . ."

"God, this is a mess," Gunnarsson says.

"My wife, Elisabet," Daniel says, in a voice that's getting increasingly unsteady. "She has a heart condition; it might, she might . . ."

"Try to stay calm," Joona says.

"My wife has an enlarged heart and . . . she was working last night. She should be here. Her phone is switched off and . . ."

21

DANIEL LOOKS AT THEM DESPERATELY, fumbling with the zipper on his jacket, and repeats that his wife has a heart condition. The dog is barking and pulling so hard at its leash that it's almost strangling itself. It coughs, then continues barking.

Joona goes over to it. He tries to calm it down as he loosens the leash attached to its collar. As soon as Joona lets go, the dog runs across the yard to a small building. Joona hurries after it. The dog is scratching at the door, whimpering and panting.

Daniel stares at Joona and the dog and starts to walk toward them. Gunnarsson yells for him to stop, but he keeps moving. His body is stiff, and his face full of despair. The gravel crunches beneath his feet. Joona tries to calm the dog down and grabs its collar to pull it back, away from the door.

Gunnarsson runs across the yard and gets hold of Daniel's jacket, but Daniel pulls free and falls to the ground, scraping his hand, then gets back up.

The dog is barking, tensing its body, and pulling at its collar.

A uniformed police officer stops in front of the door. Daniel tries to push past and calls out with a sob in his voice: "Elisabet? Elisabet! I have to . . ."

The police officer tries to lead him off to the side while Gunnarsson hurries over to Joona and helps him with the dog.

"My wife," Daniel whimpers. "My wife could be . . ."

Gunnarsson pulls the dog back toward the tree.

The dog is panting hard, kicking up grit with its paws, and barking at the door.

Joona feels a sting of pain at the backs of his eyes as he pulls on a latex glove.

A carved wooden sign beneath the low eaves of the building reads "Brew House."

Joona opens the door carefully and looks into the dimly lit room. A small window is open, and hundreds of flies are buzzing around. There are bloody paw prints from the dog all over the worn floor tiles. Without going inside, Joona moves sideways to see around the brick fireplace.

He can see the back panel of a cell phone next to a patch of blood.

As Joona leans forward through the door, the buzzing of the flies gets louder. A woman in her fifties is lying in a pool of blood with her mouth open. She's dressed in jeans, pink socks, and a gray cardigan. It's clear the woman tried to shuffle away from her attacker, but the upper part of her face and head have been caved in.

22

PIA ABRAHAMSSON REALIZES THAT SHE'S driving a little too fast.

She'd counted on getting away earlier, but the diocesan meeting in Östersund dragged on longer than she'd expected.

Pia looks at her son in the mirror. His head is lolling against the edge of his car seat. His eyes are closed behind his glasses. The morning sunlight flashes between the trees and across his calm little face.

She slows down to eighty kilometers an hour, even though the road stretches out straight ahead of her through the forest.

The roads are eerily empty.

Twenty minutes ago, she passed a truck loaded with logs, but since then she hasn't seen another vehicle.

She squints to see better.

The animal-proof fencing on either side of the road flickers past monotonously.

Human beings must be the most frightened creatures on the planet, she thinks.

This country has eight thousand kilometers of animal-proof fencing—not to protect the animals but to protect human beings. Narrow roads run through these oceans of forest surrounded on both sides by high fences.

Pia glances quickly at Dante in the back seat.

She got pregnant when she was the Hässelby parish priest. The father was the editor of the *Church Times*. She stood there with the pregnancy test in her hand, thinking about the fact that she was thirty-six years old.

She kept the child, but not the father of the child. Her son is the best thing that's ever happened to her.

Before Dante fell asleep, he was so tired that he was crying at everything. He cried because the car smelled nasty from his mom's perfume and because Super Mario had been eaten..

There are more than twenty kilometers to go until Sundsvall and another 377 before Stockholm.

Pia needs to go to the bathroom—she drank way too much coffee at the meeting. There must be an open gas station somewhere.

She tells herself that she shouldn't stop in the middle of the forest.

She shouldn't, but she's going to anyway.

She pulls over by a logging road and stops by the locked boom gate to the animal fence. Behind the barrier, the gravel road leads into the forest.

Knowing she shouldn't go out of sight of the road, she leaves the car door open so she can hear if Dante wakes up.

"Mommy?"

"Try to go back to sleep."

"Mommy, don't go."

"Sweetheart," Pia says, "I just need to pee. I'll leave the door open, so I'll be able to see you the whole time."

He looks at her sleepily. "I don't want to be alone," he whispers.

She smiles at him and pats his sweaty little cheek. She knows that she's overprotective, that she's turning him into a mama's boy, but she can't help it.

"I'll just be a second," she says cheerfully.

Dante clings to her hand and tries to stop her, but she pulls free and takes a wet wipe from the pack.

Pia gets out of the car, ducks under the barrier, and heads up the road, then turns and waves to Dante.

She shivers as she steps off the road and goes farther into the trees. Heavy forestry machinery has churned up the ground.

When she's sure she can't be seen from the road, she pulls down her underwear, steps out of them, then hoists up her skirt and squats down.

She can feel how tired she is. Her thighs start to shake, and she rests one hand on the moss that's growing on the tree trunks.

Relief courses through her, and she closes her eyes.

When she looks up again, she sees something incomprehensible. An animal has gotten up on two legs and is staggering along the logging path, hunched over.

A thick figure covered in dirt, blood, and mud.

Pia holds her breath.

It isn't an animal. It's as if part of the forest has broken free and come to life.

Like a small girl made of twigs.

The apparition stumbles but keeps walking toward the gate.

Pia gets up and follows it.

She tries to speak, but her voice has vanished.

A branch snaps beneath her foot.

Gentle rain has started to fall in the forest.

She moves slowly, as if in a nightmare; she doesn't seem to be able to run.

Between the trees, she sees that the being has already reached the car. Dirty scraps of cloth are wrapped around the bizarre girl's wrists.

Pia stumbles out onto the logging path and sees the creature sweep her purse from the seat, get in, and close the door.

"Dante," she gasps.

The car roars to life, drives over her cell phone, pulls out into the road, hitting the divider, and vanishes into the distance.

Whimpering to herself, Pia runs to the gate. Her whole body is shaking.

It's incomprehensible. The mud creature came out of nowhere—suddenly it was just there—and now the car and her son are gone.

She ducks under the gate and walks out into the big, empty road. She doesn't scream; she doesn't seem able to. The only sound is her ragged breathing.

23

THE FOREST FLICKERS PAST, AND raindrops patter against the windshield. A Danish truck driver, Mads Jensen, can see a woman standing in the middle of the road two hundred meters away. He swears to himself and honks the horn. Though he sees her flinch at the noise, she makes no attempt to get off the road. He honks again, and the woman takes a slow step forward, raises her chin, and looks up at the approaching truck.

Mads brakes and feels the heavy trailer pushing against the old cab. He presses the brake harder, the driveshaft creaks, and the whole vehicle shudders before finally coming to a stop. As the engine winds down, the rumble from the pistons gets louder.

The woman just stands there, three meters from the front of the truck. Only now does he see that she's wearing a priest's collar under her denim jacket. It stands out against her black shirt.

The woman's face is open and very pale. When their eyes meet through the windshield, tears start to run down her cheeks.

Mads puts on his hazard lights and gets out of the cab. The engine is radiating heat and a strong diesel smell. When he comes to the front of the vehicle, he sees that the woman is leaning against one of the headlights, gasping for breath.

"What happened?" Mads asks.

She looks up at him, wide-eyed. The amber glare of the hazard lights pulses over her.

"Do you need help?" he asks.

She nods, and he tries to lead her around the cab. The rain is getting harder, and it's quickly getting dark.

"Did someone hurt you?"

She resists at first, but then goes with him and climbs into the passenger seat. He closes the door behind her and hurries around to get in the driver's seat.

"I can't stay here—I'm blocking the whole road," he explains. "I have to move. Is that okay?"

She doesn't answer, but he starts the truck and switches the windshield wipers on anyway.

"Are you hurt?" he asks.

She shakes her head and claps one hand over her mouth.

"My son," she whispers. "My . . ."

"What are you saying?" he asks. "What's happened?"

"She took my son. . . ."

"I'll call the police. Is it okay if I call the police?"

"Oh God," she moans.

24

THE RAIN IS BEATING AGAINST the windshield, the wiper
blades are whipping back and forth, and the road ahead of them
looks as if it's boiling.

Pia is sitting in the warm cab high above the ground, shaking.
She can't calm down. She knows that she's not making any sense,
but now she can hear the truck driver talking to the emergency
call center. He is advised to keep driving along Highway 86, then
the 330 to Timrå, where he'll meet an emergency vehicle that
will take her to Sundsvall Hospital.

"What? What are you talking about?" Pia asks. "This isn't
about me. They have to stop my car—that's the only thing that
matters."

The Danish driver gives her a confused look, and she realizes that she needs to concentrate to make herself understood.
She has to act calmly, even though the ground has disappeared
beneath her and she's in free fall.

"My son has been kidnapped," she says.

"She says her son's been kidnapped," the driver repeats into
his phone.

"The police have to stop the car," she goes on. "A Toyota . . . a
red Toyota Auris. I can't remember the license number, but . . ."

The driver asks the emergency operator to wait.

"It's ahead of us on this road. . . . You have to stop it. My son's
only four; he was sitting in the back when I . . ."

He repeats her words to the operator, explains that her car is driving east along Highway 86, about forty kilometers from Timrå.

"They have to hurry...."

The truck slows down to pass a bent traffic light, then accelerates past a white brick building, driving parallel to the river.

The emergency call center puts the Danish driver through to a female police officer in a patrol car. She introduces herself as Mirja Zlatnek and says she's thirty kilometers away, on Highway 330 in Djupängen.

Pia takes the phone, swallowing hard to stifle the nausea she feels. She hears her own voice, calm but shaky.

"Listen," she says. "My son's been kidnapped, and the car is driving along ... Hang on...."

She turns to the driver.

"Where are we? What road are we on?"

"Highway 86," the driver says.

"How much of a head start did they get?" the police officer asks.

"I don't know," Pia says. "Five minutes, maybe?"

"Have you passed Indal?"

"Indal," Pia repeats.

"We're almost twenty kilometers from there," the driver says loudly.

"Then we've got them," the police officer says. "There are no other roads...."

When Pia hears those words, her tears start to flow. She quickly wipes her cheeks as she hears the police officer talk to a colleague. They're going to set up roadblocks on Highway 330 and on the bridge over the river. Another police officer, in Nordansjö, says he can be in position in less than five minutes.

"That's good enough," the policewoman says quickly.

The truck drives the winding road along the river through the sparsely populated part of Medelpad. Even though they can't see it, they're following the car with Pia Abrahamsson's four-year-old son in it: they know it must be ahead of them, because there are no exits. Highway 86 passes through a few isolated communities, but there are no side roads, just forest lanes that don't connect to other roads.

"I can't take this," Pia whispers.

The road they're on splits in two ten kilometers ahead of them. Just past the little town of Indal, one branch of the road crosses the river and goes almost due south, while the other continues to follow the river toward the coast.

Pia sits with her hands clasped tight, praying to God. Up ahead, police cars have set up roadblocks on the two branches of the road. One car is parked at the far end of the bridge, and the other is eight kilometers to the east.

The truck carrying the Danish truck driver and Pia Abrahamsson is passing through Indal. Through the heavy rain, they see the empty bridge over the teeming water and the blue lights of the lone police car rotating at the far end.

25

POLICE OFFICER MIRJA ZLATNEK HAS parked her patrol car across the entire width of the road. If any car wanted to get past, it would have to pull off the road and drive around with two wheels in the ditch.

In front of her is a long, straight stretch of road. The police car's blue lights flash across the wet tarmac and dark branches of the trees.

The rain is beating hard on the car roof.

Mirja sits quietly for a while, looking out the windshield and trying to think through the situation.

Visibility is poor because of the rain.

She had counted on having a very quiet day, since almost all her colleagues are busy with the case of the dead girl at the Birgitta Home. Even the National Crime Unit has been brought into the investigation.

Mirja has been developing a secret fear of the operational side of the job, although she's never actually been in a particularly traumatic situation. Maybe it's because of that time, when she tried to mediate a domestic drama that ended badly, but that was many years ago. The anxiety has crept up on her. She prefers administrative duties and crime-prevention work.

She spent the morning sitting at her desk, looking at recipes online. Elk filet wrapped in pastry, potato wedges and cream sauce with porcini mushrooms, puréed artichoke hearts. She was in the car, heading to Djupängen to look at a stolen trailer, when the call came through about the abducted boy.

Mirja tells herself that she can handle the situation with the kidnapped boy. Because the car containing the woman's four-year-old son has nowhere else to go.

This stretch of road is like a long tunnel, a trap.

The truck is following it from the other direction.

Either the car containing the boy crosses the bridge just after Indal, where her colleague Lasse Bengtsson has blocked the road.

Or it comes this way, where I'm waiting, Mirja thinks.

And ten kilometers behind the car is the truck.

Obviously, it all depends on how fast the car is driving, but within the next twenty minutes there'll be some sort of confrontation.

Mirja tells herself that the child almost certainly hasn't been kidnapped in the real sense of the word. Probably a custody dispute. The woman she spoke to was too upset to give her any coherent information, but, based on what she did say, her car must be somewhere on this road, on this side of Nilsböle.

It'll soon be over, she tells herself.

It won't be long before she can go back to her office at the station and get a cup of coffee and a ham sandwich.

But there's something worrying her: the woman spoke about a girl with arms like twigs.

Mirja didn't ask the woman's name. There hadn't been time. She assumed the emergency call center had taken all the relevant details. The fear in the woman's voice had been alarming. She had been breathing fast and described what she'd been through as incomprehensible.

Mirja reaches for the radio, waits for a moment, then calls Lasse Bengtsson.

"What's happening?" she asks.

"Torrential rain, but not much else. No cars, not a single damn … Hang on, I can see a truck, a huge articulated truck heading down the highway."

"I'll check the truck when it reaches my roadblock. It's probably the guy who called," Mirja says.

"So where the hell's the Toyota?" Lasse says. "I've been here for fifteen minutes, so it'll have to reach you in the next five minutes unless some UFO has—"

"Give me a second," Mirja says quickly, and ends the call when she sees headlights in the distance.

26

MIRJA ZLATNEK GETS OUT OF her patrol car and hunches in the downpour. She squints at the vehicle approaching through the heavy rain.

With one hand on her holstered pistol, she walks toward the vehicle, simultaneously holding her left hand up to make the driver stop.

The water coursing across the road and into the ditches looks as if it's bubbling.

Mirja sees the vehicle slow down, and she sees her own shadow bounce along the road. She hears a call on the radio in the patrol car but stays on the road. The voices over the radio are tinny, and there's a lot of crackling, but the words are still clearly audible.

"Hell of a lot of blood," a younger colleague is saying as he describes the discovery of a second body at the Birgitta Home, a middle-aged woman.

The vehicle comes closer, driving slowly, then pulls over to the edge of the road and stops. Mirja starts to walk toward it. It's a Mazda pickup with muddy tires. The driver's door opens, and a large man in a green hunting jacket and a sweater gets out. He has neatly combed shoulder-length hair and a broad face with a large nose and narrow eyes.

"Are you alone in the vehicle?" Mirja shouts, wiping the water from her face.

He nods, then looks over at the forest.

"Stay back," she says when he starts to walk closer.

He takes a tiny step back.

Mirja leans forward to look inside the truck. Water trickles down the back of her neck.

It's hard to see anything through the rain and mud on the windshield. There's a newspaper spread out on the driver's seat. She walks around and moves closer, trying to see what's lying on the narrow back seat: an old blanket and a thermos flask.

The radio in the patrol car crackles again, but she can no longer hear the words.

The shoulders of the man's hunting jacket are already dark from the rain. The sound of something scraping against metal is coming from his vehicle.

When she looks back at the man again, she sees that he's come closer. Just a little—one step, maybe. Unless she's imagining it. She's no longer sure. He's staring at her, looking her up and down, and then he frowns.

"Do you live here?" she asks.

She rubs the mud from his license plate with her foot, makes a note of it, and continues around the pickup.

There's a pink gym bag in the passenger-side footwell. Mirja keeps moving around the vehicle but keeps the big man in sight the whole time. There's something in the bed of the pickup, under a green tarp, held down by thick straps.

"Where are you going?" she asks.

He's standing still, following her with his eyes. Suddenly some blood seeps out from under the tarp.

"What do you have here?" she asks.

When he doesn't answer, she reaches over the back of the pickup. It isn't easy to reach—she has to lean on the vehicle. The man moves sideways slightly. She manages to reach the tarp with her fingertips without taking her eyes off the man. He licks his lips as she lifts it. She unfastens her pistol, then glances quickly at the back of the pickup, long enough to see the hoof of a young deer.

The man is standing completely still in the flashing blue light, but Mirja keeps her hand on her pistol as she steps back from the vehicle.

"Where did you shoot the deer?"

"It was lying on the road," he says.

"Did you make a note of where?"

He spits slowly on the road, between his own feet.

"Can I see your driver's license?" she says.

He doesn't answer and shows no sign of obeying her.

"Driver's license," she repeats, aware of the uncertainty in her own voice.

"We're done here," he says, heading for the pickup.

"You're legally obliged to report accidents involving wild animals. . . ."

The man gets in the driver's seat, closes the door, starts the engine, and pulls away. She watches him pass the police car, two of his wheels in the ditch. When he drives up onto the road again, Mirja tells herself she should have examined the pickup more closely. She should have removed the whole tarp and looked under the blanket on the back seat.

The rain is lashing the trees around her, and in the distance a crow calls from a treetop.

Mirja startles when she hears the sound of a heavy vehicle behind her. She turns around and pulls out her pistol but can't see anything except the rain.

27

MADS JANSEN IS BEING REPRIMANDED over the phone by his dispatcher. He blushes as he tries to explain the situation. Pia can hear the angry voice through the phone as the dispatcher continues yelling about coordinates and fucked-up logistics.

"But," Mads tries to say, "surely we have to help other—"

"This'll be deducted from your wages," his boss snaps. "That's all the help you're getting from me."

"Thanks a lot," Mads says, ending the call.

Pia sits beside the driver in silence as the dense forest flies by on both sides. The heavy rain sounds deafening in the cab. In the side-view mirror, Pia can see the swaying trailer and the trees they've just passed.

Mads pops some nicotine gum in his mouth and stares at the road ahead. The sound of the engine and the thud of the heavy wheels on the tarmac blur into one.

Pia looks at the calendar swaying with the motion of the cab—a curvaceous woman holding an inflatable swan in a swimming pool. At the bottom of the glossy photograph is the date, August 1968.

The road slopes downward, and the weight of the load increases the truck's speed.

Far off, between the trees, a strong blue light is flickering in the rain. A police car is blocking the road.

Pia feels her heart beat harder and faster. She stares at the police car and the woman in the dark-blue sweater waving her arm at them. Before the truck has even stopped, Pia opens the door. The sound of the engine and the tires is instantly louder.

She feels dizzy as she clambers down and hurries over to the waiting police officer.

"Where's the car?" the officer asks.

"What? What do you mean, where's the car?"

Pia stares at the other woman and tries to read her face but just gets more shaken by her serious expression. She feels as if her legs are going to give way beneath her.

"Did you see the car when you passed it?" the policewoman clarifies.

"Passed it?" Pia says weakly.

Mads walks over to them.

"We haven't seen anything," he tells the police officer. "You must have set up the roadblock too late."

"Too late? I drove up this road to get here. . . ."

"So where the hell is the car?" he asks.

Mirja Zlatnek runs back to her car and calls her colleague.

"Lasse?" she says urgently.

"I've been trying to get you," he says. "You weren't answering."

"No, I was—"

"Is everything going okay?" he asks.

"Where the hell's the car?" she asks, almost shouting. "The truck's here, but there's no sign of the car."

"There aren't any other roads," he says.

"We need to put an alert out and block the 86 in the other direction."

"I'm on it," he says, and ends the call.

Pia has come over to the police car. The rain has soaked her clothes. Mirja is sitting in the driver's seat with the door open.

"You told me you were going to get him," Pia says.

"Yes, I—"

"You told me. I believed you."

"I know, I don't understand," Mirja says. "It doesn't make sense. You can't drive fast on these roads, and there's no way the car could have gotten to the bridge before Lasse got there."

"It has to be somewhere," Pia says in a tight voice, pulling her priest's collar from her shirt.

"Hang on," Mirja says suddenly.

She calls the command center.

"This is Patrol Car 321," she says quickly. "We need another roadblock, immediately. Before Aspen, there's a small road there, you can take it from Kävsta up to Myckelsjö. . . . Yes, exactly . . . Who? Good, he'll be there in eight, ten minutes. . . ."

Mirja gets out of the car and looks along the straight road, as if she still expects the Toyota to appear.

"My boy—he's gone?" Pia asks her.

"There's nowhere they could have gone," Mirja says, doing her best to sound confident. "I understand that you're worried, but we'll get them—they must have turned off and stopped somewhere, but there's nowhere they can go. . . ."

She pauses, wiping the rain from her forehead, then takes a deep breath and goes on:

"We're closing off the last roads, and we're calling in a helicopter. . . ."

Pia unbuttons the top button of her shirt and leans one hand on the hood of the police car. She's breathing far too heavily, and her chest is pounding. She tries to calm down. She knows she should be making demands, but she can't think clearly. She feels confused and desperately afraid.

28

ALTHOUGH THE RAIN IS STILL pouring from the sky, only a few drops manage to reach the ground between the trees in the forest.

A large white police van is parked at the center of the yard at the Birgitta Home. The van acts as a command center, and a group of men and women is inside, seated around a table covered with maps and computers.

They stop discussing the ongoing murder investigation to listen to the radio communication about a boy who's been abducted. Roadblocks have been set up on Highway 330 and at the bridge at Indal, as well as at Kävsta and farther north on Highway 86. At first their colleagues sound confident, but then everything goes quiet. No communication for ten minutes, until the radio crackles again and Mirja Zlatnek reports breathlessly: "It's gone. The car's gone. . . . It should be here, but it hasn't turned up. . . . We shut down every damn road there is, but it's still vanished. I don't know what to do," Mirja says wearily. "The mother's sitting in my car. I'll try to talk to her. . . ."

The police officers sit in silence as they listen to the exchanges. Now they gather around the map on the table as Bosse Norling points out Highway 86 with his finger.

"If they blocked the road here and here, the car can't just disappear," he says. "I guess it could have driven into a garage in Bäck or Bjällsta ... or it could have gone up one of the logging trails. But it's still really weird."

"And they won't get anywhere," Sonja Rask says.

"Am I the only one thinking that Vicky Bennet might have taken the car?" Bosse asks tentatively.

The pattering on the roof has gotten quieter, but rain is still running down the van's windows.

Sonja checks several police databases: people with a criminal record, people suspected of committing a crime, and people involved in ongoing custody disputes.

"Nine times out of ten," Gunnarsson says, leaning back and peeling a banana, "problems like this sort themselves out on their own. . . . I think she had her man in the car, they had an argument, and in the end he'd had enough and dumped her at the side of the road before taking off with the kid."

"She's not married," Sonja says.

"According to the statistics," Gunnarsson goes on, "the majority of children in Sweden are now born out of wedlock."

"Here it is," Sonja says, interrupting. "Pia Abrahamsson sought sole custody of her son, Dante, and the father has tried to lodge an appeal. . . ."

"So we're dropping the possibility of a connection to Vicky Bennet?" Bosse asks.

"Try to get in touch with the father first," Joona says.

"I'll get on that," Sonja says, and goes to the back of the bus.

"Was there anything outside Vicky Bennet's window?" Joona asks.

"Nothing on the ground, but we found prints and some coagulated blood on the windowsill," one of the forensics technicians says.

"How about the edge of the forest?"

"We didn't get that far before it started to rain."

"But, presumably, Vicky Bennet ran straight into the forest," Joona says thoughtfully.

He looks at Bosse Norling, who is doing things the old-fashioned way: leaning over the map with a compass, putting its point on the Birgitta Home, and drawing a circle.

"She's not the one who took the car," Gunnarsson says. "Christ, it doesn't take three hours to walk through the forest to Highway 86 and then follow it to—"

"But it isn't easy to get your bearings at night . . . so she could very well have walked something like this," Bosse says. He points to a possible route going east around a bog, then heading north.

"The timing would fit," Joona says.

"Dante's father is in Tenerife at the moment," Sonja calls from the back of the bus.

Olle Gunnarsson swears under his breath, then goes over to the radio and calls Officer Mirja Zlatnek.

"This is Gunnarsson," he says. "Have you taken a witness statement from the mother?"

"Yes, I—"

"Do we have a description?"

"It's not easy. She's very emotional and doesn't seem to have a coherent picture of events," Mirja replies. "She's badly shaken and keeps talking about a skeleton with wiry hands that came out of the forest. A girl with blood on her face, a girl with twig-like arms—"

"But she's talking about a girl?"

"I recorded her statement, but she said lots of weird stuff. She needs to calm down before we can question her properly. . . ."

"But she keeps coming back to the idea that it was a girl?" Gunnarsson says slowly.

"Yes . . . several times."

29

JOONA STOPS THE CAR AT the roadblock on Highway 330, says hello to one of the police officers stationed there, shows his ID, then drives on beside the river.

He's been told that the girls from the Birgitta Home are being temporarily housed at the Hotel Ibis. The counselor, Daniel Grim, has been admitted to the psychiatric ward of the district hospital; the housekeeper, Margot Lundin, is at home in Timrå; and Faduumo Axmed, who works part-time as a nurse, is off duty, down with her parents in Vänersborg.

When they heard that Pia kept coming back to the idea that it was a thin girl with bandages around her wrists, everyone realized that Vicky Bennet had taken the car with the little boy in it.

"It's a mystery that she hasn't been caught in the roadblocks," Bosse Norling had said.

A helicopter was deployed, but there's no trace of the car— not in the small town and not along any of the logging paths.

It isn't really a mystery, Joona thinks. The most plausible explanation is that she managed to find somewhere to hide before she reached any of the roadblocks.

But where?

She must know someone who lives in Indal, someone who has a garage.

Joona has asked to speak to the girls in the company of a youth psychologist and someone from victim support services, and he is trying to remember the details of his first encounter with them at the home. The little redheaded girl had been watching television and banging her head against the wall. The girl named Indie had associated hands covering a face with Vicky, and then they had all started shouting and yelling at one another when they realized that she was missing. One of the girls claimed she was asleep because she took Valium. Almira spat on the floor, and Indie rubbed her face and ended up with blue eye shadow on her hand.

Joona can't help thinking that there's something about Tuula, the redheaded girl with white eyelashes. At first she yelled at them all to be quiet, but she also said something when everyone else was talking.

Tuula said that Vicky had snuck off to see her fuck-buddy.

30

THE HOTEL IBIS IS LOCATED in Sundsvall, not far from the police station. It's the sort of hotel that smells like vacuum cleaners, rugs, and stale cigarette smoke. The façade is covered with cream-colored stucco. There's a bowl of candy on the reception desk. The police have put the girls from the Birgitta Home in five adjacent rooms and have placed two uniformed officers in the hallway.

Joona strides across the worn floor.

The psychologist, Lisa Jern, is waiting for Joona outside one of the doors. Her dark hair is streaked with gray, and her mouth is thin and nervous.

"Is Tuula already here?" Joona asks.

"Yes, she is. . . . Wait a second, though," the psychologist says when he reaches for the door handle. "As I understand it, you're here as an observer from the National Crime Unit, and—"

"A boy's life is in danger," Joona interrupts.

"Tuula is barely speaking, and . . . I'm afraid my recommendation as a child psychologist is to wait until she takes the initiative herself and starts to talk about what's happened."

"There isn't time for that," Joona says, grabbing the handle.

"Wait, I . . . It's extremely important to be on the same wavelength as the children; they absolutely mustn't feel like you think they're sick or . . ."

Joona opens the door and walks into the room. Tuula Lehti is sitting on a chair with her back to the row of windows. A little girl, just twelve years old, in sweats and sneakers.

The street outside, lined with parked cars, is visible between the wooden slats of the blinds. All the tables are covered with beech veneer, and there's a fitted green carpet on the floor.

At the end of the room, a man in a blue-checked flannel shirt with neatly combed hair is looking at his phone. Joona realizes that he's from victim support services.

Joona sits down in front of Tuula and looks at her. Her eyebrows are fair, her red hair straight and greasy.

"We met very briefly this morning," he says.

She folds her freckled arms over her stomach. Her lips are thin and almost colorless.

"Fuck tha police," she mutters.

Lisa walks around the table and sits down beside the little girl's hunched frame.

"Tuula," she says gently, "do you remember when I said that I sometimes used to feel like Thumbelina? That there's nothing wrong with feeling like that, because even as an adult you can feel really small sometimes?"

"Why is everyone talking such fucking shit?" Tuula asks, looking Joona in the eye. "Is it because you're all dumb, or because you think I'm dumb?"

"Well, we probably think you're a bit dumb," Joona replies.

Tuula smiles in surprise and is about to say something when Lisa assures her that it isn't true, that the detective was just joking.

Tuula folds her arms even tighter, stares at the table, and puffs out her cheeks.

"You're definitely not dumb," Lisa repeats after a while.

"Yes, I am," Tuula whispers.

She spits a gob of saliva onto the table, then sits there silently poking at it, making it into a star shape.

"Don't you want to talk?" Lisa whispers.

"Only to the Finn," Tuula says almost inaudibly.

"What did you just say?" Lisa asks with a smile.

"I'll only talk to the Finn," Tuula says, raising her chin.

"How lovely," the psychologist replies stiffly.

Joona starts the recording, then calmly goes through the formalities: time and location, the names of those present, and the purpose of the conversation.

"How did you end up at the Birgitta Home, Tuula?" he asks.

"I was at Lövsta. . . . Some things happened that weren't that fucking great," she says, lowering her gaze. "I got mixed up with some kids who got locked up, even though I'm really too young. . . . I kept my cool, watched television, and one year and four months later I got moved to the Birgitta Home."

"What's the difference . . . compared with Lövsta?"

"It's . . . The Birgitta Home feels like a real home. . . . Rugs on the floor, the furniture's not screwed down. . . . And there aren't locks and alarms everywhere. And you get left to sleep in peace and have home-cooked food."

Joona nods and sees from the corner of his eye that the victim support services representative is still fiddling with his phone. The psychologist, Lisa Jern, is breathing through her nose as she listens to them.

"What did you have to eat yesterday?"

"Tacos," Tuula replies.

"Was everyone there for dinner?"

She shrugs. "I think so."

"Miranda, too? She had tacos yesterday evening as well?"

"Can't you just cut her stomach open and check? Haven't you done that yet?"

"No, we haven't."

"Why not?"

"We haven't had time."

Tuula smiles and starts to pull at a loose thread on her pants. Her nails have been bitten ragged, and her cuticles are torn.

"I looked in the isolation room—it was pretty intense," Tuula says, and starts to rock back and forth.

"Did you see the way Miranda was lying?" Joona asks after a while.

"Yes, like this," Tuula says quickly, putting her hands in front of her face.

"Why do you think she was doing that?"

Tuula kicks up the edge of the rug, then flattens it again.

"Maybe she was scared."

"Have you seen anyone else do that?" Joona asks lightly.

"No," Tuula says, as she scratches her neck.

"You don't get locked in your rooms, then?"

"It's kind of like an open prison." Tuula smiles.

"Do people often sneak out at night?"

"I don't."

Tuula's mouth becomes small and hard, and she pretends to fire her pointer finger at the psychologist.

"Why not?" Joona asks.

She looks him in the eye and says quietly, "I'm scared of the dark."

"What about the others?"

Joona sees Lisa listening to them. There's a pronounced frown line between her eyebrows.

"Yes," Tuula whispers.

"What do they do when they sneak out?"

The girl looks down and smiles to herself.

"They're older than you, aren't they?" Joona goes on.

"Yes," she replies, blushing.

"Do they meet boys?"

She nods.

"Does Vicky do that, too?"

"Yes, she sneaks out at night," Tuula says, leaning closer to Joona.

"Do you know who she goes to see?"

"Dennis."

"Who's that?"

"I don't know," she whispers, and licks her lips.

"But his name is Dennis? Do you know his last name?"

"No."

"How long is she usually gone?"

Tuula shrugs her shoulders and picks at a piece of tape that's hanging from the seat of her chair.

31

THE PROSECUTOR SUSANNE ÖST IS waiting outside the Hotel
Ibis beside a large Ford Fairlane. Her face is round, and she's not
wearing any makeup. She has her blond hair in a ponytail and
is dressed in long gray pants and a gray blazer. It looks as if she's
been scratching her neck, and one side of her collar is sticking up.

"Do you have any objection to my pretending to be a police
officer for a while?" she asks, blushing.

"On the contrary," Joona says, shaking her hand.

"We're busy knocking on doors, looking in garages, barns,
parking lots, and so on," she says seriously. "We're closing the net.
There aren't that many places you can hide a car. . . ."

"No."

"But it'll go a little faster now that we have a name," she says,
smiling, as she opens the front door of the Ford. "There are four
men named Dennis in the area."

"I'll follow you," he says, and gets into his Volvo.

The Ford sways as it pulls out and sets off toward Indal. Joona
follows, thinking about Vicky.

Her mother, Susie Bennet, was an addict and was homeless
before her death last winter. Vicky has lived with various foster
families and in different institutions since she was six and presumably quickly learned how to let old relationships go and how
to make new ones.

If Vicky has been sneaking out to meet someone at night, he must live fairly close. Maybe he waits for her in the forest or on a logging path. Maybe she heads down Highway 86 to his home in Baggböle or Västloning.

The asphalt is drying now; the rainwater has settled in the ditches. Though the sky is brighter, the forest is still dripping.

The prosecutor calls Joona, and he can see her looking in her rearview mirror as she talks.

"We found just one Dennis in Indal," she says. "He's seven years old. There's another one who lives out at Stige, but he's currently working in Leeds."

"Which leaves two others," Joona says.

"Yes. Dennis and Lovisa Karmstedt live in a house outside Tomming. We haven't been there yet. And there's a Dennis Rolando, who lives with his parents just south of Indal. We've paid a visit to the parents, and there's nothing there. But he owns a large workshop on Kvarnå Road that we can't get into. It's probably nothing, because we've spoken to him, and apparently he's in his car on the way to Sollefteå."

"Break the door open."

"Okay," she says, and ends the call.

The landscape opens up, and the road is lined by fields on both sides, sparkling from the recent rain. Red barns press up against the forest, which stretches off into the distance behind them.

As Joona is passing through the peaceful hamlet of Östanskär, two uniformed police officers are cutting through the heavy hinges of Dennis Rolando's workshop. A cascade of sparks sprays across the wall. The officers insert sturdy crowbars, break the door open, and go inside. The beams of their flashlights seek their way into the shadows. The workshop contains about fifty old-fashioned arcade games—Space Invaders, Asteroids, Street Fighter—all covered with dirty plastic sheeting.

Joona sees Susanne Öst talking on her phone; then she glances at him in the rearview mirror. His phone rings. Susanne tells him quickly that there's only one address left. It's not far away. They should be there in ten minutes.

He slows down and follows her as she turns right onto a road between two waterlogged meadows, then on into the forest. They approach a yellow wooden house with closed blinds in all the windows. There are apple trees growing in the well-tended garden and a blue-and-white-striped couch swing in the middle of the yard.

They pull up and walk together toward a parked police car.

Joona says hello to the two officers, then looks up at the house.

"We don't know if Vicky took the car to abduct the child, or if she just wanted a car and there happened to be a child in the back seat," he says. "Either way, we have to assume the child is a hostage."

"A hostage," the prosecutor repeats quietly.

She goes over and rings the bell, then calls out that the police will force the door open if they're not let in. Someone moves inside the house. The floor creaks, and a heavy piece of furniture topples over.

"I'm going in," Joona says.

One of the police officers stays at the front door, watching the gable side of the house, which faces the grass and the locked garage door, while the other one goes around to the back of the house with Joona.

Their shoes and pants get wet in the tall grass. There's a small flight of concrete stairs at the back of the house, leading down to a door with a smoked-glass window. When Joona kicks the door in, the frame shatters, and fragments of glass fly across the floor.

32

BROKEN GLASS CRUNCHES UNDER JOONA'S shoes as he enters a neat laundry room that's equipped with a hand wringer.

Miranda was sitting on a chair when she was murdered, Joona thinks. Elisabet was chased across the yard into the brew house and tried to crawl away before being beaten to death.

He can feel the weight of the new pistol in its holster beneath his right arm. It's a semiautomatic Smith & Wesson, .45-caliber. It's heavier than his old one and holds fewer bullets, but it's quicker with the first shot.

Joona carefully opens a creaky door and looks into an old-fashioned kitchen. There's a large ceramic bowl of red apples on the round table, and the stove smells like wood smoke. A plate of frozen cinnamon rolls is defrosting, and a drawer full of sharp knives is open.

He can see the wet garden through the blinds.

Joona comes into the hall. He hears the ceiling light tinkle as its glass prisms knock against one another. Someone's walking across the floor upstairs, making the fixture sway.

He creeps up the stairs, glancing down between the steps. There are clothes hanging in the darkness beneath the stairs.

Joona reaches the first landing and moves almost silently into a bedroom with a double bed. The blinds are drawn, and the ceiling light doesn't work.

Joona checks for possible lines of fire, then moves sideways.

On top of the colorful bedspread is the telescopic sight of a hunting rifle.

He can hear someone breathing, very close to him. Joona steps farther into the room and aims his pistol at the far corner. A man with light-brown hair is slouching behind the open wardrobe, staring at him.

The man is barefoot and wearing dark-blue jeans and a white T-shirt with "Stora Enso" on it. He's hiding something behind his back as he moves slowly to his right, toward the bed.

"I'm with National Crime," Joona says, lowering his pistol slightly.

"This is my house," the man says in a subdued voice.

"You should have opened the door."

Joona sees sweat running down the man's cheeks.

"Did you break my back door?" the man asks.

"Yes."

"Can it be repaired?"

"I doubt it," Joona replies.

There's a flicker in the mirror on the closet door. Joona sees that the man is concealing a large kitchen knife behind his back.

"I need to look in your garage," Joona says calmly.

"My car's in there."

"Put the knife on the bed and show me the garage."

The man takes the knife from behind his back and stares at it. The polished wooden handle is worn, and the blade has been sharpened many times.

"I don't have time to wait," Joona says.

"You shouldn't have broken my—"

In that instant, Joona detects movement behind him, bare feet running across the floor. He just has time to move sideways slightly, without taking his eyes off the knife, as a shadow rushes toward him from behind. Joona twists his body, raises his arm, and follows through, adding force to the blow as he hits the rushing figure, a boy, with his elbow, all the while keeping the barrel of his pistol aimed at the man with the knife. The boy sighs, and all the air goes out of him. He reaches out for support and sinks to his knees, curls up on the floor, and lies on his side, gasping.

"They're from Afghanistan," the man says quietly. "They need help, and—"

"I'll shoot you in the leg if you don't put the knife down," Joona says.

The man looks at the knife, then tosses it on the bed. Two smaller children suddenly appear in the doorway. They stare at Joona, wide-eyed.

"You're hiding refugees?" Joona asks. "How much do you get for that?"

"As if I'd take money," the man says indignantly.

"Do you?"

"No, I don't."

Joona meets the boy's dark gaze.

"Do you pay him?" he asks in English.

The boy shakes his head.

"No human being is illegal," the man says.

"You don't have to be afraid," Joona tells the older boy. "I promise I will help you if you are abused in any way."

The boy looks into Joona's eyes for a long time, then shakes his head.

"Dennis is a good man," he whispers.

"I'm glad," Joona says. He meets the man's gaze, then leaves the room.

Joona goes downstairs, all the way to the garage. He stands for a while, looking at the dusty Saab parked there. Vicky and Dante have disappeared, and there are no more places to look.

33

FLORA HANSEN IS MOPPING THE shabby linoleum floor in the apartment's entryway. Her left cheek still stings from where she was slapped earlier, and there's an odd buzzing sound in her ear. The floor has lost its shine over the years, but mopping makes it look better for a little while at least.

The smell of detergent spreads through the rooms.

Flora has beaten all the mats and has already mopped the living room, the cramped kitchen, and Hans-Gunnar's room, but she's waiting to do Ewa's bedroom until *Solsidan* starts on television. Ewa and Hans-Gunnar both watch the series and would never miss an episode.

Flora mops the floor energetically. Moving backward, she bumps into the picture she made more than thirty years ago, when she was at preschool. Each child stuck different types of pasta onto a piece of wood; then the whole thing was sprayed with gold paint.

The program's theme song comes on.

Now's her chance.

Flora feels a jolt of pain in her back as she picks up the heavy bucket and carries it into Ewa's room.

She shuts the door behind her and sets the bucket in front of it, to block the door.

Her heart is beating hard as she dunks the mop into the

bucket, squeezes out the excess water, and looks at the wedding photograph on the bedside table.

Ewa hides the key to the escritoire in the back of the frame.

Flora takes care of all the housework in exchange for being allowed to live in the spare room. She had to move back in with Ewa and Hans-Gunnar when her unemployment benefits ran out, after she lost her job as a nurse's aide.

When she was a child, Flora always thought her real parents were going to come and get her, but they were probably junkies. Ewa and Hans-Gunnar say they don't know anything about them. Flora arrived here when she was five years old and has no memories of her life before then. Hans-Gunnar has always described her as a burden, and she's been desperate to get away ever since she was a teenager. When she was nineteen, she got a job at the hospital and moved into her own apartment.

The mop drips as Flora goes over to the window and starts mopping the floor. The linoleum is black under the radiator from water damage. The old blinds are broken and hang crookedly between the inner and outer panes of glass. There is a wooden horse on the windowsill.

Flora moves slowly toward the bedside table, stops, and listens.

She can hear the television.

Ewa and Hans-Gunnar look young in their wedding photo. She's wearing a white dress; he's in a suit with a silver tie. The sky is white. A black, domed bell tower stands on a mound beside the church, sticking up behind Hans-Gunnar like a peculiar hat. Flora has never been able to put her finger on why, but she's always found the picture unsettling.

She tries to breathe calmly.

She gently leans the handle of the mop against the wall but waits until she hears Ewa laugh at something on television before picking up the photograph.

As she expected, the ornate brass key is hanging from the

back of the frame. Flora removes it from its hook, but her hands are shaking so much she drops it.

It hits the floor with a tinkle and bounces under the bed.

Flora has to reach out for support as she bends down.

She hears footsteps in the hallway and waits, lying still. Her pulse is throbbing in her temples.

The floor outside the door creaks; then everything is quiet again.

The key is nestled among the dusty cables by the wall. She reaches in and picks it up, then gets to her feet and waits a few seconds before walking over to the desk. She unlocks it, folds down the heavy lid, and pulls out one of the small drawers. Beneath the postcards from Paris and Mallorca are the envelopes where Ewa keeps the money for regular expenses. Flora opens the one with the money for next month's bills and takes half of it, puts the notes in her pocket, quickly puts the envelope back, and tries to slide the little drawer back in, but there's something jamming it.

"Flora," Ewa calls.

She pulls the drawer out again but can't see anything wrong. She tries once more, but her hands are shaking too much now.

She hears footsteps in the hallway again.

Flora pushes the drawer hard. It's slightly crooked, but it goes in, reluctantly. She closes the desk but doesn't have time to lock it.

The door to her aunt's bedroom opens, hitting the bucket so hard that water sloshes out.

"Flora?"

She grabs the mop, mumbles something, and moves the bucket. She mops the spilled water, then keeps cleaning.

"I can't find my hand cream," Ewa says.

There's a suspicious look in her eyes, and the wrinkles around her unhappy mouth are deeper than usual. She walks barefoot across the newly cleaned floor. Her yellow sweatpants are sagging, and her white T-shirt is stretched tightly across her stomach and large bust.

"It . . . Maybe it's in the bathroom cabinet. I think that's where it is, next to the hair cream," Flora says, rinsing the mop again.

The TV has cut to a commercial. The volume is louder, and shrill voices are talking about athlete's foot. Ewa stops in the doorway and looks at her.

"Hans-Gunnar doesn't like the coffee," she says.

"I'm sorry about that."

Flora squeezes out the excess water.

"He says you're refilling the package with cheaper stuff."

"Why would I—"

"Don't lie," Ewa snaps.

"I'm not," Flora mumbles, mopping the floor.

"Well, you're going to have to go and get his cup, wash it out, and make some fresh coffee."

Flora leans the mop handle against the door, apologizes, and goes into the living room. She can feel the key and the money in her pocket. Hans-Gunnar doesn't even look at her when she picks up his mug from next to the plate of cookies.

"For fuck's sake, Ewa," he cries. "It's starting again!"

His voice makes Flora jump, and she hurries out. She passes Ewa in the hall and catches her eye.

"You remember that I have to go to that employment class this evening?" Flora says.

"You still won't get a job."

"No, but I have to go—it's the rule. I'll make some fresh coffee and try to finish the floor; then maybe I can get the curtains done tomorrow."

34

FLORA PAYS THE MAN IN the gray coat. Water drips onto her face from his umbrella. He gives her the door key and tells her to leave it in the antique shop's mailbox as usual when she's finished.

Flora thanks him and hurries on along the sidewalk. The seams in her old coat have started to come loose. She's forty years old, and her girlish face radiates loneliness.

The first block of Upplands Street, closest to Oden Plaza, is lined with antique and curiosity shops. Their windows are full of chandeliers and glass cabinets, old tin toys, porcelain dolls, medals, and clocks.

Beside the security door to Carlén Antiques is a narrower door leading to a small basement. Flora tapes a sheet of white paper to the dimpled glass:

SPIRITUALIST EVENING

A steep flight of stairs leads down to the basement, where the pipes roar whenever someone above flushes a toilet or turns on the faucet. Flora has rented the room seven times to hold séances. She's had between four and six participants each time, which just covers the cost of renting the room. Though she's contacted a number of newspapers to see if they'd like to write about her ability to talk to the dead, she hasn't had any response. To prepare for this evening's séance, she placed a larger ad in the New Age journal *Phenomena*.

Flora has only a few minutes before the participants arrive, but she knows what she has to do. She quickly moves the furniture and arranges twelve chairs in a circle.

On the table in the middle, she places the small dolls in nineteenth-century costumes. A man and a woman with tiny, shiny porcelain faces. The idea is for them to evoke a sense of the past. Immediately after the séances, she hides them away, because she doesn't really like them.

She places twelve tea lights in a circle around the dolls. She pushes some strontium chloride into the wax in one of the candles with a matchstick, then conceals the hole.

She hurries over to the dresser to set the alarm on the old clock, something she tried four sessions ago. The clapper is missing, so the alarm makes only a dry hacking sound from inside the cabinet. But before she has time to wind the mechanism, the door opens from the street. The first participants are here. She hears umbrellas being shaken, then footsteps on the stairs.

Flora happens to see her own reflection in the rectangular mirror on the wall. She stops, takes a deep breath, and runs her hand across the gray dress she bought from the Salvation Army.

When she smiles, she instantly looks much calmer.

She lights some incense, then says hello quietly to Dina and Asker Sibelius. They hang up their coats and talk in subdued voices.

The participants are almost all old people who feel that death is close. They're people who can't bear what they've lost, who can't accept the idea that death might be absolute.

The front door opens again, and someone comes down the stairs. It's an elderly couple she hasn't seen before.

"Welcome," she says in a low voice from the bottom of the stairs.

Just as she's about to turn away, she stops and looks at the man as if she's seen something unusual, then pretends to shake off the feeling and asks them to take a seat.

The front door opens again, and more participants arrive.

At seven-ten, she has to accept that no one else is coming. Nine is still the most participants she's had so far, but that's still too few to allow her to replace the money she's borrowed from Ewa.

Though Flora tries to breathe calmly, she can feel her legs trembling as she reenters the large, windowless room. The participants are already sitting in a circle. They stop talking, and all eyes turn to her.

35

FLORA LIGHTS THE CANDLES ON the tray. Not until she's taken her seat does she allow herself to look at the participants. She's seen five of them before; the other four are all new. Across from her is a man who's only thirty years old or so. His face is open and handsome in a boyish way.

"Welcome, all of you," she says, and swallows hard. "I think we should start right away. . . ."

"Yes," old Asker says in his creaking, friendly voice.

"Take one another's hands to form the circle," Flora says warmly.

The young man is looking straight at her, smiling, curious. A sense of excitement and expectation begins to flutter in Flora's stomach.

The silence that settles is black and imposing, ten people forming a circle and feeling the dead gathering behind their backs.

"Don't break the circle," she tells the group sternly. "Don't break the circle, no matter what happens. If you do, our visitors may not be able to find their way back to the other side."

Most of her guests are so old that they have lost far more people than they still have. For them, death is a place full of familiar faces.

"You must never ask about the time of your own death," Flora says. "And you must never ask about the devil."

"Why not?" the young man asks with a smile.

"Not all spirits are good, and the circle is only a portal to the other side. . . ."

The young man's dark eyes glint. "Demons?" he asks.

"I don't believe that," Dina Sibelius says, smiling anxiously.

"I try to guard the portal," Flora says gravely. "But they . . . they can feel our warmth. They can see the candles burning."

The room falls silent again. The pipes are whizzing with an odd, agitated buzzing sound, like a fly caught in a spiderweb.

"Are you ready?" she asks slowly.

The participants mumble affirmatively, and Flora feels a shiver of pleasure when she realizes that there's a whole new level of concentration in the room. She imagines that she can hear their hearts beating, feel their pulses throbbing in the circle.

"I'm going to go into a trance now."

Flora holds her breath and squeezes the hands of the people on either side of her. She shuts her eyes tight, waits as long as she can, fighting the instinct to breathe until she starts to shake, and then inhales.

"We have so many visitors from the other side," Flora says after a pause.

Those who have been here before murmur supportively.

Flora can sense the young man's alert, interested gaze on her cheeks, her hair, her neck.

She lowers her face and decides to start with Violet, to help convince the young man. Flora knows her background but has made her wait. Violet Larsen is a terribly lonely person. She lost her only son fifty years ago. One evening, the boy came down with meningitis, and no hospital would take him for fear of spreading the infection. Violet's husband drove the sick boy from hospital to hospital all night. When morning came, his son died in his arms. Overcome by grief, the father died just a year later. Since then, for half a century, Violet has been a childless widow.

"Violet," Flora whispers.

The old woman turns her moist eyes toward her. "Yes?"

"There's a child here, a child who's holding a man's hand."

"What are their names?" Violet asks in a tremulous voice.

"Their names . . . The boy says you used to call him Jusse."

Violet lets out a gasp. "It's my little Jusse," she whispers.

"And the man—he says you know who he is, you're his little flower."

Violet nods and smiles. "That's my Albert."

"They have a message for you, Violet," Flora goes on. "They say they're with you every day, every night, and that you're never alone."

A large tear trickles down Violet's wrinkled cheek.

"The boy is telling you not to be sad. 'Mommy,' he says, 'I'm fine. Daddy's with me all the time.'"

"I miss you so much." Violet sniffs.

"I can see the boy. He's standing right next to you, touching your cheek," Flora whispers.

Violet is sobbing gently, and the room goes quiet again. Flora waits for the heat of the candle to ignite the strontium chloride, but it takes a while.

She murmurs to herself and thinks about whom to pick next. She closes her eyes and rocks back and forth slightly.

"There are so many here . . . ," she mutters. "There are so many. . . . They're crowding the portal, I can feel their presence, they miss you, they're longing to talk to you. . . ."

She stops speaking as one of the candles on the tray starts to crackle.

"Don't squabble at the portal," she mumbles.

The crackling candle suddenly flares bright red, and one member of the circle lets out a little scream. Flora's eyes snap open.

"You haven't been invited; wait outside," she says sternly, and waits until the red in the flame has disappeared. "I want to speak to the man in the glasses," she murmurs. "Yes, come closer. What's you name?"

She listens.

"You want it the way you usually have it," Flora says, looking up at the group. "He says he wants it the way he usually has it. Exactly as usual, with meatballs and boiled potatoes and—"

"That's my Stig!" the woman next to Flora exclaims.

"It's hard to hear what he's saying," Flora goes on. "There are so many here, they keep interrupting him."

"Stig," the woman whispers.

"He says he's sorry . . . he wants you to forgive him."

Through the hand she's holding, Flora can feel the old woman shaking.

"I've forgiven you," the old woman whispers.

36

AFTER THE SÉANCE IS OVER, Flora says a very measured farewell. She knows that people usually want to be alone with their fantasies and memories.

She goes around the room slowly, blowing out the candles and rearranging the chairs. She can still feel a lingering satisfaction in her body from everything's going so well.

She's left a box for the participants to put their money in. She counts it and confirms that it isn't enough to pay back what she borrowed from Ewa. Next week she has another spiritualist evening, and that's her last chance to earn the money back without being discovered.

Despite her advertisement in *Phenomena*, there still weren't enough participants. She's started waking up at night to stare dry-eyed into the darkness, wondering what on earth she's going to do. Ewa usually pays the bills at the beginning of the month, and that's when she's going to realize that some of the money's missing.

The rain has stopped by the time Flora emerges onto the street. The sky is black. Streetlights and neon signs shimmer in the wet tarmac. Flora locks the door and drops the key into Carlén Antiques' mailbox.

Just as she is removing the paper sign and putting it into her bag, she notices someone standing in the next doorway. It's the young man from the séance. He takes a step toward her and smiles apologetically.

"Hi, I was wondering . . . Can I get you a glass of wine somewhere?"

"I can't," she says with instinctive shyness.

"You're really great," he says.

Flora doesn't know what to say. She can feel her face getting redder and redder the longer he looks at her. "The problem is, I'm going to Paris," she lies.

"Can I just ask you a few questions?"

Now she realizes that he must be a journalist from one of the newspapers she's been trying to contact.

"I'm leaving first thing tomorrow morning," she says.

"Give me half an hour—can you manage that?"

As they hurry across the street to the nearest bistro, the young man tells her that his name is Julian Borg and that he writes for the magazine *Close*.

A few minutes later, Flora is sitting across from him at a table covered with a white paper cloth. She takes a careful sip of her red wine. Sweet and sour blend in her mouth, and warmth spreads through her body. Julian Borg picks at a Caesar salad as he looks at her curiously.

"How did this start?" he asks. "Have you always seen spirits?"

"When I was little, I thought everyone could. It didn't seem strange to me," she says, blushing because the lies come so easily.

"What did you see?"

"People I didn't know seemed to live with us. I just thought they were lonely people. Sometimes a child would come into my room and I'd try to play with her. . . ."

"Did you tell your parents?"

"I learned to keep quiet very early on," Flora says, taking another sip of wine. "It's only recently that I've realized that a lot of people actually want to be in touch with the spirits, even if they can't see them ... and the spirits need people. I've finally found my purpose. I stand in the middle and help them connect."

She looks into Julian Borg's warm eyes for a few moments.

In fact, it all started when Flora lost her job as a nurse. She saw less and less of her old colleagues, and in just one year she had lost touch with all her friends. The job center helped her get into a training program so she could become a nail technician, and there she got to know one of the other participants, Jadranka from Slovakia. Jadranka went through low patches, but when she was feeling good she used to earn extra money by taking calls for a Web site called the Tarot Hotline.

They started to socialize, and Jadranka took Flora to a big séance held by the Society of Truth Seekers. Afterward, they talked about how they could do it much better; just a few months later, they found the basement room on Upplands Street. After two séances, Jadranka's depression got worse, and she was admitted to a clinic south of Stockholm. But Flora continued holding the séances on her own.

She borrowed books from the library about healing, past lives, angels, auras, and astral bodies. She read about the Fox sisters, about the cabinet of mirrors and Uri Geller, but the person she learned most from was the skeptic James Randi, and his attempts to uncover deception and tricks.

Flora has never seen any spirits or ghosts, but she's good at saying the things people are desperate to hear.

"You use the word 'spirits' rather than 'ghosts,'" Julian says, putting his knife and fork together on the plate.

"They're the same thing," she replies. "But the word 'ghosts' sounds unpleasant and negative."

Julian smiles, and there's a disarming honesty in his eyes when he says, "I have to confess ... I have a lot of trouble believing in spirits, but ..."

"You just need to be open-minded," Flora explains. "Arthur

Conan Doyle, for instance, was a spiritualist—you know, the guy who wrote all those Sherlock Holmes books."

"Have you ever helped the police?"

"No, that . . ."

Flora blushes hard and doesn't know what to say, so she looks at her watch.

"Sorry, you need to go," he says, taking her hand across the table. "I just want to say that I can tell you want to help people, and I think that's a good thing."

His touch makes Flora's heart beat faster. She can't meet his gaze until he drops her hand, and then they go their separate ways.

37

THE RED BUILDINGS THAT MAKE up the Birgitta Home look idyllic in daylight. Joona is standing beside a huge silver birch talking to the prosecutor Susanne Öst. Raindrops sparkle in the air as they fall from the branches.

"The police are still knocking on doors in Indal," the prosecutor says. "Someone ran into a traffic light, and there's a lot of broken glass on the ground, but apart from that . . . nothing."

"I need to talk to the girls again," Joona says, thinking about the violence that played out inside the misted windows of the main building.

"I thought this business with Dennis would give us something," Susanne says.

When Joona thinks about the isolation room, he is seized by an unsettling suspicion. He tries to picture the sequence of brutal events but can only make out shadows between the pieces of furniture. The figures are transparent, fluid, almost impossible to see.

He takes a deep breath, and suddenly the room where Miranda is lying with her hands over her face becomes perfectly clear. He can see the force behind the cascade of blood, the heavy blows. He can identify every impact and see how the angle changes after the third blow. The light starts to swing. Miranda's body is covered with blood.

"But there was no blood on her," he whispers.

"What are you saying?" the prosecutor whispers back.

"I just need to check something," Joona says.

Just then, the door to the main building opens, and a small man in tight protective clothing comes out. He's Holger Jalmert, a professor of forensic science at Umeå University. He slowly removes his mask to reveal a very sweaty face.

"I'll arrange an interview with the girls at the hotel in an hour," Susanne says.

"Thanks," Joona says, and heads across the yard.

The professor is standing beside his van as he removes the protective clothing, places it in a trash bag, and seals it carefully.

"The comforter's missing," Joona says.

"So I finally get to meet Joona Linna," the professor says, opening a fresh set of disposable overalls.

"Have you been in Miranda's room?"

"Yes, I'm finished in there."

"There was no comforter."

Holger stops with a frown. "Yes, you're right."

"Vicky must have hidden Miranda's comforter in the closet or under the bed in her own room," Joona says.

"I'm just about to start in there," the professor says, but Joona is already on his way toward the building.

As the professor watches him go, he can't help thinking of what he's heard about Joona: that he's so obstinate that he can stand and stare at a crime scene until it opens up like a book.

The professor puts the bag down, then hurries after Joona, clutching the overalls.

They put the protective outfits on before they open the door to Vicky's bedroom.

"There's something under the bed," Joona confirms.

"One thing at a time," Holger murmurs, as he puts a mask on.

Joona waits in the doorway while the professor photographs and measures the room with a laser so that he can locate anything he finds using a three-dimensional set of coordinates.

On the wall above the ornate Bible passages is a poster of Robert Pattinson; there's a large bowl full of white plastic security tags from H&M on a shelf.

Joona watches Holger as he systematically covers the floor with foil, presses it down with a roller, then lifts it gently before photographing it and packing it away. He moves slowly from the door to the bed, then crosses toward the window. As he lifts the foil from the floor, the imprint of a sneaker is clearly visible on the layer of yellow gelatin.

"I need to go soon," Joona says.

"But you'd like me to look under the bed first?"

Holger shakes his head at Joona's impatience, but he carefully spreads a layer of plastic on the floor beside the bed. He kneels down, reaches one hand beneath the bed, and grabs the object underneath.

"It feels like a comforter," he says, concentrating.

He gingerly pulls a heavy comforter out onto the plastic. It's been twisted up and is drenched in blood.

"I think Miranda had it around her shoulders when she was murdered," Joona says in a low voice.

Holger folds the plastic, then pulls a large sack over the wrapped comforter. Joona looks at his watch; he can stay another ten minutes. Holger continues taking samples. He uses moist Q-tips on the dried blood, then lets them dry out before packing them.

"If you find anything that connects to either a person or a location, you must call me immediately," Joona says.

"Understood."

For the hammer under the pillow, the professor uses 120 Q-tips, which he wraps and labels individually. He collects strands of hair and textile fibers, wraps loose hairs in paper, and puts tissue samples and fragments of bone in test tubes so they can be chilled to prevent the growth of bacteria.

38

THE CONFERENCE ROOM AT THE Hotel Ibis is busy, and Joona waits in the breakfast room while the prosecutor talks to the anxious staff about acquiring another room for the interviews. A television screen is shimmering from a metal frame near the ceiling.

Joona calls his assistant, Anja Larsson, and reaches her voice mail. He asks her to find out if there's a pathologist in Sundsvall.

The television news is starting to cover the murders at the Birgitta Home. They show pictures of the police cordon, the red buildings, and the sign to the home. The killer's suspected escape route is shown on a map, and a reporter stands in the middle of Highway 86, talking about the abduction and the police's unsuccessful roadblocks.

Joona gets to his feet and is walking toward the television when the voice-over reports that the mother of the missing boy has chosen to give the kidnapper a message.

Pia Abrahamsson appears on the screen, sitting at a kitchen table with a sheet of prompts in her hand. Her face looks drawn.

"If you're hearing this," she begins, "I understand that you have been the victim of injustice, but Dante has nothing to do with that. . . ."

Pia looks directly at the camera. "You have to give him back," she whispers, her chin trembling. "I'm sure you're kind, but Dante

is only four years old, and I know how frightened he is. . . . He's
so . . ."

She looks at the sheet of paper as tears run down her cheeks.
"You can't be mean to him, you can't hit my little . . ."

She bursts into hulking sobs and turns her face away before
they cut back to the studio in Stockholm.

A forensic psychiatrist from Säter Hospital is perched at a
tall table, explaining to the news anchor just how serious the
situation is: "I haven't had access to the girl's medical records, of
course, and I don't want to speculate as to whether she may have
committed the two murders, but the fact that she's been living in
this particular group home means that it's very possible that she's
mentally ill, and even if—"

"What are the dangers?" the anchor asks.

"It's possible that she doesn't care about the boy at all," the
psychiatrist explains. "She might forget about him altogether at
times . . . but he's only four years old, and if he suddenly starts to
cry or call for his mother, she could get angry and dangerous. . . ."

Susanne Öst comes into the breakfast room to get Joona.
With a small smile, she offers him a cup of coffee and some cake.
He thanks her and follows her to the elevator, and they head up
to the top floor. They walk into an uninspiring bridal suite, with
a locked minibar and a Jacuzzi perched on battered gold paws.

Tuula Lehti is lying on the wide bed watching the Disney
Channel. The representative from victim support services nods
to them. Susanne closes the door, and Joona pulls out a pink
velvet chair and sits down.

"Why did you tell me that Vicky goes to see someone named
Dennis?" Joona asks.

Tuula sits up and clutches a heart-shaped cushion to her stomach.

"I thought that's what she does," she says simply.

"What made you think that?"

Tuula shrugs her shoulders and looks back at the television.

"Did she ever talk about someone called Dennis?"

"No." She smiles.

"Tuula, I really need to find Vicky."

She kicks the sheets and pink silk comforter onto the floor, then turns back to the television.

"Am I going to have to sit here all day?" she asks.

"No, you can go back to your room if you want," the support person says.

"*Sinä olet vain pieni lapsi,*" Joona says in Finnish: You're only a small child.

"*Ei,*" she replies, looking him in the eye.

"You shouldn't have to live in institutions."

"I like it there," she says blankly.

"Nothing bad ever happens to you?"

Her neck flushes, and she blinks her white eyelashes.

"No," she says bluntly.

"Miranda hit Indie. Did she hit you, too?"

"Oh, yeah," she mutters, and tries to squeeze the cushion.

"Why was she angry?"

"She thought I'd been snooping around in her room."

"Had you?"

Tuula licks the heart-shaped cushion.

"Yes, but I didn't take anything."

"Why were you messing around in her room?"

"I snoop around in everyone's rooms."

"Why?"

"It's fun," she replies.

"But Miranda thought you'd taken something from her?"

"Yeah, she was a little annoyed. . . ."

"What did she think you took?"

"She didn't say." Tuula smiles.

"What do you think it was?"

"I don't know, but it's usually pills. . . . Lu Chu pushed me down the stairs once when she thought I'd taken her fucking benzos."

"And if it wasn't drugs—what would she have thought you'd take?"

"Who cares?" Tuula sighs. "Makeup, jewelry . . ."

She sits on the edge of the bed again, leans back, and whispers something about a studded necklace.

"What about Vicky?" Joona asks. "Does Vicky fight?"

"No," Tuula says, smiling again.

"What does she do, then?"

"I shouldn't say, because I don't know her. I don't think she's ever spoken to me, but . . ." The girl falls silent and shrugs.

"Why not?"

"Don't know."

"But you must have seen her when she's angry?"

"She cuts herself, so you don't . . ." Tuula stops and shakes her head.

"What were you going to say?"

"That you don't have to worry about her. She'll kill herself soon; then you'll have one less problem," Tuula says without looking at Joona.

She stares at her fingers, mutters something to herself, then stands up abruptly and walks out of the room.

39

CAROLINE, THE SLIGHTLY OLDER GIRL, comes into the room with the man from victim support services. She's now wearing a long, baggy T-shirt with a kitten on it.

She smiles shyly when she says hello to Joona. Then she sits down carefully in the armchair by the brown desk.

"Tuula says Vicky sneaks out at night to meet a boy," Joona says.

"No." Caroline laughs.

"What makes you say that?"

"She doesn't do that." Caroline smiles.

"You sound very sure."

"Tuula thinks everyone's a total whore," she explains.

"So Vicky doesn't sneak out?"

"Oh, she does that," Caroline says, looking serious.

"What does she do when she gets out?" Joona asks, trying to hide his eagerness.

Caroline looks him in the eye briefly, then turns to gaze at the window.

"She sits behind the brew house and calls her mother."

Joona knows that Vicky's mother died before Vicky arrived at the Birgitta Home, but instead of confronting Caroline with this, he asks calmly, "What do they talk about?"

"Well . . . Vicky just leaves messages on her mother's voice mail, but I think ... if I've got this right, her mom never calls back."

Joona nods. No one seems to have told Vicky that her mother is dead.

"Have you ever heard of someone named Dennis?" he asks.

"No," Caroline says instantly.

"Think carefully."

She looks at him calmly, then jumps when Susanne Öst's phone buzzes with a text message.

"Who would Vicky turn to?" Joona goes on, even though the energy has gone out of the conversation.

"Her mom—that's the only person I can think of."

"Friends, boys?"

"No," Caroline replies. "But I don't know her. ... Look, we're both doing ADL, so we see each other a lot, but she never talks about herself."

"ADL?"

"Sounds like a condition, doesn't it?" Caroline laughs. "It stands for Activities of Daily Life. Only for people who are really good. You get to try going out, you tag along to Sundsvall to get the groceries, exciting stuff like that...."

"You must have talked to each other when you were doing that?" Joona prompts.

"A little, but not much."

"So who else would she talk to?"

"No one," she replies. "Except Daniel, of course."

"The counselor?"

40

Joona and Susanne leave the room and walk back along the hallway to the elevator. She laughs as they both reach for the button at the same time.

"When can we talk to Daniel Grim?" Joona asks.

"His doctor said it was too soon yesterday," she says, glancing at him. "It won't be easy. But I'll try to push back and see what happens."

They get out on the ground floor and head for the front door but stop at the reception desk when they see Gunnarsson standing there.

"Oh yes, I got a text message to let me know that the postmortem's under way," Susanne tells Joona.

"Good. When do you think we'll get the first results?" he asks.

"Go home," Gunnarsson grunts. "We don't need you here. You're not going to see any damn results, you—"

"Calm down," Susanne interrupts, surprised.

"We're so damn stupid up here that we're happy to let some fucking observer take over the whole investigation just because he comes from Stockholm."

"I'm trying to help," Joona says. "Seeing as—"

"Just shut up."

"This is my investigation," the prosecutor says, looking Gunnarsson in the eye.

"Then maybe you'd like to know that Joona Linna has Internal Affairs on his back, and that the senior prosecutor at National—"

"Are you under investigation?" Susanne Öst asks, taken aback.

"Yes," Joona replies. "But my role—"

"And here I am, trusting you," she says, her mouth contracting tightly. "I've let you in on the investigation, listened to you. And it turns out you're just a liar."

"I don't have time for this," Joona says. "I need to talk to Daniel Grim."

"I'll do that," Gunnarsson says with a snort.

"You do realize how serious this is," Joona goes on. "Daniel Grim could be the only person who—"

"I'm not working with you," the prosecutor interrupts.

"You're suspended," Gunnarsson says.

"I no longer feel like I can trust you," Susanne says with a sigh, as she moves toward the door.

"Goodbye," Gunnarsson says, following her.

"If you get a chance to talk to Daniel, you have to ask him about Dennis," Joona calls after them. "Ask Daniel if he knows who Dennis is, but, above all, ask him where Vicky might have gone. We need a name or a location. Daniel's the only person Vicky talked to, and—"

"Go home," Gunnarsson says. He waves at Joona over his shoulder and walks out.

41

DETECTIVE GUNNARSSON GETS OUT OF the elevator at Ward 52B in the West Norrland district's psychiatric clinic. A young man in a white coat comes to meet him. They shake hands; then Gunnarsson follows him down a pale-gray hallway.

"Like I said on the phone, I don't think there's much point trying to interview him yet...."

"I just want to have a little chat with him."

The doctor stops and looks at Gunnarsson for a moment before he begins to explain: "Daniel Grim is in a state of acute stress caused by trauma commonly known as arousal. It's triggered by the hypothalamus and the limbic system, and—"

"I don't give a damn," Gunnarsson interrupts. "I just need to know if he's been stuffed with drugs and if he's totally fucking out of it."

"No, he's not out of it, but I wouldn't let you see him unless—"

"We've got a double murder—"

"You know who has final say here," the doctor interrupts calmly. "If I believe the patient's recovery might be jeopardized by talking to the police, then you'll just have to wait."

"I understand," Gunnarsson says, forcing himself to speak calmly.

"But, seeing as the patient himself has repeatedly stated that he wants to help the police, I'm prepared to allow you to ask him a few questions in my presence."

"I'm very grateful," Gunnarsson says.

They set off down the hallway again and turn a corner to walk past a row of windows looking onto an internal courtyard, before the doctor opens the door to one of the patients' rooms.

Sheets and blankets are lying on the small sofa, but Daniel Grim is sitting on the floor below the window, with his back to the radiator. His face looks oddly relaxed, and he doesn't look up when they enter.

Gunnarsson pulls up a chair and sits down in front of Daniel. Eventually, he swears, breaking the silence, and crouches down next to the grieving man.

"I need to talk to you," he says. "We have to find Vicky Bennet. ... We suspect she committed the murders at the Birgitta Home, and ..."

"But I ..."

Daniel whispers something, and Gunnarsson waits for him to go on.

"I didn't hear what you said," he says.

The doctor stands and watches them in silence.

"I don't think it was her," Daniel whispers. "She's a sweet girl, and ..." He raises his glasses and wipes the tears from his cheeks.

"I know you're governed by an oath of confidentiality," Gunnarsson says. "But is there any way you could help us find Vicky?"

"I'll try," Daniel mumbles, then purses his lips together tightly.

"Does she know anyone who lives near the Birgitta Home?"

"Maybe ... I'm having trouble organizing my thoughts. ..."

Gunnarsson groans and shifts position. "You were Vicky's counselor," he says. "Where do you think she would go? Let's ignore the question of guilt, because we really don't know. But we are fairly certain that she's kidnapped a child."

"No," Daniel whispers.

"Who would she go to? Who would she get to help her?"

"When she's scared," Daniel replies in a shaky voice, "she curls up under a tree and hides. That's ... that ... What was the question?"

"Do you know of any particular hiding place?"

Daniel starts to mutter something about Elisabet's heart. He's saying he was sure it was because of the problems with her heart.

"Daniel, you don't have to do this if it's too difficult," the doctor says. "I can ask the police to come back later if you need to rest."

Daniel shakes his head quickly and tries to breathe calmly.

"Give me a few places," Gunnarsson says.

"Stockholm."

"Where?"

"I . . . I don't know about . . ."

"For fuck's sake!" Gunnarsson exclaims.

"Sorry, I'm sorry . . ."

Daniel's chin trembles, and the corners of his mouth droop, as tears well up in his eyes. He turns away and starts to sob loudly, his whole body shaking.

"She murdered your wife with a hammer and—"

Daniel hits the back of his head against the radiator so hard that his glasses fall into his lap.

"Get out of here," the doctor says sharply. "Not another word. This was a mistake. There won't be any further conversations."

42

THE PARKING LOT OUTSIDE SUNDSVALL Hospital is almost empty. The long building looks desolate in the gloomy light. It's made of dark-brown brick interspersed with white windows that look blind to the world. Joona heads through some low bushes toward the main entrance.

There's no one at the reception desk. He waits for a while until a janitor stops.

"Where's the Forensic Pathology department?" Joona asks.

"Two hundred and fifty kilometers north of here," the janitor says good-naturedly. "But if you're looking for the pathologist, I can show you the way."

They walk through deserted hallways, then take a large elevator down into the bowels of the hospital. It's cold.

The janitor pulls open a pair of heavy metal doors, and at the far end of the hallway is a sign: "Department of Clinical Pathology and Cytology."

"Good luck," the man says, gesturing toward the door.

Joona thanks him and follows the tracks left on the linoleum floor by cadaver carts. He passes the lab, opens the door, and comes straight into the white-tiled postmortem room. A large chandelier hangs from the ceiling beside the neon lights above a stainless-steel table, and the combined cold light is overwhelming. A door hisses, and two people wheel a cart in from the refrigerator room.

"Excuse me," Joona says.

A thin man in a white coat turns around. A pair of white-framed aviator glasses glint in the light. Senior Pathologist Nils Åhlén, known as "The Needle," is from Stockholm, and he is a very old friend of Joona's. The man next to him is his young apprentice, Frippe, his dyed black hair hanging in clumps over the shoulders of his coat.

"What are you doing here?" Joona asks cheerfully.

"A woman from National Crime called and threatened me," Nils replies.

"Anja," Joona says.

"I got really scared—she yelled at me. Said that Joona Linna couldn't be expected to go all the way up to Umeå to talk to a pathologist."

"But since we're here, we're taking the opportunity to go to Nordfest," Frippe explains.

"The Haunted are playing at Club Deströyer," Nils says, smiling.

"I can see how that would tip the balance," Joona says.

Frippe laughs, and Joona notices the worn leather pants beneath his coat and the cowboy boots under the bright-blue shoe covers.

"We're done with the woman . . . Elisabet Grim," The Needle says. "The only real thing to note is the wounds on her hands."

"Defense wounds?" Joona asks.

"Yes, but on the wrong side," Frippe says.

"We can take a closer look in a while," Nils says. "But first it's time to give Miranda Ericsdotter a bit of attention."

"When did they die—can you say?" Joona asks.

"As you know, body temperature sinks. . . ."

"Algor mortis," Joona says.

"Exactly. And that gradual cooling follows a curve that levels out when it reaches room temperature. . . ."

"He knows that," Frippe says.

"So, adding that to the hypostasis and rigor mortis, we can say that the girl and the woman died at roughly the same time, late on Friday."

Joona watches them roll the cadaver cart over to the examination table, count to three, and then lift the body bag. When Frippe opens it, a rancid, yeasty smell, like old blood, spreads through the room.

The girl is lying on the table in the same position she was found in: her hands over her face and her ankles crossed.

Rigor mortis is caused by an increase in calcium in the motionless muscles, which causes two different types of protein to start to combine. It almost always starts in the heart and diaphragm. After half an hour, it can be detected in the jaw; after two hours, in the neck.

Joona knows it's going to take a lot of force to move Miranda's hands from her face.

Odd ideas suddenly start to float through his head. He begins to consider the possibility that it might not be Miranda behind those hands, that her face might have been altered, that her eyes might have been damaged or removed.

"We haven't received a formal request to examine her," The Needle says. "Why does she have her hands over her face?"

"I don't know," Joona replies quietly.

Frippe is carefully photographing the body.

"I assume we're talking about a comprehensive postmortem and that you'll want a report?" Nils says.

"Yes," Joona replies.

"We should really have a secretary when we're dealing with a homicide," The Needle mutters as he walks around the body.

"You're complaining again," Frippe says, smiling.

"Yes, sorry," Nils says. He stops for a moment behind Miranda's head before moving on.

Joona thinks of what the German poet Rilke wrote about how the living were obsessed with drawing distinctions between themselves and the dead. He claimed that there were other beings, angels, that didn't notice any difference.

"The hypostasis indicates that the victim has been left lying still," The Needle mutters.

"I believe Miranda was moved immediately after the murder," Joona says. "The way I read the blood-spatter pattern, her body would have been limp when it was placed on the bed."

Frippe nods. "If it happened that early, there wouldn't be any marks."

Joona forces himself to look on while the two doctors conduct a thorough external examination of the body. He can't help thinking of his own daughter, who isn't much younger than this girl lying still in front of him.

A network of yellow veins has started to show through the white skin. Around her neck and down her thighs, the veins look like a pale river system. Her previously flat stomach has become rounder and darker.

Joona watches them work, registering the two doctors' actions. But, though he sees The Needle cut calmly through her white underpants and pack them for analysis, and listens to their conversation and conclusions, he is, at the same time, mentally back at the crime scene.

The Needle states that there is a total absence of defensive injuries, and Joona hears him discuss with Frippe the lack of soft-tissue damage.

There are no signs of a fight or common abuse. Miranda waited calmly for the killer to deliver the blows to her head; she didn't try to run, didn't put up a fight.

Joona thinks back to the bare room where she spent her last hours as he watches the two men pulling out strands of hair to test and filling tubes with blood.

Nils scrapes beneath her fingernails, then turns toward Joona and clears his throat sharply: "No traces of skin … She didn't defend herself."

"I know," Joona says.

When they start to examine the injuries to her skull, Joona moves closer and stands where he can see everything.

"Cause of death appears to be repeated blows to the head with a blunt object," Nils says when he sees how closely Joona is watching.

"From the front?" Joona asks.

"Yes, from the front, slightly off to one side," The Needle replies, pointing at the bloody hair. "Compression fracture of the temporal bone … We'll do a tomography scan, but I assume that the large blood vessels on the inside of the skull have been detached and that we'll find fragments of bone in the brain."

"Just like with Elisabet Grim, we're bound to find trauma to the cerebral cortex," Frippe says.

"Myelin in the hair," Nils says, pointing.

"Elisabet had broken blood vessels in her skull, and blood and cerebrospinal fluid had run into her nasal cavity," Frippe says.

"They were both attacked from the front; both have the same cause of death," Joona says. "The same murder weapon, and—"

"No," Nils interrupts. "They were killed with different implements."

"But the hammer …," Joona says, almost inaudibly.

"Yes, Elisabet's skull was crushed with a hammer," Nils says. "But Miranda was killed with a rock."

Joona stares at him.

"She was killed with a rock?"

43

Joona stayed in the pathology lab until he had seen Miranda's face. He felt strangely uneasy when The Needle and Frippe forced her hands away. He can't shake the notion that she didn't want to be seen after death.

Now he's sitting at Gunnarsson's desk in the Sundsvall police station reading the preliminary forensics report. Yellow light is streaming through the blinds. A woman sits a short distance away in the glow of a computer monitor. The phone rings, and she mutters irritably as she looks at the number on the screen.

One wall is covered with maps and pictures of Dante Abrahamsson, the missing boy. The bookcases on the other walls are full of files and piles of paper. The photocopier rumbles almost nonstop. A radio is switched on in the staff room, and when the pop-music station goes to a commercial break, Joona hears the announcement for the third time.

"We have a public announcement," the presenter says, before reading the description. "The police are looking for a fifteen-year-old girl and a four-year-old boy. They might be together. The girl has long blond hair, and the boy is wearing glasses, a dark-blue shirt, and dark corduroys. They were last seen in a red Toyota Auris on Highway 86, heading toward Sundsvall. Please contact the police at 114–14 if you have any information. . . ."

Joona gets up and goes into the empty staff room, changes the station to P2, then goes back to the desk with a cup of coffee.

They are playing an old recording of Birgit Nilsson singing the role of Brünnhilde in Wagner's *Ring of the Nibelung*.

Joona sits with the cup of coffee in his hand, thinking about the boy, who's been abducted by a girl who might be psychotic.

He can see them in his mind's eye, hiding in a garage, the boy forced to lie under blankets on a cement floor, tied up, with tape over his mouth.

He must be terrified, if he's even still alive.

Joona continues reading the forensics report. It's been confirmed that the keys in the lock of the isolation room belonged to Elisabet Grim, and the boots that left the bloody footprints at the crime scenes were found in Vicky Bennet's closet.

Two murders, Joona thinks. Miranda was the primary victim, but in order to get to her the killer was forced to take the keys from Elisabet.

According to the forensics team's reconstruction, an argument earlier on Friday evening could have been the trigger, although there could be a longer history of rivalry.

Vicky Bennet had taken the hammer from the shop before bedtime, along with the large boots, and then waited in her room. Once the others fell asleep, she went to see Elisabet Grim and demanded the keys. Elisabet refused and fled into the brew house. Vicky followed her and beat her to death with the hammer, took the keys, and returned to the main building, where she unlocked the isolation room and beat Miranda to death. For some reason, she laid her victim on the bed and arranged her hands over her face. Vicky then returned to her room, hid the hammer and boots, and escaped out of the window into the forest.

That's the crime-scene investigation team's version of events.

Joona knows it will take several weeks for the forensics lab to produce their results. The CSI team has simply assumed that both Miranda and Elisabet were killed with the hammer.

But Miranda was killed with a rock.

Joona can see her before him, a thin girl lying on her bunk in the isolation room, her skin as pale as porcelain. He sees her legs, crossed at the ankles, the bruises on her thigh, the cotton underwear, the little stud in her navel, the hands covering her face.

Why was she killed with a rock when Vicky had access to a hammer?

Joona stares at every single photograph from the crime scene, then imagines the chain of events, the way he usually does. He puts himself in the murderer's place and forces himself to see each horrifying choice as unavoidable.

Because, to anyone who kills another person, murder is the only possible option. The murder doesn't seem unpleasant or bestial but rational or attractive.

Sometimes the killer can't see further than the first blow. He can justify a single blow by thinking that he merely needs to vent. The next blow feels years away until it's suddenly upon him. For the murderer, death can be the conclusion to an epic saga that begins with the first blow and concludes just thirteen seconds later with the last.

All the evidence here points to Vicky Bennet. Everyone is assuming that she murdered Miranda and Elisabet, yet, at the same time, no one really seems to consider Vicky capable, either physically or mentally, of doing it.

But all people have it in them, Joona thinks, putting the report back in Gunnarsson's inbox. We see reflections of it in our dreams and fantasies. We all carry violence inside us, but most people manage to tame themselves.

Gunnarsson comes into the station and hangs up his crumpled coat. He puts his hand to his mouth and belches, then walks into the staff room. When he comes out with a cup of coffee and catches sight of Joona, he grins. "Aren't they missing you in Stockholm?"

"No," Joona replies.

Gunnarsson sniffs a pack of cigarettes, then turns to the woman sitting at the computer. "All reports come straight to me."

"Okay," she says, without looking up.

Gunnarsson mutters something.

"How did your conversation with Daniel Grim go?" Joona asks.

"Fine. Not that it's any of your business. I had to take it carefully, though."

"What did he have to say about Vicky?"

Gunnarsson makes a whistling sound with his lips and shakes his head. "Nothing that's any use to us."

"You asked about Dennis?"

"That fucking doctor was on me like he was the guy's mother. He put a stop to the whole thing."

Gunnarsson scratches his neck hard. He seems unaware that he's holding a pack of cigarettes and a lighter in his hand.

"I want copies of Holger Jalmert's report when it arrives," Joona says. "And the test results from the lab, and—"

"Okay, you need to get the fuck out of my face," Gunnarsson interrupts.

He smiles broadly at his female colleague but seems to deflate slightly when he sees the serious look in Joona's gray eyes.

"You have no idea how to find Vicky Bennet and the boy," Joona says slowly, getting to his feet. "And you have no idea how to make any progress with the murder investigation."

"I'm counting on getting information from the public," Gunnarsson replies. "There's always someone who's seen something."

44

FLORA WOKE UP JUST BEFORE her alarm clock went off. Hans-Gunnar wanted his breakfast in bed at eight-fifteen. Once he got up, Flora had to air and make his bed. Ewa sat in a chair, wearing yellow sweatpants and a nude-colored bra, watching her. Flora stood up and checked that the bottom sheet was perfectly smooth and properly tucked under the corners of the mattress. The crocheted bedspread had to be arranged with exactly the same amount of overhang on both sides, and Flora had to do it three times before it was good enough for Ewa.

Now it's lunchtime, and Flora has returned home with the groceries and cigarettes for Hans-Gunnar. She hands over the change, then stands and waits, as usual, while he checks the receipt.

"Jesus Christ, that cheese was expensive," he says unhappily.

"You told me to buy cheddar," Flora points out.

"Not if it's that damn expensive, don't you get it? If it's that much, you buy a different cheese."

"Sorry, I thought—"

She doesn't have time to finish the sentence. Hans-Gunnar's signet ring flashes in front of her face as he slaps her, hard. It happens very fast. Her ear starts to ring, and her cheek stings.

"You did say you wanted cheddar," Ewa says from the sofa. "It's hardly her fault."

Hans-Gunnar mutters something about idiots, then goes out onto the balcony to smoke. Flora puts the food away, goes back to her room, and sits on the bed. She touches her cheek gingerly and thinks about how tired she is of getting slapped around by Hans-Gunnar. Sometimes he hits her several times a day. She always knows when it's coming, because he looks at her. He never looks at her otherwise. The worst part isn't the pain but how breathless he gets when he stares at her afterward.

She can't remember his hitting her when she was little. He used to work and wasn't home much. Once, he even pointed out to her different countries on the globe in his room.

Ewa and Hans-Gunnar go out to play boules with their friends. Flora sits in her room. As soon as she hears the front door close, she looks over at the corner. On the old dresser, she keeps an ornament her teacher gave her in high school: a horse and cart made of glass. In the top drawer, she has one of the stuffed toys she had as a child, a Smurf with blond hair and high heels. The middle drawer contains a stack of neatly ironed towels. Flora lifts the towels and takes out her nice green dress. She bought it from the Salvation Army this summer. Though she's never worn it outside her room, she often tries it on when Ewa and Hans-Gunnar aren't home.

She starts to unbutton her cardigan, but then hears voices from the kitchen. It's the radio. She goes to turn it off and discovers that Ewa and Hans-Gunnar have been eating cake. The floor in front of the pantry is covered with crumbs. They've left half a glass of strawberry juice on the counter, and the bottle is still out.

Flora gets a rag and wipes the crumbs from the floor, then rinses the rag and washes the glass.

On the radio, there's a report about a murder up north. A girl has been killed in a group home for girls.

Flora rinses the rag and hangs it over the sink.

The report says that the police have no comment about the ongoing investigation, but the reporter is interviewing some of the other girls live.

"You want to know what happened, don't you? So I pushed

my way through," one girl says in a broken voice. "I didn't have time to see much, because they pulled me away from the door. I screamed, but then I realized there was no point."

Flora picks up the bottle of juice and heads for the fridge.

"Can you tell us what you saw?"

"Yes, I saw Miranda. She was lying on her bed like this, just like this—see?"

Flora stops and listens to the radio.

"She had her eyes closed?" the reporter says.

"No, like this, with both hands in front of her face, like she was—"

"God, you're such a liar!" someone shouts behind her.

Flora hears something hit the floor and feels liquid splash her legs. She looks down and sees that she's dropped the bottle. Suddenly her stomach churns, and she just makes it to the bathroom in time before she throws up.

45

WHEN FLORA COMES BACK OUT, the news is over. A woman with a German accent is now discussing autumn menus. Flora picks up the pieces of glass, wipes the spilled juice, and then stands in the middle of the floor, staring at her cold white hands. She goes to the phone in the hall and calls the police.

Flora waits, listening to the dry crackle on the line as the call goes through.

"Police," a woman answers in a weary voice.

"Hello, my name is Flora Hansen, and I'd like to—"

"Hold on," the woman says. "I didn't catch that."

"Okay," Flora says. "My name is Flora Hansen, and I have information about the murder of the girl up in Sundsvall."

There's a silent moment. Then the weary but calm voice speaks again. "What did you want to tell us?"

"Do you pay for information?" Flora asks.

"No, I'm afraid not."

"But I . . . I think I saw the dead girl."

"You mean you were there when it happened?" the police officer says quickly.

"I'm a spiritual medium," Flora says in a secretive voice. "I'm in contact with the dead . . . and I saw it all, but I think . . . I think I'd remember better if I got paid."

"You're in contact with the dead," the police office repeats tiredly. "Is that your piece of information?"

"The girl was holding her hands in front of her face," Flora says.

"For heaven's sake, that's been in all the newspapers!" the woman snaps impatiently.

Flora's heart shrinks with shame. She feels sick again. Cold sweat is running down her back. She hadn't planned what she was going to say, but she now realizes that she should have said something else. The papers had been on display at the supermarket when she was getting the food and Hans-Gunnar's cigarettes.

"I didn't know that," she whispers. "I'm just saying what I've seen. . . . I saw lots more things, things you might be interested in paying for."

"We don't pay for—"

"But I saw the murder weapon. You might think you've found the murder weapon, but that's wrong, because I saw—"

"You do know you can be fined for wasting police time?" the police officer interrupts. "It's a criminal offense. I don't mean to sound angry, but you need to appreciate that, while I'm talking to you, someone with real information could be trying to get through."

"Yes, but I—"

Flora is about to start talking about the murder weapon when the line clicks. She looks at the phone, then calls the police again.

46

Pia Abrahamsson is staying in an apartment owned by the Church of Sweden in a large wooden house in one of the leafier parts of Sundsvall. The apartment is large and beautiful. The deacons who have been bringing her food have encouraged her to talk to one of the priests, but Pia can't bring herself to do it.

She's spent the whole day driving her rental car along the same route, past the small villages, around Indal, up and down the logging roads.

Several times, she encountered police officers; they told her to go home.

Now she's lying on the bed with her clothes on, staring out into the darkness. She hasn't slept since Dante went missing. Her phone rings. She reaches for it, stares at it, then hits the mute button. It's her parents. They keep calling. Pia gazes back out into the darkness of the unfamiliar apartment.

Inside her head, she can hear Dante crying. He's frightened and asking for her. He keeps saying he wants to go home to his mommy.

She can't lie there any longer and gets up.

Pia grabs her jacket and opens the front door. She can taste blood in her mouth when she gets back in the rental car and starts driving. She has to find Dante. What if he's sitting in a ditch by the side of the road? He might have hidden under a piece of cardboard. What if the girl has just dumped him somewhere?

The roads are dark and empty. Almost everyone seems to be asleep. She tries to see into the dense darkness beyond the headlights.

She pulls in at the spot where her car was taken and sits there, her hands shaking on the steering wheel, before she turns around and starts to drive back. She heads into the small town of Indal, where the car—and Dante—probably disappeared. She drives slowly past a preschool, then turns at random onto Solgårds Road and rolls past the dark villas.

Movement under a trampoline makes her stop abruptly and get out of the car. She stumbles into the garden through a low rose hedge, scratching her legs, and goes over to the trampoline, only to find a fat cat hiding in the darkness.

She turns toward the brick house and stares at the closed blinds, her heart thudding.

"Dante?" she calls. "Dante? It's Mommy! Where are you?"

Her voice is hoarse and sad. Lights go on inside the house. Pia walks to the next house, rings the doorbell, then bangs on the door before moving on.

"Dante!" she calls as loudly as she can.

She goes from house to house, calling for her son, beating on locked garage doors with her hands, looking inside small play-houses. She scrambles through thorny undergrowth and crosses a ditch, only to find herself back on Indals Road.

She hears shrieking tires as a car brakes, and she takes a step back and falls. She stares up at the uniformed police officer hurrying over to her.

"Are you okay?"

The policewoman helps her to her feet, but Pia stares blankly at her.

"Have you found him?" Pia asks.

A second officer comes over and says they'll drive her home.

"Dante's scared of the dark," she says, hearing how weak her voice sounds. "I'm his mom, but I used to lose my patience with him—I'd force him to go back to his own bed when he came to mine. He'd stand there in his pajamas and tell me he was scared, but I . . ."

"Where did you leave your car?" the woman asks, taking Pia's arm.

"Let go of me!" Pia shouts, and pulls free. "I have to find him!" She hits the policewoman in the face and screams as they overpower her and hold her down. Though she struggles to get free, they lock her arms behind her back and hold her still. Pia feels her chin scrape the road and weeps, helpless.

47

JOONA IS DRIVING ALONG A stunningly beautiful stretch of road, past rolling fields and sparkling lakes, thinking about the lack of witnesses: no one seems to know anything about Vicky Bennet, and no one has seen anything. He reaches a white stone house, on the deck of which is a lemon tree covered with small yellow fruit, in a huge pot.

He rings the doorbell, waits, then walks around the house.

On one of the white garden chairs, beneath an apple tree in the backyard, sits Nathan Pollock, a large cast around his leg.

"Nathan?"

The thin man stiffens as he turns toward Joona. He shades his eyes with one hand, then smiles in surprise. "Joona Linna, is that really you?"

Nathan's silver-gray hair is gathered in a small ponytail over one shoulder, and he's wearing black pants and a loose-knit sweater. Nathan Pollock is a member of the National Homicide Commission, a group of six experts who work on complex murder cases throughout Sweden.

"Joona, I'm really sorry about the internal investigation. I shouldn't have taken you to visit the Brigade."

"It was my choice," Joona says, sitting down.

Nathan shakes his head slowly. "I've fallen out badly with Carlos over the fact that you're being scapegoated like this."

"Was that how you broke your leg?" Joona asks.

"No, there was an angry female bear that came rushing into the garden," Nathan replies, and grins, showing his gold tooth.

"Either that or he fell off a ladder picking apples," a high voice says behind them.

"Matilda," Joona says.

He gets up and hugs the woman, who has thick red-brown hair, and skin covered with freckles.

"Detective," she says with a smile, sitting down. "I hope you've brought some work for my dear husband before he has to start doing Sudoku."

"I might have," Joona says tentatively.

"Really?" Nathan says. He grins, scratching his leg.

"I've seen the crime scene, and I've seen the bodies, but I can't get access to any reports or test results. . . ."

"Because of the internal investigation?"

"It isn't my investigation, but I'd like to hear your opinion."

"That'll cheer him up," Matilda says, smiling, and pats her husband's cheek.

"Nice of you to think of me," Pollock says.

"You're the best detective I know," Joona replies.

He sits back down and starts to give a thorough account of what he knows about the case. After a while, Matilda leaves the table and goes back to the house. Pollock listens intently, occasionally asking questions about some of the details.

A gray tabby cat comes over and rubs against Nathan's legs, and birds sing in the trees as Joona describes the rooms and the positions of the bodies, the blood-spatter patterns, the stains and puddles, the dried blood. Nathan closes his eyes and concentrates on Joona's description of the hammer under the pillow, the bloodstained comforter, and the open window.

"Let's see," Pollock whispers. "Extreme violence, but no bite marks, no attempt at dismemberment . . ."

Joona says nothing, letting Nathan think things through for himself. Nathan has put together plenty of perpetrator profiles—and he hasn't been wrong yet.

Profiling is a way of closing in on a perpetrator by interpreting the crime as a metaphor for his psychological state. The theory is that the inner life of an individual is to some extent reflected in that person's actions and behavior. If a crime is chaotic, the criminal's mental state is chaotic, and this chaos can only be concealed if the perpetrator is a loner.

Joona watches Nathan's lips move while he thinks. Every so often, he whispers something to himself or toys unconsciously with his ponytail.

"I think I can picture the bodies ... and the spatter pattern," he says. "Okay—so, as we know, most murders are committed in the heat of the moment. Then the blood and chaos lead to panic. That's when people reach for the bone saws and trash bags ... or slide around in the blood with a scrub brush, leaving evidence everywhere."

"But not this time."

"This murderer really hasn't tried to hide anything at all."

"That same thought occurred to me," Joona agrees.

"The violence is extreme and methodical. This isn't a punishment that's gone too far; the intent in both cases was to kill ... no more, no less. Both victims are trapped in small rooms. They can't escape. . . . The violence isn't frenzied—it's more like an execution, a slaughter, even."

"We think the killer is a girl," Joona says.

"A girl?"

Joona meets Nathan's surprised gaze and shows him a photograph of Vicky Bennet.

Nathan lets out a laugh and shrugs his shoulders. "I'm sorry, but I seriously doubt that."

Matilda comes out with tea and jelly doughnuts and sits down at the table. Nathan pours three cups.

"You don't think a girl could have done this?" Joona asks.

"I've never come across anything like that," Nathan says, smiling.

"Not all girls are nice," Matilda says.

Nathan points at the photograph. "Is she known to be violent?"

"No. Quite the opposite."

"Then you're chasing the wrong person."

"We're sure she kidnapped a young boy yesterday."

"But she hasn't killed him?"

"Not as far as we know," Joona says, picking up a doughnut.

Nathan leans back in his chair and squints up at the sky. "If the girl isn't considered violent, if she has no criminal record and hasn't been the subject of a similar investigation before, then I don't think it's her," he says, looking at Joona intently.

"But if it is?" Joona persists.

Nathan shakes his head and blows on his tea. "It doesn't make sense," he replies. "I've just been reading about one of David Canter's research projects—he focuses on the role the perpetrator allocates to the victim during the crime. I've thought something similar myself—that the perpetrator uses the victim as a sort of antagonist in the drama."

"Yes . . . that's one way of putting it," Joona says.

"According to David Canter's model, covering the girl's face means that the murderer wants to turn her into an object. Men who belong to that group often use excessive violence—"

"What if they're just playing hide-and-seek?" Joona interjects.

"What do you mean?" Nathan asks, looking into Joona's gray eyes.

"The victim counts to a hundred, and the killer hides."

Nathan smiles and lets the idea sink in. "In which case, it's about the search. . . ."

"Yes, but where?"

"The only advice I have is to look in old haunts," Pollock says. "The past reflects the future. . . ."

48

CARLOS IS STANDING AT THE low window of his eighth-floor office looking out at the steep slopes of Kronoberg Park.

He doesn't know that Joona is currently walking across the park after a brief visit to the old Jewish cemetery at its far corner.

Carlos sits down at his desk again and doesn't notice the tousle-haired detective cross Polhems Street and come into the glazed entrance hall of police headquarters.

Joona passes a banner about the role of the National Police in a changing world. Benny Rubin is sitting hunched at his computer, and Joona overhears part of a conversation from Magdalena Ronander's office.

Joona has returned to Stockholm because he has been summoned to a meeting with two officers from Internal Affairs. He gets his mail and sits down at his desk. As he starts to look through the envelopes, he can't help thinking that he agrees with Nathan Pollock.

It's hard to reconcile the image of Vicky Bennet with the two murders.

Although the police don't have access to her psychiatric records, there's nothing to indicate that Vicky might be dangerous. She isn't in any of the police databases, and people who have met her describe her as withdrawn and well meaning.

Still, so far, all the forensic evidence points to her. And everything indicates that she's abducted the little boy. He may be lying in a ditch somewhere with his head smashed in. But if he's still alive, there's no time to lose. Maybe he's sitting inside the car with Vicky, in some dark garage; maybe she's shouting at him right now, working herself up into a state of violent rage.

Nathan's advice was to look to the past.

Simple and obvious, really—the past always reflects the future.

Over the course of her fifteen years, Vicky has moved plenty of times, from her homeless mother to foster homes and to children's group homes.

She's out there somewhere.

The answer could lie with any of the families she lived with. It could be buried in a conversation she had with social workers, counselors, or foster parents.

There must be people she trusted and confided in.

Joona is about to ask Anja if she's found any names and addresses when she appears in the doorway. Her bulky frame is squeezed into a tight black skirt, and, as usual, she's wearing an angora sweater. Her blond hair is in an elaborate updo, and her lipstick is bright red.

"Before I start, I just want to say that over fifteen thousand children are placed in care each year," Anja begins. "The politicians said they were introducing choice into the system when they allowed private companies to get involved. Now most children's homes are owned by venture capitalists, and the one that demands the least money gets custody.... They cut back on staffing, education, therapy, and dental care, all to make a profit...."

"I know," Joona says. "But Vicky Bennet ..."

"I thought I might try to reach her latest placement supervisor."

"Can you do that?" Joona asks.

She smiles indulgently and tilts her head. "I've already done it, Joona Linna...."

"You're brilliant," Joona says, and means it.

"Anything for you."

"I don't deserve that." Joona smiles.

"No, you're right," she says, and leaves the room.

He sits there for a few moments, then gets up and knocks on Anja's door.

"The addresses," she says, pointing to a stack of papers on top of the printer.

"Thanks."

"When the placement supervisor heard my name, he said that Sweden used to have a brilliant butterfly-swimmer with the same name," she says, blushing.

"I hope you told him that was you?"

"No, but he still told me that Vicky Bennet didn't appear in the population register until she was six years old. Her mother, Susie, was homeless and seems to have given birth to her without involving health services. Her mother was eventually taken into psychiatric care, and Vicky was placed with two voluntary carers here in Stockholm."

Joona holds the list, still warm from the printer. He looks at the dates and placements, the rows of names and addresses, from the first—Jack and Elin Frank at 47 Strand Street—to the last two, the Ljungbacken Children's Home in Uddevalla, and then the Birgitta Home, outside Sundsvall. A note indicating that the child had expressed a wish to return to the first foster family appears several times: "The child has asked to be allowed to return to the Frank family, but the family has declined."

Eventually, Vicky Bennet ended up living in institutions rather than foster homes: emergency placements, evaluation clinics, treatment centers, and group homes.

He thinks about the bloody hammer under her pillow and the blood on the windowsill.

The clenched, thin face in the photograph and the tangled fair hair.

"Can you check to see if Jack and Elin Frank still live at the same address?"

A look of amusement crosses Anja's round face, and she pouts and says, "You should try reading a few gossip magazines."

"What do you mean?"

"Elin and Jack Frank are divorced, but she kept the apartment. . . . It was her money, after all."

"So they're famous?" Joona asks.

"She does a lot of charity stuff, more than most rich people. She and Jack put a lot of money into Children's Villages, aid funds, and so on."

"So Vicky Bennet actually lived with them?"

"It doesn't seem to have gone very well," Anja replies.

Joona starts to walk out with the printouts, but he turns and looks back at Anja in the doorway.

"How can I thank you?"

"I've signed us up for classes," she replies quickly. "Promise you'll come with me."

"What kind of classes?"

"Relaxation . . . Kama Sutra something or other . . ."

49

Forty-seven Strand Street is located directly across from the Djurgården Island Bridge. It's a fancy building with an elaborate entrance and a dark, ornate stairwell.

Elin and Jack Frank were the only family Vicky wanted to go back to, even though she had only lived there a short time, but the Franks chose to reject her appeals.

When Joona rings the door with the name "Frank" embossed on a shimmering black plaque, it opens almost at once. A relaxed man with short straw-colored hair and an even suntan looks curiously at the tall detective.

"I'm looking for Elin Frank."

"Robert Bianchi. I'm Elin's consigliere," the man says, holding out his hand.

"Joona Linna, National Crime Unit."

A slight smile plays across the man's lips. "That sounds exciting, but . . ."

"I need to speak to her."

"May I ask what this is regarding? I don't want to disturb her unnecessarily. . . ."

The man trails off when he sees the cool look in Joona's gray eyes.

"Wait in the entryway, and I'll see if she's accepting visitors," he says, and disappears through a door.

The entryway is white and completely devoid of furniture. There are no closets, no objects, no shoes or coats. Just smooth white walls and a single large mirror with white-tinted glass.

Joona tries to imagine a child like Vicky in this environment. An anxious, troubled little girl who wasn't registered with the state until she was six years old. A child who had gotten used to having "home" mean the garage or underpass where you happened to spend the night.

Robert Bianchi returns, smiling calmly, and asks Joona to follow him. They pass through a large, airy living room containing several sofas and an ornamental tiled stove. Thick carpets muffle the sound of their steps as they walk through the various rooms until they reach a closed door.

"Go ahead and knock," he tells Joona with a hesitant smile.

Joona knocks and hears someone walk across a hard floor in heels. The door is opened by a slim, middle-aged woman with dark-blond hair and big blue eyes. She's wearing a thin red dress that stops just below her knees. She's beautiful, and tastefully made up, and has three rows of snow-white pearls around her neck.

"Come in, Joona," she says in a low but clear voice.

He walks into a brightly lit room containing a desk, a pair of white leather sofas, and built-in bookcases.

"I was just thinking of having some chai—is it too early for you?" she asks.

"No, that sounds great."

Robert leaves the room, and Elin gestures toward the sofas.

"Let's sit down."

She saunters over and sits down across from him. "What's this about, then?" she asks.

"Several years ago, you and your husband, Jack, acted as foster parents to a young girl. . . ."

"We helped a lot of children in different ways when . . ."

"Her name was Vicky Bennet," Joona says softly.

Something flits across Elin's controlled face, but the tone of her voice doesn't change. "I remember Vicky very well," she replies with a brief smile.

"What do you remember?"

"She was sweet and kind, and she . . ."

Elin Frank falls silent and stares ahead of her. Her hands are lying perfectly still.

"We have reason to believe she may have murdered two people at a children's home outside Sundsvall," Joona says.

Elin quickly turns her face away. Joona manages to see her eyes grow darker. She adjusts her dress over her knees with hands she can't completely keep from trembling.

"How does that concern me?" she asks.

Robert knocks and comes in with a tinkling tea tray. Elin Frank thanks him and asks him to leave the tray.

"Vicky Bennet has been missing since Friday," Joona explains once Robert has left the room. "There's a chance that she may try to contact you."

Elin doesn't look at him. She bows her head slightly and swallows hard. "No," she says in a cold voice.

"Why don't you think Vicky Bennet would contact you?"

"She'll never contact me," she replies, and gets to her feet. "It was a mistake to let you in without checking what you wanted first."

Joona starts to prepare the tea but pauses and looks up at her.

"Who do you think Vicky would turn to? Would she contact Jack?"

"If you have any more questions, you're welcome to talk to my lawyer," she says, and leaves the room.

After a while, Robert comes back in.

"I'll see you to the door," he says curtly.

"Thanks very much," Joona replies, then pours tea into both cups, picks up one of them, blows on it, and takes a cautious sip.

He smiles and takes a lemon cookie from a plate. Slowly and calmly, he eats the cookie and drinks his tea. He takes the napkin from his lap and dabs his mouth, folds the napkin, and puts it down on the table before finally getting to his feet.

Joona hears Robert's footsteps behind him as he walks through the huge apartment. He walks across the stone floor of the entrance and opens the door to the stairwell.

"Something I should mention before you leave is that it's very important that Elin isn't associated with any negative—"

"I understand what you're saying," Joona interrupts. "But this isn't about Elin Frank."

"It is to me, and it is to her," Robert counters.

"The past doesn't draw any distinctions when it comes back," Joona says, before heading down the stairs.

50

THE APARTMENT'S GYM IS LOCATED close to the largest bathroom. Elin usually runs seven kilometers each day, and she sees her personal trainer at the Mornington Health Club twice a week. In front of her treadmill is a television, which is switched off at the moment, and to her left Elin can see the rooftops and the tower of Oscar's Church.

She's not listening to music today. The only sounds are the thud of her feet, the clanking echo of the weights, the whirr of the treadmill, and her own breathing.

Her ponytail bounces between her shoulder blades. She's dressed in just a pair of sweatpants and a white sports bra. After fifty minutes, the sweat has soaked through the fabric between her buttocks, and her bra is drenched.

She thinks back to when Vicky Bennet came to her home. That was nine years ago. A small girl with fair, tangled hair.

Elin had contracted chlamydia when she was young, when she was studying abroad in France. She didn't get it treated in time and was left infertile. At the time, she wasn't concerned, because she was sure she would never want children anyway. For years, she told herself that it was just nice not to have to think about contraceptives.

She and Jack had been married only two years when he started to talk about adopting, but every time he raised the subject, she explained that she didn't want children, that they were too much responsibility.

Jack was still in love with her in those days, and he supported her when she suggested that they volunteer to help children who had problems with their own families and needed to get away for a while.

Elin called the Norrmalm branch of Stockholm Social Services, and Jack went with her to meet a social worker, who asked about their home, work, marital status, and whether or not they had any children of their own.

A month later, Elin and Jack were called in for separate in-depth interviews. They were asked a million questions, then a million more follow-up questions.

Elin can still remember the social worker's astonished reaction when she realized who Elin was. Three days after that, they got a phone call. The social worker explained that she was hoping to house a child who needed a lot of security and a calm and quiet space.

"She's six years old and . . . I think it could work. I mean, it's a question of feeling your way forward a lot of the time, but as soon as she's settled, we can recommend a number of psychologists," the woman explained.

"What's her background?"

"Her mother is homeless and mentally ill. . . . The authorities intervened when the girl was found sleeping in a subway."

"But she's okay?"

"She's mildly dehydrated, but the doctor says, other than that, she's healthy. . . . I've tried to talk to her. . . . She seems sweet but withdrawn."

"What's her name—do you know?"

"Yes, her name's Vicky Bennet."

Elin Frank starts to run faster as she gets close to the end of the workout. The treadmill whirrs louder, and her breathing speeds up. She increases the resistance for a little while, then slows down.

Afterward, she does some stretches at the ballet barre in front of the big mirror, without looking herself in the eye. Then she kicks off her shoes and leaves the room on heavy, tingling legs. Outside the bathroom, she takes off her already cold bra, drops it on the floor, pulls down her sweatpants and underwear, pushes them off with her feet, and gets into the shower.

As the warm water washes over her neck, and her muscles relax, her anxieties return. It's as if hysteria is only just below the surface, darting beneath her skin. Something inside her wants to cry and scream out loud and never stop. Instead, she composes herself and changes the temperature of the water until it's ice-cold. She forces herself to stand underneath it. She turns her face toward the jet of water until her temples ache with cold; only then does she turn the water off and dry herself.

51

ELIN LEAVES HER WALK-IN CLOSET wearing a mid-length velvet skirt and a bodysuit from Wolford's latest collection. The skin on her arms and shoulders shines through the black material with its tiny, shimmering gems. The garment is so thin that she has to wear a special pair of silk gloves when she's putting it on.

In the reading room, Robert is sitting on a lambskin-covered armchair, going through papers.

"Who was that girl the policeman was asking about?"

"No one," Elin replies.

"Anything we need to worry about?"

"No."

Robert Bianchi has been Elin's adviser and assistant for six years. He dates occasionally but has never had a long-term relationship. Elin can't help thinking he mostly just likes being seen in the company of handsome men. It was Jack's idea for her to get a gay assistant, so he wouldn't be jealous. She remembers saying that it didn't make any difference to her.

She sits down beside him, in the other armchair, and stretches out her legs to show him her high heels.

"Wonderful," he says, smiling.

"I saw the schedule for the rest of the week," she says.

"In an hour you have the reception at the Clarion Hotel Sign."

A heavy bus drives by on the street and makes the large sliding doors rattle. Elin feels Robert looking at her but doesn't look back, merely plays with the little diamond cross she's wearing on a chain around her neck.

"Jack and I took in a young girl named Vicky . . . once upon a time," she says, and swallows hard.

"Was she adopted?"

"No, she had a mother. We were just providing temporary foster care, but I . . ." She coughs and pulls the diamond cross along the necklace.

"When was this?"

"Only a couple of years before you started," she replies. "But I wasn't helping to run the business then, and Jack had only just started working with Zentropa."

"You don't have to tell me."

"I honestly think that we were prepared, as well as we could have been. We knew it wasn't going to be easy, but . . . Can you believe this country? I mean, to start with, it took forever—we kept having meetings with social workers and counselors, absolutely everything had to be examined, from our finances to our sex life—but as soon as we were accepted, it was only three days before we suddenly had a child and were left to cope on our own. It all seemed a little strange. You know, they didn't tell us anything about her; we basically got no help at all."

"Sounds typical."

"We really did want to do the right thing . . . and the girl lived here for nine months, on and off. They tried to get her back with her mother so many times, but it never ended well—once Vicky was found among some old boxes in some garage outside Stockholm."

"Tragic," he says.

"In the end, Jack couldn't handle all the nights we had to go out and rescue her—take her to the hospital, or just put her in the tub and give her some food. . . . One night, he told me I had to choose. . . ."

Elin smiles blankly at Robert. "I don't understand why he had to force me to choose."

"Because he only ever thinks about himself," Robert says.

"But we were only here as backup. I could hardly choose between him and a child who was only going to live here for a few months. It was crazy. And, of course, he knew that I was utterly dependent on him at the time."

"No," Robert says.

"But it's true, I was," Elin says. "So, when Vicky's mother got a new home, I agreed to let him call Social Services. . . . I mean, things looked pretty good for the mother that time. . . ."

Her voice breaks, and, to her own surprise, she feels tears start to fall.

"Why haven't you ever mentioned this before?"

Elin wipes her tears and lies, though she doesn't know why: "It's not a big deal, nothing I spent a lot of time thinking about."

"We all have to move on," Robert says, as if he's making excuses for her.

"Yes," she whispers, then covers her face.

"What is it?" he asks anxiously.

"Robert." She sighs and meets his gaze. "This has nothing to do with me, but that policeman who was here, he told me that Vicky has killed two people."

"Do you mean that thing that just happened up in Norrland?"

"I don't know."

"Do you have any connection to her?" he asks slowly.

"No."

"Because you can't let yourself be associated with this."

"I know. . . . Obviously, I'd like to do something to help her, but . . ."

"Keep your distance."

"Maybe I should call Jack."

"No, don't."

"He needs to know."

"Not from you," Robert points out. "It would only upset you, you know that. Every time you talk to him . . ."

She tries to smile in agreement and puts her hand on Robert's warm fingers.

"Come back tomorrow morning at eight o'clock, and we'll go through next week's schedule."

"Good," Robert says, and leaves the room.

Elin picks up her phone but waits until Robert has closed and locked the front door before she calls Jack.

He sounds hoarse and sleepy when he answers. "Elin? Do you know what time it is here? You can't just call whenever—"

"Were you asleep?"

"Yes."

"Alone?"

"No."

"Are you being honest to hurt me or to—"

"We're divorced, Elin," he interrupts.

Elin walks into the bedroom but stops when her eyes land on the large bed. "Tell me you miss me," she whispers.

"Good night, Elin."

"You can have the Broome Street apartment if you like."

"I don't want it. You're the one who likes New York."

"The police seem to think Vicky has murdered two people."

"Our Vicky?"

Her mouth starts to tremble, and tears well up in her eyes. "Yes . . . They were here, asking about her."

"That's terrible," he says quietly.

"Can't you just come back? I need you. You can bring Norah if you want; I'm not jealous."

"Elin, I'm not going to come back to Stockholm."

"Sorry I called," Elin says, and hangs up the phone.

52

Both the national department for complaints against the police and the Internal Affairs Department are based at the top of 21 Kungs Bridge. Joona is sitting in a small office with Mikael Båge, who's in charge of the investigation, and the senior secretary Helene Fiorine.

"At the aforementioned time, the Security Police conducted a raid against the Brigade, an extremist left-wing group," Båge says, then clears his throat. "The complaint alleges that Detective Joona Linna of the National Crime Unit was at the aforementioned address either simultaneously or immediately prior to—"

"That's correct," Joona replies, looking out the window at the railroad tracks and the water of Barnhusviken.

Helene Fiorine looks troubled as she puts down her pen and notepad and says, with an almost beseeching gesture, "Joona, I have to ask you to take this internal investigation seriously."

"I am," he replies distantly.

She stares into his gray eyes a little too long before nodding quickly and picking up her pen again.

"Before we conclude," Mikael Båge says, as he picks at his ear for several seconds, "I need to mention the charges raised against you in this investigation. . . ."

"It could obviously be a misunderstanding," Helene explains quickly, "that the different investigations unfortunately got in each other's way."

"But in the complaint against you," Båge goes on, looking at his finger, "it is claimed that the Security Police operation failed because you had warned members of the Brigade."

"Yes, I did," Joona says.

Helene Fiorine gets up from her chair, unsure of what to say, and just stands there, looking sadly at Joona.

"You warned the group about the raid?" Båge asks with a smile.

"They were immature youngsters," he explains. "They weren't dangerous, and they weren't—"

"The Security Police had formed a different opinion," Båge interrupts.

"Yes," Joona says calmly.

"Let's end this interview there," Helene Fiorine says, gathering her papers.

53

IT'S ALREADY FOUR-THIRTY BY THE time Joona drives past Tumba, where he once investigated a triple murder.

On the seat next to him is the list of places Vicky Bennet has lived over the years.

She must have spoken to at least one of the people she stayed with. She must have confided in someone, must have mentioned having friends somewhere if she had them.

The only thing Elin Frank had said about Vicky was that she was sweet and kind.

Sweet and kind, Joona thinks.

To the Frank family, Vicky was a troubled child, a child who needed help, someone to show kindness to.

It was about charity.

But to Vicky, Elin was her first mother after her biological mom.

Life with the Franks must have been utterly alien to her. She was warm and received regular meals. She slept in a bed and wore nice clothes. Her time with them must have been a glowing memory for years afterward.

Joona has studied the list and decided to start from the end this time. Prior to Birgitta, she was at the Ljungbacken Children's Home, and before that she spent two weeks with the Arnander-Johansson family in Katrineholm.

In his mind's eye, he sees Nils and Frippe forcing Miranda's hands away from her face. They had to make a real effort to move her rigid arms. The dead girl seemed to resist, as if she didn't want to do it, as if she were ashamed.

But her face was as calm and white as mother-of-pearl.

She had been sitting wrapped in the comforter when she was beaten with a rock, according to Nils. Six or seven times, if Joona had read the blood-spatter pattern correctly.

Then she was laid out on the bed, and her hands were positioned in front of her face.

The last thing she saw before she died was the murderer.

Joona slows down and drives through a residential area full of large houses and parks in front of a low hedge. He gets out of the car and goes to a large wooden mailbox with a brass nameplate: "Arnander-Johansson." A woman is walking around the side of the house, carrying a bucket of red apples. She seems to have a problem with her hips and grimaces occasionally in pain. She's stocky, with a large chest and thick upper arms.

"You just missed him," the woman says when she catches sight of Joona.

"Typical," he jokes.

"He had to go to the warehouse—something about shipping dockets."

"Who are we talking about?" Joona asks with a smile.

She puts the bucket down. "I thought you were here to look at the treadmill?"

"How much is it?"

"Seven thousand kronor, brand-new," she replies. She rubs one hand on her pant leg and looks at him.

"I'm from the National Crime Unit. I'd like to ask you a few questions."

"About what?" she asks in a weak voice.

"About Vicky Bennet. She stayed here briefly almost a year ago."

The woman nods sadly, gestures toward the door, then goes inside. Joona follows her into a kitchen that has a pine table with a crocheted tablecloth over it, and flowery curtains that frame the windows looking out to the garden. The grass is freshly mown, and the boundary with the next property is marked by plum trees and gooseberry bushes. There's a small pale-blue swimming pool surrounded by a wooden deck. Some inflatable toys are floating on the water.

"Vicky's run away," Joona says bluntly.

"I read about it," she whispers, putting the bucket of apples on the counter.

"Where do you think she'd go?"

"No idea."

"Did she ever talk about any friends, boys . . . ?"

"Vicky never really lived here," the woman says.

"Why not?"

"It just didn't work out," she says, and turns away.

The woman fills a pot with water and is pouring the water into the top of the coffeemaker when she suddenly stops. "It's customary to offer coffee, isn't it?" she says listlessly.

Joona looks through the window at two blond boys playing karate in the garden. They're both slim and tanned, wearing long trunks. Their game is a little too vigorous, a little too rough, but they're laughing happily.

"You foster children and young people?"

"Our daughter is nineteen, so it . . . We've done it for several years now."

"How long do the children usually stay?"

"It varies . . . and sometimes they keep coming and going," she replies, turning to face Joona. "A lot of them come from very troubled homes, of course."

"Is it hard?"

"No, not really . . . Obviously, there are fights, but it's mostly a question of being clear about boundaries."

One of the boys does a jump-kick over the swimming pool and lands with a big splash. The other strikes out at the air, then follows him into the pool with a somersault.

"But Vicky only stayed two weeks?" Joona says, and looks at the woman. She avoids his gaze and idly scratches her lower arm.

"We've got two boys," she says vaguely. "They've been here for two years. . . . They're brothers. We hoped it would work out with Vicky, but, unfortunately, we had to put a stop to it."

"What happened?"

"Nothing . . . not really, anyway. It wasn't her fault. It wasn't anyone's fault. . . . It just got to be too much; we're an ordinary family, and we just couldn't deal with it."

"So Vicky . . . Was she difficult, hard to handle?"

"No," she says weakly. "It was . . ." She trails off.

"What were you about to say? What happened?"

"Nothing."

"You've had a lot of experience," Joona says. "What would make you give up after just two weeks?"

"It is what it is."

"I think something happened," Joona says heavily.

"No, it just got to be too much for us."

"I think something happened," he repeats, in the same calm voice.

"What do you want?" she asks awkwardly.

"Please, tell me what happened."

Her cheeks turn red. The blush spreads down her neck to her chest.

"Someone came to visit," she whispers, looking down at the floor.

"Who?"

She shakes her head. Joona holds out a notepad and pen. Tears start to run down her cheeks. She looks at him, then takes the pad and starts to write.

54

JOONA'S BEEN DRIVING FOR THREE hours when he pulls up outside 35 Skrake Street in Bengtsfors. The woman had been in tears when she wrote the address on his notepad. He had to pull the pad from her hand, and when he tried to get her to say more, she merely shook her head, hurried out of the kitchen, and locked herself in the bathroom.

He drives slowly along the row of red brick houses toward the traffic circle. Number 35 is the last house in the row. The white plastic garden furniture in the tall grass has been blown over by the wind. The mailbox is overflowing with flyers from pizzerias and supermarkets.

Joona walks through the weeds by the gate and up the damp stone path toward the house.

There's a mat in front of the door with the words "Keys, Wallet, Cell Phone" on it. It's soaking wet. Black trash bags have been taped over the inside of the windows. Joona rings the doorbell. A dog barks, and after a while someone looks at him through the peephole. He hears two locks turn; then the door opens a fraction before the security chain stops it. He is struck by the smell of spilled red wine. He can't see anyone in the dark hallway.

"Can I come in for a second?"

"She doesn't want to see you," says a boy with a hoarse voice.

A dog is panting, and Joona can hear the links on its choke collar tightening.

"I need to talk to her."

"We're not buying anything," a woman calls from another room.

"I'm with the police," Joona says.

He hears footsteps inside the house.

"Is he alone?" the woman asks.

"I think so," the boy whispers.

"Can you hold Zombie?"

"Are you going to open the door, Mom?" he asks in a worried voice.

The woman comes over to the door. "What do you want?"

"Do you know anything about a girl named Vicky Bennet?"

The dog's claws scrabble at the floor. The woman closes the door and locks it. Joona hears her shout something at the boy. After a while, the door opens, ever so slightly; she's removed the security bolt. Joona pushes it open a little more and walks into the entryway. The woman is standing with her back to him. She's wearing flesh-colored leggings and a white T-shirt. Her long blond hair is hanging over her shoulders. When Joona goes to close the door behind him, the house gets so dark that he has to stop. There are no lights on.

She walks ahead of him. The sun is shining directly at the windows. Tiny holes and tears in the plastic bags light up like stars. A faint gray light permeates the kitchen. There's a box of wine on the table, and a large puddle on the brown linoleum floor beneath it. When Joona reaches the darkened living room, the woman is already sitting on a denim sofa. The dark-purple curtains reach all the way to the floor, and behind them he can see more trash bags on the windows. Even so, a weak strip of light enters the room from the garden door, falling across the woman's hand. Joona notes that her nails are neatly manicured and painted red.

"Sit down," she says calmly.

"Thanks."

Joona sits down on a large footstool across from her. When his eyes get used to the gloom, he sees that there's something not quite right about her face.

"What do you want to know?"

"You paid a visit to the Arnander-Johansson family."

"Yes."

"Why did you go and see them?"

"I warned them."

"What did you warn them about?"

"Tompa!" the woman calls. "Tompa!"

A door opens, followed by slow steps. Joona can't see the boy in the darkness, but he can feel his presence and can just about make out a silhouette over by the bookcase. The boy comes into the darkened living room.

"Turn the light on."

"But, Mom . . ."

"Just do it!"

He flicks the switch, and a large rice-paper ball lights up the whole room. The tall, slim boy stands in the strong glare with his head lowered. Joona looks at him. The boy's face looks as if he was bitten by a dog and the wound healed completely wrong. He has no bottom lip at all. His teeth are exposed, and his chin and right cheek are hollow and covered with purple scars. A deep, red groove runs from his hairline across his forehead and through his eyebrow. When Joona turns to the woman, he sees that her face is even more badly damaged. Even so, she is smiling at him. Her right eye is missing, and there are deep incisions in her face and neck, at least ten wounds. Her left eyebrow droops over her eye, and her mouth has been cut in several places.

"Vicky got angry at us," the woman says, and her smile disappears.

"What happened?"

"She cut us with a broken bottle. I didn't think a person could get that angry. She wouldn't stop. I passed out, came to, and just lay there, feeling her stab me with the broken glass. I felt each jab. Pieces broke off inside me, and that's when I realized I didn't have a face anymore."

55

The girls from the Birgitta Home have been taken from the Hotel Ibis to temporary accommodations in the small town of Hårte.

Hårte is an old fishing village. There's no church, and the school closed almost a century ago. The mine was abandoned, and the supermarket shut down when the owners got too old. But, each summer, the fishing village and its sandy beaches along the Virgin Coast come back to life again.

The six girls are going to spend a few months living in a former shop, a spacious building with a large glass-enclosed sunroom, located where the one road running through the village forks like a snake's tongue.

The girls have finished their dinner, but some of them are still by the table, looking at the calm, misty blue sea. In the large living room, Solveig Sundström is sitting with her knitting in front of the crackling fire in the open hearth.

From the living room, a cold hallway leads to a small kitchen. A guard is sitting there, positioned where he can see both the entryway and the front door, as well as the window looking out onto the lawn and road.

Lu Chu and Nina are looking for chips in the pantry but have to make do with Frosted Flakes.

"What will you do when the murderer comes?" Lu Chu asks.

The guard's tattooed hand twitches on the table, and he smiles stiffly at her. "You can feel safe here."

He's in his fifties and has a shaved head and a severe little chinstrap beard. His bulging muscles are visible beneath the dark-blue security-company shirt.

Lu Chu doesn't reply, just looks back at him as she stuffs the breakfast cereal into her mouth and chews noisily. Nina, who has been looking through the fridge, takes out a package of smoked ham and a jar of mustard.

At the other end of the house, Caroline, Indie, Tuula, and Almira are sitting around the dining table on the porch, playing a card game.

"Can I have all your jacks?" Indie says.

"Go fish!" Almira giggles.

Indie draws a card and looks at it happily.

"Ted Bundy was just like a butcher," Tuula says in a quiet voice.

"God, you really won't shut up about it," Caroline sighs.

"He went from room to room, clubbing the girls to death, like baby seals. First Lisa and Margaret, then . . ."

"Shut up," Almira says, and laughs.

Tuula smiles down at the table, and Caroline can't help shuddering.

"What the fuck's that old bag doing here?" Indie asks loudly.

The woman by the fireplace looks up, then goes back to her knitting.

"Are we still playing, or what?" Tuula asks impatiently.

"Whose turn is it?"

"Mine," Indie says.

"You're such a cheater." Caroline smiles.

"My phone's completely dead," Almira says. "I left it charging in my room, and now . . ."

"Do you want me to look at it?" Indie asks.

She removes the back of the phone, takes out the battery, and puts it back in, but nothing happens.

"Weird," she mutters.

"Don't bother," Almira says.

Indie takes the battery out again. "There isn't even a damn SIM card!"

"Tuula," Almira says sternly, "did you take my SIM card?"

"Don't know," the girl replies sullenly.

"I need it—okay?"

The woman puts her knitting down and comes into the sunroom.

"What's going on?" she asks.

"We can handle this ourselves," Caroline says coolly.

Tuula purses her lips sadly. "I didn't take anything," she whines.

"My SIM card is missing," Almira says, raising her voice.

"That doesn't necessarily mean that she took it, does it?" the woman says indignantly.

"Almira says she's going to hit me," Tuula says.

"I won't tolerate any violence," the woman warns, then sits down with her knitting again.

"Tuula," Almira says in a subdued voice, "I really do need to be able to use my phone."

"That's going to be hard, isn't it?" Tuula says, smiling back at her.

"The police think Vicky beat Miranda to death," Caroline says.

"Fucking morons," Almira mutters.

"I don't know her—none of us do," Indie says.

"Don't be stupid."

"What if she's on her way here to—"

"Shh," Tuula interrupts. She gets up and stands perfectly still, staring out into the darkness. "Did you hear that?" she says, turning to Caroline and Almira.

"No." Indie sighs.

"We'll be dead soon," Tuula whispers.

"You're so sick, you bitch," Caroline says, but can't help smiling. She grabs Tuula's hand, pulls her onto her lap, and pats her gently.

"There's no need to be scared. Nothing's going to happen," she says consolingly.

56

CAROLINE WAKES UP ON THE sofa. Gentle heat radiates from the last embers glowing in the hearth. Sitting up and looking around the dark room, she realizes that she fell asleep on the sofa and that the others went to bed and left her there.

Caroline goes over to the large windows and looks out. She can still just about make out the water beyond the black fishermen's sheds. The moon is shining above the sea behind veils of cloud. Everything is quiet.

She opens the creaky pine door and feels the cool air from the hallway on her face. Behind her, the wooden furniture creaks softly. There are deep shadows, and the doors to the girls' rooms are barely visible. Caroline takes a step into the darkness. The floor is ice-cold. Suddenly she hears something: a sigh or moan.

It's coming from the bathroom.

She approaches carefully, her heart thudding. The door is ajar. There's someone in there. She hears the strange sound again.

Caroline looks cautiously through the narrow crack.

Nina is sitting on the toilet with her legs wide apart and a look of indifference on her face. A man is on his knees in front of her with his face between her thighs. She's pulled up her pajama top so he can squeeze one of her breasts as he licks her.

"That's enough," Nina says heavily.

"Okay," he replies, and stands up quickly.

When he grabs some toilet paper to wipe his mouth, Caroline sees that it's the guard.

"Give me the money," Nina says, holding out her hand.

The guard starts to search his pockets. "Damn, I've only got eighty kronor," he says.

"Five hundred, you said."

"What the hell am I supposed to do? I've only got eighty."

Nina sighs and takes the money.

Caroline hurries past the door and slips into her cold little room. She closes the door and turns the light on. Seeing her own reflection in the black window, she realizes that she's completely visible to anyone outside and hurries over to pull the blind down. For the first time in years, she feels afraid of the dark.

Caroline shudders when she thinks about the glint in Tuula's eyes when she talked about serial killers. Little Tuula was upset and wanted to scare the others by saying Vicky had followed them to this small fishing village.

Caroline decides not to bother brushing her teeth. Nothing could persuade her to go back out into the long, dark hallway.

She moves the chair to the door and tries to push it under the door handle. With trembling hands, she stacks some old magazines underneath the chair legs so that the back of the chair presses against the bottom of the handle.

She imagines someone creeping through the hallway right outside and feels a shiver run down her spine as she stares at the keyhole.

There's a sharp bang behind her. The blinds have flown up and are spinning around with a clatter.

"God!" she gasps, then pulls them down again.

She stands motionless and listens, then turns off the overhead light and hurries into bed, where she wraps the comforter tightly around her body, waiting for the sheets to warm up.

Lying there completely still, staring at the door handle

through the darkness, she is thinking about Vicky again. Vicky seemed so shy and cautious. Caroline can't believe she did those terrible things. Before she can force herself to think about something else, she remembers Miranda's crushed head and the blood dripping from the ceiling.

Suddenly she hears tentative footsteps out in the hallway. They pause, then start up again before stopping outside her door. Through the shimmering darkness Caroline sees someone try to push the door handle. The handle stops when it hits the back of the chair. Caroline screws her eyes shut, covers her ears, and starts to pray.

57

THE RIVER HAS BEEN RUNNING high since the snow melted in the Jämtland Mountains. The hydroelectric plant has had to monitor water levels constantly so that the dams don't overflow.

After the past two weeks of heavy rain, they had to start gradually opening the floodgates to prevent a flood. More than two million liters of water are now gushing through every second.

For months, the Indals River resembled a sluggish lake, but now the current is unmistakable and strong.

The child's car seat hits the dam, drifts away, then hits again.

JOONA JOGS ALONG THE NARROW road that runs across the top of the dam. To his right, the reservoir spreads out like a shimmering floor, but to his left, a smooth concrete wall drops thirty meters straight down. It's dizzyingly high. White water froths with a roar over the black rocks far below, and water jets out of the openings in the dam with immense force.

Ahead of him, by the edge of the dam, stand two uniformed police officers and a guard from the power station, looking and pointing over the railing at the smooth surface of the water. One of the police officers is holding a boat hook.

Trash carried along on the current has started to gather around a car seat. An empty plastic bottle rolls toward the edge, knocking against some pinecones, twigs, and half-dissolved fast-food containers.

Joona looks down into the black water. The current is tugging at the car seat. The only part of it he can see is its hard gray plastic back.

It's impossible to tell if there's still a child strapped into the chair.

"Turn it over," Joona says.

The other police officer gives him a curt nod and leans over the railing as far as he can. The boat hook breaks the surface of the water and nudges a pine branch aside. He pushes the boat hook deeper under the car seat, then raises it slowly until the hook gets purchase. He pulls upward, and there's a splash as the seat finally rolls over to reveal the drenched cushion.

The seat is empty.

Joona looks at it, thinking that the child's body could have slid out of the straps and sunk to the bottom.

"Like I said on the phone, it looks like the right seat.... It doesn't seem badly damaged, but, of course, it's hard to see in detail," the police officer says.

"Make sure Forensics use a watertight bag when they pull it out."

The police officer lets go of the seat, and it slowly rolls over again.

"Meet me at the end of the bridge in Indal," Joona says, as he starts to walk back to his car. "There's a swimming spot there, isn't there?"

"What are we going to do?"

"Go swimming," Joona says.

58

JOONA GETS OUT AT THE end of the bridge and leaves the car door open. He looks down the grass slope. A floating jetty stretches out from the small sandy beach into the rushing water.

His jacket blows open in the wind, and his muscles stand out against his dark-gray shirt.

He can feel the moisture rising from the warm vegetation, and he can smell the grass and the sweetness of the willow herb.

He stops and bends over to pick up a tiny cube of glass from between the plants, then looks down at the water again.

"This is where they drove off the road," he says, indicating the direction.

One of the police officers goes to the water's edge, looks in the direction Joona is pointing, and shakes his head. "There's no sign of it, nothing," he calls back.

"I think I'm right," Joona says.

"We'll never know—there's been too much rain," the other police officer says.

"But there hasn't been any rain underwater," Joona says.

He strides down toward the water and follows the river upstream for a few meters before he sees the tire tracks under the water. The parallel lines across the sandy riverbed disappear into the black water.

"Can you see anything?" the policeman calls.

"Yes," Joona replies, and walks straight out into the river.

The cool water streams around his legs, dragging him gently sideways. He marches out with long strides. It's hard to see anything through the shimmering, gliding surface of the water. Long strands of weeds are swirling around, and the current is full of bubbles and dirt.

The policeman follows him out into the river, swearing to himself.

Joona can make out a dark shape about ten meters out.

"I'll call for a diver," the officer says.

Joona takes off his jacket and hands it to the officer.

"What are you doing?"

"I have to know if they're dead," he replies, handing the officer his pistol.

The water is freezing, and the current tugs at his increasingly heavy pants. A cold shiver runs up his legs to the base of his spine.

"There are logs in the river," the other police officer calls. "You can't swim here."

Joona wades out until the bottom slopes away sharply. When the water reaches his waist, he dives forward smoothly. His ears roar as they fill with water, and his open eyes sting from the cold. Rays of sunlight cut through the water. Mud swirls in the various currents.

He kicks his legs and glides farther out. Suddenly he sees the car. It's ahead of him, to one side of the tire tracks. The current has dragged the vehicle toward the middle of the river.

The red metal shimmers. The windshield and the two windows on the righthand side are completely missing, and water gushes through the car.

Joona swims closer, trying not to think about what he might find. He has to remain alert and try to register as many details as possible in the few seconds he can stay down there, but his brain keeps conjuring up images of Vicky in the front seat, the seat belt diagonally across her body, her arms outstretched, her mouth gaping, and her hair swirling in front of her face.

His heart is beating faster now. Visibility is poor down here.

He grabs the empty frame of the rear door's window. The current is tugging his body sideways. There's a metallic creaking sound, and as the car slides another meter away from him, he loses his grip. Mud swirls up, and he's having trouble seeing. He takes a few strokes. The cloud of mud disperses, and it's easier to see again.

Above him, some three meters away, is the sun-drenched world.

A waterlogged tree trunk is gliding just below the surface like a slow, heavy torpedo.

His lungs are starting to ache now, contracting in empty cramps. The water is moving quickly down here.

Joona grabs the empty window frame again and sees blood spread out from his hand. He forces himself down to the same level as the car door and tries to look inside. His vision is partially blocked by swirling dust and weeds.

The car is empty. No girl, no child.

The windshield is gone, the wipers hanging loose. Their bodies could have been washed out and pulled downstream.

He manages to register the area immediately around the car. There's nothing for the bodies to catch on. The rocks are smooth, and the weeds are too thin.

His lungs are screaming for oxygen, but he knows that there's always a little more time.

His body will have to learn to wait.

In the military, he had to swim twelve kilometers with a signal flag several times; he's made his way up from a submarine with an emergency balloon and no equipment; and he's swum under the ice in the Gulf of Finland.

He can manage without oxygen for a few more seconds.

With powerful strokes, he swims around the car and looks at the scene. The water is rushing past. The shadows of floating logs move quickly across the riverbed.

Vicky drove off the road here, came down the beach in the pouring rain, and went into the water. The windows had already been knocked out, probably from colliding with the bent traffic light, and the car would have filled with water instantly.

But where are the bodies?

He has to try to find the children.

Five meters out, he sees something shimmering on the riverbed—a pair of glasses, rolling farther and farther from the car, toward deeper water. He should return to the surface but tells himself he can last a little longer. His eyes flare as he swims forward, reaches out his hand, and grabs the glasses just as the water lifts them from the riverbed. He turns, kicks off, and swims upward. His vision is flickering. He needs to breathe or he's going to pass out. He breaks the surface, draws air into his lungs, and only just sees the log right before it hits his shoulder. His arm is wrenched from its socket by the heavy impact. It hurts so badly that he roars with pain and sinks below the surface again.

59

THE OTHER POLICE OFFICERS HAD managed to get a boat and were already on their way out to Joona when they saw him get hit by the log. They were able to pull him over the railing and onto the deck.

"Sorry," Joona gasps. "But I had to know. . . ."

"Where did the log hit you?"

"There are no bodies in the car," Joona says, ignoring the question, as he winces in pain.

"Look at his arm," one of the officers says.

"Shit," the other whispers.

Blood is running down Joona's wet shirt, and his arm is twisted unnaturally, seemingly hanging by the muscle alone.

They carefully take the glasses from his hand and put them in a plastic bag.

One of the police officers drives him to Sundsvall Hospital. Joona sits in the car, eyes closed, holding his wounded arm close to his body. In spite of the pain he's in, he is trying to come up with an explanation for how the car slid across the riverbed.

"The children weren't there," he says, almost in a whisper.

"The river can carry bodies a very long way in the water," the police officer says. "There's no point sending divers into the water, because either the bodies get wedged somewhere and we never find them . . . or they end up down at the power station, like the car seat."

At the hospital, two cheerful nurses care for Joona. They look like mother and daughter. Quickly and efficiently, they get him out of his wet clothes, but when they catch sight of his arm they fall completely silent. They clean and dress the wound before sending Joona off for an X-ray.

Twenty minutes later, a doctor comes into the examination room. He quickly explains that nothing is broken. Joona's shoulder is dislocated, but the good news is that his cartilage seems to be intact. Joona lies facedown on the bed with his arm hanging straight down as the doctor injects twenty milligrams of lidocaine directly into the joint. One nurse pushes Joona's shoulder blade toward his spine, and the other pushes the ball joint at the top of his arm back into place. There's a cracking sound, and Joona clenches his teeth, then slowly breathes out.

The car vanished from a stretch of highway that had hardly any other roads leading off it. The police claimed to have checked all possible hiding places, but when Joona saw the car seat in the water, he realized what they had all missed. If the car had driven into the water and been swallowed up, there was only one place that could have happened without being discovered by the police.

Just past Indal, Highway 86 turns sharply right onto a bridge across the river, but the car must have kept going straight, down the grass slope, across the sand, and out into the water. The heavy rain erased the tire tracks on the sand almost immediately. The car vanished in a matter of seconds.

60

JOONA MAKES HIS WAY DOWN to the police garage. His arm
has been stabilized and is protected by a dark-blue sling.

A large plastic tent surrounds the car that Vicky Bennet stole.
It has been raised by crane from the Indals River, packed in plastic, and moved here. All the seats have been removed and placed
next to the car. A long bench is covered with an array of items
wrapped in labeled plastic bags. Joona looks at the evidence that's
been secured: fingerprints from both Vicky and Dante, bags full
of broken glass, an empty water bottle, a sneaker that probably
belonged to Vicky, and the boy's small pair of glasses.

The door to a neighboring office opens, and Holger Jalmert,
professor of forensic science, walks into the garage with a folder
in his hand.

"You wanted to show me something?" Joona says.

"Yes, I suppose we should get it over with," Holger says with
a sigh, gesturing toward the car. "The entire windshield was
missing—you saw that for yourself—knocked out when the car
hit the streetlight. . . . But I'm afraid I've found strands of the
boy's hair on the frame."

"*Perkele*," Joona curses, feeling a great emptiness fill him.

"I know, it's tragic . . . even though we all suspected as much."

Joona looks at a photograph of the righthand side of the jagged windshield, and an enlargement showing three strands of

hair torn out at the root. The car was probably driving fast and would have hit the water hard. The evidence suggests that Vicky Bennet and Dante Abrahamsson were thrown through what remained of the windshield.

Joona reads that splinters of glass with Dante's blood on them have also been found. Joona finds it hard to imagine how the hairs could have been pulled from Dante's head if he wasn't propelled out of the car into the river. The current would have been very strong, because the dam gates were open.

Joona thinks about how Vicky Bennet's rage must have subsided. She still had the boy in the car with her and hadn't killed him.

"In your opinion, was the boy alive when they hit the water?" Joona asks quietly.

"Yes. He was probably knocked unconscious when he hit the edge of the windshield and drowned . . . but we'll have to wait until the bodies get caught in the dam."

Holger holds up a plastic bag with a red squirt gun inside. "I've got a young boy myself. . . ." He falls silent and sits down.

"I know," Joona says, putting his good hand on Holger's shoulder.

"We have to tell the mother that we're going to call off the search," Holger says, and his mouth begins to twitch sadly.

IT'S UNUSUALLY QUIET IN THE little police station. A few men in uniform are talking quietly by the coffee machine, and a woman is typing slowly on her computer. The gray daylight outside is heavy and gloomy.

When the door opens and Pia walks in, even the quiet talking stops. Pia is wearing jeans and a buttoned denim jacket that sits tightly across her chest. The nut-brown hair hanging lankly from her black beret is greasy and unwashed. She's not wearing any makeup, and her eyes look tired and scared.

Mirja quickly gets up and offers her a chair.

"I don't want to sit down," Pia says weakly.

Mirja unbuttons her shirt collar.

"We asked you to come because . . . I'm afraid we fear that . . ."

Pia puts her hand on the back of the chair.

"What I'm trying to say," Mirja goes on, "is that . . ."

"What?"

"I'm afraid we don't think they're still alive."

Pia doesn't show much reaction. She doesn't collapse; she just nods slowly and licks her lips.

"Why don't you think they're alive?" she asks in a low and strangely calm voice.

"We've found your car," Mirja says. "They drove off the road and ended up in the river. The car was found at a depth of four meters, badly damaged, and . . ."

She trails off.

"I want to see my son," Pia says in the same horribly calm voice. "Where's his body?"

"It's . . . We haven't found their bodies yet, but . . . we've made the difficult decision to call off the divers."

"But . . ."

Pia's hand flies toward her throat to clasp the crucifix hanging there, but stops at her heart. "Dante's only four," she says, perplexed. "He can't swim."

"No," Mirja says sadly.

"But he . . . he likes playing in the water," Pia whispers.

Her cheeks start to tremble. She stands there in her denim outfit, her clerical collar visible under her jacket. Very slowly, she sits down on the chair.

61

ELIN SHOWERS AFTER HER SAUNA, then walks across the smooth stone floor to the large mirror above the double sink, where she dries herself with a warm bath towel. Her skin is still hot and damp when she puts on the black kimono Jack gave her the year they split up.

She leaves the bathroom and goes through the bright rooms, across the white parquet floor, into the bedroom. She has already laid out a shimmering copper-colored dress and a pair of gold panties.

She takes the kimono off and perfumes herself, waits a few seconds, then gets dressed.

When she comes into the large living room, she sees her adviser, Robert, hide his phone. A nagging anxiety takes hold of her again, weighing heavily in the pit of her stomach.

"What is it?" she asks.

Robert's striped T-shirt has slid up, revealing his rounded stomach.

"The photographer from *Vogue* is ten minutes late," Robert says, without meeting her gaze.

"I haven't had time to watch the news," she says, trying to sound bright. "Do you know if the police have found Vicky yet?"

She's been afraid to listen to the news or read the papers for the past few days. She had to take a pill to get to sleep at ten o'clock, then another at three o'clock.

"Have you heard anything?" she repeats weakly.

Robert scratches his short hair. "Elin, I really don't want you to worry."

"I'm not, but . . ."

"No one's going to drag you into this."

"It doesn't do any harm to know what's going on," she says nonchalantly. She's composed her face again and smiles directly at him. "Am I going to have to get mad at you?"

He shakes his head and pulls his T-shirt down to cover his stomach. "I caught the end of the news on the radio on my way here," he replies. "They've evidently found the stolen car submerged in a river. . . . I think they said divers were going to start looking for bodies."

Elin quickly turns her face away. Her lips are trembling, and her heart is beating so hard it feels as if it's about to break. "That doesn't sound good," she says in an empty voice.

"Do you want me to turn the television on?"

"No, no need," she whispers.

"Obviously, it would be terrible if it turns out that they've drowned."

"Stop," Elin says.

She has to swallow. Her throat hurts, and she coughs quietly and looks down at her hands.

62

ELIN REMEMBERS THE DAY VICKY came to her as if it were yesterday. The girl stood stony-faced outside the door, her arms covered with yellowing bruises. The moment Elin saw her, she realized that Vicky was the daughter she had been longing for. She didn't even know she had been fantasizing about having a daughter.

Vicky was her own person right from the start, just as it should be.

At first, the little girl would come running to Elin's bed at night. Vicky would stop, stare at her, and turn around. Maybe she was expecting to find her biological mother to curl up with, or maybe she just changed her mind when she got there and decided she didn't want to show that she was afraid or risk being rejected.

Elin can still remember exactly how the little feet sounded as they padded away.

Sometimes Vicky wanted to sit on Jack's lap to watch television, but never on Elin's.

Vicky didn't trust her, didn't dare to, but Elin noticed that she often used to look at her in secret.

Little Vicky, the silent girl who would only play when she didn't think anyone was watching. Who wouldn't open her Christmas presents because she didn't believe those beautiful gifts were really for her. Vicky, who used to flinch away from every hug.

Elin bought her a little white hamster in a big cage full of red plastic ladders and tunnels. Vicky cared for it over Christmas vacation, but before she went back to school it had vanished without a trace. It turned out that Vicky had let it go in a park near the school. When Jack explained that it might not survive in the cold, she ran into her room and slammed the door ten times. That night, she drank a bottle of Burgundy and was sick all over the sauna. That same week, she stole two diamond rings Elin had inherited from her grandmother. She refused to say what she'd done with them, and Elin never got the rings back.

Elin could see that Jack had had enough. He started talking about how their lives were too complicated for them to provide adequate security for a child who needed so much help. He withdrew and kept to himself and stopped engaging with the little girl.

Elin realized that she was on the brink of losing him.

When Social Services made yet another attempt to rehouse the girl with her mother, Elin decided that she and Jack needed the break to work on their relationship. Vicky wouldn't even take the phone that Elin had bought her so that they could keep in touch.

Jack and Elin ate a late supper at the restaurant Operakällaren, then made love and slept undisturbed all night for the first time in months. The next morning, Jack told her that he wouldn't stay with her unless she promised to not have anything to do with Vicky.

Elin got him to call the social worker to explain that they couldn't help anymore, that they couldn't handle it.

Vicky and her mother ran away from their home in Västerås and took refuge in a small shed next to a playground. Her mom started leaving her alone at night. When she didn't come back for two days, Vicky made her way to Stockholm, all alone.

Jack wasn't home the evening Vicky showed up outside Elin's door.

Elin didn't know what to do. She remembers standing pressed against the wall in the hallway, listening as the little girl rang the doorbell and whispered her name.

In the end, Vicky started to cry and opened the mail slot.

"Please, let me come back. I want to be with you. Please, Elin, open the door. . . . I'll be good. Please, please . . ."

When Jack and Elin pulled out of the program, the social worker had warned them: "You shouldn't tell Vicky why you can't take her back."

"Why not?" Elin asked.

"Because then she'd blame herself," the social worker explained.

So Elin had stood there in silence. After what felt like an eternity, she heard Vicky's footsteps heading down the stairs—then silence.

63

ELIN STANDS IN FRONT OF the large bathroom mirror, looking into her own eyes. The indirect lighting casts sparkling reflections across her irises. She's taken two Valiums and poured herself a glass of Riesling.

In the large living room, Nassim Dubois, a young photographer from French *Vogue*, is unpacking his equipment and preparing the lighting. The actual interview was conducted last week, when Elin was in Provence for a charity auction. She sold her entire collection of French art and her Jean Nouvel–designed house in Nice in order to set up a microloan scheme for women in North Africa.

She moves away from the mirror, pulls out her phone, and dials Jack's number to tell him that Vicky's car has been found in the Indals River, even though Jack's lawyer has explained that any communication relating to Vicky should be conducted through his office. She doesn't care. She's not in love with Jack anymore, but sometimes she just needs to hear his voice.

Maybe she'll just tell him that she sold his Basquiat in the auction. But before he answers, she regrets calling and disconnects.

Elin leaves the bathroom, one hand trailing along the wall for support as she walks over to the glass doors.

She emerges onto the large deck with a languidness that could be interpreted as sensual, and Nassim lets out an impressed whistle.

"You look wonderful," he says with a smile.

She knows the copper-colored dress with the thin straps suits her. She's wearing a flat necklace of beaten white gold, which, like her earrings, casts reflections across her chin and long neck.

He asks her to stand with her back against the railing with an enormous white shawl around her shoulders. She lets it blow in the wind and watches as it fills like a sail and billows attractively behind her.

After angling a silvery reflector screen so that her face is filled with light, he takes a lot of photographs of her from a distance, then moves in closer and kneels down in his tight jeans to take a sequence of pictures with an old-fashioned Polaroid camera.

She sees that beads of sweat have appeared on Nassim's forehead. He never stops complimenting her, but his mind is clearly elsewhere, concentrating on the composition and lighting.

"Dangerous, sexy," he mutters.

"You think?" she replies with a smile.

He stops, looks her in the eye, nods, then gives her a wide, embarrassed smile.

"Mostly sexy."

"You're very sweet," she says.

Elin isn't wearing a bra, and she can feel her skin breaking out in goose bumps. Her stiff nipples are visible through the dress. She realizes she's hoping he notices and decides that she's a little drunk.

He lies down right in front of her with an old Hasselblad camera and asks her to lean forward and pout her lips as if she wanted to be kissed.

"*Une petite pomme*," he says.

They smile at each other, and Elin feels suddenly happy, almost ecstatic about his flirting.

She can see his chest clearly through his thin, tight T-shirt.

She pouts, and he takes photographs, mutters that she's the

best, that she's a top model, then lowers the camera to his chest and looks up at her.

"I could do this forever," he says frankly. "But I can tell that you're freezing."

"Let's go inside and have a whisky," she says with a nod.

64

When they get inside, they find that Ingrid has already lit the large tiled stove. They sit on the sofa, drink malt whisky, and talk about the interview, about the microloans that have become such an important tool in helping women change their lives.

The Valium and alcohol have made Elin perfectly relaxed.

Nassim tells her that the reporter was very pleased with the interview. Then he tells her that his mother comes from Morocco. "You're doing a very good thing," he says with a smile. "If my grandmother had been able to get a microloan, my mother's life would have been very different."

"I'm trying to make a difference, but ..." She falls silent and looks into his serious eyes.

"Nobody's perfect," he says, moving closer to her.

"I let a little girl down ... someone I wasn't supposed to let down ... someone ..."

He pats her cheek consolingly and whispers something in French. She smiles at him and feels intoxication tingle in her body.

"If you weren't so young, I'd fall in love with you," she says in Swedish.

"What did you just say?" he asks.

"I envy your girlfriend," she explains.

She can smell his breath—mint and whisky. Like herbs, she

thinks, looking at his neatly shaped mouth and feeling an urge to kiss him—and then realizing that it would probably scare him.

She remembers that Jack stopped having sex with her just after Vicky disappeared from their lives. She didn't understand that it was simply because he had stopped finding her attractive—she thought it was because of stress and fatigue, because they weren't spending enough time together. So she started to make an effort. She made herself look good, arranged romantic dinners, time together.

But he was no longer even looking at her.

One night, he came home and saw her lying there in her flesh-colored negligée and told her straight out that he no longer loved her. He wanted a divorce. He'd met another woman.

"Watch out, you're spilling it," Nassim says.

"Oh God," she whispers, just as she manages to spill some whisky on the dress.

"Don't worry."

He picks up a napkin, kneels down, and carefully presses it on the stain, holding it against her as his other hand goes around her waist.

"I need to change," she says, and stands up, trying hard not to fall sideways.

She can feel the Valium, wine, and whisky rushing through her brain.

He helps support her as they walk through the rooms side by side. Feeling weak and tired, she leans against him and kisses him on the neck. The bedroom is cool, the lighting subdued. Only the cream-colored lamp on the bedside table is lit.

"I need to lie down."

She doesn't say anything else as he lays her on the bed and slowly pulls off her shoes.

"I'll help you," he says in a low voice.

She pretends to be more drunk than she is, just lies still, as if she doesn't notice that he's unfastening her dress with trembling hands.

She hears his heavy breathing and wonders if he's going to touch her, if he'll exploit the fact that she's intoxicated.

She lies motionless on the bed, in just her gold underwear, looking at him through a swaying haze, then closes her eyes.

He murmurs something nervously, and his fingers feel ice-cold when he pulls off her underwear.

She squints at him as he gets undressed. His body is tanned, as if he works outdoors. He's boyishly slim and has a gray tattoo on one shoulder: an eye of Horus.

Her heart starts to beat faster when he mutters something and gets on the bed. She thinks about stopping him, but she feels flattered by his desire. She tells herself she won't let him enter her; she'll just let him look and masturbate.

She tries to concentrate on what's going on and enjoy the moment. He's breathing fast as he gently parts her thighs, and she lets it happen.

She's wet, very slippery, but at the same time she can't quite lose herself in the moment. He lies on top of her, and she feels his penis against her, warm and hard. Very slowly, she rolls away and puts her thighs together.

She opens her eyes, meets his frightened gaze, then closes them again.

Cautiously, he parts her thighs again. She smiles to herself and lets him look, then feels him on top of her, and suddenly he just slides into her.

She lets out a quiet groan and feels his heart thudding as he lies on top of her.

He's inside her now, gasping as he thrusts harder.

She feels nausea rising inside her. She'd like to be able to want him now, but he's too eager, pushing too fast and much too hard.

She starts to feel lonely and loses all desire. She lies there until he finishes and pulls out.

"Sorry, sorry," Nassim whispers as he gathers his things. "I thought you wanted . . ."

I thought so, too, she thinks, but doesn't bother to explain. She hears him getting dressed quickly and quietly and hopes he's just going to leave. She wants to get up and take a shower, then pray to God that Vicky is still alive until she falls asleep.

65

Joona is standing by the railing, looking along the high concrete wall. Water is gushing from three openings twenty meters below. Beneath them, the wall curves like an immense waterslide. Vast quantities of water crash down the wall and foam across the rocky riverbed.

His arm is still in a sling, and his jacket is draped around his shoulder. He leans out over the railing, looks down at the river, and thinks about the car with the two children in it in the heavy rain. The car hits the stoplight in Bjällsta, knocking the windshield out. Vicky is wearing her seat belt but still hits her head on the window with the force of the impact. The car is suddenly full of pieces of glass, and cold rain pours in.

A few empty moments of silence follow.

The boy starts to scream in terror. Vicky gets out of the car unsteadily, glass falling from her clothes. She opens the back door, unbuckles the car seat, and looks at the boy, checking to see if he's hurt, then tries to get him to quiet down before she drives on.

She may be planning to cross the bridge when she sees the flashing blue lights of the police car at the roadblock. She swings off the road in a panic, can't stop the car in time, and drives into the water. The abrupt impact means that Vicky's face hits the steering wheel, and she loses consciousness.

The two of them must have passed out before the car sank into the water. The current would have seized their limp bodies and swept them along the rocky riverbed.

He takes out his phone to call Carlos. The rescue diver is already standing by the power station's jetty. His blue wetsuit pulls taut across his back as he checks his breathing apparatus.

"Carlos," Joona's boss says when he answers.

"Susanne Öst wants to shut down the investigation," Joona says, "but it's not finished."

"That's always a shame, but the murderer is dead ... which means that it doesn't make financial sense to continue."

"We don't have any bodies."

He hears Carlos mutter something, and then suffer a coughing fit. Joona waits as Carlos drinks some water. He thinks about his search through Vicky's past, how he had been looking for someone she might have confided in, someone who knew where she might have gone.

"It could take several weeks for the bodies to show up," Carlos whispers, and clears his throat.

"But it's not finished," Joona objects.

"You're being stubborn again." Carlos sighs.

"I need—"

"It isn't even your case," Carlos says, cutting him off.

Joona looks down as a black log floating in the current hits the edge of the dam with a dull thud.

"Yes, it is," he says.

"Joona," Carlos says with another sigh.

"The forensic evidence may point to Vicky, but there are no witnesses, and she hasn't been convicted."

"You can't convict the dead," Carlos says wearily.

Joona thinks about the girl, and the lack of a motive, and the fact that she went back to bed after the brutal murders. He thinks about The Needle's claim that she killed Elisabet with a hammer but Miranda with a rock.

"Give me a week, Carlos," he says urgently. "I need to get a few answers before I come home."

Carlos mutters something away from the receiver.

"I can't hear you," Joona says.

"This is informal," Carlos says more loudly. "But as long as the Internal Affairs investigation is still going on, you can continue."

"What resources do I have?"

"Resources? You're still only an observer, you can't—"

"I've requested a diver," Joona says with a smile.

"A diver?" Carlos says in a alarmed voice. "Do you know what a—"

"And a dog handler."

Joona hears the sound of an engine, turns around, and sees a small gray car with a sputtering engine pull up beside his. It's a Messerschmitt Kabinenroller from the early 1960s, with two wheels in the front and one in back. The door opens, and Gunnarsson clambers out, a cigarette in his mouth.

"I decide whether or not we use divers," Gunnarsson calls, hurrying over to Joona. "This has nothing to do with you."

"I'm an observer," Joona says calmly, and walks down toward the jetty, where the diver is getting ready.

66

THE DIVER IS IN HIS fifties, showing the first signs of middle-aged weight gain, but he still has broad shoulders and powerful biceps. His wetsuit is tight around his belly and neck.

"Hasse Boman," he says by way of greeting.

"The dam gates can't be closed—there's a risk of flooding," Joona says.

"I understand," Hasse replies curtly, gazing out across the choppy water.

"The current's going to be very strong," Joona points out.

"Yes," Hasse replies with a calm look in his eyes.

"Can you handle it?" Joona asks.

"I was a mine clearer at KA1. . . . Can't be any worse than that," Hasse replies with the trace of a smile.

"Do you have nitrox in those tanks?" Joona asks.

"Yes."

"What the hell is that?" Gunnarsson asks when he reaches them.

"Like air, but with a little more oxygen," Hasse says as he pulls on his vest.

"So how long can you be down there?"

"With these—maybe two hours. . . . So no problem."

"I'm grateful to you for volunteering," Joona says.

The diver shrugs and explains: "My boy's at soccer camp in

Denmark ... place called Ishøj. ... I said I'd go with him, but you know, it's just me and him now, so extra money's always useful. ..."

He shakes his head and points at the diving mask and the camera attached to it, then at the cable that has one end attached to his lifeline and the other connected to a computer.

"I film all my dives. You'll be able to see what I see ... and we can communicate while I'm down there."

A log floats by and bumps into the edge of the dam.

"Why are there logs in the water?" Joona asks.

As Hasse pulls his equipment on, he says nonchalantly: "Who knows? Someone's probably been dumping wood that's been ruined by bark beetles."

A woman dressed in blue jeans, Wellington boots, and an open down jacket is leading a German shepherd from the parking lot toward the power plant.

"And here comes a damn bloodhound," Gunnarsson says, shivering.

The dog handler, Sara Bengtsson, walks past the winch and says something in a low voice. The dog stops instantly and sits down. Sara keeps walking without breaking stride or looking at the dog, taking for granted that she's doing what Sara has told her to.

"Thanks for coming," Joona says, shaking her hand.

Sara looks at him briefly, then pulls her hand away and digs around for something in her pockets.

"I make the decisions here," Gunnarsson says. "And I don't much care for dogs—just so you know."

"Well, I'm here now," Sara says, glancing over at the dog.

"What's her name?" Joona asks.

"Jackie," the woman says, and smiles.

"We're about to send a diver down," Joona explains. "But it would be great if Jackie could identify areas we should check. ... Do you think she can do that?"

"Yes," Sara replies, kicking at a loose stone.

"There's a lot of water and one hell of a current," Gunnarsson warns.

"Back in the spring, she found a body at a depth of sixty-five meters," Sara replies, her cheeks flushing.

"So what the hell are we waiting for?" Gunnarsson says, taking out a cigarette.

Sara doesn't appear to hear him. She's looking out across the black water. She puts her hands in her pockets and stands perfectly still before saying gently, "Jackie."

The dog immediately leaves her post and comes over to Sara. She crouches down and pats the dog on her neck and behind her ears, talking encouragingly to her, and then they start to walk along the edge of the dam.

The dog is specially trained to detect the smell of blood and decomposing lungs in dead bodies.

They pass the place where Dante's car seat was found floating. Sara gently directs Jackie's nose out across the high water.

"I don't think this is going to work," Gunnarsson says with a smile. He lights his cigarette and strokes his stomach.

Sara stops and holds up her hand when Jackie smells something. The dog stretches her long nose over the edge of the dam.

"What can you smell?" Sara asks.

The dog sniffs and moves sideways, then loses the scent and moves on along the dam.

"Hocus-pocus," the diver mutters, adjusting his vest.

The handler and the German shepherd, moving slowly along the railing, are now approaching the middle of the dam, directly above the open floodgates. Some curls of hair have come loose from the woman's ponytail and are blowing in front of her face. Suddenly the dog stops and whines, leans forward, licks her nose, then turns around on the spot anxiously.

"Is there someone down there?" Sara asks in a low voice, looking into the black water.

The dog doesn't want to stop; she walks on and sniffs around an electricity junction box, but returns to the same place and starts to whimper again.

"What is it?" Joona says, walking toward them.

"I don't know, actually. She's not giving the usual signal, but she's behaving as if . . ."

The dog barks, and the woman crouches down beside her. "What is it, Jackie?" she asks gently. "What's the matter?"

The dog wags her tail when Sara hugs her and tells her she's a good girl. Jackie whines and lies down, scratches behind her ear with her hind leg, and licks her nose again.

"What on earth are you doing?" Sara asks with a surprised smile.

67

THE DAM IS RUMBLING AND vibrating very slightly. A pile of neatly folded watertight body bags rests on top of a plastic container with flags sticking out of it that marks the boundary of the search location.

"I'll start by the power plant and search according to a grid pattern," Hasse says.

"No, we go straight down where the dog reacted," Joona says.

"So the women are in charge now, are they?" Hasse asks in a hurt voice.

Far below the relatively calm surface of the water are the openings to the spillways, each one covered with mesh that catches everything that's been swept along by the river.

The diver checks his supply of gas. He plugs the camera cable into the computer, then puts his diving mask on. Joona sees himself on the screen.

"Wave to the camera," Hasse says, and slips into the water.

"If the current's too strong, we'll stop," Joona says.

"Be careful," Gunnarsson calls.

"I'm used to diving in strong currents," Hasse says. "But if I don't come up again, you can tell my boy that I should have gone with him instead."

"We'll have a beer in the Laxen Hotel when we're done," Gunnarsson says with a wave.

As Hasse disappears into the water, the surface rocks and then settles again. Gunnarsson smiles and flicks the stub of his cigarette over the edge. They can just make out the dark form of the diver. Bubbles of air break the water's surface. The only thing visible on the computer screen is the rough concrete wall passing by in the light of the camera. The diver's heavy breathing hisses from the speaker.

"How far down are you now?" Joona asks.

"Only nine meters," Hasse replies.

"How's the current?"

"Feels like someone's pulling my legs."

Joona follows the diver's descent on the screen. The concrete wall glides upward. His breathing sounds heavier. Sometimes the diver's hands come into view on the wall, and his blue gloves glow in the light from the lamp.

"There's nothing there," Gunnarsson says, pacing anxiously.

"The dog . . ."

"It didn't indicate that it had found anything," Gunnarsson says, raising his voice.

"No, but something was bothering her," Joona replies stubbornly.

He thinks of how the dead bodies could have been carried in the water, tumbling over the riverbed, closer and closer to the fast-moving current.

"Seventeen meters . . . the current's strong as hell now," the diver says through the tinny speaker.

Gunnarsson is measuring out the lifeline as it runs over the metal railing and disappears into the water.

"It's going too fast," Joona says. "Inflate your vest."

The diver starts to inflate his vest with air from the tanks. He usually only inflates to maintain his level or rise to the surface, but he realizes that Joona is right—he needs to slow his descent, given the amount of debris in the water.

"No problem," he reports a few moments later.

"If it's possible, I want you to go down and look at the mesh," Joona explains.

Hasse moves slowly for a while, and then his speed starts to increase again. It seems as if the power plant has opened the gates even more. Trash, sticks, and leaves are drifting past his face, heading straight down.

Gunnarsson moves the camera cable and lifeline to one side as a fast-moving log hits the edge of the dam with a thud.

68

HASSE FEELS THE STRONG CURRENT dragging him straight down. He's going too fast again. The water is roaring in his ears. If there was a collision, he could break both his legs. His heart is beating quickly, and he tries to inflate his vest a bit more, but the valves are acting up.

He tries to slow his descent with his hands along the wall, and strands of weeds come loose from the concrete and drift off on the current.

He doesn't mention anything to the police officers up above, but he's starting to get worried. The suction is much stronger than he imagined. Bubbles and grit float through his narrow field of vision and vanish. Everything outside the beam of his camera light on the diving mask is completely black.

"How deep are you now?" Joona asks.

He doesn't answer. He doesn't have time to check his depth meter; he must stop his descent. He fumbles with his inflator with one hand as he tries to keep himself upright with the other.

An old plastic bag swirls past.

He's drifting down quickly now. Though he tries to reach the vent on his back, he can't reach the valve and ends up hitting his elbow against the wall. He sways badly and can feel the surge of adrenaline in his blood. He realizes that he has to regain control of his descent, and starts to panic.

"Twenty-six meters," he gasps.

"Then you're almost at the mesh," the detective says.

The water being sucked down the smooth concrete wall toward the mesh is making his legs shake uncontrollably.

Hasse, falling fast, realizes he could get skewered on a sharp branch or piece of broken wood. He's going to have to release his lead weights in order to stop, but he knows he's going to need them to regulate his ascent when he heads back to the surface.

The air bubbles from his mask are being sucked downward in a sparkling stream. The suction seems to get even stronger, and a new current appears, hitting him from behind. The water gets colder very quickly. It feels as if the whole river is pushing him toward the wall.

Through the black water, he sees a large branch, covered with leaves, heading toward him from above. The leaves brush against the concrete wall. He tries to move out of the way, but it catches on the lifeline and hits him before brushing past and disappearing into the darkness.

"What was that?" the detective asks.

"There's a bunch of stuff in the water."

With trembling hands, the diver loosens the weights from his vest and finally slows his violent descent. Badly shaken, he floats beside the concrete wall. The lamp is providing less visibility because of the soil and grit clouding the water.

He stops abruptly. His feet have hit something, and he looks down and realizes he's reached a concrete shelf—the top edge of the mesh. There are branches, leaves, trash, even a few tree trunks in front of the mesh. The suction from the spillway is so strong that movement feels impossible.

"I'm there," he says quickly. "But it's hard to see anything; there's a hell of a lot of crap down here. . . ."

He climbs cautiously down through the branches, trying to keep his lifeline free. He makes his way past a quivering tree trunk. There's a soft, dark shape moving behind a twisted pine branch. He sighs with effort as he gets closer.

"There's something down here. . . ."

69

THE WATER IS GRAY, AND bubbles stream past in front of the diver's face. Clinging to his lifeline with one hand, he reaches out with the other, trying to pull the dense branches back.

Suddenly it's right in front of his face. An open eye and a row of teeth. He gasps and almost slips, taken by surprise by how close it is. The elk's bulky body is pressed against the mesh, but its neck is caught between a thick branch and a broken oar. The head is swinging from side to side in the strong current.

"I found an elk," he says, moving backward, away from the dead animal.

"So that's what the dog was reacting to," Gunnarsson says.

"Should I come up?"

"Look around a little more," Joona replies.

"Farther down, or off to the side?"

"What's that? Right in front of you?" Joona asks.

"Looks like fabric," Hasse says.

"Can you get to it?"

Hasse can feel the lactic acid in his arms and legs. He looks slowly across all the debris in front of the mesh, trying to see between the branches, past black sprigs of pine. Everything is trembling. He tells himself that he's going to buy the new Play-Station with his earnings from this dive. He'll surprise his son with it when he comes back from soccer camp.

"A box; it's just a cardboard box. . . ."

He tries to push the sodden cardboard aside. It disintegrates, and a large piece floats off on the current and catches against the mesh.

"I'm running out of energy—I'm coming up," he says.

"What's that white thing?" Joona asks.

"Where?"

"Where you were looking just now, there was something there," Joona says. "I thought I saw something among the leaves, a bit farther down by the mesh."

"Could be a plastic bag," the diver suggests.

"No," Joona says.

"Come up now," Gunnarsson calls. "We found an elk—that's what the dog could smell."

"A sniffer dog can be unsettled by dead animals, but not like this one was," Joona says. "I think she was reacting to something else."

Hasse slowly climbs down and pulls the tangle of leaves and twigs aside. His muscles are shaking with the effort of fighting the strong current. He has to hold out one arm to brace against it. The lifeline is shaking.

"I can't find anything," he gasps.

"Abort," Gunnarsson calls.

"Should I abort?" Hasse asks.

"If you have to," Joona replies.

"We're not all like you," Gunnarsson hisses at him.

"What should I do?" the diver asks. "I need to know what to . . ."

"Keep going sideways," Joona says.

A branch hits Hasse in the neck, but he keeps on looking. He pulls away some reeds and bulrushes that are covering the bottom corner of the mesh. More debris is being sucked into the mesh. He digs faster; and then he sees something unexpected. A shoulder bag, made of white reflective fabric.

"Wait! Don't touch it," Joona says. "Move closer and shine the light on it."

"Can you see now?"

"It could be Vicky's. Put it carefully in a bag."

70

A LOG HITS THE LIFELINE before Gunnarsson can move it out of the way, and then the digital connection to the diver is gone.

"We've lost contact," Joona says.

"He needs to come up."

"Pull on the line three times."

"He's not responding," Gunnarsson says, pulling at the line.

"Pull harder," Joona says.

Gunnarsson tugs the line three more times and receives a response almost immediately.

"He replied with two tugs," Gunnarsson says.

"That means he's coming up."

"It's gone slack—he's on his way. But there are more logs coming."

"He needs to act fast," Joona replies.

Another ten logs are heading toward the dam, quickly. Gunnarsson climbs over to the outside of the railing, and Joona hauls in the lifeline with his one good arm.

"I think I can see him," Gunnarsson says, pointing.

The blue wetsuit comes into view like a flag in the wind.

Joona pulls off his sling, grabs the boat hook from the ground, and watches as the first log hits the dam two meters away and starts to spin.

Joona holds the next log back, pushing it with the boat hook, and it slides under the first; they start to roll together.

Hasse breaks the surface. Gunnarsson leans over and reaches his hand out toward him.

"Come on, get out!"

Hasse looks up at him in surprise and grabs the edge of the dam. Still holding the boat hook, Joona climbs over the railing so that he'll be able to push the logs away.

"Hurry up!" he shouts.

A log with wet black bark is approaching fast, almost hidden beneath the water.

"Look out!"

Joona drives the boat hook into the log and holds the other end in line with the edge of the dam. The momentum of the log snaps the hook's shaft, but it changes direction, missing Hasse's head by the narrowest of margins before crashing into the dam with great force. The log swings around, hitting Hasse in the back with a wet branch so hard that he is knocked back beneath the water again.

"Try to reach him!" Joona calls.

The cable gets tangled on the log, and Hasse is dragged down with it. Bubbles break the surface. The line tenses over the metal railing with a clang. The log rolls against the concrete wall. Hasse pulls out his knife and cuts the lifeline, kicks out with his legs, surfaces, and grabs Gunnarsson's hand.

Another log thuds into the previous ones, followed by three more, just as Gunnarsson drags Hasse out of the water.

When Gunnarsson has helped him remove the heavy tanks, Hasse slumps onto the ground. Joona takes the bag from him. The diver takes off his wetsuit, hands shaking. He's bruised and bleeding from scratches on his back that stain his sweaty T-shirt. Aching badly, he swears to himself as he stands up.

"This probably wasn't the smartest thing I've ever done in my life," he pants.

"But I think you've recovered something important," Joona says.

He looks at the purse in the water-filled plastic bag and watches it move, almost weightless in the murky water. Some straws of yellow grass float around with it. He gently turns the plastic bag over and holds it up against the sun. His fingers sink into the pliant plastic and touch the bag.

"We're looking for dead bodies, and you're happy with a damn purse," Gunnarsson sighs.

The sunlight passes through the plastic bag, and a shimmering yellow shadow crosses Joona's forehead. He can see dark-brown marks on the bottom of the bag. Blood. That's what the dog smelled. He's sure it's blood.

71

Joona is standing outside the locked gates of the police garage on Bergs Street in Sundsvall. He wants to talk to the forensics technicians and take a look at the bag found at the dam, but no one's answering the telephone or the intercom at the gate. The area behind the fence looks abandoned: the parking lot is empty, and all the doors are closed.

Joona gets back in his car and drives to the police station on Stor Street, where Gunnarsson is based. On the steps he meets Sonja Rask. She's not in uniform. She's wearing light makeup and looks happy.

"Hi," Joona says. "Is Gunnarsson up there?"

"Ignore him," she says, grimacing. "He feels so threatened all the time. . . . He's convinced you're trying to take his job."

"I'm just an observer."

Sonja's dark eyes sparkle warmly at him.

"Yes. I heard you walked straight into the water and swam down to find the car."

"Only to make observations," Joona says, smiling back.

She laughs, pats him on his arm, then looks embarrassed and hurries down the stairs.

Joona heads into the police station, where the radio in the staff room is switched on, as usual. Someone is talking on the phone in a monotone, and through a pair of glass doors he sees about a dozen people gathered around a conference table.

Gunnarsson is sitting at one end. Joona goes over to the door. A woman at the table meets Joona's gaze and shakes her head, but Joona walks in anyway.

"What the hell?" Gunnarsson mutters when he catches sight of him.

"I need to take a look at Vicky Bennet's bag," Joona says tersely.

"We're in a meeting," Gunnarsson says in a tone that indicates that the matter is settled. He looks down at his papers.

"Everything's out at the forensics unit on Bergs Street," Rolf Wikner explains in an embarrassed voice.

"There's no one there," Joona says.

"Just drop it, will you?" Gunnarsson snaps. "The investigation is closed, and Internal Affairs can have you for breakfast as far as I'm concerned."

Joona nods and leaves the station, then sits in his car for a while before driving toward Sundsvall Hospital. On the way, he tries to identify what it is about the murders at the Birgitta Home that's bothering him.

Vicky Bennet, he thinks. The nice girl who might not always be so nice. Vicky Bennet, who slashed a mother and son in the face with a broken bottle.

Though they were left severely disfigured, they haven't sought medical help and never reported the incident to the police.

Before Vicky drowned, she was the main suspect in two extremely violent murders.

The evidence suggests that she planned the attacks at the Birgitta Home. She waited for night to fall, killed Elisabet with a hammer to get her keys, returned to the house, unlocked the door to the isolation room, and killed Miranda.

The strange thing is that The Needle says Miranda was killed by a rock.

Why would Vicky leave the hammer in her room and use a rock instead?

Several times, Joona considered the possibility that his old friend might be wrong. That's one of the reasons he hasn't mentioned it to anyone. Nils can present his theory himself when his report is finished.

The other odd thing is that Vicky went back to bed after the murders.

Holger Jalmert had said that Joona's observation was interesting but impossible to prove. Yet Joona knows that he saw blood that had been wiped or dried on the sheet when fresh, and then smeared an hour or so later, when Vicky moved her arm.

Without witnesses, he's unlikely ever to get any definite answers.

Joona has read the Birgitta Home's log, and Elisabet Grim's last entry from that Friday night, but nothing in her brief notes gives any hint of the extreme violence in what was to come.

The other girls hadn't seen anything.

None of them really knew Vicky.

Joona has already decided that he needs to try to talk to Daniel Grim.

It's worth a try, even though he's reluctant to intrude upon someone's grief. But Daniel is the person the girls seemed to trust most, and if there's anyone who can understand what went on, it's probably him.

Joona slowly pulls out his phone, conscious of the pain in his shoulder, then dials the number and thinks back to the counselor's behavior when he arrived at the home, and how Daniel tried to hold everything together in front of the girls until he realized that Elisabet had been murdered, when his face contorted with pain and confusion.

The doctor had described his state of shock as arousal, a condition of traumatic stress that could seriously influence his ability to remember what had happened, at least for a while.

"Psychiatric ward, Rebecka Stenbeck," a woman answers after five rings.

"I'd like to talk to one of your patients. . . . His name's Daniel Grim."

"One moment."

He hears the woman tap at the keyboard.

"I'm sorry, but that patient isn't taking calls," she says.

"Whose decision was that?"

"The doctor in charge of his care," the woman replies coolly.

"Can you put me through to him instead?"

There's a click, and then the phone starts to ring again.

"Rimmer."

"My name is Joona Linna; I'm a detective with the National Crime Unit," he says. "It's very important that I speak with a patient of yours, Daniel Grim."

"I'm sorry, but it's out of the question," Rimmer replies at once.

"We're investigating a double murder, and—"

"No one is permitted to jeopardize the patient's recovery."

"I understand that Daniel Grim is going through an incredibly difficult time, but I promise—"

"In my estimation," Rimmer interrupts in a friendly tone, "the patient will be well enough to be questioned by the police before too much longer."

"When?"

"In a couple of months, I'd say."

"I really do need to have just a very short conversation with him now," Joona tries.

"As his doctor, I have to say no," Rimmer replies, in a tone of voice that doesn't invite discussion. "He was extremely upset after your colleague spoke to him."

72

FLORA HURRIES HOME WITH THE heavy bag of groceries. The sky is dark, but the streetlights haven't come on yet. Her stomach clenches when she thinks about her call to the police, how her offer had been rejected and she was left sitting there with her face burning with shame. Yet, even though the police had said it was a criminal offense to call and waste their time, she had still picked up the phone and called back to tell them about the murder weapon. Now she can't help thinking through that second conversation:

"Police," said the woman who had just given her a warning.

"My name is Flora Hansen," she said, and swallowed hard. "I called just now. . . ."

"About the murders in Sundsvall," the woman said steadily.

"I know where the murder weapon is," she lied.

"Are you aware that I'm going to have to report this call, Flora Hansen?"

"I'm a medium. I've seen the bloodstained knife. It's lying in water . . . in dark, glinting water. That was all I saw, but I . . . If I was paid, I could put myself in a trance and identify the exact location."

"Flora," the police officer said sternly, "within the next few days, you will be informed that you are suspected of having committed an offense, and the police will—"

Flora had hung up at that point.

As she passes a little halal shop, she stops and looks in the trash can for empty bottles. When she gets to her building, she notes that the lock has been smashed.

The elevator is stuck in the basement. She takes the stairs to the second floor, unlocks the door of the apartment, walks in, and turns the light on.

There's a click, but the light doesn't come on.

Flora puts the bag down, locks the door, and takes her shoes off, but when she bends down to push them aside, the hairs on her arms stand up.

The apartment suddenly feels cold.

She takes the receipt and the change from her purse and walks toward the dark living room.

She can see the sofa, the big saggy armchair, the black screen of the television. It smells electric, like dust and overheated circuits.

Without walking in, she reaches across the wallpaper for the light switch.

Nothing happens when she turns it on.

"Is anyone home?" she whispers.

The floor creaks, and a teacup rattles on its saucer.

Someone is moving in the darkness, and the door to the bathroom closes.

Flora follows the noise.

The linoleum floor is cold, like when someone's left a window open on a winter day. Just as Flora is reaching out to open the bathroom door, she remembers that Ewa and Hans-Gunnar weren't going to be home this evening: they were going to the pizzeria to celebrate a friend's birthday. Even though she knows there can't be anyone in the bathroom, she grabs the handle and opens the door.

In the gray light reflected in the bathroom mirror, she sees something that makes her quickly take a step back, gasping for breath.

A child is lying on the floor, between the bathtub and the toilet. It's a girl, and she's covering her eyes with her hands. There's a large dark pool of blood beside her head, and small red drops have sprayed across the white bathtub and up onto the wallpaper and shower curtain.

Flora stumbles over the hose of the vacuum cleaner, throws her arm out, pulling down Ewa's porcelain clown, falls backward, and hits the back of her head on the floor.

73

THE FLOOR FEELS LIKE A frozen field under Flora's back. She raises her head and stares into the bathroom.

Her heart is thudding in her chest.

She can't see the girl anymore.

There's no blood spattered on the edge of the bathtub or the shower curtain. A pair of Hans-Gunnar's jeans are lying on the floor next to the toilet.

She blinks and tells herself that she must have been mistaken.

She swallows and rests her head on the floor, waiting for her heart to calm down. The unmistakable taste of blood spreads through her mouth.

Farther along the hallway, she sees that the door to her little room is open. She shivers, and goose bumps appear all over her body.

She knows she left the door closed, because she always does.

Icy air is being sucked toward her room. She sees dust balls bouncing along the floor and watches as they get swept up in the draft in the hallway and float past two bare feet.

Flora hears herself make a peculiar moaning sound.

The girl who was lying next to the bathtub is standing in the doorway to her room.

Flora tries to sit up, but her body is numb with fear. Now she knows that she's seeing a ghost. For the first time in her life, she's seeing a real ghost.

The girl's hair looks as if it was once arranged neatly, but now it's tangled and bloody.

Flora is breathing fast and can hear her pulse beating in her ears.

The girl is hiding something behind her back as she starts to walk toward Flora. She stops with her bare feet just one step from Flora's face.

"What do I have behind my back?" the girl asks in a voice so low that her words are almost inaudible.

"You're not real," Flora whispers.

"Do you want me to show you my hands?"

"No."

"But I'm not holding anything. . . ."

A rock falls behind the girl, making the floor tremble and fragments from the broken porcelain clown bounce.

With a smile, the child holds out her empty hands.

The rock lies behind her, between her feet, dark and heavy. It has sharp edges.

The girl tentatively puts one foot on it, making it sway, then pushes it heavily to the side.

"Just die, will you?" the girl mutters to herself. "Just die."

The child crouches down, puts her pale-gray hands on the rock, and tries to get a firm grip on it, but her hands slip, and she wipes them on her dress and starts again, tipping the rock onto its side with a dull thud.

"What are you going to do?" Flora asks.

"Close your eyes and I'll be gone," the girl replies, picking up the sharp rock and raising it above Flora's head.

The rock is heavy, and its dark underside looks wet.

Suddenly the electricity comes back on. Lights go on all over the place. Flora rolls sideways and sits up. The girl is gone. She can hear loud voices from the television, and the fridge is rumbling.

She gets up and switches on more lights, then turns on the

lights in her room, opens the closets, and looks under the bed. After that, she sits down at the kitchen table. She doesn't realize how badly her hands are shaking until she tries to call the police.

The automatic exchange offers her a number of options. She can report a crime, leave information, or ask a question. This last option gives her the chance to talk to an operator.

"Police," a friendly voice says in her ear. "How can I help you?"

"I'd like to talk to someone working on what happened up in Sundsvall," Flora says in a shaky voice.

"What's this about?"

"I think ... I think I've seen the murder weapon," Flora whispers.

"I see," the receptionist says. "Then I suggest that you talk to our tipoff team. I'll put you through to them."

Flora is about to protest when she hears the line click. After just a few seconds, another woman answers.

"Police tip line, how can I help?"

Flora doesn't know if it's the woman who got angry with her when she lied about the bloody knife.

"I'd like to talk to someone working on the murders up in Sundsvall," she says.

"You can talk to me first," the voice says.

"It was a rock," Flora says.

"I can't hear what you're saying; can you speak a little louder, please?"

"The murders up in Sundsvall ... You need to look for a rock. The underside is covered with blood, and ..."

Flora stops speaking and feels sweat starting to run down her sides.

"How do you know anything about the murders in Sundsvall?"

"I ... Someone told me."

"Someone told you about the murders in Sundsvall?"

"Yes," Flora whispers.

She can hear her pulse thudding in her temples, and there's a rushing sound in her ears.

"Go on," the woman says.

"The murderer used a rock . . . a rock with sharp edges. That's all I know."

"What's your name?"

"That doesn't matter. I just wanted—"

"I recognize your voice," the police officer says. "You called and talked about a large knife before. I've filed a report against you, Flora Hansen . . . but you should contact a doctor, because you probably need help."

The policewoman ends the call, and Flora is left sitting with the phone in her hand.

74

An hour ago, Elin returned home after a long meeting with the board of Kingston, a large subsidiary, to discuss two holding companies in the United Kingdom.

She feels hot with shame when she remembers what happened with the photographer from *Vogue*. She tells herself that she needed a distraction, it was a little adventure, she needed it, it had been a long time since she last had sex. But the thought of it still leaves her writhing with embarrassment.

She grabs a bottle of Perrier from the fridge and walks through the rooms in her old pale-red sweats and a washed-out T-shirt with a faded picture of ABBA. In the living room, she stops in front of the television just in time to see a very tall woman attempt the high jump. Elin puts the bottle of mineral water on the glass table and gathers her hair into a ponytail with the scrunchie from around her wrist before going into the bedroom.

Later that evening, she'll take a conference call with her subdivision in Chicago while she gets a manicure and paraffin bath, and at eight o'clock she's due to go to a charity dinner, where she'll sit with the head of Volvo. The crown princess is going to present an award from one of the big national funds, and Roxette will be providing the entertainment.

She walks between the tall wardrobes in her walk-in closet, still hearing the sound of the television but no longer actively listening, so she doesn't realize that the news has started. She opens a few of the wardrobes and glances at the outfits. Eventually, she pulls out a metallic-green dress that Alexander McQueen designed for her.

The name Vicky Bennet rings out from the television.

She drops the dress on the floor and hurries back to the living room.

The large television has a thin white frame, so it looks as if the sharp picture is being projected directly onto the white wall. A detective named Olle Gunnarsson is being interviewed in front of a nondescript police station. He's trying to smile patiently but looks irritated. He rubs his mustache and nods.

"I can't comment on that while the investigation is still ongoing," he replies, clearing his throat.

"But you've called off the search?"

"That's correct."

"Does that mean you've found the bodies?"

"I'm not in a position to answer that."

The light from the television flickers around the room, and Elin stares at the images of the damaged car being raised from the water. The crane lifts it straight up, and it starts to sway after it breaks the surface. A serious voice explains that the car stolen by Vicky Bennet was found in the Indals River earlier in the day and that both Vicky Bennet, who is suspected of murder, and four-year-old Dante Abrahamsson are feared dead.

"The police haven't made an official statement about the discovery, but, according to sources we've spoken to, the divers have been called off, and there is no longer a national alert. . . ."

Elin doesn't hear what the newscaster says. They're showing a picture of Vicky. She's older and thinner, but she hasn't really changed. Elin feels as if her heart has stopped. She has a sudden memory of how it felt to carry the little girl when she was asleep.

"No," Elin whispers. "No . . ."

She stares at the girl's thin, pale face. At her messy, tangled hair, always so hard to fix.

She's still a child, and now they're saying she's dead. The look in her eyes is obstinate, as if she's being forced to look at the camera.

Elin moves away from the television, sways, and reaches out to the wall for support.

"No, no, no," she whimpers. "Not that, no, not that . . ."

Her last contact with Vicky was listening to her sobbing out on the landing, and now she's dead.

"No! It can't be true!" she screams.

With her heart pounding, she goes over to the illuminated display case containing the large Passover seder plate she was given by her father, which has been passed down for generations. She grabs the top of the case and pulls it over with all her strength. It crashes to the floor. The glass sides shatter, scattering shards across the parquet floor, and the beautifully decorated dish smashes.

She doubles over and curls up on the floor. She gasps for breath, thinking the same thing over and over:

I once had a daughter, I once had a daughter, I once had a daughter.

She sits up, grabs a large piece of her father's seder plate, and pulls the sharp edge hard across her wrist. Warm blood starts to flow, dripping into her lap. She pulls the sharp splinter across her wrist again and sighs with pain, then hears the lock on the front door rattle as someone opens the door and comes in.

75

JOONA IS BROWNING TWO THICK slices of steak in a cast-iron pan. He's seasoned them with coarsely ground black and green pepper. When the surface has caramelized, he transfers the steaks to the oven, adds salt, and places them on top of the potato wedges. While the meat finishes cooking, he makes a sauce from port, currants, veal stock, and some truffles.

With detached calm, he pours two glasses of Saint-Émilion.

The kitchen is full of the earthy scent of Merlot and Cabernet Sauvignon by the time the doorbell rings.

Disa is wearing a red-and-white polka-dot raincoat. Her eyes are wide open, and her face is wet with rain.

"Joona, I was thinking of testing you to see if you're as good a police officer as everyone says."

"How are you going to do that?" he asks.

"It's just a test," she says. "Do you think I look the same as usual?"

"More beautiful," he replies.

"No," she says, smiling.

"You've had your hair cut and are using the hair clip from Paris for the first time in a year."

"Anything else?"

He looks at her thin, blushing face, her glossy bobbed hair and slender body.

"Those are new," he says, pointing to her high-heeled boots.

"Marc Jacobs . . . a little too expensive for me."

"Nice."

"Nothing else?"

"I haven't finished," he says, and takes her hands in his, then turns them over and looks at her nails.

She can't help smiling when he mutters that she's wearing the same lipstick she had on when they went to Södermalm Theatre. He gently touches her earrings, then meets her gaze, holds it, and steps aside to let the light from the floor lamp shine on her face.

"Your eyes," he says. "Your left pupil isn't contracting in the light."

"Clever policeman," she says. "I had some drops put in."

"You've had your eyes looked at?" he asks.

"The vitreous body is slightly dented, but it's nothing to worry about," Disa says, and walks into the kitchen.

"Food's almost ready. The meat just needs to rest a bit longer."

"You've made it look lovely," Disa says.

"We haven't seen each other in a long time," he says. "I'm very glad you came."

They raise their glasses in a silent toast, and, as always when Joona looks at her, Disa feels hot, as if she's starting to shimmer. She forces herself to look away from his eyes, rolls the wine around the glass, inhales the bouquet, then tastes it again.

"Right temperature," she says.

Joona lays the steak and potatoes on a bed of arugula, basil, and thyme.

He drizzles the sauce carefully over the plate while thinking to himself that he should have had a serious talk with Disa a long time ago.

"How have you been?"

"Without you, you mean? Better than ever," Disa snaps.

Neither of them speaks, and she gently places her hand over his.

"Sorry," she says, and sits down. "But I get so angry with you sometimes. When I'm my worst self."

"Who are you at the moment?"

"My worst self," she says.

Joona takes a sip of the wine. "I've been thinking a lot about the past recently," he begins.

She smiles and raises her eyebrows. "Recently? You're always thinking about the past."

"Am I?"

"Yes . . . but you don't talk about it."

"No, I—"

He stops speaking abruptly, and his pale-gray eyes narrow. Disa feels a chill run down her spine.

"You asked me to dinner because we needed to talk," she says. "I'd made my mind up. I was never going to talk to you again, but then you call out of the blue . . . after several months. . . ."

"Yes, because—"

"You don't give a damn about me, Joona."

"Disa . . . think what you want about me," he says gravely. "But I want you to know that I care about you . . . I care about you, and I think about you all the time."

"You do?" she asks slowly, standing up without meeting his gaze.

"It's not you—it's other things, terrible things that . . ."

Joona watches as she puts her raincoat back on.

"Goodbye," she whispers.

"Disa, I need you," he hears himself say. "I want you."

She stares at him. Her dark, glossy bangs reach her eyelashes. "What did you say?" she asks after a pause.

"I want you, Disa."

"Don't say that," she mumbles, zipping up her boots.

"I need you; I've needed you all along," he goes on. "But I haven't been willing to put you at risk. I couldn't bear the thought that something might happen to you if we—"

"What would happen to me?" she interrupts.

"You could disappear," he explains simply, cupping her face in his hands.

"You're the one who disappears," she whispers.

"I'm being serious. I'm talking about real things that—"

She stretches up on tiptoe and kisses him on the lips, then stays close enough to feel the warmth of his breath. He feels for her mouth and kisses her tentatively several times until she parts her lips.

They kiss slowly, and Joona unbuttons her raincoat and lets it fall to the floor.

"Disa," he whispers, stroking her shoulders and back.

He presses himself against her, breathes in her silky scent, kisses her collarbone and slender neck, and ends up with her gold chain in his mouth. Then he kisses her chin and soft, moist mouth.

He feels for her warm skin inside her thin blouse. The small snaps open with a click. Her nipples are stiff, and her stomach flutters with her rapid breath.

She looks into his eyes and pulls him with her toward the bedroom. Her blouse is open, and her breasts glow, as white as porcelain.

They stop and kiss again, hungrily. His hands slide over the base of her spine, her backside, and in under her satin panties.

Disa gently pulls away. She feels the heat in her crotch and knows that she's already wet. Her cheeks flush red, and her hands tremble as she unbuttons his pants.

76

After breakfast, Disa stays in bed with a cup of coffee and reads *The Sunday Times* on her iPad while Joona showers and gets dressed.

Yesterday he decided not to go to the Nordic Museum to look at the Sami bridal crown. He spent the day with Disa instead. It wasn't planned. But he thinks that Rosa Bergman's dementia may have finally severed his links to Summa and Lumi.

More than twelve years have passed.

He has to accept that there is nothing to be scared of anymore.

But he should have talked to Disa before, should have warned her and told her about what he's afraid of, so that she could make the decision for herself.

He stands in the doorway, looking at her for a long time, before she notices; then he goes out into the kitchen and calls Professor Holger Jalmert.

"This is Joona Linna."

"I heard that Gunnarsson got unpleasant," Holger says with amusement. "I've promised him that I wouldn't send you any copies of the report."

"But you're allowed to talk to me?" Joona asks, taking his sandwich and coffee and waving at Disa, who's frowning as she reads her screen.

"Probably not," Holger says with a laugh, then turns serious again.

"Have you had a chance to look at the bag we found at the dam?" Joona asks.

"Yes, I've finished. I'm in the car, on my way home to Umeå now."

"Was there anything with writing on it inside the bag?"

"Nothing but a receipt from a newsstand."

"Cell phone?"

"Unfortunately not," Holger says.

"So what do we have?" Joona asks, scanning the gray sky above the rooftops.

Holger breathes in through his nose. When he starts to speak again, it sounds as if he's reading directly from the report: "In all likelihood, the stains on the bag are blood. I cut off a fragment and sent it to the National Forensics Laboratory. . . . There were also two different lipsticks, a stub of black eyeliner, a pink plastic hair clip, bobby pins, a wallet with a skull on it, some money, a photograph of herself, some sort of bike tool, a container of pills with no label . . . also sent for analysis . . . a blister pack of Valium, two pens . . . and, hidden in the lining of the bag, I found a butter knife that had been sharpened as keenly as a sushi knife."

"No writing, no names or addresses?"

"No, that was everything. . . ."

Joona hears Disa's footsteps on the wooden floor behind him but doesn't move. He feels the warmth of her body, shivers, then feels her soft lips against the back of his neck and her arms around his body.

WHILE DISA IS IN THE shower, Joona sits at the kitchen table and calls Solveig Sundström, who is now responsible for the girls from the Birgitta Home. She might know what medication Vicky was taking.

The phone rings eight times; then there's a click and a voice says, "This is Caroline . . . answering an ugly phone that was lying on the sofa."

"Is Solveig there?"

"No, I don't know where she is right now—can I give her a message?"

Caroline is the older girl, a head taller than Tuula. She had scars from old injections in the crook of her arm but seemed sensible, intelligent, and earnest about her attempt to change.

"Is everything okay with you all?" he asks.

"You're that detective—aren't you?"

"Yes."

Silence. Then Caroline asks tentatively, "Is it true that Vicky's dead?"

"I'm afraid we believe it is," Joona replies.

"It feels really weird," Caroline says.

"Do you know what medication she was taking?"

"Vicky?"

"Yes."

"She was incredibly thin and pretty for someone on Zyprexa."

"That's for manic episodes, isn't it?"

"I used to be on it, but now I only take Imovane, to help me sleep," the girl says. "It's a hell of a relief not to have to take Zyprexa."

"Side effects?"

"It probably varies, but for me . . . I must have gained at least ten kilos."

"Does it make you tired?" Joona asks, seeing in his mind's eye the bloodstained sheets that Vicky had slept in.

"I only had to lick it . . . Your skin starts to crawl, and when you take a little too much, you get irritated about nothing and yell at everyone. . . . I threw my phone at the wall once and pulled the curtains down. . . . But, after a while, everything changes, and it feels like you've got a warm blanket wrapped around you—you feel all calm and just want to sleep."

"Do you know if Vicky was on any other medication?"

"She probably did what most of us do and kept a little stock of all the things that actually work—Valium, Lyrica, Oxy. . . ."

There's a voice in the background. Joona realizes that the nurse has come into the room and has seen Caroline holding the phone to her ear.

"I'm going to report this as theft," the woman says.

"It rang and I answered," Caroline says. "It's a detective who wants to talk to you. . . . You're a suspect in the murder of Miranda Ericsdotter."

"Don't be stupid," the woman snaps, then takes the phone and clears her throat before speaking: "Solveig Sundström."

"My name is Joona Linna. I'm a detective with the National Crime Unit, and I'm investigating—"

The woman ends the call without a word, and Joona doesn't bother to call back, seeing that he's already found out what he wanted to know.

77

A WHITE OPEL STOPS BENEATH the flat gas-station canopy, and a woman wearing a pale-blue sweater gets out, turns toward the pump, and searches in her bag.

Ari Määtilainen looks away from the woman and sets two chunky sausages on a bed of mashed potato with bacon mayo and fried onions. He looks at the fat biker waiting for the food and explains automatically that he can help himself to coffee and Coca-Cola from the dispenser.

The many zippers on the biker's leather jacket scrape the glass counter as he leans forward to take the food.

"*Danke,*" he says, and walks off toward the coffee machine.

Ari turns the radio up slightly and sees that the woman in the pale-blue sweater is standing a little apart while the Opel's tank fills.

Ari listens as the radio gives the latest developments in the ongoing kidnapping case: "The search for Vicky Bennet and Dante Abrahamsson has been called off. The Västernorrland Police haven't released a statement, but sources indicate that the two missing children are now believed to have died on Saturday morning. There has been some criticism of the fact that the police issued a national alert. We have tried to reach the head of the National Crime Unit, Carlos Eliasson, for a comment...."

"What the hell ...?" Ari whispers.

He finds the Post-it note next to the register, picks up his phone, and dials the number for the police for the second time this week.

"Police, this is Sonja Rask," a woman's voice answers.

"Hello," Ari says. "I saw them—I saw the girl and the little boy."

"Who am I talking to?"

"Ari Määtilainen . . . I work at the Statoil gas station in Dingersjö. . . . I was just listening to the radio, and they said they're supposed to have died on Saturday morning, but that can't be true, because I saw them late Saturday night."

"Do you mean Vicky Bennet and Dante Abrahamsson?" Sonja asks skeptically.

"Yes, I saw them here that night—it was actually early Sunday morning—so they can't have died on Saturday, like they said on the radio, can they?"

"You saw Vicky Bennet and Dante Abrahamsson on . . ."

"Yes."

"Why didn't you call and tell us when it happened?"

"I did; I talked to a police officer."

Ari remembers that he had been listening to Radio Gold on Saturday night and Sunday morning. The national alert hadn't yet been issued, but the local media were asking the public to keep an eye out for the girl and the little boy.

At eleven o'clock, a semi pulled into the parking lot on the far side of the pumps. The driver stayed there and slept for three hours.

It was the middle of the night, quarter past two, when he saw them.

Ari was looking at the screen that showed the various security cameras. One of them showed the truck from a different angle. The gas station looked deserted as the large vehicle started up and drove off. Suddenly Ari saw a shape at the back of the building, fairly close to the car-wash exit. Not one but two people. He stared at the screen. The truck turned and drove toward the exit, its headlights sweeping across the big window. Ari left his place behind the counter and ran around the building, but they were already gone. The girl and the little boy were gone.

78

Joona parks in front of the gas station, 360 kilometers north of Stockholm. It's a sunny day. There's a brisk wind, and tattered advertising banners are flapping noisily. Joona and Disa were sitting and having lunch together at Villa Källhagen when he received a phone call from a nervous Officer Sonja Rask in Sundsvall.

Joona walks into the shop. A hollow-eyed man wearing a Statoil cap is arranging paperback books on a shelf. Joona looks at the menu, then at the shiny sausages rotating on the mechanical grill.

"What would you like?" the man asks.

"*Makkarakeitto*," Joona says in Finnish.

"*Suomalainen makkarakeitto*," Ari Määtilainen says with a smile. "My grandmother used to make sausage soup when I was little."

"With rye bread?"

"Yes, but, unfortunately, I only get to sell Swedish food here," he says, pointing at the hamburgers.

"I'm not actually here to eat—I'm from the police."

"Yes, that's what I figured. . . . I spoke to one of your colleagues the night I saw them," Ari says, gesturing toward the screen.

"What had you seen when you called?" Joona asks.

"A girl and a little boy out in the back here."

"You saw them on the screen?"

"Yes."

"Clearly?"

"No, but . . . I'm used to keeping an eye on what goes on here."

"Did the police come out here that night?"

"He came the next morning—Gunnarsson, his name was. He didn't think you could see anything and told me I could wipe the tape."

"But you haven't," Joona says.

"What do you think?"

"I think you store recordings on an external hard drive."

With a smile, Ari Määtilainen shows Joona into a small office next to the stockroom. There's an unfolded sofa bed, some cans of Red Bull on the floor, and a carton of buttermilk by the frost-covered window. On an old school desk sits a small laptop connected to an external hard drive. Ari Määtilainen sits down on the creaking office chair and quickly looks through the files, which are arranged by date and time.

"I'd heard on the radio that everyone was looking for a girl and a little boy, and then I saw them here in the middle of the night," he says as he clicks on one of the files.

Joona leans closer to the grubby screen, which shows four different views of the interior and exterior of the gas station. A digital clock in the corner shows the time. The gray images are completely static. Ari is visible behind the counter, and occasionally he turns the page of his newspaper and eats some fried onion rings.

"That truck had been here for three hours," Ari says, pointing at one of the images. "But it's about to leave. . . ."

A dark shadow moves inside the cab.

"Can you enlarge the image?" Joona asks.

"Hang on. . . ."

A clump of trees lights up in a white glow as the truck starts up and the headlights come on.

Ari clicks on the other external image and switches to full-screen.

"This is where you see them," he whispers.

The screen shows the truck from a different angle. It starts to move and rolls slowly forward. Ari points toward the bottom of the screen, at the back of the gas station, where the dumpsters and recycling containers are kept. The area is in deep shadow, and completely still. Then, suddenly, there's a sign of movement at the car-wash door, and they see someone, a thin figure, right by the wall.

The image is grainy and flickering. It's impossible to see a face or any other details. But it's definitely a person, and there's something else, too.

"Can the picture be improved?" Joona asks.

"Hold on," Ari whispers.

The truck turns toward the exit. Now the light from the headlights hits the garage door next to the figure. The glass flares white for a few seconds, and the back of the gas station is briefly bathed in light.

Joona sees that what he thought was one figure is a thin girl and a younger child. They watch the truck go; then everything goes dark again.

Ari points at the screen, which shows the two figures running along the dark-gray wall and disappearing out of the shot into grainy darkness.

"You saw them?" Ari asks.

"Rewind," Joona says.

He doesn't have to say which sequence he wants to look at again. Moments later, Ari replays the brightly lit fragment very slowly.

The truck barely seems to be moving now, but the light from the headlights moves jerkily through the trees and across the façade of the gas station, filling the panes of glass with white.

The smaller child is looking down, his face in shadow. The thin girl is barefoot, and it looks as if she has plastic bags over both her hands. The light gets brighter as the girl slowly raises her hand. Joona sees that they aren't plastic bags but bandages that have unraveled. They swing wetly in the strong light, and he knows that Vicky Bennet and Dante Abrahamsson didn't drown in the river.

The time stamp reads 2:14 on Sunday morning.

Somehow they got out of the car and across the fast-flowing water to the other side of the river, and then made their way 150 kilometers south.

The girl's tangled hair is framing her face. Her dark eyes flare intensely before the screen turns almost black again.

They're alive, Joona thinks. They're both still alive.

79

CARLOS IS STANDING WITH HIS back to the door when Joona walks into his office.

"Sit down," he says in an oddly expectant tone of voice.

"I've just driven back from Sundsvall, and—"

"Wait," Carlos interrupts.

Joona looks at his back in amusement and sits down on the light-brown leather chair. He looks at the shiny surface of the untouched desk, at the aquariums' reflections in the wood veneer.

Carlos takes a deep breath, then turns around. He looks different, unshaven. There are sparse patches of graying stubble on his top lip and chin. "So what do you think?" he asks with a broad smile.

"You grew a beard," Joona says slowly.

"A full beard," Carlos says happily. "Well ... I'm expecting it to thicken up soon. I'm not going to shave again. I've thrown my razor away."

"Great," Joona says curtly.

"But my beard isn't what we were going to talk about," Carlos declares. "As I understand it, the diver didn't find any bodies."

"No," Joona says, pulling out a printout from the gas station's security-camera footage. "We didn't find the bodies. . . ."

"Here we go," Carlos mutters to himself.

"Because they weren't in the river," Joona says.

"And you're sure about that?"

"Vicky Bennet and Dante Abrahamsson are still alive."

"Gunnarsson called me about the video from the gas station, and—"

"Issue another national alert," Joona interrupts.

"A national alert? You can't keep turning a national alert on and off."

"I know Vicky Bennet and Dante Abrahamsson are the people in this picture," Joona says sternly, pointing at the printout. "And it was taken hours after the car went into the river. They're alive, and we have to issue another national alert."

Carlos stretches one leg out.

"You can put the Spanish boot on me if you want, but I'm not going to report them missing again."

"Look at the photograph," Joona says.

"The Västernorrland Police went to the gas station today," Carlos says, folding the printout into a tiny square. "They sent a copy of the hard drive to the forensics lab, and two of their experts have examined the recording and have concluded that it's impossible to identify the people outside the gas station with any degree of certainty."

"But you know I'm right," Joona says.

"Okay." Carlos nods. "Let's say that you could be right—we'll see—but I'm not going to make a fool of myself by issuing a missing-person alert for someone the police believe is dead."

"I'm not backing down until—"

"Hold on, hold on," Carlos interrupts, and takes a deep breath. "Joona, the senior prosecutor is currently looking at the internal investigation into your conduct."

"But that's . . ."

"I'm your boss, and I have to take this complaint against you seriously, and I want to hear you admit that you're not in charge of the investigation up in Sundsvall."

"I'm not in charge of the investigation."

"And what does an observer do if the district prosecutor in Sundsvall decides to close the case?"

"Nothing."

"Then we're agreed." Carlos smiles.

"No," Joona says, walking out of the room.

80

FLORA IS LYING ON HER bed, staring up at the ceiling. Her heart is still racing. She was dreaming that she was in a small room with a girl who didn't want to show her face. The girl was hiding behind a wooden ladder. There was something wrong with her, something dangerous. All she was wearing was a pair of white cotton underpants. She waited for Flora to come closer, then turned away, giggled, and covered her eyes with her hands.

The previous evening, Flora had read about the murders in Sundsvall, about Miranda Ericsdotter and Elisabet Grim. She can't stop thinking about the ghost that visited her. It feels like a dream, but she knows she saw the dead girl in the hallway. The girl couldn't have been more than five years old, but in the dream she just had, the girl was the same age as Miranda.

Flora lies completely still and listens. Every creak in the furniture and floors makes her heart beat faster.

People who are afraid of the dark aren't the masters of their own homes. They creep around, wary of their own movements.

Flora doesn't know what to do. It's seven-forty-five. She sits up, then goes over to the door, opens it, and listens for noises in the apartment.

No one else is awake yet.

She creeps into the kitchen to make Hans-Gunnar's coffee. The morning sun reflects off the scratched countertop.

Flora takes a coffee filter, folds the edges, and places it in the holder. But then she hears sticky footsteps behind her and gets so scared that she holds her breath.

She turns to see Ewa standing in the doorway of her bedroom in a blue T-shirt and underwear.

"What is it?" she asks when she sees Flora's face. "Have you been crying?"

"I . . . I have to ask . . . I think I've seen a ghost," Flora says. "Have you seen her? Here in the apartment. A little girl . . ."

"What's wrong with you, Flora?"

She turns to head into the living room, but Flora puts her hand on her arm and stops her. "But this is real, I swear. . . . Someone hit her with a rock on the back of—"

"You swear," Ewa interrupts sharply.

"I just . . . Can't ghosts be real?"

Ewa grabs her by one ear, holds it tight, and pulls her forward.

"I don't understand why you like telling lies, but you do," Ewa says. "You always have, and you—"

"But I saw—"

"Shut up," Ewa hisses, twisting her ear.

"Ow . . ."

"We're not going to tolerate this," Ewa says, twisting harder.

"Please, stop. . . . Ow!"

Ewa gives Flora's ear a final twist, then lets go. Flora stands there with tears in her eyes, clutching her hand to her stinging ear, as Ewa walks to the living room. After a while, Flora starts the coffeemaker and goes back to her room. She closes the door behind her, turns the light on, and lies down on the bed to cry.

She has always assumed that mediums only pretend to see spirits.

"I don't understand anything," she mutters.

What if she really did summon the ghost with her séances? Maybe it didn't make any difference that she didn't believe in ghosts herself. When she called them and formed a circle with the other participants, the portal to the other side opened, and those who were waiting beyond could just walk through.

Because I really did see a ghost, she thinks. I saw the dead girl as a young child. Miranda wanted to show me something.

It's not impossible. She's read about how the energy of the dead doesn't disappear. Plenty of sane people have claimed that ghosts exist.

Flora tries to gather her thoughts and go through everything that's happened in the past few days.

The girl came to me in a dream, she thinks. I've dreamed about her, I know that, but when I saw her in the hallway I was awake, so it was real. I saw her standing there in front of me, and I heard her speak. I felt her presence.

Flora lies back on the bed, closes her eyes, and wonders if she fainted when she fell and hit her head on the floor.

There was a pair of jeans lying on the floor between the toilet and the bathtub.

I got scared, stumbled backward, and fell.

She is filled with a sudden sense of relief when she realizes that she could have been dreaming the first time she saw the girl.

She must have passed out on the floor and dreamed about the ghost.

That's what happened.

She shuts her eyes again and smiles to herself, but then she notices a strange smell in the room, like burned hair.

She sits up, and shivers when she sees that there's something lying under her pillow. She angles the bedside lamp and folds the pillow back. On her white fitted sheet is a large, sharp rock.

"Why didn't you close your eyes?" a high-pitched voice asks.

The girl is standing in the dark behind the bedside lamp, looking at her without breathing. Her hair is matted and dark with dried blood. The light from the lamp creates a glare, but Flora can see that the girl's thin arms are gray, and her veins form a rusty network under her dead skin.

"You aren't allowed to look at me," the girl says harshly, and turns the light out.

81

WHEN ROBERT ENTERS THE APARTMENT, he finds Elin on her knees beside the shattered display case.

"Elin, what on earth's going on?"

She gets to her feet without looking at him. Blood is running down her left arm into her hand, dripping steadily from three fingertips.

"You're bleeding. . . ."

Elin doesn't respond; she just walks across the broken glass, heading for her bedroom, until he stops her and says he'll call the doctor.

"I don't want you to, I don't care. . . ."

"Elin!" he cries anxiously. "You're bleeding."

She looks at her arm and says maybe it would be a good idea to see a doctor, then goes into her office, leaving a trail of blood behind her.

She sits down at the computer and looks up the number for the National Crime Unit, then calls the main switchboard and asks to speak to whoever is in charge of the investigation into the murders at the Birgitta Home. When the woman has connected her call, Elin repeats her question, then hears a slow intake of breath as someone taps at a keyboard.

"The investigation is being led by the district prosecutor in Sundsvall," the man explains in a high voice.

"Aren't there any police officers I could talk to?"

"The prosecutor is working with the Västernorrland Police."

"I received a visit from a detective with National Crime, a tall man with gray eyes and—"

"Joona Linna."

"Yes, that's him."

Elin picks up a pen and writes the number she's given on the front of a magazine, thanks him for his help, and hangs up.

She quickly dials the detective's number, only to be told that he's away until the next day.

Elin is about to call the district prosecutor's office in Sundsvall when her doctor arrives. He doesn't ask any questions, just washes and dresses Elin's wounds as she sits in silence. She looks at the phone, which is now lying on the August issue of British *Vogue*. Joona Linna's number is written across Gwyneth Paltrow's breasts.

82

ELIN'S FACE IS IMPASSIVE AS she heads slowly down the hall-way leading to Joona's office in police headquarters. She's wearing dark sunglasses to hide the fact that she's been crying. Her graphite-colored trench coat is open, and she's wearing a silver silk shawl over her hair. The deep cuts in her wrist ache.

Her heels click on the shabby floor. She passes a poster with the words "If you think that you're worthless and that bruises are just part of everyday life, you should talk to us." A stocky woman in a bright-red angora sweater and a tight black skirt comes out of a room and waits for her.

"My name is Anja Larsson," the woman says.

Elin tries to say that she wants to talk to Joona Linna, but she finds she can't speak. The woman smiles at her and says she'll show her to the detective's office.

"Sorry," Elin whispers.

"Don't worry," Anja says, leading her to Joona's room, then knocking and opening the door.

"Thanks for the tea," Joona says, pulling up a chair for Elin.

She sits down heavily, and Anja and Joona exchange a brief glance.

"I'll get you some water," Anja says, and leaves them.

Silence settles on the room. Elin tries to calm down enough to speak. After a little while, she says: "I know it's too late. . . ."

I know I didn't help you when you came to see me, and ... and I can guess what you think of me, and ..."

She loses the thread; the corners of her mouth turn down, and tears start to flow, running behind her sunglasses down her cheeks. Anja comes back in with a glass of water and a bunch of damp grapes on a plate, then leaves the room again.

"I'd like to talk about Vicky Bennet now," Elin says in a steady voice.

"I'm listening," he says warmly.

"She was six years old when she came to me, and I ... I had her for nine months. . . ."

"So I understand," he says.

"But what you don't know is that I let her down in an unforgivable way."

"Sometimes we have no choice," Joona says.

She takes her sunglasses off with trembling hands and looks intently at the detective sitting across from her: his fair, messy hair, his serious face, and those constantly changing gray eyes.

"I don't know how to live with what I've done," she says. "But I ... I'd like to make a proposal. . . . I'm happy to cover all the costs so that you can find the bodies, and so that the investigation can continue."

"Why would you do that?" Joona asks.

"Even if I can't make things right, at least I can ... I mean, what if she's innocent?"

"There's no evidence to support that."

"But I just can't believe ..."

Elin stops speaking, and her eyes fill with tears again.

"Because she was so sweet as a child?"

"Most of the time she wasn't." Elin smiles.

"I was starting to get that impression."

"Will you continue the investigation if I pay?"

"We can't accept money from you. . . ."

"I'm sure there's a legal way of arranging it."

"Perhaps, but it wouldn't change anything," Joona explains gently. "The prosecutor is about to close the investigation."

"What can I do?" Elin whispers desperately.

"I shouldn't be telling you this, but I'm going to investigate on my own, because I'm convinced that Vicky is still alive."

"But they said on the news . . . ," Elin whispers, then stands up with one hand over her mouth.

"The car was found at a depth of four meters, and there were blood and strands of hair on the frame of the shattered windshield," he says.

"But you don't believe they're dead?" she asks, quickly wiping the tears from her cheeks.

"I know they didn't drown in the river," he replies.

"Dear God," Elin whispers.

83

ELIN SINKS BACK DOWN IN the chair and sobs. Joona walks over to the window to give her some space. Light rain is falling, and the trees in the park are swaying in the wind.

"Do you have any idea where she might be hiding?" he asks after a while.

"Her mother sleeps in various garages. . . . I met Susie once, when she was going to try taking care of Vicky for a weekend. . . . She had an apartment in Hallonbergen at the time, but that didn't work out. They slept in the subway, and Vicky was found alone in the tunnel between Slussen and Mariatorget."

"So far, it's been difficult to find her," Joona says.

"I haven't seen Vicky for eight years, but the staff at the Birgitta Home—people who've spoken to her—they must know something," Elin says.

"Yes, well . . . ," Joona says, then falls silent.

"What?"

He meets her gaze. "The only people Vicky spoke to were the nurse who was murdered . . . and her husband, who works as a counselor. He probably knows a lot about her . . . or something helpful, at least, but he's in a very bad way, and his doctor won't let the police talk to him. There's nothing I can do about it. The doctor believes being questioned by the police would harm his recovery."

"But I'm not a police officer," Elin says. "I could talk to him."

She looks up at Joona and realizes that was exactly what he was hoping she'd say.

In the elevator down, she feels the heavy, almost drugged exhaustion that comes after a lot of crying. She thinks about the detective's voice, his soft Finnish accent. His eyes are sharp.

His assistant, Anja, called the hospital in Sundsvall and discovered that Daniel Grim was on the psychiatric ward and that the doctor responsible for his care was continuing to impose a strict ban on having the police visit or contact him for the duration of his recuperation.

Elin leaves the building, gets in her BMW, and dials the number for Sundsvall Hospital. She gets put through to Ward 52B and is told that no calls can be put through to Daniel Grim's room, but that visiting hours end at six o'clock.

She taps the address into the GPS, which tells her that it's 375 kilometers away, and that if she leaves now she'll reach the hospital at six-forty-five.

At the first set of traffic lights, Robert calls to remind her about her meeting with Kinnevik and Sven Warg in twenty minutes, over at the Waterfront Expo.

"I'm not going to make it," she says curtly.

"Shall I tell them to start without you?"

"Robert, I don't know when I'll be back, but it won't be today."

84

JOONA IS CERTAIN THAT Vicky Bennet and the little boy are alive.

A girl who has beaten two people to death, and slashed the faces of two others with a broken bottle, has now kidnapped a young boy and gone into hiding with him somewhere.

Everyone else thinks that they're already dead. No one is looking for them.

Joona thinks back to where he was with his investigation when Sonja Rask called to tell him about the security-camera footage at the gas station. He had just spoken to Caroline, one of the girls from the Birgitta Home, who told him that Vicky took Zyprexa, a medicine used to treat schizophrenia and manic episodes.

Joona has checked on the drug with The Needle's wife, a psychiatrist.

There are still too many pieces missing, he thinks. But it's possible that Vicky overdosed on Zyprexa.

Caroline had said that just licking a pill could make your skin crawl, and overdosing would make you furious.

He closes his eyes and tries to imagine Vicky demanding the keys. She would have threatened Elisabet with the hammer, gotten angry, and just started hitting her, over and over. Then Vicky took the keys from the dead woman and unlocked the door to the isolation room. Miranda was sitting on the chair with the comforter wrapped around her shoulders when Vicky went in and smashed her head in with a rock. She dragged her over to the bed and positioned her hands over her face.

And only then did Vicky's rage start to subside.

Vicky got confused, took the blood-soaked comforter with her, and hid it under her bed just as the tranquilizing effect of the drug kicked in. She probably felt incredibly tired, kicked off her boots in her closet, hid the hammer under her pillow, and fell asleep. Then, a few hours later, she woke up, realized what she'd done, got scared, escaped through the window, and ran off into the forest.

The medication could explain the rage and the fact that she fell asleep on those bloodstained sheets afterward.

But what did she do with the rock? Was there even a rock?

Once again, Joona feels very unsure. For only the second time in his life, he finds himself wondering if Nils might be mistaken.

85

At five-fifty-five, Elin enters Ward 52B, stops a nurse, and says she's there to see Daniel Grim.

"Visiting time is over," the woman replies.

"In five minutes," Elin says with a smile.

"We usually stop letting people in at five-forty-five, to keep things manageable."

"I've driven here from Stockholm," she pleads.

The nurse stops and looks at her with a hesitant expression on her face.

"If we start making exceptions for everyone, we'll have people here all hours of the day and night," she says sternly.

"Please, just let me . . ."

"You won't even have time for a cup of coffee."

"That doesn't matter," Elin assures her.

The nurse still looks dubious but gestures for Elin to follow her, heads off to the right, and knocks on the door to one of the patients' rooms.

"Thanks," Elin says, then waits for the nurse to leave before going in.

An ashen-faced middle-aged man in jeans is standing over by the window. He looks at her uncertainly as he runs one hand through his thin hair.

"My name is Elin Frank," she says gently. "I know I'm disturbing you, and I'm sorry about that."

"No, it's . . . it's . . ."

He looks as if he's been crying for days. In another context, she would have found him very attractive: friendly features, an air of maturity and intelligence.

"I need to speak to you, but I'll understand if you don't feel up to it."

"Don't worry," he says in a voice that sounds as if it might break at any moment. "The papers were all here the first few days, but I couldn't talk then, I couldn't bear to, there was nothing to say. . . . I mean, I'd like to help the police, but that hasn't gone too well, either. . . . I can't seem to focus my thoughts."

Elin tries to find a way to start talking about Vicky. She realizes that Daniel must think the girl is a monster, because she's ruined his life—it's not going to be easy to persuade him to help.

"Is it okay if I come in for a few minutes?"

"To be honest, I don't know," he says, rubbing his face.

"Daniel, I'm so sorry about what happened to you."

He whispers his thanks and sits down, then looks up.

"It hasn't really sunk in," he says slowly. "It's so unreal, because I was so worried about Elisabet's heart condition . . . and . . ."

His face goes blank, turning gray again.

"I can't imagine what you're going through," she says quietly.

"I've got a psychiatrist of my own now," he says with a broken smile. "I'd never have believed that, that I'd ever need a psychiatrist. . . . He listens to me, sits and waits while I cry. I feel . . . You know, he won't let the police question me. I'd probably have made the same decision in his shoes . . . but, at the same time, I know myself—I'll be all right. Maybe I should tell him that I think I could handle talking to them . . . not that I know if I could be of any use. . . ."

"It probably makes sense to listen to your psychologist," she says.

"Do I sound that confused?" He smiles.

"No, but . . ."

"Sometimes I think of something that I should maybe tell the police, but then I forget it again, because I ... It's strange, but I can't quite gather my thoughts; it's like when you feel really exhausted."

"I'm sure that will improve."

He wipes his nose, then looks up at her again.

"Did I ask what paper you write for?"

She shakes her head and says, "I'm here because Vicky Bennet lived with me when she was six years old."

86

Daniel blinks behind his glasses and purses his mouth, as if he's summoning all his strength to understand what she's just said.

"I heard about her on the news . . . about the car and the boy," he whispers after a while.

"I know," she replies in a subdued voice. "But . . . if she was still alive, where do you think she'd hide?"

"Why are you asking me that?"

"I don't know. . . . I'd like to know who she trusted."

He looks at her for a few seconds before asking, "You don't believe she's dead?"

"No," she replies quietly.

"You don't believe it because you don't want to," he says. "But is there any evidence to suggest that she didn't drown?"

"Don't be alarmed," she says. "But we're fairly sure she got out of the water."

"We?"

"Me and a detective."

"I don't understand. . . . Why are they saying she drowned if she . . . ?"

"They think she did—most people still believe she drowned—the police have stopped looking for her and the boy. . . ."

"But not you?"

"I might be the only person who really cares about Vicky," Elin says.

She can't bring herself to smile at him, can't bring herself to make her voice soft and amenable.

"And now you want my help to find her?"

"She could hurt the boy," Elin says tentatively. "Or someone else."

"Maybe, but I don't think so," Daniel says, looking at her with an unguarded expression. "Right from the start, I doubted that she killed Miranda. I still can't believe it. . . ."

Daniel's mouth continues moving slowly, but no sound comes out.

"What are you saying?" she asks gently.

"What?"

"You were whispering something," she says.

"I don't believe Vicky killed Elisabet."

"You don't believe . . ."

"I've worked with troubled girls for many years, and I . . . It just doesn't make sense."

"But . . ."

"In my time as a counselor, I've encountered a number of really ill patients who . . . who had it in them to murder. . . ."

"But not Vicky?"

"No."

Elin smiles and feels her eyes well up with tears; then she gets her feelings under control.

"You have to tell that to the police," she says.

"I already have. They know that I don't think Vicky is violent. Of course, I could be wrong," Daniel says, and rubs his eyes hard.

"Can you help me?"

"Did you say that Vicky lived with you for six years?"

"No, she was six years old when she lived with me," she replies.

"What do you want me to do?"

"I have to find her, Daniel. . . . You've spent hours talking to her; you must know something about her friends, boyfriends . . . anything at all."

"Yes, maybe . . . We spent a lot of time talking about group dynamics, and . . . I'm sorry, I'm having trouble getting my thoughts straight."

"Try."

"I saw her most days, and I suppose we had . . . I don't know, a couple dozen sessions. . . . Vicky, she's . . . The problem with her is that she often drifts off—in her mind, I mean. . . . I'd be most concerned that she might just leave the boy somewhere, in the middle of the road. . . ."

"Where could she be hiding? Was there ever a particular family that she liked?"

87

THE DOOR OPENS, AND THE nurse comes in with Daniel's medication for the evening. She stops abruptly, and her neck stiffens as if she's seen something indecent; then she turns to face Elin.

"What's going on?" the nurse says. "You were supposed to stay five minutes, no longer."

"I know," Elin replies. "But it's really important that I—"

"It's almost six-thirty," she interrupts.

"Sorry," Elin says, and quickly turns back to Daniel. "Where should I start looking for . . . ?"

"Get out!" the nurse shouts.

"Please," Elin says quietly, putting her hands together beseechingly. "I really do need to—"

"Are you deaf?" the nurse snaps. "I told you to leave. . . ."

The nurse curses and leaves the room, and Elin grabs Daniel's arm.

"Vicky must have mentioned places, friends?"

"Yes, of course, but I can't think of anything. I'm having trouble . . ."

"Please, try."

"I know I'm being completely useless, I should remember something, but . . ." Daniel raps at his forehead.

"How about the other girls—they must know something about Vicky?"

"Yes, they should. . . . Caroline, maybe . . ."

A man in a white uniform comes into the room with the nurse.

"I'm going to have to ask you to leave," the man says.

"Just give me a minute," Elin says.

"No, you're coming with me right now," he says.

"Please," Elin says, looking him in the eye. "This is about my daughter. . . ."

"Come on," he says, slightly more gently.

Elin's mouth quivers, and she sinks to her knees in front of them.

"Just give me a few more minutes," she begs.

"We'll drag you out if we—"

"No! That's enough!" Daniel says in a loud voice. He helps Elin up from the floor.

The nurse protests. "She's not allowed to be on the ward after—"

"Shut up," Daniel snaps, and leads Elin out of the room. "We can talk down at the entrance or out in the parking lot."

They walk together along the hallway. Though they can hear footsteps behind them, they just keep walking.

"I'm thinking of going to talk to the girls at the Birgitta Home," Elin says.

"They're not there—they've been moved," Daniel tells her.

"Where to?"

He holds a glass door open for her, then follows her through.

"To an old fishing village north of Hudiksvall."

Elin presses the button for the elevator.

"Will I be let in if I go?" she asks.

"No, but you will if I come with you."

88

Daniel is sitting next to Elin in her BMW. When they pull out onto the highway, she calls Joona.

"Sorry to bother you," she says in a slightly desperate tone.

"You can call whenever you want," Joona replies amiably.

"I'm sitting here with Daniel, and he doesn't think Vicky did those terrible things," Elin explains quickly.

"All the forensic evidence points to her, and all—"

"But it doesn't make sense, because Daniel says she isn't violent," she interrupts agitatedly.

"She's probably capable of being violent," Joona says.

"You don't know her," Elin says, almost shouting.

Neither of them speaks for a moment. Then Joona says calmly, "Ask Daniel about the drug Zyprexa."

"Zyprexa?"

Daniel looks at her.

"Ask him about the side effects," Joona says, and hangs up.

She speeds along the road, which winds from the coast into the vast forests.

"What are the side effects?" she asks in a quiet voice.

"Patients can become aggressive if they exceed the maximum dose," Daniel says factually.

"Was Vicky taking it?"

He nods, and Elin doesn't say anything.

"It's a good drug," Daniel tries to explain, but gives up.

Almost all the light from the headlights is absorbed by the trees at the edge of the forest.

"You know you said that Vicky was your daughter?" Daniel asks.

"I know," she replies. "Back at the hospital. It just slipped out. . . ."

"She was your daughter for a while, though."

"Yes, she was," Elin says, keeping her eyes on the road.

They pass Armsjön, its expanse of water glistening like molten iron in the gloom. Daniel takes a deep breath. "I was just thinking about something Vicky said when she first arrived. . . . But now I can't remember," he says, and thinks for a while. "I've got it. She talked about some Chilean friends who had a house. . . ."

He stops and looks out the side window, wiping tears from his cheeks.

"Elisabet and I were planning to go to Chile, before the 2016 earthquake. . . ."

He lets out a deep sigh and sits still, with his hands in his lap.

"You were talking about Vicky," Elin prompts.

"Oh, yes . . . What was I saying?"

"That she had Chilean friends."

"Yes . . ."

"And that they had a house somewhere."

"Did I say that?"

"Yes."

"Damn it," he mumbles. "What's wrong with me? I mean . . . this is ridiculous—I should have stayed in the hospital."

Elin smiles gently at him.

"I'm glad you didn't."

89

THE GRAVEL ROAD WINDS THROUGH the dark forest, past sunken barns and traditional farms. Eventually, the road opens up onto a landscape of rust-red houses, with the sea stretching out beyond. The Midsummer pole is still standing, decked with brown birch leaves and dead flowers. The nearest building is a large wooden house with a beautiful glass-enclosed sunroom overlooking the water. It used to be a store but has been used for the past few years as a group home.

The car rolls gently through the gates, and when Elin unbuckles her seat belt, Daniel says somberly: "You need to be prepared for . . . These girls, they've had rough lives." He nudges his glasses up his nose. "They push at boundaries and will try to provoke a reaction."

"I can handle that," Elin says. "I was a teenager myself."

"This is different, I promise," he says. "It isn't easy—not even for me. They really can be fucking awful at times."

"So what's the best way to respond if they try being provocative?" she asks, looking him in the eye.

"The best response is to be honest, and unambiguous. . . ."

"I'll remember that," she says, opening the car door.

"Wait. I just need . . . Before we go in . . . ," he says. "They have a security guard, and I think he should stick with you the whole time."

Elin smiles briefly. "Isn't that a little much?"

"I don't know, maybe. . . . I don't mean to scare you, but . . . I just don't think you should be alone with two of the girls, not even for a moment."

"Which ones?"

Daniel hesitates, then says, "Almira, and a girl named Tuula."

"Are they really that dangerous?"

He holds his hand up. "I just want you to have the guard with you when you talk to them."

"Okay."

"Don't worry," he says reassuringly. "They're all fine, really."

They get out of the car. The air is still mild and carries the smell of the sea.

"One of the girls must know something about Vicky's friends," Elin says.

"That doesn't mean they'll feel like talking."

A black slate path leads around the house to a flight of steps that go up to the porch.

Elin's red high-heeled sandals stick in the wet grass between the stones. It's late evening, but one girl is smoking in the swing by a large lilac. Her bare face and tattooed arms shine white in the gloom.

"Hello, Almira," Daniel says. "This is Elin."

"Hi." Elin smiles.

Almira looks at her but doesn't return the smile. Her thick black eyebrows meet above her large nose, and her cheeks are covered with dark spots.

"Vicky killed his wife," Almira suddenly says, looking Elin in the eye. "And once Elisabet was dead, she killed Miranda. . . . I don't think she'll stop until we're all dead."

90

ELIN AND DANIEL FOLLOW ALMIRA into an old-fashioned kitchen equipped with copper pans, rugs on the scrubbed floor, and a pantry in the corner. Lu Chu and Indie are sitting at a pine table eating ice cream straight from the carton and looking through old comics.

"Good that you're here," Indie says when she catches sight of Daniel. "You need to talk to Tuula. She's really crazy now. I think she needs to go back on the medication."

"Where's Solveig?" he asks.

"She went off somewhere," Almira replies, taking a spoon from a drawer.

"When did she go?" Daniel asks skeptically.

"Just after we'd eaten," Lu Chu mutters without taking her eyes off the comic.

"So only the security guard's here?"

"Anders," Almira says, sitting down on Lu Chu's lap. "He was only here the first two nights."

"What?" Daniel says, astonished. "What are you saying? Are you here alone?"

Almira shrugs and starts to eat some ice cream.

"I need to know," Daniel says.

"Solveig said she'd be back," Indie says.

"For heaven's sake, it's eight o'clock," Daniel says, taking out his phone.

He calls the management company and gets transferred to an after-hours number. When there's no answer, he leaves an irritated message telling them that they have a responsibility to place qualified staff on duty.

While Daniel is on the phone, Elin looks at the girls. Almira is sitting on the lap of a pretty girl with East Asian features and acne all over her round face. She's reading an old copy of *Mad* and keeps kissing the back of Almira's neck.

"Almira," Elin says, "where do you think Vicky's hiding?"

"Don't know," she replies, licking her spoon.

"Vicky's dead, for fuck's sake," Indie says. "Haven't you heard? She killed herself, and a little boy."

"Shit," Lu Chu exclaims, pointing at Elin with a smile. "I recognize you. . . . Aren't you, like, the richest person in Sweden?"

"Stop that," Daniel says.

"Fuck, I swear," Lu Chu goes on, drumming the table, and then yells out loud, "I want lots of money, too!"

"Lower your voice, please."

"I just recognized her, that's all," she says quickly. "I can say that."

"You can say whatever you want," Daniel says calmly.

"We want to know if you have any idea where Vicky was planning to hide," Elin says.

"I know she kept to herself most of the time," Daniel says. "But you talked to her sometimes, and you don't have to be best friends to have an idea where she might have gone. . . . I mean, I know what your ex's name is, Indie, for instance."

"We're back together," she says with a smile.

"When did that happen?" he asks.

"I called him yesterday, and we talked it out," she says.

"Good for you," Daniel says, smiling. "I'm glad."

"Toward the end, Vicky really only hung out with Miranda," Indie says.

"And Caroline," Daniel says.

"Because they all did ADL together," Indie adds.

"Who's Caroline?" Elin asks.

"One of the older girls," Daniel says. "She had Activities of Daily Life training with Vicky."

"I don't see why anyone's concerned about Vicky," Almira says loudly. "I mean, she slaughtered Miranda like she was a little pig."

"We don't know that," Elin tries to say.

"We don't know?!" Almira echoes harshly. "You should have seen her. She was fucking dead, I swear—there was so much fucking blood. . . ."

"Don't yell," Daniel says.

"So what? What the fuck are we supposed to say? Are we supposed to say nothing happened?" Indie says in a loud voice. "Are we supposed to say that Miranda's alive, that Elisabet's alive . . . ?"

"I just mean . . ."

"You weren't fucking there!" Almira screams. "Vicky smashed Elisabet's head in with a fucking hammer, but you think she's alive."

"Let's try to talk one at a time," Daniel says with hard-won calm.

Indie holds her hand up like a schoolgirl.

"Elisabet was a fucking junkie," she says. "I hate junkies, and I—"

Almira grins. "Just because your mom fucking overdosed—"

"One at a time, Almira," Daniel interrupts, quickly wiping the tears from his cheeks.

"I don't give a shit about Elisabet; she can burn in hell, for all I care. I don't give a damn," Indie concludes.

"How can you say that?" Elin asks.

"We heard her that night," Lu Chu lies. "She screamed for help for so long, but we just sat in bed and listened."

"She screamed and screamed." Almira grins.

Daniel turns toward the wall. Silence settles on the kitchen.

He sits motionless for a while, then wipes his face with his sleeve and turns around.

"You know you're being cruel," he says.

"Fun, though," Almira says.

"You think?"

"Yes."

"How about you, Lu Chu?"

She shrugs her shoulders.

"You don't know?"

"No."

"We've talked about situations like this," he says.

"Okay . . . Sorry, that was mean."

He tries to smile reassuringly at her but just looks upset.

"Where's Caroline?" Elin asks.

"In her room," Lu Chu says.

"Can you show us the way?"

91

AN ICE-COLD HALLWAY LEADS FROM the kitchen to a living room with an open fireplace and a dining room facing the sea. One side of the hallway is lined with doors leading to the girls' rooms. Lu Chu is walking ahead of Elin in baggy sweatpants and worn-out sneakers. She points out her own room and Tuula's before stopping in front of a door with a colorful little porcelain bell tied to the handle.

"This is Carro's room."

"Thanks," Elin says.

"It's starting to get late," Daniel says to Lu Chu. "Go and brush your teeth and get ready for bed."

She hesitates for a few seconds, then heads for the bathroom. When Daniel knocks on the door, the porcelain bell tinkles gently. The door opens, and a young woman looks at Daniel wide-eyed, then gives him a tentative hug.

"Can we come in?" he asks gently.

"Of course," she says, and holds out her hand. "Caroline."

Elin shakes the girl's thin hand, holding it in hers for a moment. Caroline's pale face is freckled and carefully made up, her sand-colored eyebrows are plucked, and her straight hair is gathered into a thick ponytail.

The wallpaper in the room is brightly patterned; there's a chest of drawers by the window, and on one wall is a picture of an old fisherman in a rain hat, smoking a pipe.

"We're here to talk about Vicky," Daniel says, sitting down on the neatly made bed.

"I was Vicky's foster mother many years ago," Elin says.

"When she was little?"

Elin nods, and Caroline bites her lip and looks out the window, which faces away from the sea.

"You know Vicky," Elin says after a while.

"I don't think she really allowed herself to trust people," Caroline says, smiling. "But I liked her. . . . She was calm and had a really sick sense of humor."

Elin clears her throat and asks: "Did she ever talk about people she met? Maybe she had a boyfriend somewhere, friends?"

"We hardly ever talk about old crap in here, because people use it as ammunition."

"Good things, then—what were her dreams, what did she want to do when she got out?"

"Sometimes we used to talk about working abroad," Caroline says. "You know, the Red Cross, Save the Children—of course, who'd employ us?"

"You were thinking of doing it together?"

"It was just talk," Caroline says patiently.

"Something I was thinking about," Daniel says, rubbing his forehead. "I was off duty that evening, but I understand that Miranda was in the isolation room—do you know why?"

"She'd hit Tuula," Caroline says factually.

"What for?"

The girl shrugs. "Because she deserved it—she keeps stealing things. She took my earrings yesterday, said they wanted to be with her instead."

"What did she take from Miranda?"

"When we went swimming, she took Vicky's bag; then, later that evening, she took one of Miranda's hair clips."

"She took Vicky's bag?" Elin asks in a tense voice.

"She gave it back, but she kept something. . . . I didn't really understand what, but it was something Vicky had been given by her mother."

"Did Vicky get angry with Tuula?" Elin asks.

"No."

"Vicky and Caroline never get involved in any arguments," Daniel says, patting Caroline's thin arm.

"Daniel, we need you," Caroline says, looking at him in an open, honest way. "You have to take care of us."

"I'll be back soon," he replies. "I want to, but I . . . I'm not quite well enough to. . . ."

When Daniel starts to pull his hand away from her arm she tries to hold on to it.

"But you *are* going to come back, aren't you?"

"Yes, I am."

They walk out, leaving Caroline standing in the middle of her room, looking abandoned.

92

DANIEL KNOCKS ON TUULA'S DOOR. They wait for a while, but there's no answer, so they start to walk back toward the living room.

"Remember what I told you before," Daniel says gravely.

The open fireplace is dark and cold. A few dirty plates have been left on the table. The harbor is dimly visible through the large windows. The rows of silvery, sun-bleached fishing sheds are reflected in the water. It's a beautiful view, but the small red-haired girl has turned her chair to face the white-painted wooden paneling instead.

"Hello, Tuula," Daniel says brightly.

The girl turns her pale eyes to them. Her hunted expression disappears, replaced by something less easily defined.

"I've got a fever," she mutters, turning to face the wall again.

"Nice view."

"Isn't it?" she replies, staring into the wall.

Elin sees her smile before she gets serious again.

"I need to talk to you," Daniel says.

"Go ahead."

"I want to see your face while we talk."

"Should I cut it off?"

"It's easier to turn your chair."

She sighs deeply, turns the chair, and sits down again with an impassive expression.

"You took Vicky's bag on Friday," Elin says.

"What?" she exclaims. "What did you say? What the fuck did you say?"

Daniel tries to smooth things over. "She was wondering—"

"Shut up!" Tuula screams.

They sit in silence, and Tuula purses her lips and picks at one of her cuticles.

"You took Vicky's bag," Elin repeats.

"You're such a fucking liar," Tuula says in a low voice, looking down at the floor.

She's sitting perfectly still, with a sad look on her face. Her body is trembling. Elin leans forward to pat her on the cheek. "I don't mean . . ."

Tuula grabs Elin's hair, picks up a fork from the table, and tries to stab Elin in the face, but Daniel manages to catch her hand in time. He holds Tuula tight as she struggles and kicks and screams: "Fucking cunt, I'm going to beat all the fucking—"

Tuula starts sobbing hoarsely, and Daniel holds her still. He sits with her on his lap, and after a while she calms down. Elin has moved away and is massaging the sore spot on her scalp.

"You only borrowed the bag, I know," Daniel says.

"There was nothing but garbage in it anyway," Tuula replies. "I should have set it on fire."

"So there was nothing in the bag that wanted to be with you?" Daniel asks.

"Just the flower button," the girl says, meeting his gaze.

"That sounds nice—can I see it?"

"A tiger's guarding it."

"Wow."

"You can nail me to the wall," she mutters.

"Was there anything else that wanted to be with you?"

"I should have set Vicky on fire when we were in the forest. . . ."

While Tuula talks to Daniel, Elin walks through the living room and out into the cold hallway. It's dark and empty. She looks back to make sure that Daniel is still talking to the girl, then goes into Tuula's small room.

93

ELIN IS STANDING IN A room with a single window. A table lamp is lying on its side on the floor, its weak glow illuminating the room.

On the wall is an embroidered sampler with the words "We are the best of each other" on it.

Elin thinks about how Tuula licked her dry lips when she tried to stab her with the fork, and how her body shook with the effort.

The room has a strangely cloying, rancid smell.

Elin hopes that Daniel realizes she's in Tuula's room and that he can keep Tuula distracted in the living room.

On the narrow cot, which has no sheets or mattress, there's a small red suitcase lying directly on the slats. Carefully, she walks over and opens it. The suitcase contains a photograph album, a few crumpled clothes, some bottles of cheap perfume, and a candy wrapper.

Elin closes the suitcase again and looks around the room. The chest of drawers has been moved half a meter away from the wall. The sheets, pillows, and comforter are behind it. Tuula has been sleeping there instead of on the bed.

Elin moves cautiously, stopping when a floorboard creaks, before reaching the chest and pulling out the drawers, but all she finds are mangled sheets and small fabric bags of dried lavender.

Though she lifts the sheets, she doesn't find anything else. She pushes the bottom drawer back softly and is just standing up again when she hears footsteps in the hallway. She stands still, trying to breathe silently, then hears the little porcelain bell on Caroline's door tinkle, before everything gets quiet again.

Elin waits a few moments, then goes around the chest of drawers and looks at the bedclothes and pillows in the gloom. The smell seems stronger now. As she lifts the mattress, a definite odor of decay rises up. There are scraps of old food on a sheet of newspaper: moldy bread, some chicken bones, brown apples, dried-up sausages, and fried potatoes.

94

TUULA MUTTERS THAT SHE'S TIRED, wriggles out of Daniel's grasp, and goes over to the big windows, where she licks the glass.

"Did you ever overhear Vicky say anything?" Daniel asks.

"Like what?"

"If she had any secret places, anywhere she . . ."

"No," she replies, turning toward him.

"But you do sometimes listen to the older girls?"

"So do you."

"I know, but I'm having trouble remembering things right now. The doctors say it's because of acute trauma," he explains.

"But it's not dangerous?"

He shakes his head but can't bring himself to smile.

"I'm seeing a psychiatrist, and I'm taking medication."

"You shouldn't be sad," she says, tilting her head to one side. "It was probably a good thing that Miranda and Elisabet were murdered . . . because there are too many people in the world anyway."

"But I loved Elisabet. I needed her, and . . ."

Tuula hits the back of her head against the window, making the glass rattle. A diagonal crack appears in one of the panes.

"I think it would be best if I went to my room and hid behind the chest of drawers," she says.

95

ELIN IS KNEELING DOWN IN front of a hand-painted trunk at the end of the bed in Tuula's room. The words "Fritz Gustavsson 1861 Harmånger" are written on the lid in an ornate font. When Elin tries to open the lid, she loses her grip and breaks a nail. She tries again, but the trunk is locked.

She hears what sounds like a window breaking in the sun-room, then, a second later, hears Tuula scream until her voice cracks.

Elin shivers and walks over to the window. There's an array of small boxes on the windowsill, some tin, some porcelain. She opens two of them. One is empty; the other contains some old packing twine.

In another porcelain jar she finds some old copper coins, then picks up a tin with a colorful harlequin on one side. She takes the lid off, tips the contents into her hand, and just has time to see some nails and a dead bumblebee when she catches sight of movement out of the corner of her eye. She looks outside again and feels her racing pulse in her temples. Everything is quiet. The weak glow from the next room is still shining on the nettles. All she can hear is the sound of her own breathing. Suddenly a figure passes through the light, and Elin drops the tin on the floor and moves to one side.

The small window is dark; she realizes that someone could be standing outside right in front of it, looking at her.

She has just decided to get out of Tuula's room when she happens to see a small sticker in the middle of the closet door. She goes over and sees that it has a picture of Tigger from *Winnie-the-Pooh* on it.

Tuula said that a tiger was guarding the flower button.

Inside the closet, a worn raincoat is hanging from a hook in front of an old-fashioned vacuum cleaner. With trembling hands, she pulls the vacuum cleaner out. Beneath it are some flattened sneakers and a grubby pillowcase. She pulls at one corner of the pillowcase and immediately feels how heavy it is.

She tips it over, and the sparkling contents rattle onto the floor: coins, buttons, hair ties, glass marbles, a glinting SIM card from a cell phone, a ballpoint pen, bottle caps, earrings, and a key chain attached to a small plate of metal with a pale-blue flower on it. Elin turns this over in her hand and sees the name "Dennis" engraved on the metal.

This must be what Caroline mentioned, the thing Vicky's mother gave her.

Elin puts the key chain in her pocket and quickly looks through the other things as she puts them back in the pillowcase. She puts everything back in the closet, presses the vacuum cleaner down on top, and adjusts the raincoat before closing the closet. She hurries over to the door, listens for a moment, then walks out.

Tuula is standing outside.

She is waiting in the gloomy corridor just a few steps away, looking at Elin without saying a word.

96

Tuula takes a step forward and shows Elin her bloody hand. Her face is pale, and there's an expectant look in her eyes. Her white eyebrows are invisible. Her red hair is hanging lankly around her face.

"Go back into the room," Tuula says.

"I have to talk to Daniel."

"We can go in together and hide," the girl says in a harsh voice.

"Why? What happened?"

"Go into the room," she repeats, and licks her lips.

"Do you want to show me something?"

"Yes," she replies quickly.

"What?"

"It's a game. . . . Vicky and Miranda played it last week," Tuula says, holding her hands in front of her face.

"I have to go," Elin says.

"Come on, I'll show you how to do it," Tuula whispers.

Elin hears steps in the hallway and sees Daniel with a first-aid box in his hand. Lu Chu and Almira come out from the kitchen. Tuula feels the back of her head and gets more blood on her fingers.

"Tuula, you were going to sit and wait on the chair," Daniel says, leading her toward the kitchen. "We need to clean the wound and see if you need stitches. . . ."

Elin stands completely still, letting her heartbeat slow down. In her pocket, she can feel Vicky's key chain.

After a while, the kitchen door opens again. Tuula walks out slowly, trailing her hand along the wooden paneling. Daniel is walking beside her, speaking in a calm voice. She nods and disappears into her room. Elin waits until Daniel comes over to her before asking what happened.

"It's nothing serious. . . . She banged her head against the window a few times until the glass broke."

"Has Vicky ever mentioned anyone named Dennis?" Elin says in a subdued voice, and shows him the key chain.

He turns it over in his hand and whispers the name to himself. "It feels like I've heard the name before," he says. "But I . . . Elin, I feel so ashamed, I'm so useless. . . ."

"You're trying. . . ."

"Yes, but who knows whether Vicky ever told me anything that could help the police? She didn't really talk much, and . . ."

He stops speaking when they hear heavy steps outside. The front door opens, and a large woman in her fifties comes in and is about to lock the door when she catches sight of them.

"You're not allowed to be here," she says, approaching them.

"My name is Daniel Grim, I'm—"

"The girls can't have visitors at this time of night," the woman interrupts.

"We're just leaving," he says. "But first we just want to ask Caroline about—"

"You're not asking anyone anything."

97

On his way up to his office, Joona looks at the key chain that Elin Frank couriered to him from Sundsvall. It's in a small plastic bag and looks like a silver dollar, but it has the name "Dennis" engraved on one side and a pale-blue flower with seven petals on the other. A sturdy key chain is attached to it through a hole at the top.

Joona turns it over several times before putting it in his jacket pocket and getting out on the fifth floor.

He's pondering why Vicky's mother would have given her a key chain with the name "Dennis" on it.

There's no record of Vicky's father's name. Maybe her mother had always known who the father was? And this was her way of telling Vicky?

Joona goes in to see Anja, to find out whether she's found anything. He doesn't even have a chance to open his mouth before she says: "There's no one named Dennis in Vicky Bennet's life at all. Not at the Birgitta Home, not at Ljungbacken, and not in any of the families she's stayed with."

"Strange," Joona says.

"I even called Saga Bauer," Anja says with a smile. "The Security Police have their own databases."

"Someone must know who this Dennis is," he says, sitting down on a corner of her desk.

"Apparently not." She sighs, drumming disconsolately at the desk with her fingernails.

Joona looks out the window. Clouds are racing across the sky.

"I'm stuck," he says simply. "I can't ask to see the report from the National Forensics Lab, I can't conduct official interviews, and I've got nothing to go on."

"Maybe you should accept the fact that it isn't your case," Anja says quietly.

"I can't," he whispers.

Anja smiles, and her round cheeks flush.

"In the absence of anything better, I want you to listen to something," she says. "And it's not Finnish tango this time."

"Why would I think that?"

"But you did, though, didn't you?" she mutters, and clicks something on her computer. "This is a phone call I received today."

"You record your calls?"

"Yes," she says in a neutral voice.

A thin female voice fills the room.

"Sorry I keep calling," the woman says, almost breathlessly. "I spoke to a police officer in Sundsvall, and he said that a detective named Joona Linna might be interested in . . ."

"You can talk to me," Anja's voice says.

"As long as you just listen, because I . . . I need to say something important about the murders at the Birgitta Home."

"The police have a dedicated line for tips," Anja explains.

"I know," the woman says quickly.

A Japanese cat is waving on Anja's desk. Joona can hear the ticking of the mechanism as he listens to the woman's voice.

"I saw the girl; she didn't want to show her face," she says. "And there was a bloodstained rock. You have to look for the rock. . . ."

"Are you saying you saw the murder?" Anja says.

The woman's heavy, short breathing is clearly audible. "I don't know why I saw her," she says. "I'm scared and I'm really tired, but I'm not crazy."

"Do you mean you saw the murder?"

"Maybe I am crazy," the woman goes on in a shaky voice, without appearing to hear Anja's question.

The call ends abruptly.

"The woman's name is Flora Hansen, and someone filed a report against her."

"What for?"

Anja shrugs her round shoulders.

"Brittis, who works the tip line, thought . . . Apparently, Flora Hansen has called in with tons of fake information, trying to get paid for it."

"Is she a regular caller?"

"No, she's only called about the Birgitta Home. . . . I thought you should hear this before she calls you, because she will. She doesn't seem likely to back down. She's still calling even though she's been reported, and now she's somehow gotten hold of my number."

"What do you know about her?" Joona asks thoughtfully.

"Brittis said Flora has a cast-iron alibi for the night of the murders. She was holding a séance attended by nine people at 40 Upplands Street here in Stockholm," Anja says with noticeable amusement. "Flora calls herself a spiritual medium and claims she can ask the dead questions if she gets paid."

"I'll go and see her," he says, heading for the door.

"Joona, I just wanted to show you that people are aware of the case," she says with a hesitant smile. "And sooner or later we'll get a tip. . . . If Vicky Bennet is alive, someone's bound to see her."

"Yes," he says, buttoning his jacket.

Anja is about to laugh, but she sees the look in Joona's eyes and realizes what he's picked up on.

"The rock," she says in a low voice. "Is that accurate?"

"Yes," he replies, looking her in the eye. "But so far the only people who know about it are me and two pathologists."

98

ALTHOUGH IT'S RELATIVELY UNUSUAL IN Sweden, the police have sought the help of spiritual mediums on a number of occasions. Joona recalls the Engla Höglund murder investigation, where a medium provided a detailed description of two murderers. The descriptions later turned out to be completely false. The real killer was eventually caught because someone who was trying out a new camera happened to take a photograph that captured the girl and the murderer's car.

A while back, Joona read somewhere that independent research had been conducted in the United States into the medium who had been consulted by the police more times than any other in the world. The report concluded that she hadn't contributed information of value to any of the 115 cases she had participated in.

The chilly afternoon sun has turned to evening shadows, and Joona shivers when he gets out of the car and walks over to a gray apartment complex with satellite dishes on the balconies. The lock on the main entrance is broken, and someone has tagged the entire entrance with pink spray paint. Joona takes the stairs up to the second floor and rings the doorbell on the apartment with the name "Hansen" on it.

A thin woman in worn gray clothes opens the door and looks at him bashfully.

"My name is Joona Linna," Joona says, showing his ID. "You've called the police several times. . . ."

"Sorry," she whispers, and looks down at the floor.

"You shouldn't call unless you have something to tell us."

"But I . . . I called because I've seen the dead girl," she says, meeting his gaze.

"Can I come in?"

She nods and leads him through a dimly lit hall with a faded linoleum floor into a small, clean kitchen. Flora sits down on one of the four chairs at the table and wraps her arms around herself. Joona goes over to the window and looks out. The façade of the building across the way is covered with plastic. The thermometer that's been screwed to the outside of the window is swaying slightly in the wind.

"I think Miranda is coming to me because she knows I'm the one who let her through when I was holding a séance," Flora begins. "But I . . . I don't really know what she wants."

"When was this séance?" Joona asks.

"I hold one every week. . . . I make my living talking to the dead," she says, and a tiny muscle starts to twitch at the corner of her right eye.

"So do I, in a way," Joona replies calmly.

He sits down across from her.

"We're out of coffee," she whispers.

"That doesn't matter," he says. "You mentioned a rock when you called. . . ."

"Miranda keeps showing me a bloodstained rock."

She indicates its size with her hands.

"So you were holding a séance," he says gently, "and then a girl appeared and told you—"

"No, it wasn't then," she interrupts. "It was after the séance, when I got home."

"And what did the girl say?"

Flora meets his gaze, and her eyes look black as she loses herself in the memory.

"She shows me the rock and tells me to close my eyes."

Joona looks at her impassively.

"If Miranda shows up again, I'd like you to ask her where the murderer is hiding," he says simply.

99

Joona removes the little plastic bag holding Vicky's key chain from his pocket, opens it, and tips it onto the table in front of Flora.

"This belongs to the suspected murderer," he says.

Flora looks at the object. "Dennis?" she asks.

"We don't know who Dennis is, but I'm wondering . . . maybe you can get something from it," he says.

"Maybe, but I . . . This is my job."

She gives an embarrassed smile, then covers her mouth with her hand and says something apologetic that he doesn't catch.

"Of course," Joona says. "How much does it cost?"

Keeping her eyes on the table, she tells him her fee for an individual half-hour sitting. Joona takes out his wallet and pays for an hour. Flora thanks him, gets her bag, and turns the light out. There's still light coming from outside, but the kitchen becomes gloomy. She takes out a tea light and a gold-embroidered black velvet cloth. Then she lights the candle, puts it in front of Joona, and places the cloth over the key chain. She closes her eyes and gently runs her hand across the cloth.

Joona watches her dispassionately.

Flora slides her left hand under the cloth and sits still; then her body starts to shake, and she takes a deep breath.

"Dennis, Dennis," she mutters.

She fingers the metal disc beneath the black fabric. The neighbors' television is clearly audible through the wall; outside, a car alarm goes off.

"I'm getting strange images . . . nothing clear yet."

"Keep going," Joona says, looking at her intently.

Flora's fair, curly hair hangs down beside her cheeks. Her blotchy skin flushes, and her eyelids twitch with the movement of her eyes.

"There's terrible power in this object. Loneliness and rage. I'm almost burning myself," she whispers. She pulls out the key chain, holds it in her palm, and stares at it. "Miranda says . . . it's hanging on a thread from death . . . because they were both in love with Dennis. . . . Yes, I can feel jealousy burning in the metal. . . ."

Flora holds the key chain in her hand for a while, then mutters that contact has been broken, shakes her head, and hands it back to Joona.

Joona gets to his feet. He had been too eager. Coming here was a waste of time. He had thought she really knew something, for reasons she didn't want to divulge. But it's obvious that Flora Hansen is just inventing things she thinks he wants to hear. Dennis belongs to a time long before the Birgitta Home.

"I'm sorry, but you're lying," Joona says, picking the key chain up from the table.

"Can I keep the money?" she asks weakly. "I can't manage; I collect cans on the subway and from the trash. . . ."

Joona puts the key chain in his pocket and starts to walk back through the hall. Flora takes out a piece of paper and follows him. "I think I saw a real ghost," she says. "I drew a picture of her. . . ."

She shows him a childish drawing of a girl and a heart and holds it up to his face, trying to make him look, but Joona brushes her hand aside. She drops it and it drifts to the floor, but he just steps over it and leaves the apartment.

100

JOONA IS STILL IRRITATED WHEN he gets to Disa's building.

Vicky Bennet and Dante Abrahamsson are alive, they're hiding somewhere, and he wasted almost an hour speaking to a mentally ill woman who lies for money.

Disa is sitting in bed with her laptop in her lap. She's wearing a white robe, and her brown hair is held back by a broad white headband.

He takes a shower in very hot water, then lies down beside her. When he leans his face against her, he can smell her perfume.

"Were you in Sundsvall again?" she asks distantly as he lets his hand run down her arm toward her narrow wrist.

"Not today," Joona replies quietly, thinking about Flora's thin, pale face.

"I was up there last year," Disa says. "Helped excavate the Women's House at Högom."

"Women's House?"

"In Selånger."

She looks up from the screen and smiles at him. "It's worth a look, if you ever get a break between murders," she says.

Joona smiles and touches her hip, tracing her thighbone toward her knee. He doesn't want Disa to stop talking, so he asks, "Why is it called the Women's House?"

"It's a burial mound, but it was raised over the ruins of a house that burned down. We don't know the full story."

"Were there people inside?"

"Two women," she replies, putting the computer aside. "I helped brush the soil from their combs and jewelry."

Joona lays his head in her lap and asks, "Where did the fire start?"

"I don't know, but there's at least one arrowhead embedded in the wall."

"So the perpetrator was outside?" he murmurs.

"Maybe the whole village stood and let the house burn," she says, running her fingers through his thick, damp hair.

"Tell me more about what you found," Joona asks, and shuts his eyes.

"We don't really know much," she says, twining a lock of his hair around her finger. "But the women who lived in the house were weavers—weaving weights have been found all over the house. It always seems funny that it's the little things, like combs and nails, that survive for thousands of years."

Joona's mind conjures up an image of Summa's bridal crown of woven birch root, and the old Jewish cemetery in Kronoberg Park, where his colleague Samuel Mendel lies all alone in his family grave.

101

Joona is woken with a gentle kiss on his lips. Disa is already dressed. She's left a cup of coffee on the bedside table.

"I fell asleep," he says.

"And slept for a hundred years," she says with a smile, and walks out into the hall.

Joona hears her close the door behind her. He pulls on his pants, then stands by the bed, thinking about Flora Hansen. He only went to see her because she had guessed right about the rock. Psychologists call this confirmation bias. Unconsciously, we tend to favor results that confirm a theory rather than contradict it. Flora called the police several times to tell them about different murder weapons, but when she mentioned the rock, he started to listen.

There were no other leads to follow.

Joona goes over to the large window and pulls back the curtain. The gray morning light still carries some of the night's gloom. The fountain in the center of Karla Plaza is pulsing and foaming monotonously. Pigeons are congregating in front of the closed entrance to the shopping center. A few people are on their way to work.

There was something desperate about Flora Hansen's eyes and voice when she said she collected cans and bottles on the subway.

Joona closes his eyes for a while, then turns back toward the bedroom and picks up his shirt from the chair.

He pulls it on distractedly.

His mind had just nudged the edge of a connection, but he's lost it. Though he tries to retrace his thoughts, he can feel it slipping further and further away.

It was something about Vicky, about the key chain and her mother.

He pulls on his jacket and goes back to stand by the window.

Was it something he saw?

He looks over toward Karla Plaza again. A bus stops to pick up passengers. Farther away, an old man with a walker is smiling at a dog sniffing a trash can. A red-cheeked woman in an unbuttoned leather jacket is running toward the subway station and startles a flock of pigeons in the square.

The subway.

It was something about the subway, Joona thinks, taking his phone out.

He almost has it; he just needs to check a few details.

While the call goes through, he walks into the entryway and puts his shoes on.

"Yes, Holger—"

"It's Joona Linna," Joona says as he leaves the apartment.

"Good morning, good morning, I've—"

"I just need to ask you something," Joona says, locking the door behind him. "You examined the bag we found at the dam, didn't you?"

"I had time to take pictures and list the contents before the prosecutor called to say that the case had been deprioritized."

"I'm not authorized to read your report," Joona says.

"There wasn't anything special," Holger says, rustling some paper. "I mentioned the knife, didn't I . . . ?"

"You said something about a bicycle tool—did you look into that?"

Joona is out in the street now, hurrying along Valhalla Boulevard toward his car.

"Yes," Holger replies. "You know what it's like with us Norrlanders—we take our time with things.... It wasn't actually a tool; it ended up being a key for a subway car ..."

"Was it ever attached to a key chain?"

"How the hell should I—?" Holger stops abruptly. "Wait, you're right, the inside of the hole has been worn smooth."

Joona thanks him and disconnects, then calls Anja. He thinks about what Elin had said, that Tuula stole things she liked from people around her: earrings, pens, coins, lipstick holders. Tuula must have removed the ugly key from the nice key chain with the pale-blue flower on it and put the key back in the bag.

"Ghostbusters," Anja answers in a bright, shrill voice.

"Anja, can you find whoever is responsible for the subway system in Stockholm?" Joona says as he drives off.

"I can consult the spirits instead—"

"It's urgent," Joona interrupts.

"Someone woke up on the wrong side of the bed," she mumbles in a hurt voice.

Joona is driving past the Olympic Stadium. "Did you know that all the subway cars are given names?" he says.

"I was sitting in Rebecka today. She was lovely and—"

"I don't think 'Dennis' is the name of a person. I think it's a subway car, and I need to know exactly where it is right now."

102

ALL OF THE SUBWAY CARS in Stockholm have numbers, just as they do all over the world, but for years they've also had names. It is said that the tradition started in 1887 with the names of the horses that used to pull carriages through the city.

Joona is pretty sure that the key Vicky was given by her mom, Susie, fits the electronic lock that opens all underground carriages, but that the key chain identified a specific car. Maybe her mother stored personal belongings in one of the conductors' cabs, or maybe she slept there sometimes.

Vicky's mother had been homeless almost her entire adult life and sometimes slept in the subway, on benches in various stations, in trains, and in the forgotten spaces between the lines, deep inside the tunnels.

Somehow she had managed to get this key, Joona thinks. It couldn't have been easy. It must have been incredibly valuable in her world.

Yet she gave it to her daughter.

And she got a key chain with the name "Dennis" on it so that the girl wouldn't forget which car to go to.

Maybe she knew Vicky was going to run away.

She had run away so many times, and managed not to be found for a long time on two occasions. The first was when she was eight years old. She went missing for seven months, until she was found with her mother in a multistory parking garage in the middle of December, suffering from hypothermia. She ran away again when she was thirteen. Vicky was missing for eleven months that time, then picked up by the police for shoplifting in the mall beside the Globe Arena.

You don't necessarily need a key to get into a subway car. An ordinary wrench of the right size would work.

Even though it's unlikely that Vicky is inside the car without the key, it may still contain clues from her time on the run, clues that could lead to her current hiding place.

Joona has almost reached police headquarters when Anja calls to say that she's spoken to the Stockholm Transport Authority.

"There is a car named Dennis, but it's been decommissioned."

"So where is it now?"

"They weren't sure," she replies. "It could be in their depot out in Rissne . . . but it's more likely to be out at the workshops in Johanneshov."

"Put me through to them," Joona says as he turns the car around.

103

JOONA IS DRIVING TOWARD JOHANNESHOV, just south of Stockholm, when a man finally answers the phone. It sounds as if his mouth is full of food.

"Underground Engineering . . . This is Kjell."

"Joona Linna, National Crime. Can you confirm that you have a car named Dennis with you in Johanneshov?"

"Dennis," the man repeats. "Do you have the carriage number?"

"No, I'm afraid not."

"Hang on, I'll check the computer."

Joona hears the man muttering to himself; then there's a clattering sound before he comes back on the line.

"There's a Denniz with a 'z' at the end. . . ."

"The spelling doesn't matter."

"Okay," Kjell says. Joona hears him swallow the mouthful of food. "I can't see it in the register. . . . It's a pretty old carriage. . . . I don't know. . . . According to our records, it hasn't been in service for the past few years."

"Where is it?"

"It should probably be here, but . . . Look, I'm going to pass you to Dick. He knows everything that's not on the computer. . . ."

Kjell's voice disappears and is replaced by an electronic buzzing. Then an older man answers, his voice echoing as if he were in a cathedral or a large metal room. "This is Dick."

"I was just talking to Kjell," Joona explains. "And he seems to think you might have a carriage named Dennis somewhere there."

"If Kjell says it's here, then it probably is—but I can go out and check, if it's a matter of life and death."

"It is," Joona says calmly.

"Are you in your car?" Dick asks.

"Yes."

"Not on your way here?"

Joona hears the sound of the man going down some metal steps, followed by the squeaking of a large, heavy door. The man sounds out of breath when he speaks again.

"I'm down in the tunnel now—you still there?"

"Yes."

"We've got Mikaela and Maria down here. Denniz ought to be here as well."

Hearing Dick's echoing steps, Joona drives as fast as he can across the Central Bridge. He thinks about the periods of Vicky's life when she's been on the run. She must have slept somewhere, somewhere she felt safe.

"Can you see that carriage yet?" he asks.

"No, this one's Ellinor . . . and there's Silvia. . . . Even the lights don't work properly down here. . . . I haven't been down here for a while," the old man says breathlessly. "Just going to turn my flashlight on . . . Right at the back, naturally . . . Denniz, old and rusty as fuck. . . ."

"Are you sure?"

"I can take a picture if you . . . What the hell? There are people inside the . . ."

"Be quiet!" Joona says quickly.

"There's someone in the carriage," the old man whispers.

"Stay back," Joona says.

"They've blocked the door with a damn gas cylinder."

The line crackles as the man moves away, breathing hard.

Joona doesn't think it's Vicky, since she no longer has her key.

Suddenly Joona hears high-pitched shouting through the phone, distant but unmistakable.

"There's a woman shouting in there," the engineer whispers. "She sounds completely insane."

"Get out of there," Joona says.

He hears the old man's footsteps and labored breathing, then the screaming again, more distant now.

"Okay, what did you see?" Joona asks.

"There was a giant welding cylinder blocking the door."

"Did you see anyone?"

"There's graffiti on the windows, but there was one large person, and one who was smaller. Maybe more, I don't know."

"You're sure?" Joona asks.

"We keep the tunnels locked, but if you're determined enough . . . well, of course, there's always a way to get in," the old man pants.

"Listen to me carefully. . . . I'm a detective, and I want you to get out of there and wait outside for the police."

104

A BLACK VAN SPEEDS THROUGH the gates of the Underground Engineering Depot, throwing up grit and a cloud of dust. The van swings around and stops in front of a green metal door.

After his conversation with Dick, Joona called the regional chief of police, and he dispatched the National Task Force. Joona explained that there was a possibility that a hostage situation might develop at the depot.

The five officers emerge from the van with a mixture of nervousness and anticipation. They're heavily equipped with boots, dark-blue overalls, bulletproof vests, helmets, protective goggles, and gloves.

Joona walks toward the group and sees that three of them are carrying green Heckler & Koch assault rifles with laser sights. They're not specialized weapons, but they're light and can empty a magazine in less than three seconds. The two other men in the group are carrying sniper rifles.

Joona shakes hands with the operational leader, the medical officer, and the three others before explaining the urgency of the situation.

"I want you to go in right away, as quickly as you can, but I want to stress that we haven't had positive identification of Vicky Bennet or Dante Abrahamsson."

When Joona arrived, moments before the team, he questioned Dick and got him to mark the positions of the various subway cars on a map of the area.

A young man with a sniper rifle in a bag by his feet raises his hand. "Can we assume that she's armed?" he asks.

"Almost certainly not with a projectile weapon," Joona replies.

"So we're expecting to encounter two unarmed children?" the young man says, shaking his head with a grin.

"We don't know what we're going to find. We never do," Joona says. He shows them the plan of a standard subway car, the same model as Denniz.

"Where do we go in?" the operational leader asks.

"The door at the front of the car is open but blocked by one or more gas cylinders," Joona says.

"Did you hear that?" the operational leader asks, turning to the others.

Joona lays the large map over the plan and points out the position of the cars.

"I think we can get close without being seen. It's a bit hard to tell, but we can definitely get this far."

"Yes, that looks reasonable."

"I know it's not a long distance, but I still want a sniper on the roof of the nearest carriage."

"That'll be me," says one of the men.

"And I can take up position here," the younger sniper says, pointing at the map.

They follow Joona to the steel door. One of the officers double-checks his reserve magazine, and Joona pulls on a protective vest.

"Our primary objective is to get the boy out of the car, and our secondary objective is to arrest the suspect," Joona explains, and opens the door. "Live fire should be targeted at the girl's legs initially, followed by shoulders and arms."

A long pale-gray staircase leads down to the sidings beneath the Johanneshov Engineering Depot, where faulty trains are left until they can be repaired.

The only thing Joona can hear behind him is the muffled noise of heavy boots and ceramic vests.

105

WHEN THE TEAM MEMBERS REACH the tunnel, they move more cautiously. The sound of their footsteps on the gravel and rusty rails echoes softly off the metal walls.

They approach a dented train giving off a peculiar smell. The cars look like dark remnants of some long-forgotten civilization. The light from the team's flashlights darts across the tunnel walls.

They're moving in single file. The tracks merge at a set of manually operated points, where a red lamp with a broken cover is giving off a dim glow. There's a dirty glove lying on the ground.

Joona gestures to the group to turn their flashlights off before they go through a narrow gap between two carriages with broken windows. A box of greased bolts sits by the wall, close to some loose cables, electrical sockets, and a grimy armature.

They're getting very close now, moving even more carefully. Joona points out one car to the older sniper. The rest of the group attaches the flashlights to their weapons and spreads out, while the sniper makes his way up to the top of the carriage without a sound, then unfolds the support of his rifle.

The rest of the group moves closer to the car at the far end of the tunnel. One of the men keeps checking the strap of his helmet, like a nervous tic. The operational leader exchanges a glance with the younger sniper and indicates a line of fire.

Someone slips on the grit, and a loose stone clatters against the rail. A sleek rat runs along the wall and disappears into a hole.

Joona walks on alone by the side of the track. He can see the car named Denniz standing in a track siding closest to the wall. Cables or ropes are hanging from the roof. When he moves sideways, he sees dim light coming from inside the dirty windows. The light is fluttering like a yellow butterfly, making the shadows keep growing and shrinking.

The lead officer loosens a shock grenade from his belt.

Joona stands and listens for a moment before moving on, with a tingling awareness that he's in the line of fire, that the snipers' rifles are aimed at his back right now.

A green metal gas cylinder has been wedged into the open doorway.

Joona approaches cautiously, going up to the carriage and crouching in the darkness. Putting his ear to the metal, he immediately hears someone shuffling across the floor.

The lead officer gestures to two of his men. They slip forward in the darkness like shapeless demons. Though they're both big men, they move almost silently. The only sounds are the muffled, watery echoes of holsters, vests, and heavy overalls. Then, suddenly, they're by his side.

Joona hasn't even drawn his own pistol, but he sees that the men from the response unit already have their fingers on the triggers of their assault rifles.

Through the car's dirty windows, Joona can see a small lamp on the floor. Its glow lights up torn boxes, empty bottles, and plastic bags.

There's a large bundle with rope around it between two of the seats.

The glow from the little lamp starts to quiver, and the whole carriage vibrates weakly. Maybe something's moving along the rails in the distance.

The walls and roof start to rumble.

Joona hears a faint whimpering sound.

He carefully draws his pistol.

At the far end of the car, a shadow is moving, as a large man in jeans and dirty sneakers crawls away.

Joona feeds the first bullet into the chamber, turns to the lead officer, and gestures for them to move in immediately.

106

THERE'S AN EXPLOSION AS THE middle door is blown off and falls on the ground. The armed officers storm the subway car.

Windows shatter, and broken glass showers the ripped seats and floor.

The man lets out a yell in a rattling voice.

The gas cylinder falls over with a heavy clang, and argon hisses out as it rolls into the car. All the internal doors in the carriage are forced open with heavy thuds.

Joona makes his way in across moldy blankets and torn, trampled newspapers. The acrid smell of the gas fills the carriage.

"Stay down!" someone roars.

The beams from the flashlights scan the car, section by section, looking between the seats and through filthy plexiglass.

"Don't hit me!" a man yells from another section.

"Don't move!"

The lead officer tapes the broken vent of the gas cylinder shut.

Joona hurries forward toward the driver's cab in the front of the train.

There's no sign of Vicky or Dante.

The carriage stinks of sweat and old food. The walls and windows are scratched and covered with graffiti. Someone's been eating fried chicken off the floor, and there are beer cans and candy wrappers between the seats. The newspaper on the floor rustles beneath his feet. The light from outside shines through the windows unevenly.

The response unit breaks open the door to the cab, and Joona goes inside. The cramped space is empty, but the walls are scratched and covered with scrawl. On the instrument panel is a syringe with no needle, some scorched foil, and an empty plastic capsule. On the narrow shelf in front of the two pedals are a bottle of Tylenol and a tube of toothpaste.

This was where Vicky's mother hid sometimes.

Joona searches some more and finds a rusty carpet knife tucked into the springs beneath the seat, more candy wrappers, and an empty jar of baby food—plum purée.

Through the side window, he sees the armed officers drag out the man in jeans. His face is furrowed, and there's a frightened look in his eyes. He coughs some blood over his beard and cries out. With his arms tied behind his back with plastic cuffs, he is forced to lie facedown on the ground, and one of the officers holds the barrel of his rifle to the back of his head.

Joona stares around the cramped space, his eyes darting over buttons and knobs, the microphone, and the lever with a polished wooden handle, but he isn't sure where he should be looking. He considers going back out into the car to search the seats, but he forces himself to stay in the cab and scan the instrument panel and driver's seat again.

Why did Vicky and her mother have keys to this cab?

There's nothing here.

He stands up and is examining the screws holding the mesh over the vent when his eyes slide sideways to a word that's been scribbled on the wall: "mom."

He takes a step back and now notices that almost all the writing and scratches on the walls are messages between Vicky and her mother. This must have been a place where they could meet without being disturbed, and when they missed each other they left messages.

Mom they were mean, I couldn't stay.
I'm freezing and need food. Have to go
back now, I'll come again on Monday.

Dont be upset Vicky! they locked me up
thats why I missed you.

Thanks for the candy.

Baby!! Im sleeping here for a while Uffe is
a pig!! If you can leave some money that wd
be grate.

Merry Christmas, Mom.

I cant keep calling you back right now.

Mom are you mad at me?

107

When Joona comes back out, the response team has turned the bearded man over. He's sitting with his back against the wall, crying, and seems very confused.

"I'm trying to find a girl and a little boy," Joona says, taking off his bulletproof vest and squatting in front of the man.

"Don't hit me," the man says.

"No one's going to hit you, but I need to know if you've seen a girl here, in this car."

"I didn't touch her, I just followed her."

"Where is she now?"

"I just followed her," he repeats, licking some blood from his lips.

"Was she alone?"

"I don't know—she locked herself in the cab."

"Did she have a little boy with her?"

"A boy? Yes, maybe . . . maybe . . ."

"Answer the question," the lead officer snaps.

"You followed her here," Joona continues. "What did she do after that?"

"She left again," he replies with a frightened look in his eyes.

"Where did she go? Do you know?"

"That way," the man replies with a helpless motion of his head toward the tunnel.

"Is she in there, in the tunnel—is that what you mean?"

"Maybe not . . . maybe . . ."

"Answer!" the officer roars.

"I can't," the man sobs.

"Can you tell me when she was here?" Joona asks cautiously. "Was it today?"

"Just now," he says. "She started shouting and . . ."

Joona rushes along the rusty tracks. The darkness ahead of him seems to move in smoky formations.

Up ahead, he can see a gate. Light is streaming in and reflecting off the damp concrete floor. The bottom of the gate is broken; he manages to squeeze under it, and suddenly finds himself outside. He's standing in the middle of the rough crushed stones surrounding about fifteen rusty sets of rails. The tracks merge together like a ponytail up ahead and curve off gently into the distance.

A thin figure is walking along the embankment. She has a dog with her. Joona starts to run after her. A train thunders past him at high speed. The ground shakes. He sees her between the wheels as he runs through the weeds at the side of the track. The ground is covered with broken glass, trash, and used condoms. There's an electrical hum, and another train approaches. Joona jumps over the track, grabs hold of the woman's thin arm, and turns her around. Taken by surprise, she tries to hit him, but he moves his head away. He loses his grip and grabs her jacket; she hits again, then pulls away and wriggles out of the jacket, drops her bag, and falls backward onto the stones.

108

Joona holds the woman down on the embankment among the thistles and cow parsley and tries to calm her down.

"I just want to talk, I don't ..."

"Get the fuck off me!" she screams, trying to pull free.

She kicks out, but he blocks her legs and holds her down. She's breathing quickly. She's very thin, with a furrowed face and cracked lips. Forty years old, maybe, though possibly only thirty. When she realizes she can't pull free, she starts whispering apologies and trying to placate him.

"Now, just take it easy," he says, letting go of her.

She glances at him timidly as she gets to her feet and picks up her handbag from the ground. Her thin arms are full of needle tracks, and on the inside of one of her arms is a badly damaged tattoo. Her black T-shirt reads "Kafka didn't have much fun either" and is extremely dirty. She wipes the corners of her mouth, looks along the rails, and takes a few steps to the side, as if to test Joona.

"Don't be scared; I just need to talk to you."

"I don't have time," she replies quickly.

"Did you see anyone else when you were back in that car?"

"I don't know what you're talking about."

"You were inside a subway car."

She doesn't answer, clenches her mouth shut, and scratches

her neck. He picks up her jacket, turns it right side out, and passes it to her. She takes it without thanking him.

"I'm looking for a girl who—"

"Leave me the fuck alone. I haven't done anything."

"I didn't say you had," Joona replies amiably.

"So what do you want with me?"

"I'm looking for a girl named Vicky."

"What does that have to do with me?"

Joona shows her a picture of Vicky.

"Don't know her," she says automatically.

"Take another look."

"Do you have money?"

"No."

"Can't you help me out with a little bit of money?"

A train crosses the bridge, rattling and letting off showers of sparks.

"I know you hang out in the driver's cab," Joona says.

"It was Susie who started that," she says, trying to shift the blame.

Joona shows her the photograph of Vicky again. "This is Susie's daughter," he says.

"I didn't know she had kids," the woman says, rubbing her nose.

The high-tension wire running alongside the track starts to hum.

"How do you know Susie?"

"We hung out around the public housing while that lasted. . . . It was fucking rough at first. I had hepatitis, and Vadim was always at me. . . . I used to get knocked around a lot, but Susie helped me. Christ, she's one tough bitch, but I wouldn't have made it through that winter without her—no chance. But when Susie died, I took her stuff, so that . . ."

The woman mutters something and digs around in her handbag, then pulls up a key like the one Vicky had in her bag.

"Why did you take that?"

"Anyone would have done it, no question. . . . I actually took it before she was dead," the woman admits.

"What's in the car?"

She wipes her mouth, mutters "Fucking hell" to herself, then takes a step to one side.

Two trains are approaching along different tracks. One is coming from Blåsut, the other from the Skärmarbrink station.

"I need to know," Joona says.

"Okay, what the hell," she says, her eyes wavering. "There was some crank and a phone."

"Do you have the phone?"

The rumbling sound and metallic clatter are getting louder.

"You can't prove it isn't mine."

The first train passes, and the ground shakes beneath their feet. A few loose stones roll down the embankment, and the weeds sway. An empty McDonald's cup rolls between the other rails.

"I just want to look at it," he calls.

"Sure," she says, laughing.

Their clothes flap in the wind. The dog barks excitedly. The woman walks backward, beside the cars as the train rushes past. She says something, then starts to run for the depot. It happens so suddenly that Joona doesn't have time to react. She obviously hasn't seen the train coming from the other direction. The noise is already deafening. The train has built up speed, but, strangely, there's no sound when the front of it hits the woman.

She just disappears under it.

Joona sees drops of blood spatter the flowers growing on the embankment as if time is moving in slow motion. The train lets out a long, eerie shriek as it brakes. The cars groan and clank, slowing down to stop. Silence settles again, and the faint buzz of insects can be heard once more. The driver stays in his seat, as if he's frozen into ice. A long streak of blood is spread over the railroad ties, leading to a dark-red lump of fabric and flesh. The smell of the brakes spreads across the area. The dog whimpers as it walks up and down the tracks, its tail between its legs, unsure of what to do.

Joona goes over slowly and picks the woman's handbag out of the ditch. The dog comes up to him and sniffs as he dumps out its contents. Candy wrappers blow off in the wind, along with a couple of banknotes. Joona picks up the black phone and then sits on a concrete pedestal by the side of the tracks.

A westerly breeze is carrying the smell of garbage from the city.

He clicks through to voice mail, calls, and hears that there are two new messages:

"Hi, Mom," a girl's voice says, and Joona realizes at once that it's Vicky. "Why don't you answer anymore? If you're in detox, I want to know. The new place is okay. I'm happy here. Maybe I said that last time. . . ."

"Message received yesterday at eleven-ten," the automated voice says.

"Hi, Mom," Vicky says in a tense, breathless voice. "Some stuff's happened, and I need to get hold of you. I can't talk long. I borrowed a phone. . . . Mom, I don't know what to do. . . . I don't have anywhere to go. I might have to ask Tobias for help."

"Message received at two-oh-five."

109

ELIN FRANK WAKES UP IN a large, strange bed. The clock on the television spreads a greenish glow across the executive suite's bedroom. The colorful drapes are visible against the blackout curtains.

She's been asleep for a long time.

The sweet scent of the flowers in the living room makes her feel slightly nauseated, and the hum of the air conditioning is spreading an uneven chill, but she's too tired to try to turn it off or call reception.

She thinks about the girls in the house on the coast. One of them must know more. There must be a witness.

The little girl, Tuula, spoke and acted as if she was boiling with rage. Maybe she'd seen something she doesn't dare speak about.

Elin thinks about how the little girl grabbed her hair and tried to stab her in the face with a fork. That should have scared her more than it did.

She slides her hand under the pillow, feeling a sting of pain from the wounds on her wrist. She thinks about how the girls ganged up on Daniel.

Elin rolls over and thinks about Daniel's face: his neat mouth and sensitive eyes. Ridiculously, she had been faithful to Jack until the mistake with the French photographer. Not that it was something she'd planned. She knows they're divorced and that he's never coming back.

Elin showers and moisturizes using the lotion provided by the hotel, puts a fresh bandage around her wrist, and, for the first time in her life, gets dressed in the same clothes she wore the day before.

The previous day's events seem almost incomprehensible now.

Elin's face is flushed with emotion as she starts to apply her makeup with slow, steady movements. Her stomach tingles when she thinks about Daniel Grim. She feels as if she's falling from a great height—and she likes it.

It was late by the time she stopped by his house in the outskirts of Sundsvall. A gravel path led into an old garden. Dark trees moved in the wind in front of a small red house with a white veranda.

If he had asked her if she wanted to go inside, she probably would have, and she would almost certainly have slept with him if she had. But he didn't ask, he was cautious and pleasant, and when she thanked him for his help he said the trip had been better than any therapy.

She felt horribly alone when she watched him walk through the low gate. She sat in the car for a while, then drove back to Sundsvall and booked a room at the First Hotel.

Her phone purrs in her bag. She hurries to answer it.

"Are you still in Sundsvall?" Joona asks.

"I'm about to check out of the hotel," Elin says, feeling a wave of anxiety rush through her. "What happened?"

"Nothing, don't worry," he says quickly. "I just need help with something, if you have time."

"What with?"

"If it's not too much trouble, I'd be very grateful if you could ask Daniel Grim about something."

"I can do that," she says. She speaks in a subdued voice but can't help smiling to herself.

"Ask him if Vicky ever mentioned someone named Tobias."

"Dennis and Tobias," she says thoughtfully.

"Just Tobias . . . That's our only lead to Vicky right now."

110

I'T'S EIGHT-FORTY-FIVE ON A BREEZY, sunny morning, and Elin is driving past the houses that line Bruks Street. She parks outside the thick hedge, gets out of the car, and walks through the low gate.

In the daylight, she can see that the house is well maintained: the black saddle roof looks new, and the ornate carpentry on the porch is bright white. This is where Daniel and Elisabet Grim lived together until Friday night. Elin shivers as she rings the doorbell. She waits for a long time, listening to the wind rustle the leaves of the large birch tree. Someone turns off a lawnmower in one of the neighboring gardens. She rings the bell again, waits a little longer, then goes around to the back of the house.

Some small birds fly up from the lawn. There's a dark-blue couch swing next to some tall lilac bushes. Daniel is lying on it, asleep. His face is very pale, and he's curled up as if he's freezing.

Elin goes over to him, and he wakes up with a start. He sits up and stares at her with a look of bewilderment.

"It's too cold to be sleeping out here," Elin says gently, sitting down.

"I couldn't go into the house," he says, moving to make room for her.

"The police called me this morning," she says.

"What did they want?"

"Did Vicky ever mention someone named Tobias?"

Daniel frowns, and Elin is about to apologize for pressuring him when he raises his hand.

"Hang on," he says quickly. "He's the guy with the attic apartment in Stockholm; she lived there for a while...." Daniel's weary face suddenly cracks into a large, warm smile. "It's 9 Wollmar Yxkulls Street."

"Are you sure?"

"I don't know how the hell I could know that. I can't remember anything. I can't even remember my parents' middle names these days."

Elin gets up from the couch-swing seat, picks up her cell phone, calls Joona, and tells him what she's found out. She hears the detective start to run while she's still talking; by the time they end the call, she hears a car door slam shut.

111

ELIN'S HEART IS BEATING FAST when she sits back down beside Daniel on the couch swing and feels the warmth of his body against her thigh. He's found an old wine cork between the cushions and is peering at it.

"We went to a wine-tasting class and started to collect wine—nothing special, but some of them were okay. I got them as a Christmas present ... Bordeaux ... two bottles of Château Haut-Brion 1970. We were going to drink them when we retired, me and Elisabet. ... So many plans ... We even saved some marijuana. We often used to joke about it, how we were going to become kids again when we got old, lots of loud music and mornings in bed."

"I should get back to Stockholm," she says.

"Yes."

They swing together on the seat for a while, and the rusty spring creaks.

"Nice house," Elin says quietly.

She puts her hand on his, and he turns his over and they lace their fingers together. They sit there in silence as the swing seat creaks slowly.

Her glossy hair has fallen across her face, and she brushes it aside and meets his gaze.

"Daniel," she murmurs.

"Yes," he replies in a whisper.

Elin looks at him, thinking that she's never needed another person's tenderness as much as she does right now. Something about the look in his eyes, his furrowed brow, is affecting her deeply. She kisses him lightly on the lips, smiles, and does it again, then takes his face in her hands and kisses him properly.

"Oh God," he says.

Elin kisses him again, scratching her lips on his stubble, then pulls her dress open and puts his hand on one of her breasts. He touches her tentatively, nudging one of her nipples.

Daniel looks incredibly vulnerable when she kisses him again, slipping one hand under his shirt, where she feels his stomach tighten with her touch.

Waves of longing roll through her. Her legs feel weak, and she wishes she could just lie on the grass with him and sit astride his hips.

She closes her eyes, pressing herself against him, and he says something that she can't hear. Her blood is pulsing within her. She feels his warm hands on her body; then he stops abruptly and pulls away.

"Elin, I can't. . . ."

"Sorry, I didn't mean to do that," she says, trying to calm her breathing.

"I just need some time," he explains with tears in his eyes. "It's too much right now. . . ."

"That's okay," she replies, trying to smile.

Elin adjusts her clothes, walks out of the garden, and gets in the car.

Her cheeks are flushed and her legs feel weak as she drives out of Sundsvall. After just five minutes, she turns onto a forest track and stops. Her heart is pounding. She looks at her face in the rearview mirror. Her eyes are glossy, her lips swollen.

Her underwear is soaked. Blood is roaring through her body. She can't remember ever feeling sexual energy like this before.

She tries to breathe calmly, then looks around the narrow forest track, slips her dress open, and pulls her underpants down over her thighs. She strokes herself quickly with both hands. Her orgasm comes fast and hard. Elin sits there gasping and sweating, with two fingers inside herself, as she looks out the windshield at the rays of sunlight through the branches of the fir trees.

112

It's starting to get dark by the time Flora heads for the recycling center behind the supermarket to look for bottles and cans. She keeps thinking about the murders up in Sundsvall and has started to fantasize about Miranda and her life at the Birgitta Home.

The Miranda in her imagination dresses provocatively, smokes, and swears a lot. Flora checks some discarded boxes in the loading bay before moving on.

She starts to imagine Miranda playing hide-and-seek with some friends outside a church.

Flora's heart beats faster when she sees Miranda covering her eyes and counting to a hundred. A five-year-old girl runs between the gravestones, laughing excitedly, already a little bit scared.

Flora stops in front of the recycling cans. She puts down her bag of empty plastic bottles and cans, goes over to the big container for clear glass, and looks inside, using her flashlight. The light dances across the broken and intact bottles. It's almost dazzling. Off to one side, Flora spots a returnable bottle. She reaches in through the hole with her arm and carefully feels around, unable to look at the same time. The recycling center is completely silent. Flora reaches a little farther and suddenly feels something touch her. It's like a gentle caress against the back of her hand; a moment later, she cuts her fingers on a piece of broken glass, snatches her arm back, and moves away.

A dog is barking in the distance; then she hears a slow crunching sound from among the glass in the large container.

Flora runs away from the recycling center, her heart pounding as she gasps for breath. Her injured fingers are stinging. She looks around, thinking to herself that the ghost had been hiding among the glass.

I see the dead girl as a young child, she thinks. Miranda is haunting me because she wants to show me something. She won't leave me in peace because I was the one who summoned her.

Flora sucks the blood from her fingertips and imagines the girl trying to grab and cling to her hand.

"There was someone there, someone who saw everything," is what she imagines the girl was trying to tell her. There weren't supposed to be any witnesses, but there were. . . .

113

Joona hurries in through the door of 9 Wollmar Yxkulls Street. He runs up the stairs to the top floor and rings the bell on the only door. His heartbeat calms down as he waits. Screwed to the door is a brass sign with the name "Horáčková" engraved on it, and immediately above that a strip of tape bearing the name "Lundhagen." He knocks hard, but there's no sound from inside the apartment. He opens the mailbox and looks inside. It's dark, but he can see that the floor is covered with mail and advertisements. He rings the bell again, waits for a while, then calls Anja.

"Can you look up a Tobias Horáčková?"

"No such person," she replies after a few seconds.

"Horáčková, at 9 Wollmar Yxkulls Street."

"Yes, Viktoriya Horáčková," she replies, after tapping at her keyboard.

"Is there a Tobias Lundhagen?" Joona asks.

"I was just going to say that Viktoriya Horáčková is the daughter of a Czech diplomat."

"Is there a Tobias Lundhagen?"

"Yes, he lives there, either on a sublet or as a renter."

"Thanks."

"Joona, wait," Anja says quickly.

"Yes?"

"Three little things ... We can't break into an apartment owned by a diplomat without a court order. ..."

"That's one thing," he says.

"You're due to see the Internal Affairs people in twenty-five minutes."

"Don't have time."

"And you have a meeting with Carlos at four-thirty."

JOONA IS SITTING PERFECTLY STILL and straight-backed in an armchair in the prosecutor's office. The head of the investigation is monotonously reading out the transcript of the first interview, which he then hands over for Joona to accept and sign.

Mikael Båge snorts noisily, passes the document to the senior secretary Helene Fiorine, then reads the transcript of Göran Stone's witness statement.

Three hours later, Joona crosses Kungs Bridge and walks the short distance to police headquarters. He takes the elevator up to the eighth floor, knocks on the door of Carlos's office, and sits down at the table where his colleagues Petter Näslund, Benny Rubin, and Magdalena Ronander are already waiting for him.

"Joona, I'm a fairly reasonable person, but enough is enough," Carlos says as he feeds his paradise fish.

"The National Rapid Response Unit," Petter says with a grin.

Magdalena sits quietly, staring down at the table.

"I think you should apologize," Carlos says.

"Because I was trying to save a little boy's life?" Joona asks.

"No, because you know you were wrong."

"Sorry," Joona says.

Petter grunts. There are beads of sweat on his forehead.

"I'm suspending you," Carlos continues. "From all active service, until the Internal Affairs investigation is over."

"Who's taking over?" Joona asks.

"The investigation into the deaths at the Birgitta Home has been deprioritized and will in all likelihood be—"

"Vicky Bennet is alive," Joona interrupts.

"And will in all likelihood be shut down tomorrow morning, once the prosecutor has made her decision," Carlos concludes.

"She's alive."

"Pull yourself together, for God's sake," Benny says. "I've looked at the recording myself, and—"

Carlos raises his hand to stop him, then says, "There's nothing to suggest that the people caught by the security camera at the gas station are Vicky and the boy."

"She left a message on her mother's voice mail yesterday," Joona says.

"Vicky doesn't have a phone, and her mother is dead," Magdalena points out.

"Joona, you're getting careless," Petter says sadly.

Carlos clears his throat, hesitates, then takes a deep breath. "I'm not enjoying this," he says slowly.

Petter is looking expectantly at Carlos, Magdalena is staring down at the table again with flushed cheeks, and Benny is doodling on a sheet of paper.

"I'll go on leave for a month . . . ," Joona says.

"Good," Carlos says quickly. "That solves . . ."

"If I can have access to an apartment first," Joona concludes.

"An apartment?" Carlos's face darkens, and he sits down behind his desk as if all the energy had drained out of him.

"It was bought seventeen years ago by the Czech diplomat to Sweden. . . . He passed it on to his twenty-year-old daughter."

"Forget it." Carlos sighs.

"But the daughter hasn't used the place in the past twelve years."

"That doesn't make any difference. . . . As long as it's owned by someone with diplomatic immunity, Paragraph 21 doesn't apply."

Anja enters the room without knocking. Her blond hair is arranged in a topknot, and she's wearing glittery lipstick. She walks over to Carlos, looks at him, then gestures toward his cheek. "Your face is dirty," she says.

"Beard?" Carlos says weakly.

"What?"

"I might have forgotten to shave," Carlos says.

"It doesn't look good."

"No," he replies, looking down.

"I need to talk to Joona," she says. "Are you finished?"

"No," Carlos says in an unsteady voice. "We . . ."

Anja leans across the desk. The red plastic beads on her necklace swing in front of her cleavage. Carlos stifles an impulse to tell her he's married as he finds himself staring at her breasts.

"Are you having some sort of breakdown?" Anja asks with genuine interest.

"Yes," he says quietly.

The others just watch as Joona gets up from his chair and follows Anja out of the room.

They head for the elevator, and Joona presses the button.

"What do you want, Anja?" he asks as they wait.

"Now you're all stressed again," she says, offering him a toffee in a striped wrapper. "I just wanted to let you know that Flora Hansen called me and—"

"I need a search warrant."

Anja shakes her head, unwraps the toffee, and feeds it to him.

"Flora wanted to return the money that you—"

"She lied to me," Joona interrupts.

"Now she just wants us to listen," she says. "Flora says there's a witness. . . . She really did sound scared this time, and kept repeating that you have to believe her, that she doesn't want any money, that she just wants us to listen."

"I have to get into that apartment on Wollmar Yxkulls Street."

"Joona." Anja sighs.

She unwraps another toffee, holds it up to his mouth, and pouts her lips. He takes the candy. Giggling delightedly, Anja quickly unwraps another one and holds it up to his lips, but it's too late—he's already gone into the elevator.

114

ON THE GROUND FLOOR OF the building at 9 Wollmar Yxkulls Street, there are now balloons hanging from one of the doors. High-pitched children's voices are singing in the courtyard. Joona opens the back door, and the glass window rattles as he glances out at the little garden, with its patch of grass and an apple tree. A table has been set in the last of the evening sun, with colorful plates and cups, balloons and streamers. A pregnant woman is sitting on a white plastic chair. She's been made up to look like a cat and is calling to the playing children. Joona feels a pang of longing in his chest. At that moment, one of the little girls breaks away from the others and runs over to him.

"Hello," she says, then pushes past and runs over to open the door with the balloons.

Her bare feet leave prints on the white marble floor in the hallway. Joona hears her call into the apartment that she needs to go to the bathroom. One of the balloons comes loose and sinks to the floor. Joona sees that there are bare footprints all over the hallway and stairwell: to and from the front door, up and down the stairs, past the garbage chute and over to the basement door.

Joona walks up to the attic apartment a second time and rings the doorbell. He stares at the brass sign with the name "Horáčková" and the yellowing tape with "Lundhagen" written on it.

The children's voices can still be heard from out in the courtyard. He rings the bell again and has just pulled out his lock-pick case when the door is opened by a man in his thirties with spiked hair.

"Tobias?"

"Who's asking?" the man replies. He's wearing a short-sleeved shirt and black jeans. His hair is stiff with gel, and his face has a yellowish tint.

"National Crime Unit," Joona says.

"No shit," the man says, smiling in surprise.

"Can I come in?"

"Now's not a good time. I'm just on my way out, but if—"

"You know Vicky Bennet," Joona interrupts.

"Maybe you'd better come in," Tobias says seriously.

Joona suddenly becomes aware of the weight of his new pistol in his shoulder holster as he goes up the short flight of steps and finds himself in an attic apartment with a sloping ceiling and dormer windows. There's a ceramic bowl full of candy on a low table. On one wall is a framed poster of a Gothic-looking woman with angel's wings and large breasts.

Tobias sits down on the sofa and tries to close a grubby duffel bag on the floor between his legs, but he gives up and leans back.

"You wanted to talk about Vicky?" Tobias says, reaching forward and helping himself to a handful of candy from the bowl.

"When did you last hear from her?" Joona asks, leafing through the unopened envelopes on a sideboard.

"Well," Tobias says with a sigh, "I don't know. It must be almost a year ago now, she called from— Damn," he says, interrupting himself when he drops some candy on the floor.

"What were you going to say?"

"Just that she called from … Uddevalla, I think it was? She talked a lot, but I don't actually know what she wanted."

"No calls in the past month or so?"

Joona opens a small wooden door leading to a closet. It contains four ice-hockey games, still in their boxes, and an old computer on a shelf.

"I really do need to get going," Tobias says.

"When did she live here?"

Tobias tries to close the large duffel again. One window looking out onto the courtyard is open slightly, and the children are now singing "Happy Birthday."

"Almost three years ago now."

"How long was she here?"

"She wasn't here the whole time, but seven months in all, I'd say," Tobias replies.

"Where else was she living?"

"Who knows?"

"You don't know?"

"I threw her out a few times. . . . Look . . . you wouldn't understand, she's only a kid, but that girl can be a real nightmare to have around the house."

"In what way?"

"The usual—drugs, stealing, suicide attempts," he says, scratching his scalp. "But I'd never have believed she could kill anyone. I've been following the story in *Expressen*. . . . I mean, it's turned into quite a story."

Tobias looks at his watch, then meets the detective's calm gray gaze.

"Why?" Joona asks after a while.

"Why what?" Tobias asks awkwardly.

"Why did you let her live here?"

"I had a hard time when I was a kid," he replies with a smile, trying once more to zip the bag.

It's full of e-readers in their original packaging.

"Can I help you with that?"

Joona holds the sides of the duffel together while Tobias zips it shut.

"Sorry about that," he says, patting the bag. "I swear, it's not my stuff. I've just been looking after it for a friend."

"Oh well, in that case," Joona says.

Tobias laughs and spits a piece of candy on the floor. He stands up and hauls the bag down the steps to the hall. Joona follows him slowly toward the door.

"How does Vicky think? Where would she hide?" he asks.

"I don't know—she could be anywhere."

"Who does she trust?" Joona asks.

"No one," Tobias replies; he opens the front door and goes out into the stairwell.

"Does she trust you?"

"I don't think so."

"So there's no likelihood she'd come here?"

Joona lingers in the small hallway and surreptitiously opens the key cabinet on the wall.

"No, but she might . . . No, forget it," Tobias says, pressing the button for the elevator.

"What were you going to say?" Joona asks, looking at the different keys.

"I really am in a hell of rush now."

Joona carefully slips a set of spare keys off their hook and puts them into his pocket before he leaves the apartment and gets into the elevator next to Tobias.

115

WHEN THEY GET OUT OF the elevator and leave the building, they hear happy cries from the garden. The balloons on the door bounce softly against one another in the draft. The two men walk out onto the sunlit pavement. Tobias stops and looks at Joona, scratches one eyebrow, and then looks off down the street.

"You almost said something about where she might try to go," Joona says.

"I don't even remember the guy's name," Tobias says, shading his eyes with one hand. "But he's kind of an extra dad to Mickan, a girl I know . . . and I know that, before Vicky moved to mine, she was sleeping on a sofa bed at his place, up on Mosebacke Plaza. . . . Sorry, I don't know why I'm saying this."

"What address?"

Tobias shakes his head and adjusts the heavy duffel bag.

"It's the little white building across from the theater."

Joona watches as Tobias disappears around the corner with the heavy bag full of stolen goods and is just thinking about driving up to Mosebacke to knock on doors when an unsettling feeling leaves him rooted to the spot. He's suddenly freezing. It's evening already, and it's been a long time since he last had anything to eat or got any sleep. A nagging headache is making it hard to keep his thoughts straight. Joona starts to move toward the car but stops quickly when he realizes what's wrong.

He can't help smiling.

It's astonishing that he didn't see it before: he must be really tired if he just noticed it now.

Maybe it was too straightforward, like the missing link in a classic detective story.

Tobias said he'd been following the case in one of the evening papers, but the whole time he was talking to Joona, he referred to Vicky as if she was still alive.

Joona has been pretty much on his own when it comes to believing that Vicky isn't dead. The newspapers have printed articles saying that Vicky and Dante drowned in the Indals River. They kept reporting on all the suffering the slow police response had caused Dante's mother and were trying to prompt her to file a complaint.

But Tobias knows that Vicky's alive.

This realization brings another observation.

Joona is now certain of what he saw, and, instead of following Tobias, he stops abruptly and hurries back toward 9 Wollmar Yxkulls Street.

His brain has summoned up the memory of the red balloon coming loose from the door. It rolled across the marble floor of the hallway, almost weightless.

The floor was crisscrossed by children's footprints. They had been playing on the stairs and chasing one another in and out of the garden.

Joona reminds himself that Vicky could still be barefoot, since she lost her sneakers in the river. He yanks the door open and rushes into the hallway and sees that his memory was correct.

Some of the larger footprints lead straight toward the basement door, but there are none leading back the other way.

116

Joona follows the footsteps to the metal door, takes out the keys he stole from Tobias, and unlocks it. With one hand he finds the light switch. The heavy door swings shut behind him, and everything goes dark before the lights come on with a flicker. The walls radiate cold, and the acrid stench of the garbage room reaches him through a vent. He stands perfectly still for a few seconds, listening, before going down the steep steps.

He finds himself in an overfull storage area and pushes past sleds, bicycles, and strollers to make it eventually into a low hallway. Insulated pipes run along the ceiling. The walls consist of the mesh doors of the storage units belonging to the various apartments.

Just as Joona turns on the lights in the hallway and walks in, there's a whirring sound beside him; he spins around to see that it's the elevator motor.

There's a strong smell of urine in the stagnant air.

Now he hears someone moving, farther inside the basement.

Joona thinks about the photograph of Vicky that has been circulated since her disappearance. It's hard to imagine that shy, blushing face transforming into something very different, full of uncontrolled rage. The only way for her to have wielded the heavy hammer would have been to hold it in both hands. He tries to imagine the scene, her striking, and blood spraying up at her face, then her hitting again and again, brushing the blood from one eye against her shoulder.

Joona tries to breathe quietly as he unbuttons his jacket with his left hand and draws his pistol. He still hasn't quite gotten used to the weight and balance of the new gun.

In one compartment, the nose of a brown rocking horse is pressed against the mesh. Behind it, Joona can see steel-edged skis, poles, and a brass curtain rod.

It sounds like someone's shuffling across the concrete floor, but he can't see anything.

He shudders at the thought that Vicky Bennet could have been hiding among the old sleds that he passed a few seconds ago and could now be sneaking up on him from behind.

Joona hears a rustling sound and quickly turns around.

The hallway is empty.

The drainage pipes running along the ceiling are gurgling.

Just as he turns back, the timed lights go out, and everything turns black. He can't see anything and reaches out one hand toward the mesh on one of the compartments. A little farther away, he can make out the glow of a light switch.

A tiny yellow light so you can find the switch.

Joona waits for his eyes to get more used to the darkness before he moves on.

Suddenly the light in the switch vanishes.

Joona stops dead, listening hard.

It takes him a moment to realize that someone is standing in front of the switch.

He crouches down carefully, to present less of a target for a blind attack.

The elevator machinery rumbles behind him, and now the light switch is visible again.

Joona moves backward and hears someone slide gently across the floor.

"Vicky," he says into the darkness.

In that instant, the door to the basement opens and he hears voices from up in the hallway as someone starts to walk down the stairs to the storage area and the lights flicker into life.

Joona seizes his chance and takes several quick steps forward. Seeing movement inside one of the compartments, he raises his pistol toward a hunched figure.

The sluggish fluorescent lights cut through the darkness. The door to the upstairs closes again, and the voices fade away.

Joona holsters his pistol, kicks the small padlock off the door to the compartment, and hurries in. The figure is much smaller than he imagined. Its hunched back is moving quickly in time with its breathing.

There's no doubt that it's Vicky Bennet.

She has tape over her mouth, and her narrow arms are pulled behind her back and tied to the mesh.

Joona hurries over, intending to undo the rope. She's just standing there, panting for breath with her head bowed. Her tangled hair is hanging down in front of her dirty face.

"Vicky, I'm going to get you—"

Without any warning, she kicks him hard in the forehead just as he's bending down. The kick is so powerful that he stumbles back. Hanging from her bound arms, she kicks him in the chest, almost dislocating her shoulders in the process. She kicks again, but this time Joona blocks her foot with his hand. She screams behind the tape, kicks out again, and throws herself forward so hard that an entire section of mesh comes loose. Tugging hard with both hands, Vicky tries to grab a metal bar as Joona knocks her to the concrete floor. He holds her down with one knee and cuffs her wrists before untying the rope and removing the tape.

"I'll kill you!" Vicky shrieks.

"I'm a detective with the—"

"Rape me, then, I don't care, I'll come after you and kill you—"

"Vicky," Joona repeats, raising his voice, "I'm a detective, and I need to know where Dante is."

117

Vicky Bennet is breathing rapidly through her half-open mouth, staring at him with dark eyes. Her face is streaked with blood and dirt, and she looks unbelievably tired.

"If you're a police officer, you have to stop Tobias," she says hoarsely.

"I just spoke to Tobias," Joona explains. "He left to sell some e-readers that he—"

"The bastard!" she gasps.

"Vicky, you know I have to take you to police headquarters."

"Yeah, what the hell, do whatever you want, I don't care...."

"But first ... first you have to tell me where Dante is."

"Tobias took him. And I believed him," Vicky says, turning her face away. Her body starts to shake. "I believed him again, I..."

"What are you trying to say?"

"You won't listen anyway," she says, looking at Joona with wet eyes.

"I'm listening now."

"Tobias promised to get Dante back to his mother."

"He hasn't done that yet," Joona says.

"I know, and I believed him. ... I'm so fucking stupid, I ..."

Her voice breaks, and panic shines in her eyes. "Don't you get it? He's going to sell him—he's going to sell Dante."

"What do you—"

"Don't you understand what I'm saying? And you let him go!" she yells.

"What do you mean by sell?"

"There isn't time! Tobbe, he ... he's going to sell Dante to people who will sell him on again, and you'll never be able to trace him after that."

They hurry through the storage area and up the steep steps. Joona holds Vicky's thin arm as he pulls out his phone and calls the Regional Communications Center.

"I need a car to 9 Wollmar Yxkulls Street to pick up a murder suspect," he says quickly. "And I need assistance finding someone who's suspected of kidnapping. . . ."

They rush out through the door, down the steps, and onto the sunlit pavement. Joona points to his car and explains to the duty officer who has taken the phone call: "His name is Tobias Lundhagen, and ... Hang on," Joona says, and turns to Vicky. "What kind of car does he have?"

"A big black one." She holds her hand up. "I'd recognize it if I saw it."

"What make?"

"No idea."

"What does it look like? An SUV, a minibus, a van?"

"I don't know."

"You don't know if it's—"

"What the fuck? I don't know!" Vicky shouts.

Joona ends the call and puts his hands on her shoulders, looking her in the eye.

"Who's he going to sell Dante to?" he asks.

"I don't know! God, I don't know. . . ."

"So how do you know he's going to sell him? Did he say that? Did you hear him say it?" Joona asks, looking into her anguished eyes.

"I know him. . . . I . . ."

"What is it?"

Her voice is thin and breaking with stress when she replies: "The slaughterhouse district; we need to go to the slaughterhouse district."

"Get in the car," Joona says tersely.

They run the rest of the way, Joona yelling at her to hurry up; she gets in with her hands still cuffed behind her back. He starts the car, then pulls away quickly. Loose grit flies up behind the tires. Vicky falls sideways as Joona turns sharply onto Timmermans Street.

With a nimble movement, Vicky slips her cuffed hands under her backside and legs so that they're in front of her instead.

"Put your seat belt on," Joona says.

They speed up to ninety kilometers an hour, brake sharply, and slide onto Horns Street.

A woman stops in the middle of a pedestrian crossing, looking at something on her phone.

"Moron!" Vicky shouts.

Joona passes the woman on the wrong side of the road and is heading straight for a bus before he swerves back into the right lane. He accelerates as they drive past Maria Square. By the church, a homeless man stops poking through a trash can and walks straight out into the road ahead of them with his crumpled bag over his shoulder.

Vicky gasps and hunches up. Joona swerves sharply into the bike lane as a car heading the other way honks its horn loudly. Joona speeds up again, ignoring the traffic lights, turns right, and puts his foot down as they head into the Södermalm Tunnel.

The light from the lamps on the walls pulses monotonously inside the car. Vicky's face is still, almost stony. Her lips are cracked, and she has a thin layer of dried mud on her skin.

"Why the slaughterhouse district?" Joona asks.

"That's where Tobias sold me," she replies.

118

THERE'S NOT MUCH TRAFFIC IN the Södermalm Tunnel, and Joona is driving very fast. Dry sheets of newspaper swirl in the air in front of the large ventilation units.

From the corner of his eye, he can see that Vicky is biting her nail.

The radio makes a strange crackling noise when Joona requests police and ambulance backup. He tells them that it's likely to be at the slaughterhouse district in Johanneshov but that he doesn't have a precise address yet. "I'll get back to you," he says as the car thunders over the shredded remnants of an old tire.

They continue to head through the long, curved tunnel as yellow bands of light flash past.

"Drive faster," she says, putting her hands against the dashboard as if to protect herself in case they crash.

The light pulses across her pale, dirty face.

"I said I'd pay him back double if he could lend me money and get me a passport. . . . He promised to get Dante back to his mother . . . and I trusted him, can you believe it? After everything he did to me . . ." She hits herself on the head with both hands. "How the fuck can anybody be so fucking stupid?" she says quietly. "All he wanted was Dante. . . . He beat me with a pipe and locked me up. I'm so fucking stupid. . . ."

They pass beneath Nynäs Road and skirt around the Globe

Arena, which sits like an off-white moon beside the soccer stadium.

Beyond the mall, the architecture quickly becomes squat and functional. They drive into a large fenced area full of industrial buildings and parked trailers. In the distance, a neon sign is lit up above the two lanes of the road, white lettering on a red background: SLAUGHTERHOUSE DISTRICT.

The barriers are open, and they drive into the complex on thundering tires.

"Where now?" Joona says as they drive alongside the gray warehouse.

Vicky bites her lip as she looks around frantically.

"I don't know."

119

Even though the sky is dark, the labyrinthine industrial park is lit up with streetlights. Almost all activity has stopped for the day, except that, at the end of one of the side streets, a crane is squealing and creaking as it loads a blue container onto a truck.

Joona drives quickly past a dirty building with a buckled sign advertising pork chops and is approaching some green tin buildings behind closed steel gates.

They pass a yellow-brick building with a loading bay and some rusting containers, then swing behind the central abattoir.

There's no one in sight.

They drive onto a darker street lined with large ventilation drums, garbage containers, and old trolleys.

A van with a pornographic motif painted on its side is standing in the parking spaces beneath a sign reading "Meaty Sausages for You."

There's a rumbling sound as they drive over an uneven drain cover. Joona turns left, skirting a crooked fence. Some seagulls fly up from a stack of pallets.

"There! That's it!" Vicky shouts. "That's his . . . I recognize the building, too—they're in there!"

A black van with an American Confederate flag across its rear window is parked in front of a large liver-brown building with dirty windows and metal shutters. On the other side of the road, four cars are parked in a row. Joona drives past, swings left, and stops in front of another brick building. Advertising banners are fluttering in the wind from three flagpoles.

Without saying anything, Joona takes out his key, removes the cuff from one of Vicky's hands, and fastens it to the steering wheel before he leaves the car. She looks at him darkly but doesn't protest.

Through the windshield, she watches the detective run, illuminated by a streetlight. In the strong wind, grit and trash are flying through the air.

There's a narrow alleyway with loading bays, metal staircases, and containers for discarded meat between the buildings.

As Joona approaches the door, he stops to glance back and look around at the deserted industrial park. In the distance, a forklift is driving around inside a hangarlike building.

He walks up a metal staircase, opens the door, and finds himself in a hallway with a linoleum floor, where he walks past three thin-walled offices. A dusty plastic lemon tree is sticking up out of a white pot full of small clay balls. There's still some tinsel left over from Christmas draped through its branches. A framed butcher's license from 1943 is hanging on the wall, issued by the Emergency Wartime Committee in Stockholm.

A laminated sign about hygiene and recycling rules is hanging on the steel door at the end of the hallway. Someone has scrawled "handling of cocks" across the regulations. Joona opens the door a couple of centimeters, listens, and hears voices some distance away.

Very carefully, he peers into a large processing room where the sides of pork are butchered. The light reflects dimly off the yellow-tiled floor and stainless-steel benches. A bloodstained plastic apron is hanging out below the lid of a trash can.

He silently draws his pistol, and his heart starts to beat a little faster at the smell of gun grease.

120

With his pistol in his hand, Joona creeps into the room, crouching behind the large machines. The cloying smell of the drains and scrubbed rubber mats hits his nose. He realizes he never gave the Regional Communications Center an address. He assumes they've probably reached the slaughterhouse district, but it will take them a while to find Vicky.

A memory flares up. Joona was eleven years old when the principal came to get him from his classroom, took him out into the hallway, and told him, with tears in her eyes, that his father had died. His father was a beat officer and had been killed on duty when he went into an apartment and got shot in the back. Even though it was against regulations, his father had gone into the apartment alone.

Now Joona doesn't have time to wait for backup.

As he moves forward silently, he starts to hear voices more clearly.

"No, he has to wake up first," a man says in a low, gruff voice. "Give it a little longer."

Joona recognizes the boyish tone of Tobias's voice.

"What the fuck were you thinking?" another man asks.

"I just wanted him to stay nice and calm," Tobias says softly.

"He's almost dead," the gruff man says. "I'm not paying until I know he's okay."

"We'll wait another two minutes," the third man says.

Joona keeps moving; when he reaches the end of the row of machinery, he sees the boy, lying on the floor on a gray blanket. He's wearing a crumpled blue hoodie, dark-blue pants, and a small pair of sneakers. His slack face has been washed, but his hair and hands are dirty.

Beside the boy stands a large man with a huge beer gut, wearing a leather vest. His face is running with sweat, and he's pacing, tugging at his white beard and sighing irritably.

Something drips on Joona. The clamp on the end of a hose hasn't been fixed properly. The dripping water trickles across the tiled floor to a drain a short distance away.

The fat man walks around restlessly and looks at the time; a drop of sweat falls from the end of his nose. He crouches down beside the boy with a sigh.

"We can take some pictures," says a man whose voice Joona hasn't heard before.

Joona doesn't know what to do. He thinks there are four men in the room, but he doesn't know if they're armed.

He could use the Rapid Response Unit right now.

The light reflects off the fat man's face as he pulls the sneakers off Dante's feet. His small striped socks come off as well and fall to the floor. His rounded heels bounce on the blanket.

When the man's huge hands start to unbutton the boy's jeans, Joona can't hold back any longer. He stands up from his hiding place.

Without even trying to conceal his presence, he walks out between the butchers' benches, which are covered with a wide variety of freshly sharpened knives. He keeps his pistol pointing at the floor.

His heart is thudding from anxiety.

Joona knows he isn't following the rules, but he can't wait any longer; he just strides out into the open.

"What the hell . . . ?" the fat man says, looking up.

He lets go of the boy but stays on his knees.

"You're all under arrest for kidnapping," Joona says, and kicks the fat man hard in the chest.

Sweat flies off the man's face as he is thrown backward. He tumbles helplessly into the cleaning buckets, rolls backward over the drainage gulley, and manages to pull down a box of ear plugs before crashing into the bulky skinning machine.

Joona hears the safety catch of a gun being released, and a moment later he feels the end of the barrel against his back, just below his shoulder blades. He stands perfectly still, because he knows that the bullet would go straight through his heart if the pistol was fired now.

A man in his fifties with a blond ponytail and a pale-brown leather jacket approaches from one side. He moves smoothly, like a bodyguard and is aiming a sawed-off shotgun at Joona.

"Shoot him!" someone cries.

The fat man is lying on his back, gasping for breath. He rolls over and tries to get up but loses his footing. Then he gets unsteadily to his feet and disappears from Joona's field of vision.

"We can't stay here," Tobias whispers.

Joona tries to look at the reflections in the metal of the butchers' benches and machinery, but it's impossible to see how many men are standing behind him.

"Put your gun down," a calm voice says.

121

Vicky is still sitting in the passenger seat of Joona's car. She bites her dry lips as she stares at the reddish-brown building. She's holding the steering wheel with her hand to stop the cuff from digging into her wrist.

Whenever she gets angry or scared, her world goes blank. It's like a flash of reflected light. It darts around before vanishing again.

Vicky shakes her head, screws her eyes shut for a few seconds, then looks again.

She doesn't know how much time has passed since the detective went into the slaughterhouse. Maybe Dante's already lost; maybe he's already disappeared into the black hole that swallows children.

She tries to stay calm but realizes she can't just wait in the car.

A rat scampers along the damp wall and disappears down a drain.

The man driving the forklift at the end of the road finished work earlier. He closed the two huge doors of the hangar and locked up before he left.

Vicky looks at her hand and the smooth metal holding her captive.

He promised to take Dante back to his mother.

She lets out an anguished moan.

How could she trust Tobias again? If Dante disappears, it will be all her fault.

She turns to check whether she can see anything through the rear window. All the doors are closed, and there's no one in sight, just the yellow fabric of a torn awning flapping in the wind.

She tugs at the steering wheel with both hands, trying to break it, but it's no use.

"Shit . . ."

Breathing hard, she bangs her head against the headrest.

The detective should have been back by now.

Suddenly there's a loud bang, like an explosion.

The clattering echo fades away; everything is quiet again. She looks around but can't see anything. The area is deserted.

What are they doing?

Her heart is thudding in her chest.

Anything could be happening in there.

She starts to breathe faster, and in her mind's eye she sees a lone child sobbing with fear in a roomful of strange men.

The image appeared out of nowhere—she has no idea what it's about.

Vicky stretches and tries to look in through the windows of the building, feeling the panic growing inside her as she tries to pull her hand free. It's impossible. Pulling harder, she just winces with pain; the metal slides a short way over the back of her hand and stops. Breathing through her nose, she leans back, puts one foot on the wheel and the other on the edge of the handcuff, then kicks out as hard as she can.

Vicky screams out loud as the metal tears the skin on her hand and her thumb breaks. But her hand is free.

122

THE PRESSURE OF THE PISTOL barrel disappears from Joona's back as soon as he gives his weapon to Tobias.

Rapid footsteps move away, and he turns around slowly.

A short man in a gray suit and glasses backs away a little farther. He's aiming a black Glock at Joona while his left hand hangs by his hip. It looks oddly inert. At first Joona wonders if it's injured, then realizes that it's a prosthetic.

Tobias, standing behind a dirty bench, is holding Joona's Smith & Wesson, but he doesn't seem to know what to do with it.

To his right, the blond man is pointing the sawed-off shotgun at Joona.

"Roger," the short man says to the one with the shotgun, "you and Micke take care of the policeman once I leave."

Tobias is standing over by the wall, staring at him with eyes darkened by stress.

A young man with cropped hair and camouflage pants walks up in front of Joona, holding a "Carlo," a homemade submachine gun assembled with parts from different weapons. Joona isn't wearing a bulletproof vest, but if he had to choose which of the weapons in the room to be shot with, it would be this one. Though Carlos do sometimes have the same firepower as normal automatic weapons, they're often very badly made.

A red dot is hovering on Joona's chest.

The Carlo is fitted with laser sights, like the ones police officers used a few years ago.

"Lie down on the ground with your hands behind your head,"
Joona says.

The man with cropped hair grins. The red dot slips down to
Joona's crotch, then moves back up to the top of his chest.

"Micke, shoot him," Roger says, still aiming at Joona with the
sawed-off shotgun.

"We can't leave any witnesses," Tobias agrees, wiping his
mouth nervously.

"Put the kid in the car," the man with the prosthetic hand tells
Tobias in a low voice, then walks out of the room.

Without taking his eyes off Joona, Tobias goes over to Dante
and drags him unceremoniously across the tiled floor, by his
hoodie.

"I'll be there shortly," Joona calls after him.

There are maybe six meters between him and Micke, who's
holding the Carlo.

Joona takes a very small step closer to him.

"Stand still!" the young man shouts.

"Micke," Joona says calmly, "if you lie down on the floor with
your hands behind your head, you'll get out of this okay."

"Just shoot the cop!" the man named Roger calls out.

"Do it yourself," Micke whispers.

"What?" Roger says, lowering the shotgun. "What did you
say?"

123

THE YOUNG MAN WITH THE Carlo is breathing quickly and shallowly. The red dot of the laser sight is quivering on Joona's chest. It disappears for an instant, then comes back, moving erratically.

"I can see that you're scared," Joona says, moving toward him.

"Shut up, just shut up," Micke says, backing away.

"The red dot's shaking."

"Shoot him, for fuck's sake!" Roger roars.

"Put the gun down," Joona says.

"Shoot!"

"He won't shoot," Joona tells him.

"No? Well, I will," Roger says, raising the shotgun. "I'm happy to shoot you."

"I don't think so," Joona says with a smile.

"You want me to? Okay, I'll do it!" he yells, coming closer. "You want me to do it?"

Roger strides toward Joona. He has a Thor's hammer dangling from a chain around his neck. He holds the sawed-off shotgun out in front of him, puts his finger on the trigger, and aims at Joona.

"I'm going to blow your head off," he snarls.

Joona lowers his eyes and waits until the man is right in front of him before he thrusts his hand out, grabs the short barrel, pulls the gun toward him, then swings it around and hits Roger in the cheek with the butt of the gun. Roger's head snaps sideways with the impact. The man stumbles into the Carlo's line of fire. Joona stands behind him, aims between his legs, and fires the shotgun. The blast is deafening. The gun jolts from the weight of the charge, and the shot passes between the man's legs and hits Micke's left ankle with immense force. His foot is torn from his leg and rolls under the conveyor belt.

As blood squirts across the floor from his shattered stump, Micke fires the homemade submachine gun. Six bullets slam into Roger's chest and shoulder. Micke collapses to the floor, screaming. The rest of the bullets hit the ceiling and ricochet off the pipes and struts.

The metallic clatter continues until the magazine is empty, and then the only sound is Micke's howls of pain.

The short man with the prosthetic hand comes running in and is just in time to see Roger sink to his knees and lean forward, his ponytail hanging across one cheek. He rests his hands on the floor in front of him as a steady stream of blood pours from his chest, through the grille on the floor, and into the gulley for pigs' blood.

Joona quickly darts behind some machinery. He hears the man with the Glock kick a rattling trolley out of the way, breathing hard through his nose as he comes after Joona.

Joona moves backward, opens the shotgun, and sees that it was loaded with only one cartridge.

The young man is crying for help, panting and screaming.

Just ten steps away, Joona sees a doorway leading to a refrigerated storage room. Behind the yellowing strips of clear plastic, he can see sides of pork hanging in tightly packed rows.

He reasons that there ought to be a door leading to the street and the loading bay at the other end of the cold store.

124

AT THE END OF THE red-brown building is a black metal door that's been wedged open with a rolled-up newspaper.

A white sign reads: "Larsson's Charcuterie and Butchers' Products."

Vicky moves closer, stumbling slightly on the metal grille in front of the door. Blood drips from her wounded hand onto the newspaper as she goes inside the building.

She has to find Dante. That's her only plan.

Without trying to stay hidden, she walks into a locker room with a row of wooden benches in front of some dented red metal lockers. A poster of a smiling Zlatan Ibrahimović is taped to the wall.

She hears a scream through the walls. A man crying for help.

Vicky looks around the locker room, opens some lockers randomly, and pulls out some dusty plastic bags, then looks in the trash can. Among the discarded chewing tobacco and candy wrappers, she sees an empty glass soda bottle.

The man screams again, sounding more tired this time.

"Shit," Vicky whispers. She picks the bottle up and clutches it tightly in her right hand as she makes her way through the other door into a refrigerated storage room full of pallets and packaging machines.

She runs as quietly as she can toward a large garage door.

While she's running past the pallets of shrink-wrapped boxes, she glimpses movement from the corner of her eye and stops.

She looks around and sees a shadow moving behind a bright-yellow forklift. Breathing as silently as she can, she creeps forward, moves around behind the forklift, and sees a man leaning over a bundle lying on a blanket.

"I feel sick," a high-pitched child's voice says.

"Can you stand up, little guy?" the man asks.

She takes a step toward them. The man turns around, and Vicky sees that it's Tobias.

"Vicky? What are you doing here?" he asks with a surprised smile.

She moves closer, warily. "Dante?" she asks softly.

The boy looks at her as if he can't quite see her face.

"Vicky, take him out to the van," Tobias says. "I'll follow you out in a minute."

"But I'm—"

"Just do what I say and everything will be fine," he snaps.

"Okay," she says tonelessly.

"Now, hurry up—get him out to the van."

The boy's face is gray, and he lies down on the blanket again. His heavy eyelids sink lower, then close.

"You'll have to carry him." Tobias sighs.

"Yeah," Vicky says. She walks over and smashes the glass bottle over Tobias's head.

At first he just looks surprised, as he staggers and falls to one knee. He puts his hands to his head in amazement, then looks at the blood and broken glass on his fingers.

"What the fuck are you . . ."

She lunges at him with the jagged remains of the bottle and hits the side of his neck, twists, and feels his warm blood on her fingers. The rage that fills her is so powerful that she feels intoxicated. Fury burns inside her. She jabs at him again and hits his right cheek.

"You should have left the boy alone!" she yells.

Aiming for his eyes, she thrusts the bottle forward. He fumbles and manages to grab her jacket, pulls her toward him, and punches her hard in the face. She falls backward, her field of vision shrinks, and everything goes black for a fraction of a second.

As she falls, she remembers the man who paid Tobias. She remembers waking up with a terrible pain in her crotch and finding out later that she had damaged ovaries.

She lands on her back with a gasp but manages to stop her head from hitting the floor. She blinks, and her sight comes back. She gets to her feet—wobbles but keeps her balance. Blood is trickling from her mouth. Tobias has found a plank with nails sticking out of it on the floor and is trying to stand up.

Vicky's left hand is burning with pain from her broken thumb, but she's still clutching the remains of the broken bottle in her right hand.

She walks forward and stabs Tobias hard in his outstretched hand, getting her own blood in her eyes. She starts to stab randomly, hitting him in the chest and forehead. The remnants of the bottle shatter and she cuts her hand, but she goes on swiping at him until he falls to the floor and doesn't move.

125

Vicky can't run anymore, but she keeps walking with Dante in her arms. She feels as if she's going to throw up. She's lost feeling in both arms and is worried about dropping the boy. She stops and tries to change her grip, but she loses her footing and falls to her knees, hard. Vicky lets out a sigh and gently puts Dante down on the floor. He's fallen asleep again. His face is extremely pale, and she can barely hear his breathing.

They're going to have either to get out or to find somewhere to hide.

She tries to gather her strength. Clenching her teeth, she grabs Dante's jacket and drags him toward a large trash can. It might be possible to squeeze in behind it. Dante whimpers, and his breathing suddenly becomes unsettled. She pats him and sees his eyes open for a second before closing again.

They're only ten meters away from a large garage door with a glass door next to it, but she doesn't have the strength to carry him anymore. Her legs are still shaking from the exertion. All she really wants to do is lie down behind Dante and go to sleep, but she knows she can't do that.

Though her hands are bleeding, she can't feel anything: her arms are still numb.

She can see the empty street through the door.

She sinks onto one knee, breathing heavily, and tries to gather

her thoughts. She looks at her hands, then at Dante, brushes his hair from his face, and leans forward.

"Time to wake up now," she says.

He blinks; at the sight of her blood-streaked face, he looks scared.

"Don't worry," she says. "It doesn't hurt. Have you ever had a nosebleed?"

He nods and licks his lips.

"Dante, I can't carry you anymore. You're going to have to walk the last little bit," Vicky says, feeling a stifled sob in her throat.

"I just want to sleep," he says with a yawn.

"You're going home now. It's over. . . ."

"What?"

"You're going home to your mom," she says, and her exhausted face breaks into a wide smile. "You just need to walk a little way."

He nods, rubs his head with his hands, and sits up.

At the far end of the storeroom, something falls to the ground with a clatter. It sounds as if metal pipes are rolling across the floor.

"Try to stand up now," Vicky whispers.

The two of them get to their feet and start walking toward the glass door. Every step is unbearable, and Vicky realizes she's not going to make it. Suddenly she sees the flashing blue lights of the first police car. It's followed by others, and Vicky thinks, We're safe.

"Hello?" a man calls in a gruff voice. "Hello?"

His voice echoes off the walls and the high ceiling. Vicky feels dizzy and has to stop, but Dante keeps walking.

She leans her shoulder against the cold metal of the container.

"Go out through the door," she says in a muted voice.

Dante looks at her and is about to walk back to her.

"No, go outside," she tells him. "I'll follow you in a second."

She sees three uniformed police officers run in the wrong

direction, toward a building on the other side of the road. Dante keeps heading for the door. He takes hold of the handle and pulls, but nothing happens.

"Hello?" the man calls, closer now.

Vicky spits some bloody saliva on the floor, clenches her teeth, tries to calm her breathing, and starts to move again.

"Stuck," Dante says, tugging at the handle.

Vicky's legs are shaking underneath her, and she feels her knees are going to buckle, but she forces herself to walk the last steps. Her hand stings with pain as she grabs the handle and pulls. The door doesn't move, even when she shoves it; it's locked. When she tries to bang on the glass, it makes almost no sound. There are four police cars parked outside, their blue lights sweeping across the buildings, glinting off the various windows. She tries waving, but none of the officers see her.

Heavy steps thud across the storeroom floor behind them, rapidly getting closer. Vicky turns around to see a fat man in a leather vest heading for them with a smile on his face.

126

Pig carcasses are hanging close together from a belt mounted just below the ceiling. The smell of the meat is dulled by the cold.

Joona moves between the sides of pork in a crouch, going farther and farther in, as he looks around for something to use as a weapon. He can hear muffled screams from the processing room, followed by some rapid thuds. When he tries to see his pursuer through the thick strips of plastic covering the doorway, he can make out a blurred figure in front of the benches. At first he seems to be as wide as four men, then he gets thin again.

He's coming closer, fast.

And he's clearly holding a pistol in his right hand.

Joona backs away, ducks down, and looks around on the floor beneath the pig carcasses. Over by the far wall is a white bucket, a pipe of some sort, and some dirty rags.

He can work with the pipe.

He starts to move cautiously in that direction but has to stop and pull back when the short man pushes the strips of plastic aside with his prosthetic hand.

Joona stands still, catching glimpses of the man reflected in the narrow chrome lintels. He sees the man enter the cold store, holding the pistol out in front of him as he looks around.

Joona takes a few silent steps toward the wall and tucks in

behind one of the carcasses. In that position, he can no longer observe his pursuer—but he can still hear his footsteps and breathing.

Fifteen meters away is a door, which probably leads to a loading bay. Joona could run down the passageway between the hanging carcasses, but just before he reached the door there would be several seconds when he would be an open target to the man with the gun.

Several seconds too many, Joona thinks.

He hears slow, shuffling steps, then a heavy thud. One of the pigs starts to sway, and the hook connecting it to the belt in the ceiling creaks.

Joona takes the last few steps to the wall and crouches down beside one of the cold-storage units. His pursuer's shadow is gliding across the concrete floor ten meters away.

Time is starting to run out.

The man with the prosthetic hand will find him soon. Joona sidles along the wall and sees that the pipe is made of plastic—it's useless as a weapon. He's about to move back when he sees that there are several tools in the old bucket: three screwdrivers, a pair of pliers, and a knife with a short, sturdy blade.

Joona cautiously picks the knife out of the bucket, making a slight scraping sound as the blade slips against one handle of the pliers. Trying to read his pursuer's movement from the sound of his steps, he realizes that he has to get away.

A shot goes off and thuds into a side of pork with a dull thump, half a meter from Joona's head.

127

THE POLICEMAN IS UNARMED AND scared, the man thinks as he brushes his bangs aside with his prosthetic hand.

He stops, raises the pistol, and tries to see past the animal carcasses.

He must be scared, he repeats to himself.

He might be hiding now, but the man knows that soon the policeman will try to make a run for the door leading to the street.

His own breathing is faster than normal. The air feels cold and dry in his lungs. He coughs weakly, turns around, glances at the pistol, then looks up again. He blinks hard. Did he just see something over by the wall, behind that cold-storage unit? He starts to run along the row of carcasses.

All he has to do is catch up with the policeman and shoot him at close range. First shot at his body, second through his temple.

He stops when he sees that the aisle by the wall is empty. There's just a white bucket and some rags on the floor.

He turns abruptly and starts to retrace his steps, then stops and listens.

All he can hear is the nasal sound of his own breathing.

He pushes one side of pork with his false hand, but it's heavier than he expected. He has to give it a good shove to get it to swing. His arm starts to ache again when the prosthetic presses against his stump.

The hooks up at the ceiling creak. The pig swings to the right, and he can see into the next aisle.

There's nowhere he can go, the man thinks. He's trapped in a cage. All he has to do is keep an open line of fire to the door in case the policeman tries to get out, while also keeping an eye on the plastic-covered opening to the processing room to stop him from going back that way.

His shoulder is starting to tire, and he lowers the pistol for a little bit. He knows he risks losing vital seconds, but the gun will shake if his arm gets too tired.

Moving forward slowly, he catches a glimpse of what he thinks is the man's back, raises the pistol, and fires. The recoil kicks back, and the percussive powder burns his knuckles. Adrenaline rushes through him, making his face feel cold.

He moves sideways but realizes that he was wrong: it was a just a side of pork hanging crookedly.

This is starting to go seriously wrong, he thinks. He has to stop the policeman; he can't let him get away, not now.

So where the hell is he? Where is he?

The ceiling creaks, and he looks up at the beams and struts. Nothing. He backs away and puts his foot down wrong, ending up with one shoulder resting against a side of pork, feeling the cold dampness of the meat through his shirt. The carcass is sparkling with tiny drops of condensation. He feels sick. There's something not right about this. The stress is starting to catch up with him, and he's not going to be able to stay in here much longer.

As the man continues to move backward, he sees a fleeting shadow on the wall and raises the gun.

Suddenly the carcasses start to sway, all of them at once. As they begin to quiver, their outlines blur. With an electronic whirring sound from the ceiling, the machinery rattles, and the heavy sides of pork start to move as one along the belt, causing a cold draft.

The man with the pistol turns around, his eyes scanning the room, trying to cover all angles at the same time.

It should have been simple, buying a Swedish boy the police already thought was dead. He wouldn't have to go farther than Germany or Holland to get a good price for him. But it's not worth the effort now.

The pigs stop abruptly, and sway slowly. A red lamp is glowing on the wall. The policeman has pressed the emergency stop button.

The room is quiet again.

What the hell am I doing here? the man asks himself.

He tries to calm his breathing as he moves slowly closer to the red light, crouching in an attempt to see between the carcasses.

The door to the street is still closed.

He turns to look at the other exit, and in that instant he finds the tall policeman standing right in front of him.

The man feels a cold shiver run down his spine.

128

JOONA MIRRORS THE SHORT MAN'S movement, taking a step forward and deflecting the gun so it ends up pointing at the ceiling. He grabs the man's wrist and slams it against one of the carcasses, twists the pistol out of his grasp, then drives the knife straight through the man's hand as hard as he can.

Joona lets go of the knife and takes a step back.

The man is panting hard, fumbling for the handle of the knife with the lifeless fingers of his prosthetic hand, but he gives up. He's stuck and realizes that he needs to stand perfectly still to lessen the excruciating pain. His hand is skewered high above his head. Blood is running down his wrist and underneath the sleeve of his shirt.

Without giving him another glance, Joona picks up the pistol and walks out.

The air in the large processing room feels very warm after the refrigerated storage room as he hurries toward the door where Tobias vanished with Dante. Quickly checking the pistol, he sees that there's a bullet in the chamber; there are probably more in the magazine. He opens the green metal door and finds himself in a large storeroom full of loaded pallets and forklifts.

Light is coming in through the dirty windows close to the ceiling.

He can hear a rattling, groaning sound.

Joona works out where it's coming from and runs over to a large trash can. Blue light is playing across the floor from a glass door. He raises the pistol and moves around the container. The fat man in the leather vest is kneeling on the floor with his back to Joona. He lets out a load groan as he slams Vicky's head onto the floor. A short distance away Dante is curled up, crying in a high, desolate voice.

Before the fat man has time to get up, Joona is on him. He grabs the man's throat under his beard with one hand and pulls him to his feet, away from Vicky. He gives him a shove and breaks his collarbone with the pistol, then pushes him back again, letting go of his throat, and kicks him hard in the chest, so that he lurches back, straight through the glass door.

The fat man falls backward into the street in a shower of broken glass and ends up lying there bathed in blue light.

Three uniformed policemen run over, weapons drawn, aiming at the man on the ground, who clutches his chest with one hand as he tries to sit up.

"Joona Linna?" one of the officers asks.

They stare at the tall detective standing in the remains of the shattered door, splinters of glass still falling from the top of the frame.

"I'm just an observer," Joona says.

He tosses the Glock on the ground and goes over and kneels down beside Vicky. She's lying on her back, gasping for breath. Her arm is lying at an unnatural angle. Dante has stopped crying and looks at Joona in astonishment as he gently strokes Vicky's cheek and whispers that it's over now. A steady trickle of blood is running from her nose. Joona crouches down and holds her head completely still. She doesn't open her eyes and doesn't react when spoken to, although her feet are twitching.

129

THE FIRST PARAMEDICS ON THE scene took care to immobilize Vicky's head with a neck brace before they lifted her onto a stretcher.

As Joona informed the lead officer about the situation, two police patrols made their way into the building from different directions.

In the refrigerated storage room they discovered a silent, pale man with his right hand pinned to a hanging side of pork. The police officer who found him called in the paramedics, then had to get a colleague to help him pull the knife out. The blade squeaked against the animal's ribs before coming loose with a sigh. The man lowered his hand, pressed it to his stomach with the prosthetic, then staggered and slumped down onto the floor.

The last to be found was Tobias Lundhagen, who had hidden among the trash in the darkness of the storeroom with his badly cut face. He was bleeding profusely, but his injuries weren't life-threatening, although he would be left badly disfigured. He tried to crawl farther in among the trash; when the police pulled him out by his legs, he was shaking with terror.

CARLOS HAS ALREADY BEEN INFORMED of developments out in the slaughterhouse district when Joona calls him from the ambulance.

"One dead, two seriously injured, and three more requiring hospitalization," Carlos reads.

"But the children are alive, they made it. . . ."

"Joona." Carlos sighs.

"Everyone said they'd drowned, but I—"

"I know. You were right, you were definitely right," Carlos interrupts. "But you're under investigation and had been given other orders."

"So I shouldn't have bothered?" Joona asks.

"Exactly."

"I couldn't do that."

The ambulance makes a sharp turn toward the emergency room at Södermalm Hospital and turns its sirens off.

"The prosecutor and her people are in charge of the interviews, and you are now formally on leave."

Joona assumes that the internal investigation is going to get worse and that they may even decide to press charges against him, but all he can feel right now is immense relief at rescuing Dante from a terrible fate.

When they reach the hospital, he climbs out of the ambulance on his own, but then they make him lie on a trolley. They fold the sides up and wheel him off to an examination room.

While he's being checked over and patched up, he tries to find out about Vicky Bennet's condition, and then, instead of waiting to be X-rayed, he goes to find the doctor responsible for her care.

Dr. Lindgren, a very short woman, is staring at a coffee machine with a frown on her face. Joona explains that he needs to know if Vicky can be questioned today. The short woman listens without meeting his gaze. She presses the button for mocha, waits for her cup to fill, then says that she performed an emergency CAT scan of Vicky's brain to check for possible intracranial bleeding. Vicky has suffered a serious concussion, but, luckily, there's no hematoma.

"Vicky needs to stay in the hospital for observation, but

there's no reason why she can't be questioned first thing tomorrow morning if it's important," the woman explains, then walks away with her cup.

District Prosecutor Susanne Öst is driving down to Stockholm. She's decided to arrest the girl. At eight o'clock tomorrow morning, she's planning to conduct the first interview with Vicky Bennet, the fifteen-year-old girl suspected of two counts of murder and one of kidnapping.

130

Joona shows his ID and says hello to the young police officer standing guard outside Room 703.

Vicky is sitting up in bed. The curtains are open, and her face is covered with dark cuts and bruises. Her head has been bandaged, and the hand with the broken thumb is now in a cast. Over by the window stands Susanne Öst, the prosecutor from Sundsvall, with a second woman. Without bothering to acknowledge their presence, Joona goes straight over to Vicky and sits down in the chair by the bed.

"How are you feeling?" he asks.

She looks at him groggily and asks, "Did Dante get home to his mom?"

"He's still in the hospital, but his mom's with him; she hasn't left his side."

"Is he hurt?"

"No."

Vicky nods, then stares in front of her.

"How are you feeling?" Joona asks again.

She looks at him but doesn't get a chance to answer before the prosecutor clears her throat. "I must ask Joona Linna to leave the room now," she says.

"And now you have," Joona replies, without taking his eyes off Vicky.

"You don't have any involvement in this investigation," Susanne says, raising her voice.

"They're going to ask you an awful lot of questions," Joona explains to Vicky.

"I want you to be here," she says quietly.

"I can't stay," Joona replies plainly.

Vicky whispers something to herself, then looks at Susanne.

"I'm not talking to anyone unless Joona's here," she says stubbornly.

"He can stay if he keeps quiet," the prosecutor replies.

Joona looks at Vicky and tries to figure out a way of getting through to her.

Two murders are an immense burden to carry.

Anyone else her age would already have crumbled, would be crying and confessing everything, but this girl seems to have a crystalline shell. She never really lets anyone in. She forms alliances quickly but remains distant and is always in control of the situation.

"Vicky Bennet," the prosecutor begins with a smile. "Like I said, my name is Susanne, and I'm the person who's going to be talking to you, but before we start I want to let you know that I'm going to record everything we say so that we can remember it afterward . . . and so I don't have to do so much writing, which is handy, because I'm pretty lazy. . . ."

Vicky isn't looking at her and shows no reaction to her words. Susanne waits a few seconds, still smiling, then states the time, the date, and the names of those present in the room for the recording.

"I have to do that before we start," she explains.

"Do you understand who we are?" the other woman asks. "My name is Signe Ridelman, and I'm your legal representative."

"Signe's here to help you," the prosecutor says.

"Do you know what a legal representative is?" she asks.

Vicky nods almost imperceptibly.

"I need an answer," Signe says patiently.

"I understand," Vicky says quietly, then suddenly smiles.

"What's so funny?" the prosecutor asks.

"This," Vicky says, slowly pulling the narrow tube out from the crook of her elbow, then watching as the dark blood trickles down her pale arm.

131

THE LIGHT FIXTURE IN THE ceiling of the hospital room hums quietly. Vicky is emotionless as the nurse applies a new bandage.

"I'm going to ask you some questions," Susanne Öst says. "And I want you to tell me the truth."

"And nothing but the truth," Vicky whispers with her head bowed.

"Nine days ago . . . you left your room at the Birgitta Home in the middle of the night," the prosecutor begins. "Do you remember that?"

"I didn't count the days," the girl says in a toneless voice.

"But you remember leaving the Birgitta Home in the middle of the night?"

"Yes."

"Why?" Susanne Öst asks. "Why did you leave?"

Vicky pulls at a loose thread on the bandage around her hand.

"Had you done it before?" Susanne asks.

"What?"

"Left the Birgitta Home in the middle of the night?"

"No," Vicky says in a bored voice.

"Why did you do it on this occasion?"

When the prosecutor doesn't get an answer, she just smiles tolerantly and asks, in a gentler tone of voice, "Why were you awake in the middle of the night?"

"Don't remember."

"If we go back a few more hours—do you remember what happened then? Everyone went to bed, but you were awake; what were you doing?"

"Nothing."

"You did nothing until you suddenly left in the middle of the night—don't you think that sounds a bit strange?"

"No."

Vicky stares out the window. Clouds drift across the sky in front of the sun.

"Now, I want you to tell me why you left the Birgitta Home," Susanne says in a more serious tone of voice. "Because I'm not going to give up until you tell me what happened. Do you understand?"

"I don't know what you want me to say," Vicky replies quietly.

"I know it's hard, but you still need to tell me."

The girl looks up at the ceiling and her mouth moves, as if she were searching for words, before she says in a dreamy voice: "I killed . . ."

She falls silent.

"Go on," Susanne says, sounding tense.

Vicky licks her lips and shakes her head.

"You can tell me," Susanne says. "You said you killed . . ."

"Yeah, right . . . There was an annoying fly in my room, and I killed it and . . ."

"Oh, for God's sake . . . ! Sorry, I didn't mean that . . . but don't you think it's strange that you remember killing a fly, but you can't remember why you left the house?"

132

THE PROSECUTOR AND SIGNE RIDELMAN have requested a
short break and left the room. Vicky Bennet is sitting up in the
hospital bed, swearing quietly to herself.

"Couldn't agree more," Joona says, sitting down on the chair
beside the bed.

She looks up and gives him a brief smile. "I keep thinking
about Dante," she says weakly.

"He's going to be okay."

She's about to say something else, but she stops herself when
the prosecutor and lawyer come back in.

"You've admitted to running away from the Birgitta Home in
the middle of the night," the prosecutor says with renewed vigor.
"In the middle of the night. Straight into the forest. That's not
the kind of thing people normally do. You had a reason for running away, didn't you?"

Vicky lowers her gaze and licks her lips but says nothing.

"Answer me," Susanne says, raising her voice.

"Yeah . . ."

"Why did you run away?"

The girl shrugs.

"You did something that's hard to talk about, didn't you?"

Vicky rubs her face hard.

"I have to ask you these questions," Susanne says. "You might think it's unpleasant, but I know everything will feel much better if you just confess."

"Will it?"

"Yes."

Vicky shrugs her shoulders again, looks up to meet the prosecutor's gaze, and asks, "What do you want me to confess?"

"What you did that night."

"I killed a fly."

The prosecutor stands up abruptly and leaves the room.

133

SAGA BAUER OPENS THE DOOR to the senior prosecutor's room at Internal Affairs at eight-fifteen. Mikael Båge, who's in charge of this investigation, gets up politely from his chair.

Saga's hair is still damp after her shower, and her long blond locks, into which she's wound colorful ribbons, curl across her back and shoulders. She has a Band-Aid across the bridge of her nose but is still strikingly beautiful.

Saga has already run ten kilometers this morning and is wearing what she always does: a hoodie from the Narva Boxing Club, faded jeans, and sneakers.

"Saga Bauer?" the internal investigator asks with a broad smile.

"Yes," she replies.

He goes over and shakes hands with her.

"Forgive me," he says. "But I—I'm sure you've heard it before, but if I was twenty years younger . . ."

Mikael Båge is blushing; he sits down on a chair and loosens his tie slightly before looking up at Saga again.

The door opens, and Senior Prosecutor Sven Wiklund walks in. He shakes hands with them both, then stops in front of Saga as if he's about to say something, but he just nods and sets a pitcher of water and three glasses on the table before he sits down.

"Saga Bauer, detective with the Security Police," Mikael says.

Sven pours water into the glasses.

"You've been asked to provide a witness statement," Mikael continues, tapping a folder. "Because you were present at the incident in question."

"What do you want to know?" she asks.

"The complaint against Joona Linna concerns ... Well, he's suspected of having warned—"

"Göran Stone is really fucking stupid," she interrupts.

"There's no need to get upset," Mikael says.

Saga vividly remembers how both she and Joona made their way inside the headquarters of a clandestine group of left-wing extremists. Daniel Marklund, the Brigade's expert at hacking and surveillance, gave them information that helped save Penelope Fernandez's life.

"So you don't consider the Security Police operation a failure?"

"I do, because it was, but I was the one who warned the Brigade."

"Well, this complaint has been filed against—"

"Joona's the best police officer in the country."

"Loyalty is all well and good, but this is serious. We're going to press charges against him."

"Then you can go to hell!" Saga snaps.

She gets up, overturning the table. The glasses and pitcher hit the floor, spreading water and broken glass across the room. She snatches Mikael's folder from his hand, empties its contents on the floor, then leaves the room, slamming the door.

134

SAGA IS STILL SWEARING TO herself when she emerges onto Kungs Bridge. She forces herself to walk slower as she tries to calm down. Her phone rings, and she answers when she sees it's her boss.

"We've received a request from National Crime," Verner says in his deep voice. "I've had a word with Jimmy and Jan Petters-son, but neither of them can take it. . . . I don't know if Göran Stone is suitable, but . . ."

"What's it about?" she asks.

"Questioning an underage girl . . . She's mentally unstable, and the head of the investigation needs someone trained in interview techniques."

"I can understand your asking Jimmy," Saga says, aware of the jagged note of irritation in her voice, "but why Jan Pettersson? Why would you ask Jan Pettersson before talking to me? And as for Göran . . . how can you begin to think that . . ."

Saga forces herself to stop. She can still feel the aftereffects of her outburst a few minutes ago. "Look, I'm the one who went down to Pullach and did the BND's training course, and—"

"Please—"

"I'm not done," she interrupts. "You know perfectly well that I sat in when Muhammed al-Abdaly was cross-examined."

"But you weren't lead interviewer."

"No, but I was the one who . . . Oh, what's the point?"

She disconnects and contemplates handing in her notice tomorrow morning. Her phone rings again.

"Okay, Saga," Verner says slowly. "You can give it a try."

"Shut up!" she yells, and switches her phone off.

CARLOS SPILLS FISH FOOD ON his desk when Anja forcefully throws the door open. He is just starting to sweep the dry flakes into his hand as his phone rings.

"Could you put it on speaker?" he asks her.

"It's Verner," Anja says, and presses the button.

"Hi there," Carlos says brightly, brushing his hands above one of the aquariums.

"It's Verner. Sorry it took such a long time."

"No problem."

"Look, Carlos, I've done my best, but I'm afraid all my best guys are on loan to Alex Allan at the Joint Intelligence Committee," Verner says, and clears his throat. "But there's one female agent . . . I think you've met her, Saga Bauer. . . . She could at least sit in and . . ."

Anja leans toward the phone and snaps, "She could sit in and look pretty, couldn't she?"

"Hello?" Verner says. "Who am I talking—"

"Oh, just shut up!" Anja snarls. "I know Saga Bauer, and I can tell you right now that the Security Police don't deserve her!"

135

THE POLICE OFFICER POSTED IN the hallway looks at Saga Bauer's ID and blushes. He tells her that the patient will be back soon and holds the door open for her.

Saga takes a few steps inside and stops in front of the two people waiting in the empty room. The bed is gone, but the IV stand is still there.

"Excuse me," the woman in the gray suit says.

"Yes?" Saga says.

"Are you a friend of Vicky's?"

Before Saga can say anything, the door opens and Joona comes in.

"Joona," she says in surprise, smiling broadly as she shakes his hand. "I thought you'd been suspended."

"I have," he confirms.

"Good to know," she says.

"The internal investigators are doing a great job," he says, grinning so hard that dimples appear in his cheeks.

The prosecutor Susanne Öst walks up to Saga with a confused expression on her face. "Security Police?" she asks. "I thought perhaps . . . I mean, I asked for . . ."

"Where's Vicky Bennet?" Saga asks.

"Her doctor wanted to perform another CAT scan," Joona says, then goes to stand at the window with his back to the room.

"This morning, I decided to charge Vicky Bennet," the prosecutor says. "Obviously, it would be good to get a confession before the custody hearing."

"You're planning to press charges?" Saga asks in surprise.

"Look," Susanne says dryly. "I was there. I saw the bodies. Vicky Bennet is fifteen years old, but she's in a league way beyond what juvenile homes can provide."

Saga smiles skeptically. "But a prison sentence—"

"Don't take this the wrong way," the prosecutor interrupts, "but I was expecting to get an experienced interviewer."

"I'm sure you were," Saga says.

"You can take a shot, though. You should definitely get a chance."

"Thanks," Saga says through clenched teeth.

"I've been here half a day already, and I can tell you that this isn't a normal interview," Susanne says, taking a deep breath.

"In what way?"

"Vicky Bennet isn't scared—she seems to enjoy mind games."

"How about you?" Saga asks. "Do you enjoy mind games?"

"I don't have time for her games—or yours, either," the prosecutor says sternly. "Tomorrow I'm in court for the custody hearing."

"I've listened to the first session, and I don't get the impression that Vicky Bennet is playing," Saga says.

"It's just a game," the prosecutor insists.

"I don't think so. Murder can be traumatic even for murderers— their memories can be like separate islands with fluid boundaries."

"So what did the Security Police teach you about that?"

"The lead interviewer should presume that all perpetrators want to confess and be understood," Saga replies, deliberately ignoring Susanne's provocative tone.

"Is that all?" the prosecutor asks.

"I tend to think that a confession is linked to a feeling of power—the person confessing has power over the truth," Saga goes on amiably. "That's why threats don't work, whereas friendliness, respect, and—"

"Just don't forget that she's suspected of committing two extremely brutal murders."

136

VICKY BENNET IS WHEELED INTO the room by two nurses. Her face is badly swollen now, and her cheeks and forehead are covered with dark scabs. Her arm is still bandaged, and there's a cast around her broken thumb. The bed is put back into position, and the drip is reattached to the stand. Vicky is lying on her back with her eyes open, ignoring the nurses' attempts to make small talk. The look on her face is sad and heavy.

The safety rails of the bed are pulled up, but the straps hang loose.

When the nurses leave the room, Saga notices that there are now two police officers standing guard in the hallway.

Saga waits until the girl looks at her before walking over to the bed.

"My name is Saga Bauer, and I'm here to help you remember the past days."

"Are you some sort of counselor, then, or what?"

"Detective."

"Police?"

"Yes, Security Police," Saga replies.

"You're the most beautiful person I've ever seen."

"That's a nice thing to say."

"I've cut beautiful faces before now," Vicky says, smiling.

"I know," Saga replies calmly.

She takes out her phone and switches on the recording function. She quickly says the date, time, and location, then the names of the people in the room, before turning to Vicky and looking at her. After a while, she says, without any artifice, "You've been through some terrible things."

"I've seen the papers," Vicky replies, and swallows a couple of times. "I've seen my picture, and Dante's . . . and I've read things about myself."

"Do you recognize the things they wrote?"

"No."

"Tell me what happened instead, in your own words."

"I've been running and walking and freezing . . . frozen."

Vicky looks at Saga curiously, licks her lips, and then appears to search inside herself—either for memories that match what she's said or for lies that might explain it.

"I don't know anything about why you ran, but I'll listen if you decide you want to tell me," Saga says slowly.

"I don't want to," Vicky mumbles.

"How about we start with the day before that?" Saga goes on. "I know a little about that. I know you had lessons in the morning, but apart from that . . ."

Vicky closes her eyes, then, after a short pause, says, "It was normal, just routines and boring chores."

"Don't you usually have activities in the afternoons?"

"Elisabet took everyone down to the lake. . . . Lu Chu and Almira went skinny-dipping, even though we're not allowed to, but that's just what they're like," Vicky says with a sudden smile. "Elisabet got annoyed with them, so everyone else started to take all their clothes off."

"But not you?"

"No . . . and not Miranda or Tuula, either," Vicky says.

"So what did you do instead?"

"I paddled at the edge of the water and watched the others playing."

"What did Elisabet do?"

"She took all her clothes off and went swimming." Vicky smiles again.

"What about Tuula and Miranda?"

"They sat and threw pinecones at each other."

"And Elisabet went swimming with the others?"

"She swam the way old ladies do."

"How about you? What did you do?"

"I went back to the house," Vicky says.

"How did you feel that evening?"

"Fine."

"You felt fine? But, then, why did you hurt yourself? You cut yourself on your arms and stomach."

137

THE PROSECUTOR HAS BEEN SITTING on a chair, following the conversation with intense concentration. Saga is looking at Vicky's face and sees it become darker now, harder, for a few seconds. The corners of her mouth turn down, and there's a cold look in her eyes.

"It says in the notes that you cut your arms," Saga explains.

"Yeah, but it was nothing. . . . We were watching TV, and I felt a little sorry for myself and cut myself with a piece of a broken plate. . . . I had to go to the office to get patched up. I like it when that happens. Because Elisabet is calm, and she knows I need soft gauze bandages around my hands, or, rather, my wrists . . . Because it always feel disgusting afterward, when I think about the open veins and everything . . ."

"Why did you feel sorry for yourself?"

"I was supposed to have a talk with Elisabet, but she said she didn't have time."

"What did you want to talk about?"

"I don't know; nothing, really. It was just my turn for a talk with her, but all my time got used up because Miranda and Tuula were fighting."

"That doesn't sound very fair," Saga says.

"Anyway, I felt sorry for myself and cut myself and got patched up."

"So you got some time alone with Elisabet after all."

"Yeah," Vicky says with a smile.

"Are you Elisabet's favorite?"

"No."

"Who is her favorite?" Saga asks.

Vicky quickly lunges out with the back of her hand, but Saga merely rolls her head back without moving her body. Vicky can't understand what happened, how she managed to miss, or how the police officer has managed to press her hand very gently against Vicky's cheek.

"Are you feeling tired?" Saga asks, letting her hand rest soothingly against the girl's cheek.

Vicky looks at her and holds the hand in place for a moment before suddenly turning her face away.

"You usually get twenty milligrams of Zyprexa before you go to bed," Saga continues after a while.

"Yes."

The girl's voice is now monotonous and dismissive.

"What time?"

"Ten."

"Were you able to get to sleep then?"

"No."

"If I've understood correctly, you weren't able to sleep all night."

"I don't want to talk anymore," Vicky says, resting her head heavily on the pillow and closing her eyes.

"That's enough for today," her lawyer says, getting up from her chair.

"We've got twenty minutes left," the prosecutor objects.

"My client needs to rest," Signe Ridelman says, going over to Vicky. "You're tired, aren't you? Would you like me to get you something to eat?"

The lawyer talks to Vicky, and the prosecutor stands by the window, listening to her voice mail with a blank face.

Saga is about to stop the recording when she happens to catch Joona's eye and hesitates. His eyes look remarkably gray—like ice melting in the spring. Then he walks out of the room. Saga asks Signe Ridelman, Vicky's lawyer, to wait, and follows Joona a little way down the hall. He's waiting for her by the door to the fire escape.

"Did I miss something?" she asks.

"Vicky slept in her bed with bloodstained clothes on," Joona tells her quietly.

"What?"

"It's not in the crime-scene report."

"But you spotted it?"

"Yes."

"So she did sleep, after the murders?"

"I don't have access to the lab results, but one thought I had is that she gave herself an overdose of her medication because she was feeling bad. It's easy to think that it would help, but it doesn't—it just makes you more and more restless, until you end up in a rage. We don't know anything yet, but maybe she wanted to get revenge on Miranda for using up all her conversation time, or maybe she was angry with Elisabet for letting Miranda get away with it. Or maybe it's about something else entirely. . . ."

"So you're thinking that one possible scenario is that she killed Elisabet, took the key, opened the door to the isolation room, killed Miranda, and then fell asleep?"

"Yes, because the evidence points to two distinct aspects of the crime in the isolation room—uncontrollable rage, and concern, almost sadness."

Joona looks directly at Saga, his eyes heavy and thoughtful. "Once Miranda was dead, the rage faded away," he says. "She tried to arrange Miranda's body—laid her on the bed and put her hands over her eyes. Then she went back to her own room just as the tranquilizing effect of the medication kicked in."

138

WHEN SAGA RETURNS TO THE patient's room, the prosecutor tries to explain that the remaining fifteen minutes are too little time to accomplish anything useful. Saga just nods, then goes over to the foot of the bed. Signe Ridelman looks at her curiously. Saga waits with her hands on the metal bed frame until Vicky meets her gaze.

"I thought you were awake all night," Saga begins, very slowly. "But Joona says you slept in your bed for a while before you left the Birgitta Home."

Vicky shakes her head, and her lawyer tries to intervene: "Today's session is over, and . . ."

Vicky whispers something and scratches one of the scabs on her cheek. Saga knows she has to get her to talk about what happened next. It doesn't have to be much, just a few honest words about her flight through the forest and the boy's abduction. The more the interviewer can get the subject to talk about the events surrounding the crime, the more likely he or she is to confess to everything.

"Joona isn't usually wrong," Saga says with a smile.

"It was dark, and I was lying in bed while everyone was screaming and slamming doors," Vicky whispers.

"You're lying in bed and everyone's screaming," Saga says, nodding. "What are you thinking? What do you do next?"

"I'm scared, my heart is beating really hard and fast, and I lie there completely still under the covers," Vicky says, without looking at anyone in the room. "It's really dark ... but then I realize that I'm wet. . . . I think I've wet myself or got my period or something. . . . Buster is barking, and Nina is screaming something about Miranda, and I switch the light on and see that I have blood all over me."

Saga forces herself not to ask about the blood or the murders. She can't try to force a confession; she has to just go with the flow.

"Do you start screaming, too?" she asks in a neutral voice.

"I don't think so. I don't know. I couldn't think," Vicky goes on. "I just wanted to get away from it all, disappear. . . . I sleep with my clothes on—I always have—so I just grab my bag, put my shoes on, climb out through the window, and walk off into the forest. . . . I'm scared, and I go as fast as I can, and the sky gets lighter, and after a few hours it's easier to see through the trees. I just keep going, and then I see a car. . . . It's almost new; it's just sitting there abandoned; the door's open, and the keys are in it. . . . I know how to drive—I spent a whole summer doing it— so I just get in the car and start driving. . . . And then I feel how exhausted I am, and how my legs are shaking. . . . I'm thinking of driving to Stockholm and getting some money so I can go and stay with my friend in Chile. . . . Then, suddenly, there's a bang, and the car spins around and the side hits something. . . . Bang, then silence . . . I come around—my ear's bleeding—and I look up. There are pieces of glass everywhere. I've driven into a damn traffic light. I don't know how, but the windows are gone, and the rain's coming straight into the car. . . . The engine's still running, and I'm alive. . . . I put my hand on the gearshift, reverse, and then keep driving. . . . The rain's blowing into my face. And then I hear someone crying, and I turn around and see that there's a kid sitting in a car seat in the back, a little boy. It's crazy—I have no

idea how he got there. . . . I shout at him to shut up. The rain just
keeps pouring down. I can hardly see at all, but just as I'm about
to turn the corner and drive across the bridge, I see flashing blue
lights across the river. . . . I panic and spin the steering wheel,
and we go off the road. It all happens too fast—we're rushing
down the riverbank. I try to brake, but the car just keeps going,
into the water, and I hit my head on the wheel. Water crashes
over the hood into the car, and we just keep going, farther
out into the river. . . . Everything gets dark when we start to sink,
but I find some air up by the roof and crawl back toward the
boy, I manage to get his seat belt off and pull the whole car seat
out through the windshield. We're already a long way down, but
the car seat floats and pulls us up to the surface, and we float
down the river and manage to get out on the opposite bank. . . .
We're soaked through, my bag and shoes are gone, but we start
walking. . . ."

Vicky pauses to catch her breath. Saga detects movement
from the prosecutor but doesn't take her eyes off Vicky.

"I told Dante we were going to find his mom," Vicky goes on
in a shaky voice. "I held his hand, and we walked and walked,
and sang a song from his preschool about an old man who wore
his shoes out. We were walking along a road with lampposts
on the sides. . . . A car stopped, and we got in the back seat. . . .
The man looked at us in the mirror and turned the heater up
and asked if we wanted to go to his house and get some food
and new clothes. . . . We would have gone if he hadn't checked
us out in the mirror and said we could earn some cash, too. . . .
When he stopped for gas, we snuck out and started walking
again instead. . . . I don't know how far we got, but there was an
IKEA truck parked at a rest stop near a lake, and on one of the
picnic tables we found a bottle and a plastic bag full of ham-
burger rolls. But before we could grab the bag, a guy asked if
we were hungry. . . . He's from Poland, and he gives us a ride all

the way to Uppsala. . . . I borrow his phone and call my mom. . . . Over and over, I tell myself that I'll kill him if he touches Dante, but he just lets us sit there quietly and sleep—he doesn't want anything. He just drops us off, and we catch the train and take it the last part of the way to Stockholm, hiding in the baggage car. . . . I don't have my key for the subway anymore, and I don't know anyone there now, it's been such a long time. . . . I spent a few weeks with a couple who lived at Midsommarkransen, but I can't remember their name. I do remember Tobias, though—of course I remember him—and I remember that he lived on Woll-mar Yxkulls Street, and that I used to get off at the Mariatorget station, and . . . I'm so fucking stupid, I really am."

She rolls over and buries her face in the pillow.

139

SAGA STAYS WHERE SHE IS at the end of the bed, looking at Vicky, who's lying very still on her stomach, running one finger along the side of the bed.

"I'm thinking about the man in the car," Saga says, "the one who wanted you to go back to his house with him. . . . I'm almost positive your instincts were right and that he was dangerous."

Vicky sits up and looks into Saga's pale-blue eyes.

"Do you think you could help me track him down when we're done with all this?" Saga asks.

Vicky nods and swallows hard, then lowers her gaze and sits there quietly with her arms wrapped tightly around her, covered in goose bumps. It isn't easy to see how this thin, fragile girl could have smashed two people's heads in.

"Before we go any further, I just want to say that it does usually feel better when you tell the truth," Saga says.

She feels a tingling sense of calm, the way she usually does in the boxing ring. She knows she's very close to getting a full, honest confession. She can feel the change in the room—it's there in their voices, in the warmth, in the moistness of Vicky's eyes. Saga pretends to write something in her notepad, then looks at the girl as if she's already confessed to the murders.

"You went to sleep in those bloody sheets," Saga says softly.

"I killed Miranda," Vicky whispers. "Didn't I?"

"You tell me."

Vicky's mouth trembles, and the wounds on her face flare darker as she blushes.

"I can get so angry," she says, and puts her hands over her face.

"Did you get angry with Miranda?"

"Yes."

"What did you do?"

"I don't want to talk about it."

Her lawyer rushes up to her. "You know you don't have to say anything, don't you?"

"I don't have to," Vicky repeats to Saga.

"This interview is over," Susanne says in a decisive voice.

"Thanks," Vicky says.

"She needs time to remember," Saga says.

"But we have a confession," Susanne says.

"I don't know," Vicky mumbles.

"You've admitted that you killed Miranda Ericsdotter," Susanne says, raising her voice.

"Don't yell at me," Vicky says.

"Did you hit her?" Susanne persists. "You hit her, didn't you?"

"I don't want to talk anymore."

"The interview is over," Vicky's lawyer says sharply.

"How did you hit Miranda?" the prosecutor demands sternly.

"It doesn't matter," Vicky replies, a sob catching in her throat.

"Your fingerprints were found on a bloody hammer that—"

"I can't fucking talk about it—don't you understand?"

"You don't have to," Saga says. "You have the right to remain silent."

"Why did you get angry with Miranda?" the prosecutor asks loudly. "So terribly angry that you—"

"I will be reporting this," Signe Ridelman says.

"How did you get into Miranda's room?" the prosecutor asks.

"I unlocked the door," Vicky replies, trying to get out of the bed. "But I can't answer any more questions about—

"How did you get the keys?" the prosecutor snaps.

"I don't know, I—"

"Did Elisabet have them?"

"I borrowed them," she replies, standing up.

"Did she want to lend them to you?"

"I smashed her head in!" Vicky screams.

She grabs the drip stand and hits the prosecutor in the shoulder with it as hard as she can; the bag of fluid comes loose, hits the wall, and bursts.

140

Joona and Saga get between Vicky and the others and try to calm her down. The liquid from the burst IV runs down the wall. Vicky is breathing hard, looking at them with frightened eyes. She has cut herself on something and is bleeding profusely from one eyebrow. Nurses and the two police officers rush in and force her down onto the floor. There are four of them, and she starts to panic and struggle frantically to pull loose, screaming and kicking a cart over.

Vicky is forced onto her stomach and given an injection in one buttock. She screams hoarsely but soon calms down.

A couple of minutes later, they lift her onto the bed. Still crying, she is trying to say something but is slurring her words too badly for anyone to understand her. One of the nurses supervises the process of strapping her down. First her wrists and ankles are tied to the rails on the sides of the bed, then her thighs; finally, the thick straps are placed across her chest in a star pattern. The sheets and the nursing staff's white clothes are stained with Vicky's blood, and the room is a complete mess.

Joona knows that the prosecutor is watching him and that he can't get involved, but he doesn't like the way things are going. Now there won't be any more interviews before the custody hearing. It would have been better to hold off on the legal proceedings until the interview process was complete and the results from the forensics lab were in. But Susanne Öst has decided to press formal charges against the girl and request that she be remanded in custody the next day.

If Saga had been given a little more time, Vicky would have told her the truth. Now all they have is a confession. Even though any good defense attorney will argue that it was forced, as long as the forensic evidence supports it that may not matter too much, he thinks as he leaves the room.

He walks along the hallway; a strong smell of disinfectant is coming from an open door.

Something about this case is still troubling him. If he disregards the rock, he really hasn't had too much difficulty imagining the scenario. It holds together, even though it's far from perfect. The sequence of events is still developing, as if in some pulsating shadow world.

He really needs to see all the material—the postmortem reports, the forensics results, and all the test results from the lab.

Why were Miranda's hands covering her face?

He can remember exactly how the blood-spattered room looked, but he'd like to be able to see the crime-scene reports in order to dig deeper into the sequence of events.

Susanne heads for the elevators and stops next to Joona. They nod to each other. The prosecutor looks happy.

"Now everyone hates me for pushing too hard," she says as they walk into the elevator and she presses the button. "But a confession carries a hell of a lot of weight, even though sometimes things get a little out of control."

"What's your impression of the forensic evidence?" Joona asks.

"So compelling that I've opted for the second-highest charge."

The elevator reaches the ground floor, and they get out together.

"Could I see the report?" Joona asks, stopping.

Susanne looks surprised, then says, after a moment's hesitation, "There's no need."

"Okay," Joona says, starting to walk away.

"Do you think there are holes?" the prosecutor asks, trying to keep up with him.

"No," Joona replies curtly.

"I should have the crime-scene report here," she says, opening her briefcase.

Joona goes out through the glass doors, and behind him he can hear the prosecutor rooting through her papers, then starting to run. He's already reached his car by the time she catches up with him.

"It would be great if you could take a look at it today," she says breathlessly, holding out a thin leather folder to Joona. "I'll get you some preliminary results from the lab and the postmortem reports."

Joona looks her in the eye, nods, and tosses the folder onto the passenger seat before he gets in.

141

Joona is sitting alone in the back room of Il Caffè to read the report. Susanne's provocative behavior during the interview had been a big mistake. He doesn't believe that Vicky took Dante on purpose—it doesn't fit the picture he has of her—but for some reason she killed Miranda and Elisabet.

Why?

Joona opens the folder, hoping it contains the answer.

Why does Vicky sometimes get so incredibly angry and violent? It can't just be her medication. She didn't start taking it until she arrived at the Birgitta Home.

He leafs through the papers.

Crime scenes reflect the perpetrator. There are small fragments of the motive hidden in the spatter pattern of blood across the walls and floor, in the overturned furniture, the footprints, and the positions of the bodies. Nathan Pollock would probably say that a comprehensive approach to a crime scene can be much more important than securing evidence, because the perpetrator always assigns particular functions to the victim and the scene. The victim plays a role in the perpetrator's internal drama, and the scene is like a stage, with scenery and props. A lot of things may be random, but there's always some connection to that inner drama, something that can be linked to the motive.

Joona reads the report of the crime-scene investigation for

the first time. He spends a long time studying the evidence and analysis.

The police had done a good job, far more thorough than what they're required to do.

A waiter with a knitted hat comes over carrying a large mug of coffee on a tray, but Joona is so deep in thought that he doesn't notice him. A young woman with a pierced lip smiles as she tells the waiter that she saw Joona order the coffee.

Although the final results from the lab aren't included in the file, Joona can see that the evidence is clear-cut: the fingerprints on the hammer are Vicky Bennet's. The level of probability is judged to be the highest possible, +4.

Nothing in the crime-scene analysis contradicts what he saw for himself at the scene of the murders, although a lot of his own observations aren't included—such as the way the increasingly coagulated blood had been smeared across the sheets over a period of at least an hour. Nor does the report say anything about the way the backward spatter pattern on the walls changes angle after three blows.

Joona reaches out for the coffee, drinks it down, and studies the photographs again. He looks slowly through the bundle, concentrating hard on each one in turn. Then he picks out two photographs of Vicky's room, two of the isolation room, where Miranda was found, and two of the old brew house, where Elisabet was found. He moves the coffee cup and everything else off the table and lays out the six pictures, then stands up and tries to see them all at the same time, looking for new, unexpected patterns.

After a while, Joona turns all the photographs over except one. He looks carefully at this last picture, trying to return to the room in his memory, dredging up the smells, the atmosphere. The photograph shows Miranda's slender body. She's lying on the bed in a pair of white cotton underpants, with both hands over her face. The flash from the camera makes her body and the sheets dazzlingly white. The blood from her shattered head forms a dark pattern on the pillow.

Suddenly Joona sees something he wasn't expecting.

He takes a step back, bumping into the table. The empty coffee cup falls to the floor.

The girl with the pierced lip looks down at her table, smiling.

Joona leans over the photograph of Miranda. He's thinking about his visit to see Flora Hansen. He had been annoyed at wasting his time on her. When he was leaving, she followed him into the hall, repeating that she really had seen Miranda, and saying that she had drawn a picture of the ghost. She showed him the drawing but dropped it when he brushed her hand aside. The paper drifted to the floor. Joona took a quick look at the childish sketch as he stepped over it to leave.

Now that he's studying the photograph of Miranda's arranged body, he tries to remember Flora Hansen's drawing. It had been done in two stages: first just a stick figure, and then the limbs had been filled in. Some of the outline of the girl's body was shaky, and some parts of the drawing were very vague. The head was too large, out of proportion. The mouth was only visible because the girl was holding her unfinished, skeletal hands in front of her face. The picture was a reasonable match with the descriptions that had appeared in the tabloids.

But what the papers hadn't said was that Miranda had been hit on the head and that her blood had seeped onto the bed around her head. No pictures from the crime scene had been released. The press wrote about the hands in front of her face, they speculated, but they didn't know anything about the injuries to her head. The entire investigation has been kept strictly confidential in the lead-up to custody proceedings.

"You've just realized something important, haven't you?" the girl at the next table says.

Joona looks into her eyes and nods before looking back at the color photograph on the table.

What he realized when he was looking at Miranda's body in the photograph was that Flora had drawn a dark heart next to the girl's head, just like the dark pool of blood.

Same size, same place.

As if she really had seen Miranda lying on the bed.

It could still be a coincidence, but if he really is remembering Flora's drawing accurately, the resemblance is striking.

142

THE BELLS OF GUSTAV VASA Church are ringing when Joona meets Flora outside Carlén Antiques on Upplands Street. She looks terrible—tired and pasty. A faded but large bruise is clearly visible on one cheek, and her eyes are dull and heavy. On a narrow door next to the antique shop, a small sign announces an evening of spiritualism.

"Do you have the drawing with you?" Joona asks.

"Yes," she replies, unlocking the door.

They go down a flight of steps to the basement. Flora turns the lights on and enters the room on the right.

"I'm sorry I lied," Flora says, looking in her bag. "I didn't feel anything from the key chain, but I . . ."

"Can I just see the drawing?"

"I saw Miranda," she says, handing him the sheet of paper. "I don't believe in ghosts, but . . . she was there."

Joona unfolds the paper and looks at the childish drawing. It looks as if the girl is lying on her back. She's holding her hands in front of her face, and her hair is loose. No bed or other furniture is depicted. His memory was correct. Beside the girl's head is a dark heart, positioned right where Miranda's blood had seeped out and soaked into the sheet and mattress.

"Why did you draw a heart?"

He sees Flora lower her eyes and go red in the face.

"I don't know, I don't even remember doing it. . . . I was just scared; I was shaking all over."

"Have you seen the ghost again?"

She nods.

Joona tries to figure out how all this fits together. Could Flora have guessed everything? If the rock was a guess on her part, she must have realized that her guess was correct: it isn't that hard to read people's reactions. And if the rock was right, then it was really only logical to assume that Miranda had been hit in the head with it and that there would be blood on the bed.

But she didn't just draw blood, she drew a heart, he thinks. And she wouldn't have done that if she were trying to deceive him.

It doesn't make sense.

She must have seen something.

It looks as if she saw Miranda on the bed very hazily, or very briefly, and then she drew what she had seen without really thinking about it. The image of Miranda with the bloodstain by her head just stuck. She sat down and drew what she saw. She remembered the supine body and the hands in front of the face and the fact that there was something dark next to the girl's head.

A dark shape.

When she drew the picture, she interpreted the shape as a heart without thinking about the logic.

Joona knows that Flora was nowhere near the Birgitta Home when the murders were committed and that she has no connection to anyone involved or anything that's happened.

He looks at the drawing again and tests a different theory: what if Flora was told something by someone who was there?

Perhaps a witness told her what to write.

A childish witness who interpreted the blood as a heart.

In which case, all this talk about ghosts is just Flora's way of protecting the witness's identity.

"I want you to try to contact the ghost," Joona says.

"No, I can't—"

"How does it usually work?"

"I'm sorry, but I can't do this," she says, in a very composed voice.

"You need to ask the ghost if she saw what happened."

"I don't want to," she whispers. "I can't do it anymore."

"I'll pay you," he says.

"I don't want money, I just want you to listen to me."

"I am listening," Joona says.

"I honestly don't know what's going on, but I don't think I'm crazy."

"I don't think you're crazy, either," he replies seriously.

As she looks at him, she wipes tears from her cheeks. Then she stares ahead of her and swallows hard.

"I'll give it a try," she says quietly. "But I don't actually believe in . . ."

"Just try."

"You'll have to wait in there," she says, pointing to a smaller room. "Miranda usually only comes when I'm completely alone."

143

Flora sits absolutely still and watches the detective close the door behind him. A chair creaks when he sits down; then everything is quiet. She can't hear anything: no cars, no dogs barking, and nothing from the room where the detective is waiting.

Only now does she realize how tired she is.

Flora doesn't know what to do. She isn't sure if she should light the candles and incense, so instead she just sits there, closes her eyes for a few seconds, then looks at the picture.

She remembers how her hands were shaking when she drew what she'd seen, and how she had trouble concentrating. She kept looking around the room to see if the ghost had come back.

Now she looks at the picture. She's no good at drawing, but it's clear that the girl is lying on the floor. She sees the small crosses and remembers that they were supposed to represent the fringe of the bath mat.

Flora's hand had slipped when she was drawing, making one of the girl's thighs as thin as a bone.

The fingers in front of her face are no more than lines. The straight mouth is visible behind them.

The chair in the next room creaks again.

Flora blinks hard and stares at the drawing.

It looks as if the fingers have slid apart slightly, so that Flora can see one of the girl's eyes.

Flora looks at her.

She jumps when the pipes rumble and looks around the little room. The couch is black with shadows, the table tucked away in a dark corner.

When she looks at the drawing again, the eye isn't visible. A fold in the thin paper runs right across the girl's face.

Flora's hands shake as she tries to smooth the paper. The girl's thin fingers are covering her eyes. Only part of her mouth is visible.

The floor suddenly creaks behind her, and Flora turns around quickly.

No one is there.

She looks at the drawing again until she has tears in her eyes. The heart hanging over the girl's head has fluid edges now. She looks at the tangled hair, and then goes back to the fingers in front of the face. Instinctively, Flora snatches her hands away from the paper when she sees that the mouth is no longer a straight line.

It looks like it's screaming.

Flora leaps up from her chair, panting hard, and stares at the drawing, at the screaming mouth behind the fingers. She is about to call for the detective when she sees the girl for real.

She's hiding in the cabinet by the wall, as if she's trying to stay as well hidden as possible. But the door won't close when she's in there. The girl is standing completely still with her hands in front of her face. Then her fingers slip apart, and she looks at Flora with one eye.

Flora stares at the girl.

She's saying something behind her hands, but it's impossible to make out the words.

Flora walks closer.

"I can't hear," she says.

"I'm pregnant," the girl says, and takes her hands from her face. She reaches to the back of her head, then pulls her hand away, looks at the blood, and staggers. A steady stream of blood is pouring from the back of her head, running down her back and onto the floor.

Flora's mouth opens, but before she has time to say anything, her head shakes and her thin legs give way.

Joona hears the crash from the next room and rushes in. Flora is lying on the floor in front of a half-open cabinet. She sits up and looks at him in confusion.

"I saw her. . . . She's pregnant. . . ."

Joona helps Flora up. "Did you ask what happened?"

Flora shakes her head and looks at the empty cabinet.

"No one must see anything," she whispers.

"What did you say?"

"Miranda said she was pregnant," Flora sobs, moving backward.

She wipes her tears, looks at the cabinet again, then leaves the room. Joona picks her coat off a chair and follows her. She's already halfway up the steps leading to the street.

144

FLORA IS SITTING ON THE step outside Carlén Antiques, buttoning her coat. Her cheeks have some color back in them, but she still isn't speaking. Joona is standing on the sidewalk with his phone pressed to his ear. He's calling The Needle at Karolinska University Hospital.

There's a loud crackle in Joona's ear.

"Yes?"

"I've got a quick question," Joona says.

"Frippe's fallen in love," Nils says in his tight, nasal voice.

"Great," Joona says calmly.

"I'm just worried he'll get hurt," The Needle says. "Do you know what I mean?"

"Yes, but—"

"What did you want to ask?"

"Was Miranda Ericsdotter pregnant?"

"Definitely not."

"You remember, the girl who—"

"I remember them all," he replies sharply.

"Do you? I never knew."

"You never asked."

Flora is on her feet and is muttering to herself.

"Are you sure she—"

"I'm absolutely sure," The Needle interrupts. "She wasn't even capable of getting pregnant."

"She wasn't?"

"Miranda had a large cyst on one of her ovaries."

"Well, now I know. Thanks very much. . . . Say hi to Frippe."

"Will do."

Joona ends the call and looks at Flora. Her smile slowly fades.

"Why do you do this?" Joona asks gravely. "You said the murdered girl was pregnant, but she couldn't even get pregnant."

Flora gestures vaguely toward the door to the basement.

"I remember that she—"

"But it wasn't true," Joona interrupts. "She wasn't pregnant."

"What I meant," Flora whispers, "what I meant is that she said she was pregnant. But it wasn't true, she wasn't. She just thought she was, she thought she was pregnant."

"*Jumala,*" Joona sighs in Finnish, and starts walking up Upplands Street toward his car.

145

THE FOOD IS A LITTLE too expensive, and Daniel feels embarrassed when he looks at the wine list. He asks Elin if she'd like to choose, but she just smiles and shakes her head. He clears his throat slightly, asks the waiter about the house wine, but changes his mind before he has time to answer; instead, he asks if the waiter could recommend a red to go with the food. The young man looks at the wine list and suggests three wines in different price brackets. Daniel picks the cheapest, saying that a South African Pinot Noir will do fine.

The waiter thanks him and takes the list and menus away with him. Farther inside the restaurant, a family are having a meal.

"You didn't have to invite me out to a restaurant," she says.

"I wanted to," he says with a smile.

"It's very nice of you," she says, drinking a sip of water.

A waitress comes over to swap the cutlery and glasses, but Elin continues talking as if she weren't there. "Vicky's legal representative has pulled out," she says quietly. "But my family lawyer, Johannes Grünewald—he's already on the case."

"That's good," Daniel says reassuringly.

"There won't be any more interviews for a while. They say she's confessed," Elin says, and clears her throat carefully. "I know that Vicky looks the part. Foster homes, running away, institutions, violent mood swings—everything points to her. But I still think she's innocent."

"I know," Daniel says.

She lowers her head when the tears start to flow. Daniel gets up, goes around the table, and puts his arms around her.

"I'm sorry to talk so much about Vicky," she says, shaking her head. "It's just that it feels like we're the only people who don't think it was her. . . ."

"Elin," he says earnestly, "I don't really know what I think. But the Vicky I got to know could never do something like this."

"Can I ask you . . . Tuula seems to have seen Vicky and Miranda together," Elin says.

"That night?"

"No, earlier . . ."

Elin falls silent, and Daniel holds her shoulders, trying to look her in the eye.

"What is it?" he asks.

"Vicky and Miranda were playing some game . . . holding their hands in front of their faces," Elin says. "I didn't tell the police, because it would just make them suspect Vicky even more."

"But, Elin . . ."

"It doesn't necessarily mean anything," Elin says quickly. "I'll ask Vicky when I get the chance. . . . I'm sure she'll be able to explain what they were doing."

"But if she can't?"

He stops speaking when he sees the waiter approach with their bottle of wine. Elin wipes her eyes, and Daniel goes back to his chair, puts his napkin on his lap, and tastes the wine with a trembling hand.

"Good," he says, a little too fast.

They sit in silence as the waiter pours the wine, thank him quietly, and then, once they're alone again, glance tentatively at each other.

"I want to help Vicky again, officially," Elin says.

"You've made up your mind?" he asks.

"Don't you think I can do it?" she says, smiling.

"Elin, it's not about that," he says. "Vicky has suicidal tendencies.... She's better than she was, but she still demonstrates a serious tendency to self-harm."

"She cuts herself? Is that what she does?"

"She's better, but she still cuts herself, and she's on medication ... and in my opinion she needs someone with her twenty-four hours a day."

"So you wouldn't recommend me as an official source of support?"

"She needs professional help," Daniel says gently. "I mean, I don't think she even got enough help at the Birgitta Home. We didn't have the money, but ..."

"What does she need?"

"Twenty-four-hour care," he replies simply.

"And therapy?"

"I only had an hour a week with the girls, two with some of them, but that's nowhere near enough if you ..."

Elin's phone rings, and she apologizes, but when she sees that it's Johannes Grünewald, she takes the call at once.

"What's going on?" she asks quickly.

"I checked, and it's true that the prosecutor has decided to push for a custody hearing without any further interviews," the lawyer says. "I'm going to talk to the court about the timing, but we need a few more hours."

"Is Vicky going to accept our help?"

"I talked to her, and she told me I could act as her representative."

"Did you mention me?"

"Yes."

"Did she say anything?"

"She's ... They've got her on a lot of medication, and ..."

"What exactly did she say when you mentioned my name?" Elin persists.

"Nothing," Johannes replies bluntly.

Daniel sees a sudden flash of pain cross Elin's beautiful, smooth face.

"Meet me at the hospital," she says into the phone. "It makes sense to talk about it directly with her before we go any further. When can you be there?"

"Twenty minutes should be enough. . . ."

"See you there," she says, ending the call, and then looks at Daniel's puzzled face.

"Okay . . . Vicky has accepted Johannes as her lawyer. I need to go over there now."

"Now? You don't have time to eat first?"

"It sounded really good," she says, getting to her feet. "We'll have to have dessert afterward instead."

"Sure," he says quietly.

"Can you come with me to the hospital?" she asks.

"I don't know if I'm up to that," he replies.

"I don't mean to see her," she says quickly. "I was just thinking . . . I'd feel calmer if I knew you were waiting outside."

"Elin, it's just . . . I haven't reached a point where I can think about Vicky. It's going to take time. Elisabet is dead . . . and even though I can't believe it was Vicky, I . . ."

"I understand," Elin says. "Maybe it wouldn't be such a good idea."

"Although maybe it would be," he says hesitantly. "Maybe it would help me start to remember."

146

VICKY TURNS HER FACE AWAY when Saga enters the room. The girl has white straps across her ankles, wrists, and chest, like a snowflake.

"Remove the straps," Saga says.

"I can't do that," the nurse says.

"They should be scared of me," Vicky whispers.

"Did you have to lie like this all night?" Saga asks, sitting down on the chair.

"Mm-hmm . . ."

Vicky lies completely still, with her face turned away, her body almost inert.

"I'm going to meet your new lawyer," Saga says. "The custody hearing is set for this evening, and he needs the transcript of our interview."

"I just get so angry sometimes."

"The official interviews are over for now, Vicky."

"Am I allowed to say anything?" she asks, looking into Saga's eyes.

"It's probably best if you ask your lawyer for advice before you—"

"What if I want to?" she interrupts.

"Of course you can speak, but we won't record the conversation," Saga says calmly.

"It's like when there's a really strong wind," Vicky says. "Everything just ... I get a roaring sound in my ears, and I have to get swept along with it or I'll fall."

Saga looks at the girl's shredded fingernails, then says in a calm, almost indifferent tone, "Like when the wind's blowing."

"I can't explain. ... It's like, once, when they hurt Simon, a little boy who ... We'd been placed in the same foster home," Vicky says, her mouth trembling. "The eldest boy in the family—he was their real son—he was really mean to Simon, he used to torment him. Everyone knew about it, I'd told the social worker, but no one cared. ..."

"What happened?" Saga asks.

"I went into the kitchen. ... The older boy had forced Simon's hands into boiling water, and the mother was there, she was just watching, with a scared look in her eyes. I saw it all and just went really weird, and then I was hitting them, and I cut their faces with a bottle. ..."

Vicky suddenly pulls hard at the straps, her body tensing; she relaxes with a gasp when there's a knock at the door.

A man with gray hair and a dark-blue suit walks into the room. "I'm Johannes Grünewald," he says, and shakes Saga's hand.

"Here's the transcript," Saga says.

"Thanks," Johannes says, without looking at the document. "I've just reached an agreement with the district court to postpone the custody hearing until tomorrow morning."

"I don't want to wait," Vicky says.

"I can sympathize, but I've got more work to do." He smiles. "And then there's someone here who I want you to meet before we go through all the questions."

Vicky stares wide-eyed at the woman coming toward her. Elin looks nervous. Her lips tremble as she looks at the girl strapped to the bed.

"Hi," she says.

Vicky slowly turns her face away and lies like that while Elin removes the straps.

"Is it okay if I sit down?" she asks, her voice thick with emotion.

Vicky's eyes become bright and hard. But she still doesn't speak.

"Do you remember me?" Elin whispers.

Her throat hurts from all the words lodged inside and the tears that are welling up.

Vicky touches Elin's wrist, then pulls her finger back.

"We've got the same bandage, you and me," Elin says, smiling, and her eyes instantly fill with tears.

Vicky still doesn't say anything, just closes her mouth and turns her face away again.

"I don't know if you remember me," Elin goes on. "You lived with me when you were younger—just for a little while, but I've never stopped thinking about you. . . ."

She takes a deep breath, and her voice breaks again. "And I know that I let you down, Vicky. . . . I let you down, and . . ."

Elin looks at the child in the bed, at her tangled hair, frowning forehead, the dark rings under her eyes, the wounds on her face.

"I know I'm nothing to you," she goes on in a weak voice. "Just one of all the people who passed through your life, who let you down. . . ."

Elin falls silent and swallows hard before she continues: "The prosecutor wants you to be remanded in custody, but I don't think that would be good for you; I don't think it's good for anyone to be locked up."

Vicky shakes her head almost imperceptibly. Elin notices this, and there's fresh eagerness in her voice when she says, "So it's important that you listen to what Johannes and I tell you."

147

THE HEARING IS IN A simple meeting room, furnished with varnished pine tables and chairs. About twenty journalists have already gathered in the glass atrium, and large television vans are parked outside, on Polhems Street.

The night's heavy rain has streaked the triple-glazed windows, and there are wet leaves stuck to the white sills.

Susanne Öst looks pale and tense in her new suit and low black pumps. A heavyset uniformed police officer is standing by the wall next to the door. The judge, an older man with big, bushy eyebrows, sits behind the desk.

Vicky is sitting between Elin and her lawyer, Johannes, leaning forward on her chair as if she had a stomachache. She looks exhausted and extremely small.

"Where's Joona?" she whispers.

"He wasn't sure he'd be able to come," Johannes says calmly.

The prosecutor looks exclusively at the judge when she says, with a somber expression, "I'd like to request that Vicky Bennet be remanded in custody, because she is suspected on reasonable grounds of the murders of Elisabet Grim and Miranda Ericsdotter, and also suspected on reasonable grounds of the abduction and kidnapping of Dante Abrahamsson."

The judge jots something down, and the prosecutor presents

a spiral-bound binder of papers, then starts to go through the findings of the investigation thus far.

"All of the forensic evidence points directly at Vicky Bennet, and at her alone," she begins. She pauses for a moment, then presents the findings of the crime-scene investigation. With thinly veiled enthusiasm, she gives an account of the biological evidence and prints:

"The boots that were found in Vicky Bennet's wardrobe match the prints found at the scenes of both murders, blood from both victims has been found in the suspect's room and on her clothes, and Vicky Bennet's bloody handprints were found on the windowsill."

"Why do they have to say everything out loud?" Vicky whispers.

"I don't know," Elin says.

"If you'd care to turn to the appendix of the report from the National Forensics Laboratory," Susanne says to the judge. "Illustration 9 shows the murder weapon. . . . Vicky Bennet's fingerprints were found on the handle, shown in detail in Illustrations 113 and 114. Comparative analysis confirms that Vicky Bennet used the murder weapon."

The prosecutor clears her throat and waits while the judge looks at the pages in question, then goes on to cite the conclusion of the full postmortem report: "Miranda Ericsdotter died as a result of being struck on the head by a blunt instrument, compression fracture of the temporal bone and—"

"Susanne," the judge interrupts, not unkindly, "this is a custody hearing, not the actual trial."

She nods. "I know, but, bearing in mind the age of the suspect, I believe that a slightly more comprehensive presentation is justified."

"As long as it doesn't exceed reasonable boundaries," the judge says.

"Thank you." The prosecutor smiles, then continues to describe the injuries suffered by the two victims, the positions in which they lay according to the hypostasis seen on the bodies, and Elisabet Grim's attempts to defend herself.

"Where's Joona?" Vicky asks again.

Johannes puts a reassuring hand on her arm and whispers that he'll try calling him if he doesn't arrive before the break.

148

When they gather again to resume the custody proceedings after the break, Joona still hasn't appeared. Johannes shakes his head when Vicky gives him a questioning look. She's very pale and sits there quiet and hunched. The prosecutor describes how the police believe Vicky followed Elisabet to the brew house and murdered her in order to get the keys to the isolation room.

Vicky sits with her face bowed, tears dropping onto her lap.

The prosecutor describes the second murder, then Vicky's flight through the forest, the theft of the car, the impulsive kidnapping, her eventual arrest in Stockholm, and her violent outburst during the interview, when she had to be restrained.

The sentence for kidnapping is four years to life, and for murder there's a minimum sentence of ten years.

Susanne makes Vicky out to be very dangerous and prone to extreme violence, but not a monster. In an effort to forestall the defense, she mentions Vicky's more positive aspects several times. The prosecutor's argument is skillfully presented, and she concludes by reading from the transcript of the interview: "During the third session, the detainee confessed to both murders," the prosecutor says slowly, leafing through the transcript. "I quote: 'I killed Miranda,' then, in response to my question about . . . about whether Elisabet Grim was willing to lend her her keys, the detainee replied: 'I smashed her head in.'"

149

WITH A WEARY EXPRESSION ON his face, the judge turns to Vicky and Johannes and asks if they have any objections to the prosecutor's proposal. Vicky looks very upset as she stares at him. She shakes her head, but Johannes forces the smile from his face as he explains that he'd like to go through everything one last time to make sure that the court doesn't miss anything.

"I didn't think we'd get off that lightly with you in the room," the judge replies calmly.

In his response, Johannes opts not to address the forensic evidence or the question of Vicky's guilt. He repeats the positive things Susanne Öst said about Vicky and emphasizes several times how young she is.

"Even if Vicky Bennet and her previous representative were prepared to accept the interview, the prosecutor ought not to have done so," Johannes says.

"The prosecutor?"

The judge looks extremely curious until Johannes walks over to him and points out Vicky Bennet's response in the transcript of the recorded interview. The prosecutor has highlighted the words "I killed Miranda" in yellow.

"Please, read her reply out loud," Johannes asks.

"'I killed Miranda,'" the judge reads.

"The whole reply, not just the highlighted words."

The judge puts on his glasses and reads: "'I killed Miranda—didn't I?'"

"Does that look to you like a confession?" Johannes asks.

"No," the judge says.

Susanne stands up. "But the next answer," she tries to say. "The next confession—"

"Quiet," the judge interrupts.

"Perhaps we should let the prosecutor read it out loud?" Johannes suggests.

The judge nods, and Susanne's face starts to sweat as she reads in a trembling voice, "'I smashed her head in.'"

"That sounds like a confession," the judge says, turning to Johannes.

"Look a little earlier in the transcript," Johannes says, pointing at the document.

"'This interview is over,'" the judge reads.

"Who says that the interview is over?" Johannes asks.

The judge runs his finger across the transcript, then looks at the prosecutor.

"It was me," the prosecutor replies quietly.

"And what does that mean?" the judge asks.

"That the interview is over," Susanne replies. "But I just wanted to—"

"Shame on you," the judge interrupts sharply. "Using this in custody proceedings is a breach of Swedish law, Article 40 of the UN Convention on the Rights of the Child, and the Council of Europe's declaration on children's rights."

150

Susanne Öst sits down heavily, pours water into her glass but spills some on the table, wipes it away with her sleeve, then drinks with a shaky hand. Only when she hears Johannes call in Daniel Grim does she realize that she's going to have to reduce the strength of the charges filed against Vicky to stand any chance of having her remanded in custody.

Elin tries to catch Vicky's eye, but the girl just sits there with her face lowered.

Johannes gives Daniel Grim a glowing introduction, emphasizing the many years he has spent working at the Birgitta Home and other institutions. Vicky looks up for the first time and tries to look Daniel in the eye, but he's just staring in front of him with his mouth clenched.

"Daniel," Johannes says. "I'd like to ask you how well you think you know Vicky Bennet."

"Know . . . ," Daniel repeats thoughtfully. "Well, it's . . ."

He falls silent and Vicky starts to scratch one of the wounds on her arm.

"Is there any psychologist or counselor who knows her better than you do?"

"No," Daniel whispers.

"No?"

"No, well . . . it's hard to judge, of course, but I think I've had more sessions with her than anyone else."

"Has it been long since your last session?"

"No."

"You had an hour of cognitive behavioral therapy with her every week until she ran away, didn't you?" Johannes asks.

"Yes ... and I've also been involved in her Activities of Daily Life training."

"To help prepare her for a return to normal life," Johannes explains to the judge.

"It's a big step," Daniel adds.

Johannes becomes pensive, looks at Daniel for a few moments, then says in a serious voice, "I have to ask a difficult question now."

"Okay."

"It's been said that much of the forensic evidence suggests that Vicky Bennet was involved in the murder of your wife."

Daniel nods almost imperceptibly, and a somber atmosphere settles on the room.

Elin tries to read the look in Daniel's eyes, but he's not looking in her direction. Vicky's eyes are red, as if she's trying not to cry.

Johannes stands still, with the same calm expression on his face, and doesn't take his eyes off Daniel. "You were Vicky Bennet's counselor," he says. "Do you believe she's the person who murdered your wife?"

Daniel Grim looks up. His lips are very pale, and his hand is shaking so badly that he knocks his glasses askew when he tries to wipe the tears from his eyes.

"I haven't spoken to any of my colleagues. I haven't felt up to it," he says weakly. "But in my opinion ... I simply can't believe that Vicky Bennet could have done this."

"How have you reached that opinion?"

"Vicky responded well to both therapy and medication," he goes on. "But it's more than that. You get to know people when ... She doesn't fantasize about violence, and she isn't violent, not in that way."

"Thank you," Johannes says gently.

151

Everyone takes their seats after the break for lunch. Johannes is last in. He's holding his phone in his hand. The judge waits until the room is quiet, then sums up the first part of proceedings: "The prosecutor is no longer requesting that the suspect be held for both murders but is still requesting that she be remanded in custody for the charge of kidnapping."

"Yes, we can't overlook the fact that Vicky Bennet kidnapped Dante Abrahamsson and held the little boy captive for just over a week," Susanne says determinedly.

"Just one thing," Johannes Grünewald says.

"Yes?" the judge asks.

The door opens, and Joona walks into the small hearing room. His blond hair is sticking straight up. A woman and a small boy in glasses follow him but stop just inside the door.

"Joona Linna," Johannes says.

"I know who he is," the judge says, leaning forward with interest.

"These are the old men I was telling you about," Joona says, turning to the boy, who's hiding behind the woman's legs.

"They don't look like trolls," the boy whispers with a smile.

"Don't you think so? Look at that one?" Joona says, pointing at the judge.

The boy laughs and shakes his head.

"Say hello to Dante and his mom," Joona says to the room.

Everyone says hello, and when Dante catches sight of Vicky, he gives her a cautious wave. She waves back, and her face lights up with a heartbreaking smile. The prosecutor closes her eyes for a few seconds and tries to breathe calmly.

"You waved at Vicky—but isn't she mean?" Joona asks.

"Mean?"

"I thought she was really mean?" Joona says.

"She gave me piggybacks, and I got all her Hubba Bubba."

"But didn't you just want to go back to your mom?"

"That wasn't possible," he replies slowly.

"Why wasn't it possible?"

The boy shrugs his shoulders.

"Tell them what you said at home," Pia says to her son.

"What?" he whispers.

"That she called," she reminds him.

"She called," Dante says.

Pia nods. "Tell Joona."

"Vicky called, but wasn't allowed to go back," the boy says, looking at Joona.

"Where did she call from?" Joona asks.

"From the truck."

"Did she borrow a phone in the truck?"

"I don't know," Dante says, with another shrug.

"What did she say on the phone?" Joona asks.

"That she wanted to go back."

Dante's mother picks him up and whispers something to him, then puts him down again when he starts to wriggle.

"What does that mean?" the judge asks.

"Vicky Bennet borrowed the phone belonging to a driver working for IKEA. His name is Radek Skorża," Johannes Grünewald explains. "Joona Linna has traced the call. It was made to the Birgitta Home and was forwarded automatically to the care provider's switchboard. Vicky spoke to a woman called Eva Morander. Vicky asked for help and repeated that she wanted to return to the home. Eva Morander remembers the call, and says she wasn't aware of who she was speaking to, and told the girl that they were unable to deal with individual cases at the head office."

"Do you remember this, Vicky?" the judge asks.

"Yes," Vicky says simply. "I just wanted to go back—I wanted them to take Dante home to his mom—but they said I wasn't welcome anymore."

Joona walks over to stand next to Johannes.

"It might seem unusual for a detective to support the defense," he says, "but I'm confident that Vicky Bennet was telling the truth about her flight when she was questioned by Saga Bauer. I don't believe this was a kidnapping—just a terrible accident. That's why I went to talk to Dante and his mother, and that's why I'm here. . . ."

He turns to look at the girl's un-made-up face—her bruises and cuts—with his sharp gray eyes.

"But the murders are different, Vicky," he says solemnly. "You might think you can stay silent, but I'm not going to give up until I know what happened."

152

THE CUSTODY HEARING ENDS JUST twenty minutes later. Looking very red in the face, the prosecutor Susanne Öst has to withdraw her request for Vicky to be remanded in custody, pending the kidnapping charge.

The judge leans back in his chair and declares that Vicky Bennet will not be remanded in custody for the murders of Elisabet Grim and Miranda Ericsdotter and that she is therefore free to go until such time as the prosecutor presses charges.

Vicky is staring at the table, and Elin sits very straight in her chair as she listens with a neutral expression on her face. Responsibility for Vicky Bennet until the start of her trial would have reverted to a care provider, except that Social Services has already accepted Elin Frank as her guardian.

When the judge turns to Vicky and tells her that she's free to go, Elin can't help breaking into a broad, grateful smile, but after the hearing, Johannes takes Elin aside and warns her: "You're her guardian now, but, remember, she's still suspected of having committed two murders."

"I know she's innocent," Elin replies, and a shiver runs down her spine when she realizes how naïve she must sound to him.

"It's my job to warn you," Johannes says carefully.

"Even if Vicky was involved . . . I still think she's too young to go to prison," Elin tries to explain. "Johannes, I can give her the best care in the world. I've already employed professionals, and I've asked Daniel to help, since she feels comfortable with him. . . ."

"That's good," he says gently.

"We'll have to work out exactly what would be best for her. But I will never let her down again. I can't do that."

153

While Johannes Grünewald talks to the journalists in the press room, Elin and Vicky leave Stockholm in a four-wheel-drive SUV.

Elin's left hand rests on the wheel, and the amber glow from the instrument panel lights up her fingers.

Bach's first cello suite is playing through the speakers, telling a gentle autumnal story.

The eight lanes of the highway pass between Haga Park, where the crown princess lives in her palace, and the huge cemetery where the famous activist August Palm is buried.

Elin looks at Vicky's calm face and smiles to herself.

In order to avoid media attention, they have decided to spend the time leading up to the trial in Elin's home in the mountains, a huge house on the slopes of Tegefjället, just outside Duved.

Elin has arranged for Vicky to have people on hand twenty-four hours a day. Bella is already in the house, Daniel is coming in his own car, and the nurse will be arriving tomorrow.

Vicky took a shower at the hospital, and her hair smells like cheap shampoo. Elin has bought her several pairs of jeans and plenty of shirts, underwear, socks, sneakers, and a waterproof jacket. Vicky has put on a pair of black Armani jeans and a chunky gray sweater from Gant. The rest of the clothes are still in their bags on the back seat.

"What are you thinking about?" Elin asks.

Vicky doesn't answer. She just stares out at the road, through the windshield. Elin turns the music down slightly.

"You're going to be found not guilty," Elin says. "I know you will. I'm sure of it."

The suburbs disappear behind them, and fields and forest take over.

Elin offers Vicky some chocolate but gets only a brief shake of the head in response.

"I'm so happy Daniel is coming with us," Elin says.

"He's good," Vicky whispers.

Daniel, driving his own car, is somewhere ahead of them. Elin saw his car at Norrtull but has fallen behind since then.

"Is he better than the counselors you've seen before?" she asks.

"Yes."

Elin turns the volume down a little further.

"So you'd like him to continue to work with you?"

"If I have to."

"I think it would probably be a good idea to keep going with the treatment for a while."

"Then I want Daniel."

The farther north they drive, the more advanced the autumn is. It's as if the seasons are changing at an accelerated rate. The green leaves become yellow and red. They fall like shimmering lakes around the trunks of the trees and swirl across the highway.

"I need my things," Vicky suddenly says.

"Your things?"

"My things, everything . . ."

"I think they moved anything the police didn't want to that house the other girls are living in," Elin says. "I can get someone to collect them. . . ."

She looks at the girl and thinks that this might be important to her.

"Or we could drive up there now, if that would make you feel better?"

Vicky nods.

"Would you like that? Okay, I'll talk to Daniel," Elin says. "It's pretty much on the way."

154

It's already starting to get dark when Elin turns right toward Hårte and pulls in behind Daniel's car. He's just taken out a pink cooler and waves them over. They get out and stretch their legs, then each eat a cheese sandwich and have a drink, looking out across the railroad tracks and fields.

"I called the counselor on duty in the home," Daniel tells. "She didn't think it was such a great idea for you to go in and see the others."

"But what harm could it do?" Elin asks.

"I don't want to see them anyway," Vicky mutters. "I just want my stuff."

They get back into their cars. A winding road leads them past lakes and traditional red-painted barns, through forests, to the coastal plain.

They park in front of the building where the girls are currently living. A black naval mine stands beside an old gas pump, and there are seagulls perched on the telephone poles.

Vicky unbuckles her seat belt but stays in the car. She watches Elin and Daniel walk across the road and up to a large red building, where they disappear from sight behind the dark lilac bushes.

There's a faded Midsummer pole where the road divides. Vicky gazes out at the tranquil sea, then picks up the box holding the new cell phone Elin has given her. She breaks the seal, lifts the lid, takes the phone out, and carefully peels the plastic from the screen.

THE GIRLS ARE STANDING AT the windows when Daniel and Elin go up the steps to the large deck. Their temporary counselor, Solveig Sundström, is already standing at the front door. It's immediately apparent that she isn't happy about the visit. She makes it very clear that, unfortunately, they can't stay for dinner.

"Can we come in and say hello?" Daniel asks.

"Preferably not," Solveig says. "It would be better if you just told me what you've come to get, and I'll go in and look for it."

"There are a lot of things," Elin tries to explain.

"I can't promise anything. . . ."

"Ask Caroline," Daniel says. "She's usually on top of things."

While Daniel asks how the other girls are, and if any of their medication has been changed, Elin stands and looks at the girls through the window. They're jostling one another, and she can hear their voices through the glass, sounding as if they're underwater. Lu Chu pushes to the front and waves. Elin waves back, then sees Indie and Nina standing together. They keep pushing each other, taking turns to look and wave. The only one who isn't visible at all is Tuula, the little red-haired girl.

VICKY INSERTS THE SIM CARD in the phone, then looks up. A shiver runs down her spine. She can't help thinking she just saw something from the corner of her eye, outside the car. Maybe it was just the wind blowing the lilac leaves.

It's darker now.

Vicky looks at Daniel's car, at the Midsummer pole, the hedge, the fence and grass in front of the dark-red house.

A solitary lamp is shining from a mast at the end of the pier, its light glinting off the black water.

Old frames for cleaning fishnets stand in a meadow closer to the harbor. They look like rows of linked soccer goals.

Now Vicky sees a red balloon rolling across the grass in front of the house where the girls are staying.

She puts the phone back in its box and opens the car door. The air is mild and carries the smell of the sea. A lone gull cries in the distance.

The balloon rolls away across the grass.

Vicky walks cautiously toward the house, then stops to listen. Light from one of the windows is falling across the yellow leaves of a birch tree.

She can hear a vague mumbling sound a little farther away. Vicky wonders if someone is out in the darkness. She continues walking quietly along the path. There's a row of dead sunflowers at the end of the building.

The balloon rolls under a volleyball net and catches on a hedge.

"Vicky?" a voice whispers.

She turns around quickly but can't see anyone.

Her pulse speeds up, and the surge of adrenaline in her blood sharpens all her senses.

The swing creaks on its springs, rocking slowly. The old weathervane on the roof is spinning around.

"Vicky!" a sharp voice hisses, very close by.

She turns to her right and stares into the darkness with her heart pounding. It takes her a few seconds to see the thin face. It's Tuula. She's practically invisible, standing among the lilac bushes. She's clutching a baseball bat in her right hand. It's heavy, and so long that it's resting on the ground. Tuula licks her lips and stares at Vicky with bloodshot eyes.

———

ELIN LEANS ON THE RAILING of the veranda, trying to see if Vicky is still in the car, but it's too dark. Solveig has come back, and Daniel is talking to her. Elin hears him try to explain that Almira needs counseling and tends to react badly to stronger antidepressant medication. He asks again if he can go inside, but Solveig says the girls are her responsibility now. The front door opens, and Caroline comes out onto the deck. She gives Daniel a hug and says hello to Elin.

"I've packed Vicky's things," she says.

"Is Tuula in there?" Elin asks in a tense voice.

"Yes, I think so," Caroline replies, somewhat surprised. "Shall I get her?"

"Please, if you wouldn't mind," Elin says, trying to appear calm.

Caroline goes back inside and calls for Tuula. Solveig looks at Elin and Daniel with barely concealed hostility.

"If you're hungry, I can ask one of the girls to get you some apples," she says.

Elin doesn't answer. She just walks down the steps and out into the garden. Behind her, she hears voices calling for Tuula.

The garden seems darker back here. The trees and shrubs cut out almost all the light.

The swing is creaking.

She's trying to breathe quietly, but her heels click on the garden path as she hurries around the corner.

The leaves in the big lilac bush rustle. It sounds like a hare darting away. The branches move; then, suddenly, Vicky is standing in front of Elin.

"God!" Elin gasps.

They look at each other. The girl's face is very pale in the weak light. Elin's pulse is throbbing in her ears.

"Let's get back to the car," she says, leading Vicky away from the house.

She looks over her shoulder, keeping her distance from the dark trees as she hears quick footsteps behind them. She keeps walking with Vicky, out of the garden. She doesn't look back again until she reaches the road and sees Caroline hurrying after them with a large plastic bag in one hand.

"I couldn't find Tuula," she says.

"Thanks anyway," Elin says.

Vicky takes the bag and looks inside.

"I think most of it's there, although Lu Chu and Almira wanted to play poker for your earrings," Caroline says.

When Elin and Vicky drive off in the big black car, Caroline stands and watches them go with a sad expression on her face.

155

ELIN SEES THE LIGHTS OF Daniel's car in the rearview mirror the entire time they're on the highway. There's hardly any traffic, just the occasional truck, but it takes them three hours to reach the ski resorts anyway. In the darkness along the sides of the mountains, they see the static ski lifts and the tall pillars of the cable car at Åre. Six kilometers before Duved, they turn off onto a road that leads up into the mountains. Leaves and dust swirl in the beam of the headlights. The narrow gravel road leads diagonally up the mountain.

They slow down, pull off the road between two gateposts, and continue the last bit of the way to a large, modernist house. It's made of cast concrete, with angular terraces, and huge windows hidden behind closed aluminum shutters.

Both Elin and Daniel drive into a huge garage. A small blue Mazda is already parked there. Daniel helps Elin carry the bags in. Several lights are already on inside the house. Elin goes straight in and presses a button. There's a whirring sound, and the shutters covering all the windows begin to creak as the metal slats start to separate. Light from the driveway filters in through hundreds of small holes; then the metal shutters start to rise.

"It's like being inside a safe," Elin says.

A short while later, everything is silent again, and the dark mountain scenery is now visible through the vast windows. Tiny pricks of light from other buildings look like shimmering dots in the darkness.

"Wow," Vicky says as she gazes out.

"Do you remember Jack, the man I was married to?" Elin asks, going over to stand beside her. "He built this. Well, maybe not 'built'—he didn't exactly do it himself—but ... he said he wanted a bunker with a view."

An older woman in a green apron appears from the floor above.

"Hello, Bella, I'm sorry we're so late," Elin says, giving her a hug.

"Better late than never," the woman says, smiling, then tells Elin she's made up the beds in all the rooms.

"Thanks."

"I didn't know if you were going to buy any food on the way, so I bought a bit of everything. Enough to manage for a few days, anyway."

Bella lights a fire in the large hearth, and Elin walks her to the garage and says good night. The doors close once the blue car has left, and she comes back inside. Daniel has started to prepare some food, and Vicky is sitting on the sofa, crying. Elin hurries over and kneels down in front of her.

"Vicky, what is it? Why are you so upset?"

The girl just gets up and locks herself in one of the bathrooms. Elin hurries back to Daniel. "Vicky locked herself in the bathroom," she says.

"Do you want me to talk to her?"

"Yes, quickly, please!"

Daniel goes with her to the bathroom door, knocks, and tells Vicky to open the door.

"No locked doors," he says. "Remember that?"

Just a few seconds later, Vicky comes out with moist eyes and returns to the sofa. Daniel exchanges a glance with Elin and then sits down beside Vicky.

"You were upset when you first arrived at the Birgitta Home, too," he says after a short pause.

"I know.... I really should be happy," she replies without looking at him.

"Arriving in a new place ... it's also the first step toward leaving it," he says.

Vicky swallows hard, her eyes start to well up again, and she lowers her voice so that Elin can't hear what she says:

"I'm a murderer."

"I don't want you to say anything like that unless you're absolutely sure that it's true," he says calmly. "And I can hear in your voice that you're not sure."

156

FLORA POURS STEAMING-HOT WATER INTO the bucket and, even though she hates their smell, pulls on the rubber gloves. The detergent turns the water a greenish-gray color, and a clean smell spreads through the little apartment. Cool air is coming in through the windows, the sun is shining, and the birds are singing.

After the detective left her outside the antique shop, Flora had just stood there. She should have been getting ready for the séance, but she was afraid to go back down on her own and waited for the first participants. As usual, Dina and Asker Sibelius were fifteen minutes early. Flora pretended that she was a little late, and they went downstairs with her and helped arrange the chairs. By five minutes after seven, nineteen participants had arrived.

Flora went on for longer than usual, giving them time, pretending to see kindly old ghosts, happy children, and forgiving parents.

Very carefully, she managed to find out from Dina and Asker why they came to the séances. Their adult son had been left in a coma after a bad car accident, and they accepted medical advice to switch off his life-support machines and sign the forms for organ donation.

"Imagine if he doesn't find the Lord," Dina whispered.

But Flora talked to the son and assured them that he was bathed in light and that it had been his dearest wish to let his heart, lungs, corneas, and other organs live on.

Afterward, Dina kissed her hands, cried, and kept repeating that she was the happiest person on the planet.

Now Flora energetically mops the linoleum floor and breaks into a sweat.

Ewa is at her sewing circle with some of the neighbors, and Hans-Gunnar is watching an Italian soccer match with the sound turned up loud.

She rinses the mop, squeezes the water out of it, then stretches her aching back before continuing.

Flora knows that Ewa will open the envelope in her escritoire on Monday morning to pay that month's bills.

"Pass the fucking ball, Zlatan!" Hans-Gunnar yells in the living room.

Her shoulders ache when she carries the heavy bucket to Ewa's bedroom. She closes the door, blocks it with the bucket, goes over to the wedding photograph to get the brass key, then hurries over to the escritoire and unlocks it.

A loud bang makes Flora start.

It was just the mop falling over, its long handle hitting the floor.

Flora listens for a second, then opens the desk. Her hands are shaking as she tries to pull out the little drawer. It's stuck. She looks through the pens and paper clips and finds a small penknife. She carefully slips the blade into the gap above the drawer and tries very gently to pry it open.

Very slowly, the drawer slides out a few centimeters.

She hears a scraping sound very close to her. A pigeon outside the window, its claws slipping on the tin sill.

Flora inserts her fingers into the drawer and pulls it out. The postcard from Copenhagen is crumpled. She takes out the envelope, opens it, and puts exactly the right amount of money back inside. She puts everything back in place, tries to smooth out the postcard, slips the drawer back in, adjusts the pens and knife, closes the desk, and locks it.

She walks quickly over to the bedside table and has just picked up the wedding photograph when the door to Ewa's bedroom flies open. The bucket tips over, and the water gushes out across the floor. Flora feels her feet become wet and warm.

"You little fucking thief!" Hans-Gunnar shouts as he marches in, bare-chested.

She turns toward him. His eyes are wide open, and he's so angry that he's just lashing out blindly. The first blow hits her shoulder, and she doesn't really feel it. But then he grabs her hair and hits her with his other hand, a hard slap on the side of her neck and chin. The next blow hits her on the cheek. She falls and feels some of her hair being pulled out. The wedding photograph hits the floor, and the glass shatters. She lies on her side as the water from the bucket soaks into her clothes. The pain in her cheek and eye is so intense that she can hardly breathe.

Flora feels sick and rolls over onto her stomach, trying not to throw up. Her vision flares. She notices that the photograph has slid out of the frame and is lying facedown on the wet floor. On the back are the words "Ewa and Hans-Gunnar, Delsbo Church."

In that instant, Flora remembers what the ghost whispered to her. Maybe she'd dreamed it? She can't remember. Miranda had whispered something about a tower that rang like a church bell. The little girl had shown her the wedding photograph, pointed at the black bell tower in the background, and whispered, "She's hiding there, she saw everything, she's hiding in the tower."

Hans-Gunnar is looming over her, panting for breath, when

Ewa comes into the bedroom, still wearing her outdoor clothes. "What's going on here?" she asks in an anxious voice.

"She stole our money," he says. "I knew it!"

He spits at Flora, picks the brass key off the floor, and goes over to the desk.

157

Joona is sitting in his office with all the material from the custody hearing laid out in front of him. It will probably be enough to secure a guilty verdict.

His phone rings, and Joona probably wouldn't have answered if he'd looked at the screen first.

"I know you think I'm lying," Flora says breathlessly. "Please, don't hang up. You have to listen to me. I'm begging you, I'll do anything you want if you'll just listen to me."

"Calm down and tell me."

"There's a witness to the murders," she says. "A real witness, not a ghost. I'm talking about a real witness who's hiding."

Hearing the hysteria lurking just beneath her voice, Joona tries to calm her down: "That's good," he says gently. "But the investigation—"

"You have to go there," she interrupts.

He doesn't know why he's listening to this person. Possibly because she sounds so desperate.

"Where exactly is the witness?" he asks.

"There's a bell tower, a black bell tower next to Delsbo Church."

"Who told you—"

"Please, she's there; she's scared, and she's hiding there."

"Flora, you have to let the prosecutor do—"

"No one's listening to me."

Joona hears a man's voice in the background, shouting at her to get off his phone; then there's a banging sound.

"This little conversation's over," the man says, and hangs up.

Joona sighs and puts his phone down on the desk. He can't figure out why Flora is continuing to lie.

After Vicky was charged, the investigation was put on the back burner, and all that's left is for the prosecutor to compile the evidence before the trial.

I missed out on this case, Joona thinks, feeling an odd sense of desolation. It was already over by the time I got access to the reports and expert statements.

If Vicky overdosed on her medication, that could cause both her violent behavior and her sudden need to sleep.

But he can't let go of the rock.

The Needle's report states that the murder weapon was a rock, but no one has tried to follow that line of inquiry, because it doesn't fit the other facts.

He decides not to let go of the case just yet. A wave of stubbornness makes him look through the test results from the forensics lab again and read the pathologist's report. He reads the paragraph about the injuries to Elisabet's hands carefully before he goes on.

The light wanders slowly across Joona's corkboard, which has pinned to it the notification of the internal investigation, and Disa's latest postcard—a picture of a chimpanzee wearing lipstick and heart-shaped glasses.

While Joona reads, the shadow of the plant in the window moves slowly toward the bookcase.

There was nothing unusual in Miranda's abdominal cavity, and her heart, lungs, and other organs were in good condition.

Joona holds one finger on the postmortem report and leafs through the test results from the forensics lab, where he reads that Miranda's blood group was type A and showed traces of venlafaxine, a component of many antidepressants, but was otherwise normal.

Joona returns to the postmortem and reads that her thyroid gland was grayish red and contained normal levels of colloid, and that her adrenal glands were yellow and of normal size. The urinary ducts are of normal appearance. The bladder contains approximately one hundred milliliters of clear pale-yellow urine. The mucous membrane is pale. Joona leafs through the lab results to find the urine sample. There were traces of the sedative nitrazepam in Miranda's urine, and the hCG level was unusually high.

Joona jumps to his feet, grabs his phone, and calls The Needle.

"I'm sitting here looking at the forensics report, and Miranda had a high level of hCG in her urine," he says.

"Yes, obviously," Nils Åhlén replies. "The cyst on her ovary was so—"

"Hang on a second," Joona interrupts. "Don't pregnant women have high hCG levels?"

"Yes, but like I said—"

"So, if Miranda took a pregnancy test, she'd think she was pregnant."

"Yes," Nils says. "She'd definitely get a positive result."

"So Miranda might have believed she was pregnant?"

As Joona walks quickly along the hallway, he calls Flora's home number. He hears Anja call out behind him but doesn't stop. There's no answer. Joona repeats to himself that Flora had changed her mind, and said that the girl who had appeared to her had only believed that she was pregnant.

"What I meant is that she said she was pregnant," Flora had said. "But it wasn't true, she wasn't. She just thought she was."

Joona calls the number again, and he's just walked through the revolving door when a voice answers breathlessly, "Hans-Gunnar Hansen."

"My name is Joona Linna, I work with the National Crime Unit, and . . ."

"Did you find my car?"

"I need to talk to Flora."

"What the fuck?" the man exclaims. "If Flora was here, then I wouldn't be asking about my fucking car, would I? She's the one who stole it, and if the police can't—"

Joona abruptly ends the call and runs the rest of the way to his black Volvo.

158

ELIN SLEPT IN THE ROOM next to Vicky's with the doors open last night. She kept waking at the slightest sound and getting up to check on the girl. When morning comes, she stands in the doorway for a while, watching her sleep, before she heads to the kitchen.

Daniel is standing at the stove, making scrambled eggs. The room smells like coffee and freshly baked bread. The view through the huge picture windows is immense. Round-topped mountains, shimmering lakes, and valleys of red and yellow trees.

"The view is almost too much," he says with a smile. "It kind of hurts my heart."

They embrace, and he kisses her head gently several times. She breathes in his scent and feels her stomach start to glow with sudden happiness.

A timer beeps on the counter, and Daniel pulls away to take the bread out of the oven.

They sit down to eat, every now and then reaching for each other's hands across the table.

The views take their words away. They drink their coffee in silence, just looking out the windows.

"I'm so worried about Vicky," Elin eventually says in a low voice.

"It'll be okay."

She puts her cup down. "You promise?"

"I just need to get her to talk about what happened," he says. "I'm worried that her feelings of guilt are making her more and more self-destructive.... We really do need to keep a close eye on her."

"The nurse's bus gets into Åre in an hour. I'll drive down and pick her up," Elin says. "Should I ask Vicky if she'd like to come? What do you think?"

"I don't know; I think it would be best if she stayed here," he says.

"Yes, we just got here, after all," Elin agrees. "I can't help feeling worried.... You'll have to stay with her the whole time."

"She knows she's not even allowed to close the door when she isn't going to the bathroom," Daniel says.

At that moment, Elin sees Vicky through the window. She's walking by herself out on the grass, kicking the red leaves. Her long hair is hanging down her back, and her thin body looks as if it's freezing. Elin grabs her cardigan from the back of the chair and goes out to give it to Vicky.

"Thanks," the girl whispers.

"I'm never going to let you down again," Elin says.

Without a word, Vicky takes her hand and squeezes it. Elin's heart beats hard with joy, but the lump in her throat stops her from speaking.

159

THE SKY IS UNUSUALLY DARK when Joona pulls off the highway. He's assuming that Flora took the car to drive to Delsbo Church in Hälsingland.

He can still hear her agitated voice when she told him that a witness was hiding in the bell tower.

Joona can't make any sense of her. It's as if she's getting the truth mixed up with lies, without knowing it. Despite the many lies Flora has told, he can't quite shake the feeling that she knows something about the murders at the Birgitta Home.

Perhaps this witness is another one of her lies, but if there's a chance it's true, he can't afford to miss it—a witness would be crucial.

The low rain clouds turn the fields gray and the pine trees almost blue. He pulls off onto a narrow road. Autumn leaves swirl across the street, and the road is so uneven and winding that it's difficult to maintain any speed at all.

He turns onto a straight avenue leading to Delsbo Church. Now he can see a large field through the trees. A solitary combine is making its way across the field in the distance. Its blades cut across the ground like a scythe.

When he's almost at the church, he sees a car that crashed into a tree. The hood is crumpled, and one of the windows is broken. The engine is still running, the driver's door is open, and the rear lights are glinting off the grass.

Joona slows down, but when he sees that the car is empty he drives past it. Flora must have jumped out, he thinks, and headed for the church on foot.

Joona gets out of his car and hurries up the gravel path. The tarred bell tower stands on a small mound a short distance from the church.

The sky is so dark, it looks as if it could start raining at any moment.

The huge bell hangs beneath the tower's onion dome. In the distance he can see the fast-flowing river, black and foaming.

The bottom of the bell tower is covered with dark wooden shingles. The door is open, and inside, a steep wooden ladder leads up to the bell.

"Flora?" Joona calls out.

160

Flora walks over and stops in the dark doorway of the bell tower, next to Joona. Her face is sad, and her big eyes are tired and wet.

"There's no one here," she says, biting her lip.

"Are you sure?"

She starts to cry, and her voice breaks. "Sorry, but I thought . . . I was so sure . . ."

She steps down and whispers "Sorry" again without looking at him, then holds one hand over her mouth as she starts to head slowly back to the car.

"How did you find your way here?" Joona asks, following her. "Why did you think the witness would be here?"

"My adoptive parents' wedding photograph—the tower is in the background."

"But what does that have to do with Miranda?"

"It was the ghost that said . . ."

Flora stops speaking abruptly.

"What is it?" Joona asks.

He thinks back to Flora's drawing of Miranda, with her hands over her face and the dark blood beside her head. She hadn't drawn the blood like someone trying to deceive; it was more like someone who saw something but no longer remembered exactly what.

Outside Carlén Antiques, Flora had talked about the ghost as if it was a memory.

A memory, he repeats to himself, looking at Flora's pale face.

Yellow autumn leaves are drifting through the air, and in that instant Joona realizes how everything fits together. It's as if a curtain is opened and light streams into a large room. He's found the key to unlocking the whole mystery.

"It's you," he whispers, and his own words send a shiver through him.

He realizes that Flora is the witness at the bell tower.

She's the witness, but it wasn't Miranda she saw being murdered.

It was another girl.

Someone who was killed in exactly the same way.

Another girl, but the same murderer.

The realization is startling and is followed by the stab of a sudden migraine. For a long moment, he feels as if a pistol shot is passing through his head. He reaches out for support and hears Flora's anxious voice through the darkness, and then the pain vanishes.

"You saw everything," he says.

"You're bleeding," she says.

Some blood is running from his nose, and he finds a paper napkin in his pocket.

"Flora," he says, "you're the witness in the tower."

"But I didn't see anything."

He presses the napkin to his nose.

"You've just forgotten it."

"But I wasn't there. You know that—I've never been to the Birgitta Home."

"You saw something else. . . ."

"No," Flora whispers, shaking her head.

"How old is the ghost?" Joona asks.

"Miranda is maybe fifteen when I dream about her ... but when she comes to me when I'm awake, when it's like she's actually in the room, she's younger."

"How much younger?"

"About five years old."

"How old are you now, Flora?"

She starts to feel scared when she looks into his strangely gray eyes.

"Forty," she replies quietly.

Flora has been describing a murder she witnessed as a child, but she has consistently believed she was talking about the murders at the Birgitta Home.

Joona knows he's right. He takes out his phone and calls Anja. Flora saw what she had forgotten or suppressed many years ago. That's why the memories have been so confusing and powerful.

"Anja," he says, the moment she picks up the phone, "are you in front of your computer?"

"Where else would I be?" she asks, sounding amused.

"Will you check to see if anything happened in Delsbo around thirty-five years ago?"

"Anything in particular?"

"Involving a five-year-old girl."

While Anja taps at her keyboard, Joona watches Flora go over to the church, run her hand across the wall, and walk around the porch. He follows her to keep her in sight. A hedgehog scurries off between the gravestones.

Beyond the avenue, a combine harvester is still moving across the field, surrounded by a cloud of dust.

"Yes," Anja says, breathing through her nose. "There was a death.... Thirty-six years ago, the body of a five-year-old girl was found at Delsbo Church. That's all it says. The police concluded that it was an accident."

Joona sees Flora turn and look at him with a heavy, curious expression.

"What was the name of the police officer in charge of the investigation?"

"Torkel Ekholm," Anja replies.

"Can you try to find an address?"

161

TWENTY MINUTES LATER, JOONA PARKS the car beside a
narrow gravel road. He and Flora open an iron gate and walk
through a leafy garden to a red wooden house with white eaves.
The autumn vegetation is full of buzzing insects. The sky is an
unsettled yellow, threatening rain and thunder. When Joona
rings the doorbell, an earsplitting ringing sound echoes across
the garden.

There's a shuffling sound; then the door is opened by an old
man wearing a cotton undershirt, suspenders, and slippers.

"Torkel Ekholm?" Joona asks.

Leaning on his walker, the man looks at them through watery
eyes. They can see a hearing aid tucked behind his big, wrinkled
right ear.

"Who's asking?" he says in a barely audible voice.

"Joona Linna, detective with the National Crime Unit."

The man squints at Joona's ID and can't hold back a strange
little smile. "National Crime Unit," he whispers, and gestures
vaguely for Joona and Flora to enter. "Come in, we can have
coffee."

They sit down at the kitchen table while Torkel goes over to
the stove. He speaks very quietly and seems to be almost completely deaf.

A clock on the wall is ticking loudly, and above the kitchen sofa hangs a well-maintained elk-rifle, a Remington. An embroidered sampler with the text "Contentment Is a Happy Home" has come partly loose from its frame, and its corners are drooping.

The man scratches his chin and looks at Joona through the gloom of the kitchen.

When the water is boiling, Torkel Ekholm gets out three cups and a jar of freeze-dried instant coffee.

"You get lazy with old age," he says with a shrug, handing Flora the teaspoon.

"I'm here to ask about a very old case," Joona says. "Thirty-six years ago, a girl was found dead at Delsbo Church."

"Yes," the old man says without meeting Joona's gaze.

"An accident?"

"Yes," he replies tersely.

"That's not what I think," Joona says.

"That's good to hear," the old man says.

His mouth starts to shake as he pushes the bowl of sugar lumps toward the detective.

"You remember the case?" Joona asks.

The spoon tinkles when the old man tips coffee granules into his cup and stirs it. His eyes, looking at Joona, are bloodshot. "I wish I could forget it, but some cases . . ."

Torkel Ekholm stands up, goes over to a dark desk by the wall, and unlocks the top drawer. He explains in an unsteady voice that he has kept his notes from the case for all these years. "I knew you'd find me one day," he says, so quietly that it's almost impossible to hear.

162

A drowsy fly is buzzing against the window in the little kitchen. Torkel nods toward the papers lying on the table in front of the them. "The dead girl's name was Ylva; she was the daughter of the groundskeeper at Rånne Manor. . . . By the time I got there, they'd already laid her on a sheet. I was told that she'd fallen from the bell tower. . . ."

The old policeman leans back in his chair, making the wood creak. "There was blood on the base of the tower. They pointed and I looked, but it didn't make sense."

"Why did you drop the investigation?"

"There were no witnesses, so I didn't have a thing. I kept asking, but I wasn't getting anywhere. In the end, they didn't want me to upset the gentry over at Rånne anymore. They fired the groundskeeper and . . . that was . . . I've got a picture Janne took—he worked for *Arbetarbladet,* we used to use him as our crime-scene photographer."

The old policeman shows them a black-and-white photograph. A small girl is lying on a sheet, with her hair loose. Beside her head is a black bloodstain exactly the same as the one in Miranda's bed, in the same place.

The stain looks almost like a heart.

The little girl's face is relaxed, her cheeks are childishly chubby, and her mouth looks as if she's asleep.

Flora stares at the picture and feels for her hair with one hand; all the color drains from her face. "I didn't see anything," she whimpers, then starts to cry with her mouth open.

Joona moves the photograph away and tries to calm Flora, but she gets up and takes the picture from Torkel. As she wipes the tears from her cheeks, she stares at the photograph, leaning against the counter. She doesn't notice when she knocks an empty beer bottle into the sink.

"We were playing the close-your-eyes game," she says in a subdued voice.

"The close-your-eyes game?"

"We had to close our eyes and cover our faces."

"But you looked, Flora," Joona says. "You saw who hit the little girl with the rock."

"No, I had my eyes closed. . . . I . . ."

"Who hit her?"

"What did you see?" Torkel asks.

"Little Ylva . . . she looked so happy, covering her eyes with her hands, and then he hit her. . . ."

"Who?" Joona asks.

"My brother," she whispers.

"You don't have a brother," Joona says.

Torkel starts to shake, and his cup falls off his saucer.

"The boy," he mutters. "Surely it wasn't the boy?"

"What boy?" Joona asks.

Flora's face is white, and tears are streaming down her cheeks. The former policeman tears off a paper towel and gets up heavily from his chair. Joona sees her shake her head, but her mouth is still moving.

"What did you see?" Joona asks. "Flora?"

Torkel walks over to her and hands her the paper towel.

"Are you little Flora? The younger sister who wouldn't speak?" he asks gently.

163

FLORA'S CHILDHOOD MEMORY OVERWHELMS HER. She leans against the drainboard, feeling as if her legs are going to give way when she remembers what she saw.

The sun was shining on the grass outside the church. She was covering her face with her hands. The light was shining through her fingers, giving the two others shiny yellow edges.

"Oh God," she whimpers, sinking to the floor. "God . . ."

She remembers seeing her brother hit the little girl with a rock.

The memory is so vivid that it feels as if the children are standing there in the kitchen.

She hears the thud and sees Ylva's head shake.

Flora remembers how the girl fell to the grass. Her mouth opened and closed, her eyelids trembled, she muttered confused words, and he hit her again.

He hit her as hard as he could. And screamed that they all had to close their eyes. When Ylva stopped moving, he moved her hands to her face and repeated that she had to keep her eyes closed.

"But I didn't have my eyes closed . . ."

"Are you Flora?" the old policeman asks again.

Between her fingers, Flora saw her brother stand up with the rock in his hands. Very calmly, he told Flora to keep her eyes closed, because they were playing the close-your-eyes game. He came closer with the bloody rock and held it up in the air. She pulled back just as he went to hit her. The rock cut her on the cheek and hit her shoulder hard; she fell to her knees but got up and started to run.

"Are you little Flora who lived at the Rånne place?"

"I can hardly remember anything," she replies.

"Who's her brother?" Joona asks.

"People called them 'the kids from the children's home' even though they'd been adopted by the people in the big house," the former policeman says.

"And their name was Rånne?"

"Rånne, the timber baron. . . . We just called them 'the gentry,'" Torkel replies. "It was even in the paper when they adopted two children—a noble act of charity, they wrote—but after the accident the girl moved away. . . . The boy stayed on his own."

"Daniel," Flora says. "His name is Daniel."

Joona's chair scrapes the floor as he gets up from the table and leaves the house without a word. With his phone clutched to his ear, he runs through the garden, past the yellowing leaves under the trees, out through the gate to his car.

"Anja, listen to me. I need your help, it's urgent," Joona says, getting in the driver's seat. "See if Daniel Grim has any connection to a family called Rånne in Delsbo."

Joona barely has time to switch the car's radio on to alert the National Communications Center before Anja comes back with the answer.

"Yes, they're his parents."

"Find out everything you can about him," Joona says.

"What's this about?"

"Girls," Joona replies.

164

ELIN IS DRIVING CAREFULLY DOWN the steep gravel road toward Åre to pick up Vicky's nurse. One of the side windows is open, and fresh air fills the car. The long, thin lake gleams darkly below. The mountains are lined up like gigantic Viking burial mounds, gently rounded and covered in vegetation.

She thinks of how Vicky took her hand and squeezed it. Everything is getting better again.

Just as the narrow road leads her below a rock face, her phone buzzes in her bag. She drives a little farther, then pulls off the road and takes out her phone with an uneasy feeling. It's Joona Linna. Though she doesn't really want to hear whatever he has to say, she still unlocks the phone with trembling fingers.

"Hello?" she says.

"Where's Vicky?" the detective asks.

"She's up here, with me," she replies. "I've got a house in Duved that—"

"I know, but can you see her right now?"

"No, I—"

"I want you to go and get Vicky right now, put her in the car, and drive to Stockholm. Just you and Vicky. Do it right away. Don't pack anything—just walk straight out to the car and—"

"I'm already in the car!" Elin shouts, feeling panic growing in her chest. "Vicky's back at the house with Daniel."

"That's not good," Joona says, and she can hear the tone in his voice, a tone that makes her feel sick with worry.

"What's happened?"

"Listen to me. . . . Daniel murdered Miranda and Elisabet."

"That can't be true," she whispers. "He's watching Vicky while I go to the bus station."

"Then it's probably too late," Joona says. "Just get yourself out of there. That's my advice to you as a police officer."

Elin stares out at the sky through the windshield. It's no longer white. The clouds are low, skimming the mountaintops, black and heavy with rain.

"I can't just abandon her," she hears herself say.

"The police are on their way, but it will take a while for them to get there."

"I'm going back," she says.

"Okay," Joona says, "but be careful. . . . Daniel Grim is very, very dangerous, and you'll be completely alone with him until the police arrive. . . ."

But Elin is no longer thinking. She turns the car around and starts to drive back, up the steep road, with the gravel rattling beneath the car.

165

VICKY IS ON HER BED, downloading apps onto her phone, when Daniel comes in. He sits down on the white leather armchair beside the bed.

Outside, the mountain landscape is laid out before them, with Ullådalen and the peaks of Åreskutan etched against the sky.

"Did it feel wrong yesterday?" Daniel asks. "I mean . . . just sitting and waiting in the car while we got your things?"

"No . . . I get that no one wants to see me," she replies, still fiddling with her phone.

"When I went into the house, Almira and Lu Chu were playing that game where you have to close your eyes, the blind game," Daniel lies. "I know Miranda taught you that game."

"Yes," she replies.

"Do you know how Miranda learned it?" Daniel asks.

Vicky nods and takes out the phone's charger.

"I sometimes use the game in therapy sessions," Daniel says. "It's a trust exercise."

"Miranda fed me chocolate." Vicky smiles. "And then she drew a heart on my stomach and . . ."

Vicky suddenly stops herself. She thinks about what Tuula told her in Hårte, when she was outside, in the lilac bushes.

"Did you tell anyone about the game?" Daniel asks, looking at her.

"No," she replies.

"I just wondered...."

Vicky looks down and thinks about Tuula, standing there in the darkness with the baseball bat in her hand, saying that the murderer only kills whores. Only whores needed to worry about getting their skulls smashed in, she whispered. It was typical of Tuula to say weird, horrible things. Vicky tried to smile, but Tuula said she found a pregnancy test in Miranda's bag when she took her necklace. Vicky's immediate reaction when she heard that was to assume that Miranda had had sex with one of the guys they met at ADL.

But now she realizes it must have been Daniel.

Vicky knew something was wrong when Miranda showed her what to do, because Miranda was only pretending that it was fun. She giggled and broke off pieces of chocolate, but all she wanted to do was find out if Vicky had experienced the same things she had, without actually telling her what had happened.

Vicky remembers Miranda's attempts to sound nonchalant when she asked if Daniel had ever come into her room to play.

"Miranda didn't say," Vicky tries to say, glancing up at Daniel's eyes for a moment. "She never said anything about what you used to do in therapy sessions...."

Vicky's cheeks turn red as she realizes how everything fits together. Daniel must be the person who killed Miranda and Elisabet. The murders had nothing to do with whores. Daniel killed Miranda because she was pregnant.

Maybe Miranda had already told Elisabet everything.

Vicky tries to breathe calmly. She doesn't know what to say, so she picks at her cast.

"It was ..."

Daniel leans forward, picks up the phone from her lap, and puts it in his pocket.

"Therapy—it's really all about trusting each other," Vicky continues, even though she knows that Daniel has already realized she's not telling him the truth.

He knows she's figured out that he killed Miranda and Elisabet with a hammer and pinned the blame on her.

"Yes, that's an important step in therapy," Daniel says, watching her carefully.

"I know," she whispers.

"We could try it now, you and me. Just for fun," he says.

She nods, thinking with growing panic that he's decided to kill her. Her heartbeat is thudding in her ears, and sweat is trickling from her armpits. He helped get her released and has come with them to Elin's house to find out how much she knows, to make sure he wasn't going to be exposed.

"Close your eyes," he says with a smile.

"Now?"

"It's fun."

"But I . . ."

"Just do it," he says sternly.

She closes her eyes and covers her face with her hands. Her heart is pounding with fear. He's doing something in the room. It sounds as if he's pulling the sheet from the bed.

"I need to go to the toilet," she says.

"Soon."

She sits there with her hands over her face and starts when he pulls a chair across the floor. But, though she hears a scraping sound, she keeps her hands in front of her face.

166

ELIN IS DRIVING AS FAST as she possibly can up the steep slope. A key chain is rattling in the tray beside the gearshift. The branches of a tree whip against the windows and roof. She brakes at a sharp bend and almost skids. The tires slip across the loose stones, but she pushes the clutch down, gets around the bend, and accelerates again.

The car jolts and rumbles. Meltwater has carved deep grooves in the road.

She keeps driving up the mountain, a little too fast, and then tries to slow her speed slightly as she approaches the turn to her house. But as she turns sharply right, the side of the car scrapes the gate, and the left side-view mirror flies off. She puts her foot down again, and it feels as if the car is leaving the ground when she reaches the top of the slope.

She drives the last, straight stretch of road toward the house and brakes hard, kicking up a cloud of dust. Elin leaps out of the car with the engine still running and rushes into the house. The blinds are down. It's completely dark, and she stumbles over shoes and ski boots in the gloom as she hurries into the large living room.

"Vicky!" she calls.

Elin turns on the lights and runs up the stairs, slipping and hitting her knee on one of the steps in the process. She rushes to Vicky's room, but the door is locked. Elin bangs on the door and hears the hysteria in her own voice when she screams: "Open the door!"

There's no sound from inside the room, and Elin leans over to look through the keyhole. A chair is lying on the floor, and shadows are moving jerkily across the walls.

"Vicky?"

She takes a step back and kicks at the door. Nothing happens, apart from a dull thud. She kicks again, then runs to the next room, but the key isn't in the lock. She moves on to the next door, fumbles with her hand, and manages to pull the key out. Then she rushes back, knocking over a glass sculpture, which falls to the floor with a loud crash. Her hands are shaking so badly that she has trouble inserting the key in the lock. She uses both hands, manages to turn it on her second attempt, and throws the door open.

"Oh God!" she whispers.

Vicky is hanging from a twined bedsheet tied to the wooden beam. Her mouth is gaping open, her face drained of color. Her feet are moving gently in the air. She's still alive. Her toes are reaching for the floor, half a meter below, and she's clutching at the noose with her fingers.

Elin doesn't think. She just rushes over to Vicky and lifts her up as high as she can.

"Try to pull loose," she sobs, holding Vicky's thin legs.

The girl struggles with the sheet, and her body jerks. She needs oxygen and is starting to panic as she fights to loosen the noose.

Suddenly Elin hears Vicky inhale some air and cough. Gasping deeply, she tenses her body.

"I can't get it off," Vicky says, still coughing.

Elin stands on tiptoe and tries to lift her up higher.

"Try to pull yourself up!"

"I can't...."

The noose tightens again. Vicky can't get enough air, and her body starts to convulse in her panic. Elin's arms are starting to shake from the effort of holding her up. But she can't give up. She tries to reach the overturned chair with her foot so she can climb up on it. No, it's impossible. Vicky is wet with sweat, and her body is twitching spasmodically. When Elin tries to change her grip, Vicky is just too heavy. Numbing weakness is creeping up on her, but even so she manages to lower one hand slightly, get a better grip, and lift Vicky a little higher. Exerting the last of her strength, Vicky finally manages to pull the noose over her head. She coughs hard, and they sink to the floor together.

Vicky's neck looks blue, and she's breathing very shallowly, but she's breathing, she's alive. Elin kisses her cheeks and strokes the hair from her sweaty face with a trembling hand, and whispers to her not to try to speak.

"It was Daniel...."

"I know. The police are on their way," Elin whispers. "You need to stay here. I'll lock the door, but you have to stay absolutely quiet."

167

ELIN LOCKS THE DOOR BEHIND Vicky and feels her body shaking as she goes down the stairs. Her arms and legs feel numb from the exertion. Then her phone buzzes, and she sees that she's received a text from Vicky's phone:

Sorry, but I can't lie anymore. Don't be sad. Love, V

Elin feels sick and anxious. Thoughts are spinning through her head. It's impossible to understand what's happening. Daniel must have just texted her from Vicky's phone. She walks cautiously into the dark living room. The blinds have been lowered throughout the house, in fact.

A shadow falls across the floor. It's Daniel. He's standing on the staircase to the lower floor; he must have come up from the garage. She knows she has to try to delay him until the police arrive.

"She's done it," Elin says. "Vicky locked the door to her room. It took too long. I don't understand. . . ."

"What are you saying?" he asks slowly, looking at her blankly.

"She's not breathing. . . . Can we go outside? We have to call someone," she whispers.

"Yes," he replies, coming closer.

"Daniel . . . I don't understand."

"Don't you?"

"No, I . . ."

"After she killed you, Vicky went to her room and hanged herself," he says.

"What are you saying?"

"You shouldn't have come back so soon," Daniel says.

Elin sees that he's hiding an ax behind his back. She starts to run for the front door, but there's no time—he's right behind her—and she turns right abruptly instead, toppling a chair behind her. He trips, giving her a slight advantage, and she runs past the kitchen and into the hallway. His footsteps are getting closer. There's nowhere to hide. She hurries into Jack's old bedroom, locks the door behind her, and presses the button to activate the blinds.

I'm not going to be able to get outside, she thinks. It would take too long.

The motor whirrs, and there's a creaking sound as the aluminum slats start to separate and light filters through the small holes.

Elin lets out a shriek when the first swing of the ax hits the door. The blade penetrates the wood next to the lock, then pulls sideways and back.

Slowly, the blinds start to rise. A narrow strip of window is visible by the time the ax strikes a second time.

She can't wait—she has to move on—so she hurries across the floor and into Jack's bathroom as Daniel kicks at the bedroom door. The wood cracks, and long splinters splay out around the lock, and the door flies open.

Elin catches sight of herself in the large mirror as she rushes through the bathroom, past the bathtub, shower, and sauna, and out through the other door into Jack's office. It's dark, and she trips over the low document-cabinet. Old files fall to the floor. Her hands fumble across the desk, and she pulls out a drawer, tips out the pens, and grabs the letter opener.

The blinds in the bedroom have finished opening, and it's

quiet now. She hears something fall into the large bathtub. Daniel is coming after her. Elin kicks off her shoes, creeps barefoot into the hallway, and closes the door behind her.

She's thinking she might be able to sneak around behind Daniel and go through the shattered door into Jack's bedroom again, where she could try to open the window.

She takes a few steps but changes her mind and rushes farther along the hallway instead.

"Elin!" he roars behind her.

The door to the larger guest room is locked. When she turns the key, the lock sticks. She glances backward and sees Daniel approaching. He's not running, but his strides are long. He's so close she can smell his sweat. A shadow passes quickly across the door as she yanks at the handle. She throws herself sideways and hits her cheek against a picture.

The ax misses her head, and the blade hits the concrete wall behind her. There's a sharp clanging sound, and the ax deflects so sharply that Daniel loses his grip on it. It hits the floor with a crash.

168

Now the lock clicks, and Elin shoves the door open with her shoulder and stumbles into the room. Daniel follows, trying to grab her. She turns around and stabs him with the letter opener. It hits him in the chest, but the wound is superficial. He grabs her by the hair and drags her down to the floor with such force that she hits the table and knocks the lamp off.

He pushes his glasses farther up his nose, then retrieves the ax. Elin crawls beneath the wide bed.

She hopes that Vicky is staying hidden, because she's starting to think that she might just be able to hold out until the police arrive.

She can see Daniel's legs and feet as he walks around. She shrinks back and feels him climb up onto the bed. The mattress and struts creak. Not knowing which way she should go, she tries to stay close to the middle.

Suddenly he grabs her foot, and she screams. He's off the bed now and drags her out. Though she tries to hold on, she stands no chance. Still holding her ankle, he raises the ax. She kicks him in the face with her other foot. He loses his glasses and lets go; he staggers backward into the bookcase, pressing a hand to one of his eyes and staring at her with the other.

She crawls out and rushes toward the door. From the corner of her eye, she sees him bend over and pick up his glasses. She runs past Jack's old room and into the kitchen, hearing Daniel's heavy steps behind her in the hallway.

Thoughts are flying through her head. The police should be here by now—Joona said they were on their way.

Elin snatches up a saucepan from the drying rack as she runs through the kitchen, then dashes through the living room, opens the door to the garage, and throws the saucepan down the steps.

As she hears it clatter down the staircase, she heads upstairs instead.

Daniel reaches the door to the garage but isn't fooled: he can hear her steps going upstairs. She's running out of options. Though she's out of breath, Elin keeps going up, past the floor where Vicky is hiding, making sure to climb the stairs more slowly, trying to lure Daniel away from the girl and up to the top floor.

Elin knows she only has to hold out until the police arrive. She has to manage this somehow, to keep Daniel occupied so that he doesn't go back to Vicky's room.

The staircase creaks behind her under Daniel's feet.

She reaches the top floor. It's almost completely dark. She hurries over and grabs the poker from the fireplace. The other tools rattle on the stand. Elin walks to the middle of the floor and smashes the ceiling lamp with one blow. The large frosted glass chandelier falls to the floor and shatters with a loud crash. The shards of glass scatter across the floor; then the room is silent.

The only sound is the heavy footsteps on the stairs.

Elin hides in the darkness beside a bookcase, just to the right of the doorway.

Daniel is panting as he climbs the last steps. He's in no hurry. He knows she can't escape from the top floor.

Elin tries to breathe more quietly.

Daniel stands still with the ax in his hand, staring into the dark room, then flicks the light switch.

There's a click, but nothing happens.

169

Standing in the darkness, Elin clutches the poker with both hands. The adrenaline in her blood is making her tremble, but she feels strangely powerful.

Daniel is breathing softly, moving very cautiously farther into the room.

She can't see him, but she can hear the crunch of glass beneath his feet.

Suddenly there's a click, followed by an electrical whirring sound. Light starts to filter through the tiny holes between the slats of the shutters. Daniel is standing just inside the door, waiting, as the blinds slowly rise and light fills the room.

There's nowhere to hide.

He stares at her, and she backs away, holding the poker out toward him.

Clutching the ax in his right hand, he glances at it, then starts to walk toward her.

She strikes at him with the poker, but he moves out of the way. Breathing hard, she aims the poker at him again. Her foot stings when she stands on a piece of broken glass, but she doesn't take her eyes off Daniel.

The ax swings in his hand.

She lunges again, but he moves aside.

His eyes stare at her impassively.

Just then, he makes a rapid, unexpected move with the ax. The side of the blade hits the poker—there's a dull clang as metal strikes metal. The poker falls from her hand and clatters to the floor.

She has nothing to defend herself with now and backs away with the bewildering realization that she's not going to get out of this. Mortal dread courses through her body, making her feel strangely detached and apathetic.

Daniel follows her.

She looks at him. Though he meets her eyes, there doesn't seem to be any depth to his gaze.

She backs away until she hits the large window. Behind her, the smooth concrete façade drops three and a half floors down to the deck.

Elin's feet are bleeding, and her shuffling red footprints stand out on the pale wooden floor.

She's run out of fight. All she can do is stand still. She knows that she should try to bargain with him, promise him something, get him to talk.

Daniel is breathing harder now, and he looks at her for a few seconds, licks his lips, then quickly takes the last few steps toward her. He raises the ax and strikes. Instinctively, she moves her head aside. The ax crashes into the window. She feels the thick glass shake behind her back and hears a splintering sound as it starts to crack. Daniel raises the ax again, but before he has time to swing it, Elin leans backward, pressing her whole weight against the large window, until she feels it give way. Her stomach lurches. She falls back through the air, surrounded by glass and sparkling fragments. Elin Frank closes her eyes and doesn't even notice when she hits the deck.

Daniel leans one hand against the window frame and looks down. Pieces of glass are still falling from the sill. Elin is lying far below. There's glass everywhere. A steady stream of dark blood is spreading across the deck from her head.

Daniel's breathing calms down. The back of his shirt is wet with sweat.

The view from the top floor is breathtaking. The peak of Tyskhuvudet feels incredibly close, and the chalet at the top of Åreskutan is draped in autumn mist. The flashing blue lights of a number of emergency vehicles are clearly visible heading up the road from Åre, but the road toward Tegefors is empty.

170

Joona realized why Elisabet had defensive injuries on the wrong sides of her hands.

They had been covering her face.

Daniel doesn't leave any witnesses—no one is allowed to see what he does.

After warning Elin, he called and asked for police and an ambulance to be dispatched to Duved. The helicopters were already busy up in Kiruna, and it would take the emergency vehicles at least half an hour to reach the house.

There was no way Joona could get there in time—it was more than three hundred kilometers from Delsbo to Duved.

He shut the car door and had just switched on the engine when Carlos called and asked why he suddenly suspected Daniel Grim.

"Thirty-six years ago, he killed a child in exactly the same way as the girl at the Birgitta Home," Joona replies as he drives slowly down the gravel road.

"Anja's shown me photographs of the accident at Delsbo." Carlos sighs.

"It was no accident," Joona says stubbornly.

"And what leads you to connect the two cases?"

"Both victims were covering their faces when they—"

"I know Miranda was," Carlos interrupts. "But I'm sitting here with the pictures from Delsbo in front of me, for God's sake. The victim is lying on a sheet, and her hands are—"

"The body was moved before the police arrived at the scene," Joona says.

"How do you know that?"

"I just know," he says.

"Is this your usual stubbornness, or did your fortune-teller tell you all this?"

"She's an eyewitness," Joona replies in his dark Finnish accent.

Carlos laughs wearily and then takes a more serious tone: "The statute of limitations has already run on it. We've got a prosecutor leading the investigation against Vicky Bennet, and you're under investigation by IA."

Once Joona was back on Highway 84 and heading toward Sundsvall, he contacted the Västernorrland Police and asked for a patrol car and forensics team to be sent to Daniel Grim's home. Via the comms unit, he heard that the Jämtland Police expected to be at Elin Frank's house in ten minutes.

171

THE FIRST PATROL CAR STOPS in front of Elin's house. One of
the officers goes over to the large SUV and switches the engine
off while the other draws his pistol and walks toward the front
door. Another police car pulls into the driveway, followed by an
ambulance.

The lights from the second ambulance are already visible on
the steep drive.

The large house looks oddly shut up. The windows are covered by metal blinds.

Everything is disconcertingly quiet.

With their pistols drawn, two police officers enter through
the front door. A third officer stays by the cars; the fourth moves
around the house, heading slowly up a broad flight of white concrete steps.

The house doesn't seem to be inhabited.

The police officer walks out onto a deck, past a set of outdoor
furniture, and then he sees the blood, the broken glass, and the
two figures.

He stops.

A pale-faced girl with cracked lips and tangled hair is looking
up at him. The look in her eyes is almost black. She's kneeling
down beside the apparently lifeless body of a woman. A pool
of blood has spread out around them. The girl is holding the

woman's hand in both of hers. Her mouth is moving, but the police officer can't hear what she's saying until he gets closer.

"She's still warm," Vicky whispers. "She's still warm. . . ."

The police officer lowers his gun, takes out his radio, and calls the paramedics.

The paramedics silently bring two stretchers over. Immediately concluding that the woman has a fractured skull, they lift her carefully onto the stretcher, even though the girl won't let go of her. Vicky holds the woman's hand tightly between hers as heavy tears roll down her cheeks.

The girl is also seriously injured. She's bleeding badly from her knees and legs from sitting in the broken glass, her neck is swollen and bruised, and her vertebrae are probably damaged, but she refuses to lie on a stretcher, and it's obvious that she has no intention of leaving Elin's side.

They need to get going, so they make a quick decision: they let the girl sit and hold Elin Frank's hand while they drive to Östersund, where a helicopter ambulance will take them to Karolinska Hospital.

172

JOONA IS DRIVING ACROSS SOME old railroad tracks when the coordinator of the operation in Duved finally answers his phone. His voice sounds shaken, and he is speaking with someone else in the police van with him as he talks to Joona.

"It's a little chaotic right now … but we're on the scene," he says, and coughs.

"I need to know if—"

"No, for God's sake. … It needs to be before Trångsviken and Strömsund!" the coordinator shouts at someone.

"Are they alive?"

"Sorry, I need to get the roadblocks set up."

"I'll wait," Joona says, as he passes a truck.

He hears the coordinator put the phone down and direct patrol cars to set up the roadblocks.

"Okay, I'm back," the man says eventually.

"Are they alive?" Joona asks again.

"The girl's condition isn't serious, but the woman is … Her condition is critical. They're preparing for an emergency operation at Östersund Hospital before she's transferred to Karolinska."

"And Daniel Grim?"

"There's no one else in the house. … We're setting up road-blocks now, but if he goes for one of the smaller roads … we don't have the resources to …"

"Helicopters?" Joona asks.

"We're liaising with the rangers up in Kiruna, but it's all taking too long," the coordinator says in a voice that's rough with fatigue.

Joona drives into Sundsvall. Elin Frank went back to her house, despite his warning. It's impossible to imagine what she did when she got there, but she evidently got back in time. Though she is seriously injured, Vicky is still alive.

There's a possibility that Daniel Grim will get caught in one of the roadblocks, especially if he doesn't realize they're looking for him. But if he manages to slip through, it will take him at least two hours to get back to his house. By then the police need to have set a trap for him.

And before that, a preliminary forensics search of the house needs to be completed, Joona thinks.

He slows down and stops behind a patrol car on Bruks Street. The front door of Daniel Grim's house is open, and two uniformed officers are waiting for him in the entryway.

"The house is empty," one of them says. "Nothing unusual so far."

"Is the forensics technician on the way?"

"Give him ten minutes."

"I'll take a look around," Joona says, walking in.

Joona moves quickly around the house without knowing what he's looking for. He opens cupboards, pulls out drawers, glances inside a wine cellar, moves on to the kitchen, looks in the cabinets, fridge, and freezer. Then he runs upstairs and pulls off the tiger-striped bedspread, turns the mattress upside down, opens the closet, pushes Elisabet's dresses aside, and taps the wall, before kicking some old shoes out of the way so he can pull out a box of Christmas decorations. He goes into the bathroom, looks in the cabinet full of aftershave, medicine, and makeup, then goes all the way down to the basement, looks at the tools on the wall, tries the locked door to the boiler room, pulls the lawnmower aside, lifts the drain, and looks inside the bags of compost, before finally heading back upstairs.

He stops in the middle of the house and looks out through the window at the hammock in the garden. In the other direction, the front door is still open, and Joona can see the two police officers waiting by their car.

Joona closes his eyes and thinks about the hatch in the bedroom that leads to the attic, the locked door to the boiler room in the basement, and the fact that the wine cellar under the stairs should have been bigger.

There's an old-fashioned sign on the narrow door under the stairs with the words "Sobriety and Humor" on it. He opens it and looks inside the wine cellar once more. There are around a hundred bottles in racks on a high wooden shelf, and an obvious space behind the shelf, at least thirty centimeters between it and the outside wall. He pulls at it, removes the bottles at either end, and finds a sliding latch right at the top. Very carefully, he swings the whole shelf back on its hinges. The smell of dust and wood hits him. The space inside is almost empty, but on the floor is a shoebox with a heart painted on its lid.

Joona takes out his phone, photographs the box, then pulls on a clean pair of latex gloves.

173

THE FIRST THING JOONA SEES when he lifts the lid of the box is a photograph of a girl with strawberry-blond hair. It isn't Miranda. It's another girl, maybe twelve years old.

She's holding her hands over her face in the picture.

It's just a game. Her mouth is smiling, and her sparkling eyes are visible between her fingers.

Joona gently lifts the photograph out and finds a dried wild rose.

The next photograph shows a girl curled up on a brown sofa, eating potato chips. She's looking questioningly at the camera.

Joona turns over a bookmark in the shape of an angel and sees that someone's written "Linda S" in gold ink on the back.

On top of a bundle of photographs held together by a rubber band lies a lock of light-brown hair, a pink silk bow, and a cheap ring with a plastic heart on it.

He looks through the pictures of different girls. Somehow they all remind him of Miranda, but most of them are considerably younger. Some of them have their eyes closed or are covering their faces with their hands.

A young girl in a pink ballet dress and legwarmers is covering her face. Joona turns the picture over and reads "Dear Sandy." The words are surrounded by a lot of hearts drawn with red and blue pens.

A girl with short hair is making a face at the camera. Someone has scratched a heart and the name "Euterpe" into the glossy surface of the photograph.

At the bottom of the box is a polished amethyst, some dried tulip petals, some candy, and a piece of paper with childish writing on it: "Daniel + Emilia."

Joona picks up his phone and holds it in his hand for a moment as he looks at the photographs. Then he calls Anja.

"I don't have anything," she says. "I don't even know what I'm looking for."

"Deaths," Joona says, looking at a photograph of a girl with her hands over her face.

"Yes, but I'm afraid ... Daniel Grim has worked as a counselor at seven different institutions for vulnerable girls in Västernorrland, Gävleborg, and Jämtland. He has no convictions and has never been suspected of any crime. There are no internal reports filed against him—not even any notes."

"I see," Joona says.

"Are you sure you have the right person? I've done a few comparisons. . . . During the periods he's been there, the homes have actually seen lower mortality rates than the national average."

Joona looks at the pictures again, at all the flowers and hearts. It would almost have been cute if a small boy had hidden the box.

"Isn't there anything unusual or unexpected?"

"Over the years, just over two hundred and fifty girls have passed through the institutions where he's worked."

Joona takes a deep breath. "I have seven first names," he says. "The most unusual name is Euterpe. Is there a Euterpe anywhere?"

"Euterpe Papadias," Anja says. "Suicide at Fyrbylund, that children's home in Norrköping. But Daniel Grim has no connection there."

"Are you sure?"

"Before she was moved to Fyrbylund, there are just a few brief notes about her bipolar disorder, self-harm, and two serious suicide attempts."

"Was she moved there from the Birgitta Home?" Joona asks.

"Yes, she was moved in June 2009. . . . Then, on July 2 of that same year, just two weeks later, she was found in the shower with her wrists slashed."

"But Daniel wasn't working there then?"

"No," Anja replies.

"Any girls by the name of Sandy?"

"Yes, two . . . One of them is dead, an overdose of pills at an institution in Uppsala. . . ."

"He's written 'Linda S' on the back of a bookmark."

"Yes, Linda Svensson . . . reported missing seven years ago, after returning to a school in Sollefteå . . ."

"They all die somewhere else," Joona says heavily.

"But . . . is he the one doing all this?" Anja whispers.

"Yes, I think so," Joona replies.

"Dear God . . ."

"Do you have a girl called Emilia?"

"Yes . . . I've got an Emilia Larsson, who left the Birgitta Home. . . . There's a photograph. . . . Her arms are sliced open, from her wrists up to her elbows. . . . He must have cut her arms and stopped her from calling for help, then blocked the door and watched her bleed to death."

Joona goes out and sits in the car. The world is showing its darker side again, and he feels immense sorrow.

He looks at the beautiful trees outside, takes a deep breath, and tells himself that the police are going to hunt Daniel down.

Joona talks to the coordinator of the operation in Duved, and finds out that the roadblocks will remain in place for another two hours but that the lead officer no longer believes that Daniel will get caught in any of them.

Joona thinks about the pictures of the girls Daniel Grim

picked out. He seems to have felt a childish infatuation for them. Among the pictures were hearts, flowers, candy, short messages. His little collection was pink and bright, whereas the reality was a nightmare.

The girls in the institutions and group homes were locked in—some of them may have been strapped down and heavily medicated—when he forced himself upon them.

And they had no one but him to talk to.

No one would listen to them, and no one would miss them.

He's picked girls with a history of self-harm, and so many suicide attempts behind them that their relatives have given up and already begun to think of them as dead.

Miranda was an exception. He killed her before she was moved, in a panic. Maybe the murder was triggered by her belief that she was pregnant?

174

TORKEL EKHOLM'S WIFE'S INFLUENCE IS still visible in the fabrics, in the hand-sewn embroidery on the faded tablecloths. But the crocheted hems of the curtains are now gray with dust, and the knees of Torkel's trousers have worn thin.

The clock on the wall ticks on laboriously. On the table in front of Flora are all of Torkel's notes, the newspaper clipping about the accident, and the death notice.

The old man tells Flora all he can remember about the logging baron Rånne, and the family's manor house, their forests and fields, how they couldn't have children, and about their decision to adopt Flora and her brother, Daniel. He tells her about the groundskeeper's daughter, Ylva, who was found dead beneath the bell tower, and about the silence that spread across Delsbo.

"I was so little," Flora says. "It never occurred to me that they might be memories. I thought I'd just imagined those children...."

Flora thinks back to all the times she thought she was going crazy after she heard about the murders at the Birgitta Home. She couldn't stop thinking about what had happened, the girl with her hands over her face. She dreamed about her, saw her everywhere.

"But you were there," he says.

"I tried to explain what Daniel did, but everyone just got angry. . . . When I told them what had happened, Daddy took me into his office and said that all liars end up burning in a sea of fire."

"At last I've got my witness," the old policeman says quietly.

Flora remembers being terrified of burning up, of having her hair and clothes catch fire. She thought her whole body would turn as dry and black as the wood in the stove if she told anyone what Daniel had done.

Torkel slowly sweeps the crumbs from the table.

"So what happened with the girl?" he asks.

"I knew Daniel liked Ylva—he always wanted to hold her hand, gave her raspberries. . . ."

She trails off as she once again sees the strange yellow fragments of memory flicker, as if they were about to catch fire.

"We were playing the close-your-eyes game," she goes on. "When Ylva closed her eyes, he kissed her on the mouth. . . . She opened her eyes, laughed, and said that now she was going to have a baby. I laughed, but Daniel got . . . He told us we weren't allowed to look . . . and I could hear that his voice sounded funny. I peeked between my fingers, the way I always did. Ylva looked happy as she closed her eyes, and I saw Daniel pick up a rock from the ground and hit her and hit her. . . ."

Torkel lets out a deep sigh and then lies down on the narrow kitchen sofa. "I see Daniel sometimes, when he comes to visit Rånne. . . ."

When the old policeman has fallen asleep, Flora very carefully takes the hunting rifle down from the wall and leaves the cottage.

175

FLORA WALKS DOWN THE NARROW avenue leading to Rånne Manor with the heavy rifle in her arms. Black birds are perched in the yellowing treetops.

Flora feels as if Ylva is walking beside her. She remembers how they used to run around with Daniel here on the estate.

She has always thought it was a dream. The beautiful house they were brought to, with bedrooms of their own and flowery wallpaper—she remembers now. The memories have risen from the depths. They were buried deep in the black soil, but now they're standing right in front of her.

The old cobbled courtyard looks just the same as it used to. There are several cars parked over by the garage. She walks up the wide flight of steps, opens the door, and goes inside.

It feels strange to walk through the familiar house, with its huge chandelier and dark Persian carpets, carrying a loaded weapon in her hands.

No one has seen her yet, but she can hear voices coming from the dining room.

As she goes through the succession of four drawing rooms, she can already see them sitting at the table in the distance.

She changes her grip, resting the barrel in the crook of her arm, clutching the butt, and putting her finger on the trigger.

Her former family is talking and eating. No one is looking in her direction.

There are fresh-cut flowers in the tall vases in the window alcoves. She detects movement from the corner of her eye and spins around with the gun raised. It's her own reflection in a huge, uneven floor-to-ceiling mirror, aiming the rifle at herself. Her face is almost gray, and the look in her eyes is raw and wild.

With the rifle aimed in front of her, she walks through the last drawing room and straight into the dining room.

The table is adorned with the fruits of the harvest: small sheaves of wheat, bunches of grapes, plums, and cherries.

Flora remembers that it's Thanksgiving Day in Sweden.

The woman who was once her mother looks thin and frail. She's eating slowly, with trembling hands, a napkin spread out across her lap.

A man Flora's own age is sitting between the older couple. She doesn't recognize him, but she knows who he is.

Flora stops in front of the table, and the floor creaks beneath her feet.

The father is the first to notice her.

When the old man sees her, a strange calmness settles over him. He puts his knife and fork down and sits up, as if he wants to take a good look at her.

The mother turns to look at what he's staring at and blinks several times when the middle-aged woman with the shiny rifle steps forward out of the gloom.

"Flora," the old woman says, dropping her knife. "Is that you, Flora?"

She stands there with the rifle in front of their lavish table and can't bring herself to answer. She just swallows hard, looks the mother briefly in the eye, then turns toward the father.

"Why did you come here with a gun?" he asks.

"You made me into a liar," she replies.

The father smiles briefly and joylessly. The wrinkles on his face make him look bitter and lonely. "Anyone who lies shall be cast into the lake of fire," he says wearily.

She nods and hesitates for several seconds before asking her question: "You knew Daniel killed Ylva, didn't you?"

The father slowly wipes his mouth on the white linen napkin.

"We had to send you away because you told such terrible lies," he says. "And now you're back, telling lies again."

"I'm not lying."

"You admitted it, Flora. . . . You admitted to me that you had just made it all up," he says quietly.

"I was four years old, and you were yelling that my hair would burn if I didn't admit I was lying, you screamed that my face would melt and my blood boil . . . so I said I was telling lies, and then you sent me away."

176

FLORA SQUINTS AT HER BROTHER, who is sitting at the dining table with the light behind him. She can't tell if he's meeting her gaze—his eyes look like frozen wells.

"Go now," the father says, and goes back to eating.

"Not without Daniel," she replies, pointing at him with the rifle.

"It wasn't his fault," the mother says weakly. "I was the one who—"

"Daniel is a good son," the father interrupts.

"I'm not saying he isn't," the mother says. "But he . . . You don't remember, but we were sitting and watching a play on television the night before it happened. It was Strindberg's *Miss Julie*, and of course she feels such lust for the servant . . . and I said it would be better—"

"What's this about?" the father interrupts.

"I think about it every day," the old woman goes on. "It was my fault, because I said it would be better for the girl to die than get pregnant."

"That's enough."

"And just when I said that . . . I saw that little Daniel was staring at me," she says with tears in her eyes. "Of course, I was only talking about Strindberg's play. . . ."

Her hands are shaking badly when she picks her napkin up.

"After that business with Ylva ... a week had passed since the accident, it was nighttime, and I was about to say Daniel's bedtime prayers with him. ... He told me that Ylva was going to have a baby. He was only six years old—he didn't understand."

Flora looks at her brother. He pushes his glasses farther up his nose and looks at his mother. It's impossible to make out what he's thinking.

"You need to come with me to the police and tell the truth," Flora says to Daniel, aiming the rifle at his chest.

"What good would that do?" the mother says. "It was an accident."

"We may have been playing," Flora says without looking at her. "But it was no accident."

"He was only a child!" the father bellows.

"Yes, but he's killed again. ... He killed two people at the Birgitta Home. One was a fourteen-year-old girl, and she was found with her hands covering her face, and—"

"You're lying!" the father screams, slamming his fist on the table.

"No. *You're* all lying," Flora whispers.

Daniel stands up. Something has happened to his face. Maybe it's cruelty, but it looks more like disgust and fear. A mixture of emotions.

His mother pleads, tries to hold Daniel back, but he removes her hands and says something Flora can't hear.

It sounds as if he's swearing at her.

"Let's go," Flora says to Daniel.

The father and mother stare at her. There's nothing more to say. She walks out of the dining room with her brother.

177

FLORA AND DANIEL LEAVE THE manor and walk down the broad flight of steps, across the yard, and down toward some outbuildings.

"Keep moving," she mutters when he slows down.

They follow the driveway around the big red barn to get to the field. Flora keeps the rifle trained on Daniel's back the whole time. She's starting to remember fragments of her two years at the manor, but she also knows that there was a time before that, when she lived in a group home with Daniel, though that time is completely black.

But before everything else, there must have been a time when she was with her mother.

"Are you going to shoot me?" Daniel asks softly.

"I could," she replies. "But I want us to go to the police."

The sun comes out from behind the heavy rain clouds and dazzles her for a moment. Once her eyes have gotten used to the glare, she realizes that her hands are sweating. She wishes she could wipe them on her pants, but she's afraid to let go of the rifle.

A crow calls in the distance.

They pass two tractor tires and an old bathtub in the grass and follow the gravel track as it makes a wide curve around the big, empty barn.

It's a long detour through the large field.

The sun is shaded by the barn when they reach the other side of it.

"Flora," he mumbles, sounding bewildered.

Her arms are starting to tire, and her muscles ache.

The road to Delsbo is visible in the distance as a pencil line across the yellow fields.

Flora prods Daniel between the shoulders, and they walk on.

She quickly wipes the sweat from her hand and then puts her finger back on the trigger.

Daniel stops and waits for the barrel to touch him again before continuing past a concrete pedestal with rusty iron rings set into it. Weeds are growing along the cracked edge.

Daniel has started to limp and is walking slower and slower.

"Just keep walking," Flora says.

He holds one hand out and lets it slide through the tall weeds. A butterfly takes off and drifts up into the air.

"I was thinking we could stop here," he says, slowing down. "This was the old slaughterhouse, back when we kept cattle. . . . Do you remember the slaughtering mask and the way they used to kill the animals?"

"I'll shoot if you stop," she says, feeling her finger tremble on the trigger.

Daniel pulls a pink bell-shaped flower from its stem, stops, and turns toward Flora to give her the flower.

She steps back, thinking that she has to shoot, but she's not quick enough. Daniel grabs the barrel and jerks the rifle toward himself.

Flora is so taken aback that she doesn't even have time to pull back when he hits her hard in the chest with the butt of the rifle, knocking her flat on her back. She gasps for breath, coughs, and gets to her feet again.

They stand facing each other. Daniel looks at her with a distant expression in his eyes.

"You probably shouldn't have peeked," he says.

With a languid gesture, he lowers the barrel of the gun so it's pointing at the ground. She doesn't know what to say. A surge of angst twists her stomach when she realizes that she's probably going to die.

Small insects are crawling among the weeds.

Daniel raises the rifle again and looks her in the eye. He presses the barrel against her right thigh, and it looks almost unintentional when he suddenly fires it.

The blast is so loud that it rings in her ears.

The jacketed bullet passes straight through Flora's thigh muscle. She doesn't really experience any pain; it's more like a cramp.

The recoil forces Daniel to take a step back, and he watches Flora fall, no longer able to support her weight with her right leg.

She tries to break her fall, but her hip and cheek hit the ground, and she lies there, her nostrils full of the smell of straw and gunpowder.

"Now cover your eyes," he says, aiming the rifle at her face.

Flora lies on her side as blood bubbles from her thigh. She turns to look at the large barn, and her vision fades for a moment. The landscape, with the yellow fields and big red barn, spins around her as if she were on a carousel, making her feel sick.

Her heart is beating so fast that she's finding it hard to breathe. She coughs and forces herself to take a deep breath.

Daniel is standing over her with his back to the sun. He prods her on the shoulder with the barrel of the rifle, making her fall onto her back. A stab of pain from her thigh makes her gasp. He looks at her and says something she can't hear.

She tries to lift her head, and her gaze slips across the ground, past the weeds and concrete pedestal with the iron rings.

Daniel moves the rifle across her body, pointing it at her forehead, then moving down her nose to her mouth.

She feels the hot metal against her lips and chin. Her breathing is extremely fast. Warm blood is pumping out from her thigh. She looks up at the bright sky, then at the top of the barn, blinking and trying to make sense of what she sees. A man is running through the barn, through the striped light.

She tries to say something but has no voice.

The barrel of the rifle moves toward her right eye, and she closes her eyes, feels the tentative pressure against her eyelid, and doesn't even hear the loud blast.

178

JOONA DRIVES SOUTH TOWARD DELSBO. He hasn't been able to stop thinking about Daniel and his box of photographs for a second.

At first glance, the contents seem almost innocent. Perhaps the opening phase had resembled a flirtation—all kisses, longing glances, and passionate words.

But when the girls moved on, Daniel didn't hesitate to show his other side. He bided his time, then secretly visited them and murdered them. Their deaths were rarely entirely unexpected. He gave them overdoses when drug abuse was in their medical history and slit the wrists of those who had a history of cutting themselves.

Private group homes are run for profit and have presumably done all they could to hush up the deaths in order to avoid scrutiny from Social Services. And no one has ever drawn any connection to the Birgitta Home and Daniel Grim.

But it was different with Miranda. He deviated from his pattern, most likely because he panicked when Miranda thought she was pregnant. Maybe she threatened to expose him.

Daniel can't bear the thought of witnesses. He's always gone to great lengths to get rid of them.

With a nagging sense of unease, Joona phones Torkel Ekholm, tells him he'll be there in ten minutes, and asks if Flora's ready to go home.

"Sorry, I fell asleep after tea," the old policeman says. "Give me a second."

Joona hears Torkel put the phone down, cough, then shuffle across the floor. He's already driving across the bridge at Badhus Island when the old man picks up the phone again.

"There's no sign of Flora," he says. "And my rifle's gone, too. . . ."

"Do you have any idea where she might have gone?"

The line goes quiet for a moment. Joona thinks about the little cottage, the kitchen table covered with notes and photographs.

"Maybe to the manor?" Torkel replies.

Instead of going to Torkel's house, Joona turns sharply right onto the highway and puts his foot down. He requests police backup and an ambulance. On the short stretch of road beside the water, he hits a speed of 180 kilometers an hour before he has to brake, and turns right through the gateposts and into the narrow drive leading to Rånne Manor.

The gravel rattles beneath the car as the tires thud across the uneven surface.

From a distance, the large white building looks like an ornate ice sculpture, but the closer he gets, the darker it appears.

Joona pulls up sharply and leaves his car in the yard. He's surrounded by a cloud of dust. He runs toward the main entrance but suddenly catches sight of two figures some distance away, just as they go around the end of a wall and disappear behind a large red barn.

Even though he only caught a glimpse of them, Joona knows at once what he saw: Flora was pointing the gun at Daniel's back. She's planning to march him across the field, the shortest route back to the road toward Delsbo.

Joona starts running along the gravel track, past the freestanding wing of the manor, and down the slope past the outbuildings.

Flora's walking too close to Daniel, he thinks. Her brother could easily take the rifle from her. She isn't prepared to fire. She doesn't want to fire—she just wants to know the truth.

Joona leaps over the remains of an old fence and slips on the loose gravel but manages to keep his balance.

He tries to keep them in sight through the slatted red walls of the barn. The black gates are open, and sunlight is flickering between the planks.

He runs past a rusty gas tank, toward the barn, when he hears the crack of the rifle. The echo bounces between the building and fades away across the fields.

Daniel must have overpowered Flora.

The way around the barn and the wall is too long. There's no time. Perhaps it's already too late.

179

Joona draws his pistol as he runs into the empty barn. The slats along the sides are shimmering from the light streaming in from every direction.

Joona runs across the dry grit floor of the barn, sees the yellow field glint between the planks, then catches sight of the two figures behind the barn.

Flora is lying motionless on the ground, and Daniel is standing over her with the rifle aimed at her face.

Joona stops and holds his pistol out in front of him. The distance is still too great. Through the gaps in the planks, he sees Daniel tilt his head and press the barrel of the rifle to Flora's face.

Everything happens very quickly.

The sights of his pistol tremble before Joona's eye. He aims at Daniel's torso, follows his movements, and squeezes the trigger.

There's a bang; the recoil jolts his arm, and the powder scorches his hand.

The bullet from the pistol passes between two of the planks in the wall. A small cloud of dust swirls in the light in the gap.

But Joona doesn't stop to see if he hit his target; he keeps on running through the barn. He can no longer see the two figures. The stripes of light flicker past. Joona kicks open a narrow back door, racing through waist-high weeds to emerge into the yard behind the barn.

Daniel has dropped the rifle on the ground. He didn't manage to fire it a second time: the bullet from Joona's pistol hit him before he could pull the trigger.

Daniel is walking across the yard toward the huge field, clutching his stomach with one hand. Blood is running through his fingers and down his pants. He hears Joona behind him and turns around unsteadily, gesturing toward Flora, who's lying on her back, gasping for breath.

Joona keeps walking toward Daniel with his pistol aimed at his chest.

The sunlight gleams on Daniel's glasses as he sits down on the ground.

He groans and looks up.

Without saying anything, Joona kicks the rifle away, grabs Daniel's arm, and drags him several meters across the yard. He cuffs him to one of the iron rings in the concrete pedestal, then hurries over to Flora.

She hasn't passed out but is staring up at him with a strangely fixed expression. She's bleeding heavily from her thigh, and her face is pale and sweaty. She's starting to slip into shock, and her breathing is very fast and shallow.

"I'm thirsty," she whispers.

Flora's pant leg is soaked with blood, and more is still bubbling out. There isn't time to apply a tourniquet. He places both hands around her thigh and presses his thumbs down hard just above the wound, right on her femoral artery. The warm flow of blood slows at once. He presses harder and looks at Flora's face. Her lips are white, and her breathing is extremely shallow. Her eyes are closed, and he can feel how fast her pulse is.

"The ambulance will soon be here," he says. "It's going to be okay, Flora."

Behind his back Joona hears Daniel trying to say something. He turns around and sees an old man walking toward him, wearing a black coat over a dark suit. His footsteps as he approaches Daniel are strangely heavy. The man's solemn face is gray, and there's a desolate look in his eyes as he meets Joona's gaze.

"Just let me hold my son," he says in a gruff voice.

Joona can't release the pressure on Flora's thigh. He has to stay where he is if he wants to save her life.

When the man walks past him, Joona can smell gas. The old man's coat is drenched in it, and he's holding a box of matches as he walks on with numb slowness.

"Don't do it," Joona calls out.

Daniel stares at his father and tries to crawl away, jerking, trying to pull his hand through the cuff.

The old man looks at Daniel struggling to get away. His fingers shake as he takes out one of the matches, closes the box, then holds the match against the side.

"She's lying," Daniel whimpers.

His father barely has time to strike the match before he is enveloped in blue light. A ball of bright-blue flame closes around him. The heat hits Joona's face. The burning old man staggers, leans over his son, and embraces him. The grass starts to burn around them. The old man holds on tight. Daniel struggles, then gives up. Flames envelop them both. The fire twists upward. A pillar of black smoke and glowing embers rises into the sky.

180

BY THE TIME THE FIRE behind the big barn was put out, all that remained were two charred corpses: blackened bones, meshed together and smoldering.

The paramedics drove away with Flora just as the old woman emerged from the house. The lady of the house stood completely still in the yard, as if she had frozen to the spot a moment before the pain hit her.

Joona is driving back to Stockholm, listening to the weekly book-club program on the radio, as he thinks about the hammer and the rock again, the murder weapons that have been troubling him so much. Now everything seems much clearer. Elisabet wasn't killed because the murderer wanted to get her keys. Daniel had his own keys to the isolation room. Elisabet must have seen him. He murdered Elisabet because she was a witness to the first murder.

Rain starts to hit the windshield, as hard as pellets of glass. The evening sun shines through the drops, and white steam rises from the road.

Daniel probably went to see Miranda when Elisabet was sleeping, knocked out by her pills. And she did what he wanted. She had no choice. She would get undressed and sit on her chair with the comforter around her shoulders to keep her warm. But something went wrong that night. Maybe Miranda told him she was pregnant, or maybe he found a pregnancy test in the bathroom.

And he panicked, his old panic from long ago.

Daniel didn't know what to do—he felt hunted and suffocated. He pulled on the boots that always stood in the hall, went out and found a rock in the garden, demanded that she close her eyes, and hit her.

She wasn't supposed to see him—she had to be covering her face with her hands, just like little Ylva.

He always had plenty of time to plan the other girls' deaths, but Miranda's was carried out in panic. He beat her to death without knowing how he was going to get out of the situation.

And at some point—while he was forcing Miranda to cover her face, beating her with the rock, moving her to the bed, covering her face again—Elisabet saw him.

Daniel chased after Elisabet, saw her go into the brew house, grabbed a hammer from the shed, and followed her in. He told her to cover her face, and he hit her.

Only when Elisabet was dead did he get the idea of pinning the blame on the new girl, Vicky Bennet. He knew she would be asleep, because she was heavily medicated.

Daniel was in a hurry in case anyone woke up. He took Elisabet's keys and went back into the house, left them in the lock of the isolation room, then quickly planted the evidence in Vicky's room and smeared blood on her sleeping body before he left.

He probably sat on a trash bag or newspaper in his car when he drove back to his house, and burned his clothes when he got there.

From then on, he made sure he was never too far away, so he could check whether anyone had seen or knew anything. He was able to play both the helpful counselor and the devastated victim.

Joona is approaching Stockholm. The radio program is almost over. They've been discussing some novel.

Joona turns the radio off and thinks through the latter part of the investigation.

When Vicky was arrested and Daniel found out that Miranda had told her about the blind game, he realized that he would be caught if Vicky got the chance to talk through everything that had happened in detail—just seeing a psychologist who asked the right questions would be enough. So Daniel did all he could to help get Vicky released from custody, which would allow him to arrange her suicide.

Daniel had spent years working with troubled girls, children who had no security, no parents. Consciously or unconsciously, he was drawn to and fell in love with girls who reminded him of the very first one. Daniel exploited the girls, and when they were moved to another facility, he made sure they could never tell the truth about what had happened.

As Joona slows down at a traffic light, he feels a shiver run down his spine. He's met a number of murderers in his life, but when Joona thinks about how Daniel wrote reports and diagnoses and laid the groundwork for the deaths of these girls long before he went to see them for the last time, he can't help wondering if Daniel is one of the worst.

181

THERE'S A COLD MIST IN the air when Joona Linna walks across Karla Plaza from his car to Disa's apartment.

"Joona?" Disa says when she opens the door. "I almost didn't think you'd come. I have the television on. They haven't stopped talking about what happened out in Delsbo."

Joona nods.

"So you caught the murderer," Disa says with a little smile.

"If that's the right description," Joona says, thinking about the father's burning embrace.

"How's that poor woman who kept calling you? They said she'd been shot."

"Flora Hansen," Joona says, walking into Disa's home.

His head hits the lampshade, and the light starts to sway across the walls. Joona finds himself thinking about the young girls in Daniel's box again.

"You're tired," Disa says gently, pulling him along by the hand.

"Flora's brother shot her in the leg, and . . ."

He doesn't notice when he stops talking. He tried to clean himself up at a gas station, but his clothes are still smeared with Flora's blood.

"Go and take a bath, and I'll get some food," Disa says.

"Thanks." Joona smiles.

Just as they're heading through the living room, the news

shows a picture of Elin. They both stop. A young reporter explains that Elin Frank has been operated on overnight and that her doctors are now optimistic. Elin's adviser, Robert Bianchi, appears on-screen. He looks drained and has tears in his eyes as he smiles and says that Elin is going to make it.

"What happened?" Disa whispers.

"She fought the murderer on her own and saved the girl who . . ."

"Dear God," Disa says quietly.

"Yes, Elin Frank is . . . She's . . . she's quite remarkable," Joona says, putting his hands on Disa's thin shoulders.

182

JOONA IS SITTING WITH A blanket around him while they eat chicken vindaloo and lamb tikka masala at Disa's kitchen table.

"Good . . ."

"My mom's secret Finnish recipe," she says, laughing.

She tears off some naan and passes the rest to Joona. He looks at her with smiling eyes, drinks some wine, and tells her more about the case. Disa listens and asks questions, and the more he tells her, the calmer he feels inside.

He tells Disa about Flora and Daniel, siblings who ended up in a group home at a very young age.

"So they really were brother and sister?" she asks, refilling their glasses.

"Yes . . . and it was a big deal when the wealthy couple at Rånne adopted them."

"I can imagine."

They were just young children when they played with the groundskeeper's daughter. Daniel had a crush on little Ylva. Joona thinks back to Flora's wide-eyed account of Daniel kissing Ylva when they were playing the blind game.

"The little girl laughed and said now she was going to have a baby," Joona says. "Daniel was only six years old, and for some reason he panicked. . . ."

"Go on," Disa whispers.

"He ordered both the girls to close their eyes; then he picked up a heavy rock and killed Ylva."

Disa has stopped eating, and her face is pale as she listens to Joona describing how Flora fled and told her father what had happened.

"But their father loved Daniel and defended him," Joona says. "He demanded that Flora take back her accusations. He threatened her by saying that all liars would be thrown into a sea of fire."

"So she retracted?"

"She said she was lying, and because she'd told such wicked lies, she was sent away from the house forever."

"Flora took back her accusations . . . and lied about lying," Disa says thoughtfully.

"Yes," Joona says, reaching across the table to touch her hand.

Flora, a very small child, soon forgot her previous life, her adoptive parents, and her brother.

Joona can see how Flora built a whole life around lies. She lied to keep other people happy. It wasn't until she heard about the murders at the Birgitta Home on the radio, about the girl with her hands over her face, that the past started to come back to her.

"But what about her memories?" Disa asks, gesturing to Joona to help himself to more food.

"I actually called Britt-Marie on the way here to talk about that," Joona says.

"The Needle's wife?"

"Yes . . . She's a psychiatrist. She didn't seem to think it was strange at all. . . ."

He explains to her that memory loss is often associated with post-traumatic stress disorder. High levels of adrenaline and stress-related hormones can affect long-term memory. After particularly traumatic experiences, memories can be buried almost intact deep within the brain. They get hidden away and remain untouched by emotion because they were never processed. But with the right stimulus, the memory can suddenly pop up as physical sensations and images.

"At first Flora was just shaken up by what she'd heard on the radio, without knowing why. She thought she could make some money by tipping off the police," Joona says. "But when her actual memories started to break through, she thought they were ghosts."

"Perhaps they really were ghosts, in a way," Disa suggests.

"Maybe." He nods. "Either way, she began to tell the truth, and Flora ended up being the witness who unlocked the entire mystery."

Joona stands up and blows out the candles on the table. Disa walks up to him, makes her way inside the blanket, and embraces him. They stand there just holding each other for a long time. He breathes in her scent and feels the vein pulsing in her slender neck.

"I'm so scared something's going to happen to you. That's why I've been keeping my distance," he says.

"What could happen to me?" she says, smiling.

"You could disappear," he replies seriously.

"Joona, I'm not going to disappear."

"I used to have a friend named Samuel Mendel," he says quietly, then falls silent.

183

Joona walks out of police headquarters and up the steep path across Kronoberg Park, over the hill to the old Jewish cemetery. With practiced hands, he unfastens the wire holding the gate closed, opens it, and goes inside.

Among the dark gravestones is a more recent family grave bearing the words "Samuel Mendel, his wife, Rebecka, and their sons, Joshua and Reuben."

Joona puts a small round stone on the top of the gravestone, then stands with his eyes closed. He can smell the damp soil and hear the park's leaves rustling as the wind blows through the treetops.

Samuel Mendel was a direct descendant of Koppel Mendel, who, against Aaron Isaac's wishes, bought this cemetery in 1787. Even though it officially stopped being used in 1857, it has remained the last resting place for Koppel Mendel's family for all these years.

Samuel was a detective, and Joona's first partner in the National Crime Unit. He and Joona were very close friends. Samuel was only forty-six years old when he died, and Joona knows that he's lying alone in the family grave, even though the headstone says otherwise.

Joona and Samuel's first big case together also turned out to be their last.

Just an hour later, Joona is back at Internal Affairs. He's sitting in a room with Mikael Båge, the head of the investigation, the secretary Helene Fiorine, and the prosecutor Sven Wiklund.

The yellow light from outside glints off the polished furniture, and reflects off the glass bookcases containing handsomely bound law books.

"I now need to decide whether or not to press charges against you, Joona Linna," the prosecutor says, putting one hand on a thick pile of papers. "This is the material I've got to go on, and there's nothing in here that helps your case."

His chair creaks as he leans back and meets Joona's calm gaze. The only sounds in the room are the rasp of Helene Fiorine's pen and her shallow breathing.

"As I see it," Sven Wiklund goes on dryly, "your only chance of avoiding prosecution is a really good explanation."

"Joona usually has an ace up his sleeve," Mikael Båge says in a low voice.

Out in the clear sky, the vapor trail from an airplane is slowly dissipating. Their chairs creak, and Helene swallows audibly and puts her pen down.

"All you have to do is explain what happened," she says. "Maybe you had a good reason for preempting the Security Police raid."

"Yes," Joona says.

"We know you're a good police officer," Mikael says with an embarrassed smile.

"I, on the other hand, am a stickler for the rules," the prosecutor says. "I'm the sort of man who crushes people for breaking the rules. Don't make me crush you here and now."

That's as close to a plea as Helene has ever heard Sven Wiklund make.

"Your entire future's in the balance, Joona," the head of the investigation whispers.

Helene's chin starts to tremble, and Mikael's forehead is shiny with sweat. Joona meets the senior prosecutor's gaze and finally starts talking.

"The decision was mine, and mine alone, as you already know," he begins. "But I do actually have an answer that you might . . ."

Joona breaks off when his phone buzzes. He looks at the screen automatically, and his eyes turn as dark as wet granite.

"I'm sorry," he says somberly. "But I really have to take this call."

The other three look on in bemusement as he answers and listens to the voice at the other end.

"Yes, I know," he says quietly. "Yes . . . I'll come at once."

Joona ends the call and gives the senior prosecutor a lingering look, as if he's forgotten where he is.

"I have to go," Joona says, and leaves the room without another word.

184

ONE HOUR AND TWENTY MINUTES later, the scheduled flight lands at Härjedalen Sveg Airport, and Joona immediately takes a taxi to the Blue Wings care home. This is where he tracked down Rosa Bergman, the woman who was following him outside Adolf Fredrik's Church, the woman who asked him why he was pretending that his daughter was dead.

Joona gets out of the taxi and walks quickly up to the cluster of yellow buildings, through the main entrance, and straight to Maja's ward.

The nurse he met last time waves to him from the reception desk. The light coming through the blinds makes her curly hair shine like copper.

"That was quick," she says. "I've been thinking about you, and we've had your card pinned up behind the desk, so I called—"

"Is it possible to talk to her?" Joona interrupts.

His tone disconcerts the woman, and she brushes her hands on her pale-blue tunic.

"Our new doctor was here the day before yesterday. She's a young woman—from Algeria, I think. She changed Maja's medication and . . . Well, I've heard about it, but I've never seen it myself before. . . . The old dear woke up this morning and kept saying very clearly that she needed to speak to you."

"Where is she?"

The nurse leads Joona to the cramped room with closed curtains and leaves him alone with the old woman. Above a narrow desk hangs a framed photograph of a young woman sitting next to her son. The mother has her arm around the boy's shoulders, serious and protective.

Several heavy and expensive items of furniture line the walls: a dark desk, a dresser, and two gilded pedestals.

Rosa Bergman is sitting on a daybed with deep-red cushions. She's crisply dressed in a blouse, skirt, and knitted cardigan. Though her face looks swollen and wrinkled, there's a completely new focus in her eyes.

"My name is Joona Linna," he says. "You had something you wanted to tell me."

The woman nods and gets to her feet with effort. She opens a drawer in her bedside table and takes out a Gideon Bible. She holds the spine and shakes the pages above the bed. A small, folded piece of paper falls onto the bedspread.

"Joona Linna," she says, picking up the paper. "So you're Joona Linna."

He doesn't answer, but he starts to feel a migraine burn into his temple like a red-hot needle. "How can you pretend your daughter is dead?" Rosa Bergman asks.

The old woman's eyes go to the photograph on the wall.

"If there was some way I could have had my boy here still . . . If you knew what it's like to see your child die . . . Nothing in the world could have made me abandon him."

"I didn't abandon my family," Joona says tersely. "I saved their lives."

"When Summa came to me," Rosa goes on, "she didn't tell me about you, but she was broken. . . . It was worse for your daughter, though. She stopped talking, didn't speak for two years."

Joona feels a shiver run all the way up his spine to his scalp.

"Were you in contact with them?" he asks. "You weren't supposed to have any contact with them."

"I couldn't just let them disappear," she says. "I felt so incredibly sorry for them."

Joona knows Summa would never mention his name unless something was horribly wrong. There wasn't supposed to be any connection between them at all. Nothing, ever. That was the only way to survive.

He leans against the desk, swallows hard, and looks at the old woman again.

"How are they?" he asks.

"This is serious, Joona," Rosa says. "I usually see Lumi once a year or so. But . . . I . . . I've become so very confused and forgetful."

"What happened?"

"Your wife has cancer, Joona," Rosa says slowly. "She called me and said she was going to have an operation, but that she probably wasn't going to recover. . . . She wanted you to know that Lumi will be taken into foster care by Social Services if she . . ."

"When was this?" Joona asks through clenched teeth, his lips white. "When did she call?"

"I'm afraid it might be too late," she whispers. "I've been so forgetful and everything. . . ."

She finally hands him the crumpled note with the address on it, then stares down at her arthritic hands.

185

JOONA HAS TO FLY BACK to Stockholm and change planes to get to Helsinki. The whole thing feels like a dream. He sits in his seat and stares through the veils of cloud at the rippled surface of the Baltic Sea. People serve him drinks and snacks and try to talk to him, but he can't bring himself to respond.

Memories are dragging him down.

Nineteen people had disappeared. At first it just looked like a strange coincidence, but when none of the missing people reappeared, the case was given top priority.

Joona was the first person to claim that the police were dealing with a serial killer.

Working with Samuel Mendel, he managed to track and catch Jurek Walter red-handed out in Lill-Jan's Forest while he was forcing a fifty-year-old woman back into a coffin in the ground. She had already been in the coffin for two years but was still alive.

The extent of the nightmare became apparent in the hospital. The woman's muscles had atrophied, she was deformed by pressure sores, and her hands and feet had suffered frostbite. After further examination, her doctors concluded that not only was she suffering from extreme psychological trauma but she was badly brain-damaged.

Joona knows you can't kill the devil, but twelve years ago he and Samuel managed to cut one of his fingers off when they caught the serial killer Jurek Walter.

Joona sat in court when Jurek was sentenced to secure psychiatric care and placed in a secure unit twenty kilometers north of Stockholm.

Joona will never forget Jurek Walter's wrinkled face when he turned to look at him.

"Now Samuel Mendel's two sons are going to disappear," Jurek said in a weary voice while his defense lawyer gathered his papers. "And Samuel's wife, Rebecka, will disappear. But . . . No, listen to me, Joona Linna. The police will look for them, and when the police give up, Samuel will go on looking, but when he eventually realizes that he'll never see his family again, he'll kill himself."

Joona had stood up to leave.

"And your little daughter," Jurek Walter went on, looking down at his fingernails. "Lumi will disappear. And Summa will disappear. And when you realize that you're never going to find them, you're going to hang yourself."

One Friday afternoon a couple of months later, Samuel's wife drove from their apartment in Liljeholmen to their summerhouse on Dalarö. She had their two sons, Joshua and Reuben, in the car with her. When Samuel arrived at the house a few hours later, his wife and children weren't there. The car was found abandoned on a nearby forest track, but Samuel never saw his family again. One chill March morning a year later, Samuel Mendel went down to the beautiful beach where his boys used to swim. The police had stopped looking eight months earlier, and now he, too, had given up. He drew his service pistol from his shoulder holster and shot himself in the head.

186

Joona and Summa had been planning a road trip: up to Umeå, past Storuman, across to Mo i Rana in Norway, then back down the west coast. Now they were on their way to a hotel that lay in the middle of Dalälven and were going to visit a safari park nearby the following day.

Summa changed the station on the radio and murmured happily when she found one playing relaxed piano music, the notes all blending into one another. Joona reached back to make sure that Lumi was sitting in her car seat the right way and hadn't slipped her arms out of the straps.

"Daddy," she said sleepily.

He felt her little fingers in his hand. She held him tight but let go when he pulled back.

They passed the turnoff to Älvkarleby.

"You're going to love Furuvik Wildlife Park," Summa said quietly. "Chimpanzees and rhinocer—"

"I already have a monkey!" Lumi cried from the back seat.

"What?"

"I'm her monkey," Joona said.

Summa raised her eyebrows. "It suits you."

"Lumi's taking care of me—she says she's a nice vet."

Summa's sandy-brown hair was hanging over her face, half hiding her thick dark eyebrows. The dimples in her cheeks grew deeper.

"Why do you need a vet? What's wrong with you?"

"I need glasses."

"Did she say that?" Summa laughed, and leafed through her newspaper, not noticing that he was driving along a different road and they were already north of the Dala River.

Lumi had fallen asleep, with her doll pressed to her cheek.

"Are you sure we don't need to reserve a table?" Summa suddenly asked. "Because I want to sit on the deck tonight to see the whole river outside the window. . . ."

The road was narrow and straight, the forest crowding in.

It wasn't until he turned off toward Mora that Summa realized something was wrong. "Joona, we've gone past Älvkarleby. Weren't we going to stop there? I'm sure we said we were going to stop in Älvkarleby."

"Yes."

"So what are you doing?"

He didn't answer, just stared at the puddles on the road glowing in the afternoon sun. Without warning or signal, a truck pulled out into the passing lane.

"We said we . . ."

She fell silent, breathing through her nose, then went on in a frightened voice: "Joona? Tell me you haven't been lying to me. Tell me."

"I had to," he whispered.

Summa looked at him, and he could sense how upset she was, but she still made an effort to speak quietly so she wouldn't wake Lumi.

"You can't be serious," she said tersely. "You can't just . . . You said there was no danger anymore; you said it was over. You said it was over, and I believed you. I thought you'd changed, I really believed that. . . ."

Her voice broke, and she turned away to look out the side window. Her chin was trembling, and her cheeks turned red.

"I lied to you," Joona admitted.

"You weren't allowed to lie to me, you weren't allowed to. . . ."

"No . . . And I'm so, so sorry."

"We can run away together. That would work—that would work fine."

"You have to understand. . . . Summa, you really have to understand. . . . If I thought that was possible, if I had any other choice, I'd—"

"Stop it," she interrupted. "The threat isn't real. It's not true—you're seeing connections that aren't there. Samuel Mendel's family has nothing to do with us, don't you get that? There's no threat to us."

"I've tried to explain how serious it is, but you won't listen."

"I don't want to listen. Why would I want to?"

"Summa, I have to . . . I've arranged everything. There's a woman named Rosa Bergman. She's waiting for you up in Malmberget. She'll give you new identities. You're going to be fine."

His hands had started to shake. His fingers were slippery with sweat on the steering wheel.

"You really are serious," Summa whispered.

"More serious than I've ever been," he replied heavily. "We're on our way to Mora, where you'll be catching the train to Gällivare."

He could hear that Summa was doing her best to sound composed. "If you leave us at that station, you've lost us. Do you understand that? There's no way back after that." She looked at him with moist, stubborn eyes.

"You'll have to tell Lumi that I'm working overseas," he went on in a subdued voice, hearing Summa start to sniff.

"Joona," she whispered. "No, no . . ."

He just stared ahead of him, out at the wet road, and swallowed hard.

"And in a few years," he went on, "when she's a little older, you'll have to tell her I'm dead. You must never, ever contact me. Never come to find me. Do you understand?"

Summa could no longer hold back the tears.

"I don't want this, I don't want this. . . ."

"Neither do I."

"You can't do this to us," she wept.

"Mommy?"

Lumi had woken up, and her voice sounded frightened. Summa wiped the tears from her cheeks.

"There's nothing to worry about," Joona told his daughter. "Mommy's just sad because we're not going to the hotel by the river."

"Tell her," Summa said in a louder voice.

"Tell me what?" Lumi asked.

"You and Mommy are going on a train," Joona said.

"What are you going to do?"

"I have to work," he replied.

"But I thought we were going to play vet and monkey."

"He doesn't want to," Summa said harshly.

187

JOONA SLOWED DOWN IN FRONT of the yellow station. He parked the car, opened the trunk, and lifted out the large wheeled suitcase.

"You took your things out last night?" Summa asked in a subdued voice.

"Yes."

He nodded and looked off toward the railroad.

Summa came over and stood next to him. "Your daughter needs you in her life."

"I don't have a choice," he replied, looking back through the car's rear window.

Lumi was pressing a big, soft doll into her pink backpack.

"You've got plenty of choices," Summa went on. "But instead of fighting, you're just giving up. You don't even know if the threat is real. I can't get my head around this."

"Can't find Lollo," Lumi was muttering to herself.

"The train leaves in twenty minutes," Joona said tersely.

"I don't want to live without you," Summa said quietly, trying to take his hand. "I want everything to be the way it was."

"I know."

"If you do this to us, you'll be alone."

He didn't answer. Lumi climbed out of the car, dragging her backpack along the ground. A red barrette was dangling loosely from her hair.

"Are you going to lead a completely solitary life?"

"Yes," he said.

The northernmost inlet of Lake Siljan glinted between the trees on the other side of the tracks.

"Say goodbye to Daddy now," Summa said blankly, nudging her daughter forward.

Lumi stood still, with a dark expression on her face, staring at the ground.

"Hurry up," Summa said.

Lumi looked up for a couple of seconds and said, "Bye-bye, monkey."

"Do it right," Summa said irritably. "Say goodbye nicely."

"Don't want to," Lumi replied, clinging to one of her mother's legs.

"Do it anyway," Summa said.

Joona crouched down in front of his little daughter. His forehead was shiny with sweat.

"Can I have a hug?"

She shook her head.

"Here comes the monkey with his long arms," he joked.

He picked her up and felt her little body resist; then she started to laugh in spite of herself, even though she could tell something was wrong. She tried to kick and get down, but he held her tight, just for a moment, just to inhale the smell of her hair and neck.

"Silly!" she shouted.

"Lumi," he whispered against her cheek. "Never forget that I love you more than anything."

"Come on, now," Summa said.

He put his daughter down and tried to smile at her. Summa looked at him with a horrified, rigid expression, then took Lumi's hand and pulled her toward herself.

They waited for the train in silence. There was nothing more to say. Downy dandelion seeds drifted slowly across the tracks.

188

HE DROVE FOR 140 KILOMETERS without thinking. His head was full of white noise, and he felt frighteningly detached.

Eventually, he arrived.

He turned into a large industrial park in Ludvika, down by the deserted harbor, next to the power station. A large gray van was already parked between two huge piles of sawdust. Joona stopped next to it. He suddenly felt remarkably calm and realized that he was in some form of shock.

He got out and looked around. The Needle was waiting in the darkness next to the van door. He was wearing white overalls, and his face looked clenched and haggard.

"So—are they gone now?" he asked in the sharp tone of voice he always used when something had upset him.

"They're gone," Joona confirmed bluntly.

Nils nodded. His white-rimmed glasses sparkled coldly in the faint light from a streetlight in the distance.

"You didn't give me a choice," he said bitterly.

"That's true," Joona said. "You don't have a choice."

"We'll both get fired for this," Nils said.

"Maybe," Joona replied.

They headed for the back of the van.

"There are two of them; I called as soon as they came in."

"Good."

"Two of them," The Needle repeated, almost to himself.

Joona remembered waking up a couple of days ago, next to his wife and daughter, because his cell phone was buzzing in his jacket out in the hall.

Someone had sent him a text. When he got up and saw it was from Nils, he immediately understood what it was about.

They had come to an understanding. As soon as Nils came across two suitable bodies, Joona would take off with Summa and Lumi on the pretext of finally taking the vacation they had talked about for so long.

Joona had been waiting to hear from Nils for almost three weeks. Time was starting to run out. He was keeping watch over his family, but he wouldn't be able to do it forever. Jurek Walter was a patient man.

Joona knew that the text meant he was going to lose his family. But he also knew that it meant he could finally give Summa and Lumi real protection.

Nils opened the two rear doors of the gray van to reveal two stretchers covered with white sheets, one bearing a large figure, the other a smaller one.

"A woman and a girl. They died in a single-car accident yesterday morning," Nils said, and began to pull one of the stretchers out. "I've spirited them away," he explained quickly. "They don't exist, not a trace. I deleted everything."

He groaned as he pulled the bodies out. The stretcher's frame unfolded with a clatter as its small wheels touched the ground.

Without further ceremony, Nils unzipped one of the body bags.

Joona gritted his teeth and forced himself to look.

Inside lay a young woman with her eyes closed and a perfectly calm expression on her face. Her chest was horribly crushed. Her arms looked as if they were broken in several places, and her pelvis was badly contorted.

"Their car went off a bridge," Nils said in his sharp, nasal voice. "Her chest is crushed because she wasn't wearing her seat belt. Possibly because she was trying to pick something up for her daughter. I've seen it before."

Joona looked at the woman. There was no sign of pain or terror, nothing in her face that gave any indication of what had happened to her body.

When he turned to look at the little girl's face, his eyes filled with tears.

Nils muttered something to himself and covered the bodies again.

"Well, then," he said. "Catharina and Mimmi will never be found, never be identified."

He lost his train of thought for a moment, then went on angrily: "The girl's father has been going to all the hospitals looking for them, all night. He even called my department. I had to talk to him." Nils pressed his lips together. "They'll be buried as Summa and Lumi. . . . I'll organize fake dental records."

He gave Joona one last probing look but got no response. Together, they moved the bodies to Joona's car.

189

It felt unreal to drive a car with two dead bodies as passengers. The roads were dark. A badger stared at Joona from the roadside with glowing eyes, hypnotized by the headlights.

When he reached the hill he had chosen, he began to arrange the bodies. He moved the woman's body to the driver's seat and strapped the girl into Lumi's car seat, hearing only his own strained breathing and the soft sound of their dangling arms and legs hitting the seats.

He leaned in, released the hand brake, and set the car in motion. Slowly, it began to roll down the hill, while he walked beside it. Every so often, he would lean in and adjust the steering wheel. As it gained speed, he started to run. With a dull crunch, the car crashed into a thick pine tree. There was shriek of metal as the front folded around the tree. The woman slumped against the dashboard. The little girl's body jerked hard in the car seat.

Joona took the gas can from the trunk and poured gas over the seats, the girl's padded overalls, and the woman's shattered body.

It was getting hard to breathe.

He had to stop and calm himself down. His heart felt as if it were trying to break into his throat.

Joona mumbled a few words to himself, then pulled the little girl out again. He walked up and down with her in his arms, holding her tight, rocking her, and whispering in her ears. Then he put her on her mother's lap in the front of the car.

He quietly closed the car door and emptied the last of the tank over the vehicle. One of the rear windows was open, and through it he set fire to the back seat.

Like an angel of death, the fire spread through the inside of the car.

He caught a glimpse of the woman's incomprehensibly calm face as her hair burned.

The car, wedged against the tree, was now completely alight. The flames were loud with ragged, shrieking cries and weeping.

It was as if Joona suddenly woke up. He rushed toward the car to get the bodies out. Though he burned his hands on the door, he eventually managed to open it, and the fire inside the car billowed out. He tried to get to the woman, but her jacket was burning fiercely. Her slender legs looked as if they were twitching in the flames.

Daddy, Daddy. Help me, Daddy.

Joona knew it wasn't real—he knew they were already dead—but he still couldn't bear it. He reached his hand in through the flames and held the girl's hand.

At that moment, the heat made the car's gas tank explode. Joona experienced a weird crunching sound as his eardrums burst. He felt blood pour from his nose and ears, and he was thrown backward; his head hit the ground. His brain was flaring and roaring. Before his vision faded, he saw the burned embers of the leaves drifting slowly through the air.

190

Joona stares out through the window and doesn't hear the flight attendant announce that they will shortly be arriving at Helsinki International Airport.

Twelve years ago, he cut off one of the fingers of the devil incarnate, and as a punishment he was sentenced to live alone. It's a high price, but he has always felt that it wasn't enough. He knows the punishment has been too lenient, that the devil has just been biding his time before taking something else from him, waiting for him to think that everything has been forgiven and forgotten.

Joona hunches up in his seat and tries to calm his breathing. The man in the next seat looks at him anxiously. Sweat is dripping from Joona's forehead.

This isn't a migraine—it's the other thing, the great darkness behind everything, Joona thinks.

He caught the serial killer Jurek Walter. That's not the kind of thing that can be forgotten, and it will never be forgiven.

It wasn't worth it.

For the past twelve years, the strictly isolated bunker in the Secure Criminal Psychology Unit at Löwenströmska Hospital has been home to the aging Jurek Walter. He is not allowed to have any visitors or meet other patients, but Joona knows that Jurek hasn't given up his thoughts of revenge.

Joona is on his way to find Summa and Lumi. He's on his way to do something unforgivable. As long as Jurek Walter thinks they're dead, they're safe, but he could be leading a serial killer to his family at this very moment.

JOONA LEFT HIS CELL PHONE in Stockholm. He's using a fake passport and paying cash for everything. When he gets out of the taxi, he walks two blocks before stopping in a doorway and searching for signs of life in the dark windows of their apartment.

He waits for a while, then goes to a café farther down the street, pays ten euros to borrow a phone, and calls Saga.

"I need help," he says in a voice that's on the brink of breaking.

"Where are you? Everyone's looking for you! It's absolute chaos here. . . ."

"I need help with something."

"Okay," she says, her voice suddenly calm and focused.

"Once you've given me the information," Joona goes on, "you have to make absolutely sure that you erase every trace of the search."

"Okay," she says quietly, without any hesitation.

Joona swallows hard, looks at the little note Rosa Bergman gave him, then asks Saga to check if a woman named Laura Sandin at 16 Liisan Street in Helsinki is still alive.

"Can I call you back?" she asks.

"Preferably not. I'll wait while you search," he replies.

The minutes that follow are the longest of his life. He looks at the dust on the counter, the espresso machine, the scuff marks on the floor.

"Joona?" Saga eventually says.

"I'm here," he whispers.

"Laura Sandin was diagnosed with liver cancer two years ago. . . ."

"Go on," Joona says, as he feels sweat start to trickle down his back.

"Looks like she had an operation last year. And she . . . but . . ." Saga whispers something to herself.

"What is it?" Joona asks.

Saga clears her throat and says, with a hint of stress in her voice, as if she's only just realized that this is somehow extremely important: "She underwent a second operation very recently, last week. . . ."

"Is she alive?"

"It looks like it. . . . She's still in the hospital," Saga says gently.

191

WHEN JOONA REACHES SUMMA'S ROOM, it's as if everything slows down. The distant sounds of televisions and conversation get slower and slower.

Very gently, he opens the door and walks in.

A thin woman is lying in the bed, facing away from him.

A cotton curtain is pulled across the window. Her frail arms are on top of the covers. Her dark hair is sweaty and dull.

He doesn't know if she's asleep, but he has to see her face. He walks closer. The room is completely silent.

THE WOMAN WHO WAS KNOWN in a different life as Summa Linna is extremely tired. Her daughter has spent the entire night sitting up with her and is now sleeping in the visitors' room.

Summa sees the weak daylight filter through the thin curtain and thinks about how human beings are ultimately alone. She has several good memories that she usually tries to find when she's at her most lonely and afraid. When they gave her the anesthetic before the operation, she conjured up those memories.

The incredibly light summer nights when she was a child.

The moment her daughter was born, and held her finger in her hand.

Her wedding on a summer's day, with the bridal crown her mother had woven from birch roots.

Summa swallows and feels the beat of her heart. She's so terribly afraid of dying and leaving Lumi alone in the world.

The stitches from the operation sting when she rolls over. She closes her eyes, then opens them again.

She has to blink several times before she realizes that her message must have reached him.

Joona is leaning over her, and she reaches up and touches his face, then runs her fingers through his thick, fair hair.

"If I die, you need to take care of Lumi," she whispers.

"I promise."

"And you have to see her before you go again," she says. "You have to see her."

He puts his hands against her cheeks and strokes her face. Whispers that she's as beautiful as she ever was. She smiles at him. Then he's gone, and Summa is no longer afraid.

THE VISITORS' ROOM IS SIMPLY furnished. There's a television on the wall, and a pine table covered with cigarette burns sits in front of a sagging sofa.

A fifteen-year-old girl is lying asleep on the sofa. Her eyes hurt from crying so much, and one cheek is striped from the pattern on the cushion. She wakes up abruptly with a strange feeling. Someone's put a blanket over her. Her shoes have been taken off and are lined up neatly on the floor next to her.

Someone had been in there with her. In her dream there was someone sitting with her, very gently holding her hand.